Howard Jacobson was born in 1942, brought up in Manchester, and read English at Cambridge. He has taught English at Selwyn College, Cambridge, Sydney University and Wolverhampton Polytechnic, and is the co-author – with Wilbur Sanders – of *Shakespeare's Magnanimity*. His first novel, *Coming From Behind*, is also available in Black Swan. With his wife, Rosalin, he spends the summers in Cornwall, and the winters in London.

Author photograph by Tony Errington

Also by Howard Jacobson

COMING FROM BEHIND

and published by Black Swan

Peeping Tom

Howard Jacobson

BLACK SWAN

PEEPING TOM

A BLACK SWAN BOOK   0 552 99141 4

Originally published in Great Britain by
Chatto & Windus/The Hogarth Press

PRINTING HISTORY

Chatto & Windus/The Hogarth Press edition
published 1984
Second impression, with corrections,
published 1984
Black Swan edition published 1985
Black Swan edition reprinted 1985
Black Swan edition reprinted 1986

This book is set in 11/12 pt Mallard

Black Swan Books are published by
Transworld Publishers Ltd., Century House,
61 - 63 Uxbridge Road, Ealing, London W5 5SA,
in Australia by Transworld Publishers
(Aust.) Pty. Ltd., 26 Harley Crescent,
Condell Park, NSW 2200, and in New
Zealand by Transworld Publishers (N.Z.)
Ltd., Cnr. Moselle and Waipareira Avenues,
Henderson, Auckland.

Made and printed in Great Britain by the
Guernsey Press Co. Ltd., Guernsey, Channel Islands.

For Rosalin –
who instigated, hatched and reared this, and
looked to me to legitimize it merely.

Prologue

*Remember to keep faith with those three great sources
of your strength: Earth, Sea and Air. Walk barefoot on
the Earth whenever you can. Learn to swim, and return
to the Sea from which all life originally came. And
always wear as few clothes as possible. It is important to
allow the Air to circulate freely around those parts of
the body which are not usually exposed to it.*

*And don't forget: it is no good working on your body if
your mind is drugged with cigarettes and television.*

Lance Tourney, *Lad of Destiny: A Boy's
Guide to Health and Confidence*

Signs are, even to my drugged eye, that the village is
finally coming out of winter. I am not witnessing a return
to robustness and sanity exactly – that's too much to
expect down here, so far from the soundness of cities, so
deep into the obsessional neurosis of Nature – but there
is an atmosphere of fragile convalescence abroad, as if
the patients have been allowed their first unaccompa-
nied turn around the walled gardens of the institution.

The wind has dropped. The water in the harbour
rocks itself, brooding on its delusions. The squinting sea
birds look as if they believe they might just eat again.
Those hoteliers who changed wives or husbands at the
start of the off-season – hoteliers are always the most
romantic and expectant inhabitants of any remote
place – have changed back again and are freshening up
their Vacancy notices. Autographed copies of this
year's print run of Lionel Turnbull's pamphlet (Lance

7

Tourney is, of course, a pen-name) have started to appear in the post office and the village stores, and Lionel himself has begun those naked ritualistic swims which will continue every morning now until the Atlantic freezes over again. And already the first serious walkers of the season have arrived in their fetishistic boots and with their Ordnance Survey maps in protective plastic packets tied around their necks like bibs.

I meet them in the early morning during my penitential walks along the harbour walls or out on the cliff paths, and although they all nod me a bracing greeting or wave their blackthorn sticks, I can see that I am an extraneity and a blemish for them. In my long sleek-piled fur coat (resembling ocelot and bought on an Austin Reed charge account) and my Bally slip-on snakeskin shoes decorated, rather tastefully I've always thought, with a delicate gold chain and having the added advantage of slightly built-up heels, I am not what they have taken a week off work and kissed goodbye to their children and strapped methane stoves to their backs to find. At a stroke I domesticate the cliffs for them. Many of them, I fancy, will spend the rest of the day in a pet, not even noticing the wild sea below; fearing that at the next precipitous turn of the path, beneath the overhanging crags, above the foaming waterfall, they will come upon more like me, wearing jewels and stoles, contradicting one another in broken accents, and picnicking on smoked salmon sandwiches from the boot of a white Daimler. That's the extent to which I have blotted their landscape.

But if my being here is a disagreeable shock to them, imagine what it is to me!

I have just been sitting on the rocks watching a group of schoolgirls watching Lionel Turnbull preparing for a swim. Whether Lionel saw the schoolgirls or whether the schoolgirls saw me it is impossible to say. We were all, in our own ways, separately engrossed. With the exception of a neat square rug of hair on his chest and

8

back Lionel is a smooth man. Bobbing about in the water he is indistinguishable from the brown seals he has befriended. Anyone familiar with rustic persiflage will be able to imagine the sorts of jokes that circulate about Lionel and his relations with those seals. For all the influx of summer tourists this is still essentially a farming community – there isn't anything that farmers find improbable.

Once he had peeled off his posing pouch which he wears under his exercise briefs which he wears under his swimming trunks which he wears under his perambulating shorts, Lionel stood for a while with his legs apart and his arms raised, for the purpose, I guessed, of letting the air circulate around those parts which had been stored away all winter. Then, with slow rhythmic movements, he began the sort of examination of himself that is recommended to women for the location of unfamiliar lumps in the breasts; except that he didn't confine himself to one area, but examined his neck and his armpits also, and the region of his lumbar ganglion and his prostate, his rib cage, his kidneys, his liver, and, with lingering deliberation, his testicles. This was too much for the schoolgirls who, being visitors to the village, had never before seen an adult male standing on argillaceous rock and rolling his balls minutely around the outstretched palm of his hand.

It puzzled me also, I must confess, although I didn't almost fall into the sea with laughter, because if those were cancer lumps Lionel Turnbull was searching for then he must have let himself go quite badly over the winter. Chapter V of *Lad of Destiny* states categorically that cancer is merely a consequence of lifestyle, being ascribable entirely to smoking, television, and bad bodily habits. From the confident manner in which he plunged finally into the water I deduced that he had found nothing in his body that shouldn't have been there, but it has not gone without my noticing it that he thought he might.

There is something about this part of the world – it

might be the light or the towering cliffs or the perpendicular fields and meadows – all offering incomparable
opportunities for high profile – that attracts exhibitionists. A year and a half ago a whole family of them
took a winter let on a small holiday cottage in the harbour. Grandmother, mother, two sons, and a daughter-
in-law. That's only approximate – domestic confusion
as to who is related to whom and how is not uncommon
in this neck of the woods. The rule of thumb seems to be
that if a person sharing your house looks twice your age
then there is a good chance it is your parent and
oughtn't, therefore, to make a habit of sharing your
bed – at least not until you're married; otherwise it's
fairly open slather. Anyway, in the case of the family of
exhibitionists, I can say for sure that there were three
women and two men, and that the National Trust didn't
take at all kindly to the manner in which they disported
themselves both within the cottage and without it. Just in
case that sounds unreasonable, let me make it clear that
the cottage stood inside the area designated as the harbour, and that the harbour is the property of the
National Trust. Gossip had it that they received an official typed complaint on Trust notepaper, in response to
which the grandmother (if that *was* who she was) sent
back a signed group photograph of them all lined up
against the harbour wall in a state of Nature, the women
concealing their ultimate immodesty behind their
National Trust membership cards and the two men more
flagrant in their National Trust ties. Was it the colour of
their skins, she sent a covering note to enquire, that the
Trust found out of keeping? This was a sly allusion to an
argument which was occupying the attention of the village at the time, on the issue of the colour of the motor
cars the Trust preferred the villagers to own. For that
jibe alone their emmet foreignness and impudicity might
have been forgiven, but the youngest son, the ostensibly
unmarried one, went and blew it.

As long as he merely roamed the cliffs, in his earrings
and his bright orange wig, with his ornithologist's binoc-

ulars strapped around his neck and his cock hanging out of his trousers, nobody gave him any trouble. If you came upon him unexpectedly he would immediately put his glasses to his eye. Whether this was exquisite tact or complete confusion as to his role – an inability to make up his mind whether he was a shower-off or a looker-on – who could say? For my part I was never very interested in him. But Camilla – there! I've named her at last, my beloved and much-missed Camilla, whose spirit fills and frets this place for me – Camilla was, in that perverse way of hers, entirely sympathetic to him. Unforgiving of just about everybody, enraged by the smallest omissions of her friends, she was massively tolerant of aberrations. And according to her, this was an aberration every bit as massive as her tolerance. He had shown it to her in a queue at the post office once, and she had understood immediately how tragically limited were his options. 'You've no idea what an enormous size it is,' she tried to explain to me. 'I can see why he has to show it, the poor bugger. There's absolutely nothing else he could possibly do with it.'

Well, she was wrong there. One thing he could do with it was to trundle it up the hill to the village school, poke it through the protective railings, and get the children – girls or boys, he didn't much care which – to measure it. And that was how, one afternoon, the village parents found him: standing on the old slate wall, one arm hooked around a cast iron railing, his binoculars pointing out to sea, his trousers open, and all their pretty ones gathered round him with their tiny rulers and protractors.

Camilla was a Parish Councillor again that year, but although she liked to make matters of public morality her own there was nothing she could do, even in her official capacity, to soothe parental wrath. This was not the sort of subject, either, that she was likely to be at her most understanding about. She didn't throb parentally herself. She didn't much care for children. And she certainly didn't believe they were in possession of any innocence worth troubling oneself to protect.

11

'The only thing you've got to worry about,' she told the near murderous mother of one little girl, 'is what this has done to her expectations. I myself don't see how men can be anything but one big disappointment to her after this.'

'I very much doubt that the experience will turn Colin into a homosexual,' she assured the harbour master's wife. 'But if it does, look on the bright side – one more homosexual in the world means one less compliant wife and mother.'

It took the police though, not Camilla's reassurances, to forestall the terrible vengeance demanded by outraged decency and to escort the five frightened flashers safely from the village.

It seems to be doing me some good, forcing myself to remember actual words that Camilla spoke. Her presence has been getting unhealthily generalized and diffused of late, particularly when I'm out walking the cliffs or following the course of rambles that we used to take together deep into the Valency Valley. There has been a touch of Heathcliff about me recently, I fear, that is if someone who is called Barney Fugleman and what's more *looks* as he if is called Barney Fugleman can approximate to such a gentile, such a Christian, such an English, such an essentially *Cornish* spinster's fantasy. But then why not? Might it not be possible to show, without going so far as to claim Jewish parentage for her Liverpudlian gypsy foundling, that it was precisely someone such as me, swarthy and saturnine and inhospitable and liable to vent my spleen on other people's pets, that the poor girl dreamed about, my fur coat and Bally shoes notwithstanding, in the back room of that draughty rectory? It's not out of the question. I've stirred the imagination of more than one lonely bookish vicar's daughter in my time. Either way, it's a surprise to me how morbid I've become. I listen to voices in the wind for God's sake! I trudge moors. I haunt country graveyards. Dogs I have always wanted to kick and I might myself, at any time, have hung up Isabella Linton's – the more the worms writhe, and all that – but now, I swear, and this is absolutely uncharacteristic of me, if I knew what an ash tree looked like or where one was to be found I could very easily fall to dashing my head against it.

To convey the extremity of my condition let me tell you that I toyed, for longer than I care to admit, with the notion of having all Camilla's words printed in a different type-face – in something thin and spectral and wraith-like, in tribute to her rarity and other-worldliness and ventriloquial genius. The only thing that changed my mind was the realization that Camilla herself would have hated it. She didn't see herself as a wraith. And she loathed every kind of tricksiness. Her preference, in all things, was always for simplicity and directness. As indeed, when I am myself, is mine. This was one of the many fastidiousnesses that united us. Together we were very choosy in our ideas of what constituted good art. We couldn't stand, in just about equal measure, novels that took an interminable time telling you who was telling the story and how he came by it, both of us being perfectly at home with the convention of invisible omniscient narrators, no matter what people said about the breakdown of social certainty and the consequent necessary fictiveness of fabulists. We had no patience for films that could in any way be described as experimental, enigmatic, or surreal; and we could not abide plays that were about tramps, lunatics, savages without language, the terminally infirm, or the problem of writing plays. When I think of the number of theatres we stormed out of together and the quantity of paperbacks we tossed into the fire to keep us warm in winter, or into the sea to keep us young in spring, my heart aches.

Stuck out here, so far from the civilizing amenities, all efforts to keep in touch with written or spoken English were labours of love. We had to drive for an hour to find an even moderately well-stocked bookshop. If we wanted to see a play in the West End we had to set out early in the morning, leaving food for the cats, messages

13

for the milkman, and the telephone number of the hotel we were staying at in case anyone important to us died while we were away. And yet before ten minutes of the first scene had elapsed we were up out of our seats – often on the front row, sometimes in a box – and into the nearest bar. We weren't particularly interested in drinking; we just wanted somewhere quiet to sit where we could talk over the insult that had just been delivered to our intelligence. We didn't just sneer; we discussed and analysed conscientiously. Our conversations on these occasions were almost certainly the best things on anywhere in London.

In the second of our summers together (the really good one) I think we must have seen as many as twenty-five plays without getting to the final act of any of them. One – I suppose it must have been a Pinter – we walked out of before a single character had even said anything. On top of that we consigned to the flames or the waves one Gunter Grass, two John Fowles, a Nabokov, a John Berger, three Doris Lessings, a Gore Vidal, two John Barths, and the whole of Jorge Luis Borges. I remember that I even tossed in a Norman Mailer but Camilla dived in – she was a stupendous diver – and rescued him. I think she detected my unclean unliterary motive. I knew that she had a soft spot for Norman Mailer and that for him she might leave me. We were very much in love that summer. We had a ball.

I didn't worry too much about Norman Mailer. There didn't seem any realistic danger of his turning up here with a rucksack, so far from the jazz and the booze and the hot bitches and the hellish stench of home. It was already stretching probability that I should be here, and I was not, more's the pity, Norman Mailer, I did not have his rival distractions, and I had come for a purpose.

Of course the village has had its share of literary celebrity. Even leaving aside Lance Tourney, Camilla and myself, and the dozens who are at this very moment scribbling down their dreams in low-rent fishermen's

14

cottages all around the harbour, this spot is consecrated by one who came and courted here, and roamed and wrote awhile, and returned famously, full of remorse and rhyme. Many of those who visit today, whose mornings I interrupt and spoil up on the cliffs, are on a sort of pilgrimage and have come to inspect the church and walk the valley, to see the stiff escarpments, to stride the purple strand, to lose themselves in the flounce flinging mists. Don't think that you detect any irony; you won't hear a word against such pilgrims from me. After all, Camilla made her living out of them. And I welcome tourists for the very reason that the National Trust fears them: there is a good chance they will eventually wear away the countryside.

Let them come in their thousands. It's not their fault, individually, that they cannot read a word of the melancholy poems and novels they have journeyed here in order to topographically reconstruct. The whole culture conspires to blind them. Camilla was always very wary of my conspiracy theories; she believed she could smell in them the airless odour of ghetto fears. But we differed not a jot about this one: some rural plot it is, hatched over the centuries in countless village halls and parlours, that convinces the English there is an indissoluble connection between literature and lakes, between meaning and mountains, between poets and peasants, between honesty and haylofts. I remember one long hot afternoon, sitting with Camilla on the little wooden bridge halfway up the valley, dangling our bare feet in the water, discussing this and related topics. It must have been a very hot day because I do not take willingly to uncovering my feet. I always like to feel that I am fully dressed and ready for flight. Another ghetto fear. I think the pretext – for our discussion, not my barefootedness – was the news we'd received that morning that Lilian Stinsford, a woman who occasionally worked for Camilla at the school, had been taken into hospital and was not expected to return from it. Lilian Stinsford had been a blooming energetic

15

townswoman brought down here, kicking and screaming every inch of the way, by a husband in retreat from
the modern world. He put her in a white thatched cottage in sight of the sea, gave her advice, babies, and
more advice, and scratched together a pittance himself
painting birds on local slate and selling them to the
tourists he abhorred. They became a familiar sight
around the village, Ken and Lilian Stinsford, once their
children grew up and got the hell out, he stooping to
croon over some marvel of growth or colour in the
hedgerows, his face contorted into a horrible simu-
lacrum of simple pleasure, she always a foot or two
behind and to leeward of him, tossing pebbles into the
fields or swiping at flowers with the stick he'd carved
and insisted that she carried, her hair a pure white, her
eyes puffed out with the poison of unused life. 'And not
once has that man paused to consider the wrong he's
done her,' I recall Camilla saying. 'Not once in the thirty
years he lived here. But then why should he? Who or
what in this place could ever plant the idea of erroneousness in his mind? He goes out into his garden in the
morning, feels the pulse of God beating evenly in the soil,
detects the same unhurried rhythm in his own breast
and in that of his goats and chickens, and therefore
knows that his poor frenzied wife is the anomaly, not
him. Women don't have a chance in Nature, Barney. The
heat and the tempo are against them. Nature belongs to
men. Look at a ploughed field – have you ever seen anything more brutal or tyrannical in your life? All farmers
are fascists, Barney. By instinct. The only future for
women is in the cities. Not that there's any future for
poor Lilian.'

I can still see Camilla swinging her legs as she spoke,
absently kicking the surface of the stream, her toes
painted a deep Clytemnestra purple, frightening away
the summer flies that had paused to feed and cool off.

'Admit I'm right,' she said, after I'd failed to respond.
'Admit that there isn't a single person in the village that
isn't sorry for Ken for being stuck with a neurotic wife.

Decent old Ken who just wanted to paint birds and collect worms in peace. Admit that the assertion of the male will begins, like everything else, in the country.'

What could I say? I wouldn't have argued with her if I'd wanted to. She looked brown and strong and immovable. And I was sitting on the very edge of the bridge. True, the stream was shallow, but I couldn't swim an inch and was quite capable of drowning in a hip bath. And anyway, I didn't wish to quarrel with her. I didn't think anything good came out of Nature either. Even food had nothing to recommend it to my taste until all trace of the earth had been grilled or sautéed out of it. I was the last person to argue that it wasn't the same with human beings.

I nodded and smiled, but before I could get around to shaping a fuller answer we were disturbed by a couple of wonder-struck students from Camilla's summer school. Camilla had founded the school three or four years earlier – before my time, that is – on the shrewd hunch that there would be some amongst the annual literary pilgrims who would welcome serious organization, the provision of expert lectures, properly researched and conducted rambles, and above all the opportunity to meet like-minded enthusiasts in an atmosphere conducive to devotional exchanges of findings and opinions. On perfect days like this Camilla sent everybody off in different directions, with copies of the poems, in order to find the field where and the bridle path from whence and the high cliff whither. Well, wasn't this the little bridge on which? Yes, yes, it was. How clever of them to have recognised it! And had they also noticed on the way the selfsame small weir and the very stepping-stone? Camilla was marvellously encouraging and informative. To an untrained eye she even appeared to have a passion for her subject. But then he was her living.

Long after the ecstatic intruders had left us – Camilla had sent them next in search of the stony stile – we remained quiet, brooding separately. It really must have

17

been a marvellous day, because I can distinctly remember taking off my tie and rolling up my shirt sleeves and commenting on how nice it was out here. Such avid naturism was not called out of me without good reason. But my words served only to remind Camilla of her theme. Her anger against mankind in general had been aggravated, it seemed, by her being forced to recall the one man in particular, that presiding genius who had grieved upon this little bridge. 'And when the woman has been bullied and harried unto death,' she said, assuming that I had been following all her silent thoughts or that I was smart enough to fill in the gaps myself, 'when she has attained to the only peace and independence she is likely ever to have known, then along he comes again with his bent back and his remorse and his generous gift of guilt, making *her* death yet one more triumph for *him*, muscling in once more on whatever dignity or sympathy or attention happens to be going. Another Hamlet taking on all-comers in Ophelia's grave. Fucking men with their obtrusive fucking guilt!'

I didn't take it personally at the time – I seemed a long way from country graveyards then – but there is no possibility of my not noticing now that some of the flak from Camilla's firing was meant to come my way. Guilt was one of my words. It helped me to understand myself. I believed I carried it in every pocket and that the weight of it was the reason I bent slightly at the knees. It's certainly the reason I'm not entirely upright now.

Don't mistake me, though. The guilt I've always been interested in is not the usual variety of cosmic unworthiness. I'm not a self-hater. I don't wonder what such a creature as I is doing crawling across the face of the earth. I don't feel that I'm largely to blame for starving Africans or camps of futureless refugees. What I'm referring to is a very particular sense of having let women down, not just the odd woman and not merely at random, but as it were the whole sex, systematically.

Perhaps a fragment of family history will help me to

explain more exactly what I mean.

On the night he was married my father turned in his sleep, slipped both his hands inside the pure white nightdress of his softly slumbering wife – this is my mother I'm talking about: I have the right to heightened language – and murmured, 'Lucetta, ah Lucetta, comme tu est douce! Que je t'aime!'

This was a surprise to both of them, for not only could my father speak no French, my mother's name was Rachel.

To this day my father swears that he was as innocent as Adam of knowledge of any other woman, had never even heard of anyone called Lucetta, and that his whispering for her in his first sleep as a husband was just another example of that atrocious luck that has dogged him all his life when it comes to remembering my mother's name. God knows whether he is telling the truth. Certainly my mother did her best to understand the sorts of associative confusions that might have been behind her receiving anniversary flowers accompanied by a card 'To my darling Rose', and gifts of jewellery on her birthday 'For Golda'. But I know for a fact that she had never been happy about the letters my father sent her all those years ago from Germany – he had entered Hamburg with the British 2nd Army, just a month before my fifth birthday – addressed to 'Liebe Helga'.

In fairness to him it must be said that he has made no better a job of remembering the names of my wives. The only time he got my first one's right was on the day I was marrying my second. 'Here's to Barney and Sharon,' he proposed, raising a tumbler of champagne, for all the world the proudest and the happiest of fathers-in-law; only Sharon had not, for reasons to do with good taste, been invited. Camilla – how vividly I recollect it! – roared with amusement. But she was capable of doing something like that while having her own thoughts.

The odd thing about this idiosyncrasy of my father's is that names are in a sense his living. I've never known what precisely he does in that comfortable room of his in

Somerset House, directly above a Tuscan column and with wide views over the Thames, except that he is involved in some way with births and birth certificates. In earlier times, when his job was new to him and he had a young family to entertain, he would come home, take off his coat, and without further preliminary explanations rattle off the latest batch of cruel and comic christenings, the day's dirty tricks that parents had played upon their children. 'Ivor Soredick,' he would say, as we all fussed around him, bringing him tea and helping him off with his shoes. 'Greta Warmley, Eva Brick, Nelson McCollum, Noah Arkwright, Ava Crisp, Russell Spring, Albert Bridge, Clyde Banks, Treta Wright, Atossa Day.' And after supper, if we were lucky, he might remember some more. 'Mavis Sphincter, Nola Blower, Rosina Hattrick, Yule Grocock, Rosy Titball, Neil Downs, Melvyn Bragg, Carrie Waters, Ellen Evans, Willie Wanklyn, Montague Gaylord, Butch Walker, Patricia Plaything.'

On some nights he would go on for hours. There is no possibility that he could have made these names up. There were too many of them. And we never caught him out repeating any. He simply remembered them. He saw them once and he never again forgot them. From which it must follow that there was nothing organically wrong with his memory. Some other explanation must therefore be found for why he so often suffered amnesia when he came to address or give something to his wife, and why he so frequently confused her with other women, real or imaginary, who might or might not have enjoyed some separate and individual existence in his life.

Guilt, of course, is where I'm heading, guilt husbandly and filial, guilt personal and atavistic, but I've no objection to pausing briefly, on the way, at guilt's greatest ally, love. 'Twice or thrice had I loved thee,' I tried to convince Camilla on countless cliff walks or valley rambles, 'Before I knew thy face or name.' But I was never successful. 'You'd say that to anyone,' she told me, 'you've said it to I'll never know how many others.'

20

Which showed how far she was from grasping what I was telling her. It wasn't her fault. No member of her sex can ever understand how, for a man, love is a continuum. They cannot bear the idea that all previous women are but a dream of them, because that must mean that they themselves are but a dream of someone else. It's no coincidence that Plato was a man.

'I don't want to be a part of your continuum, thanks very much,' Camilla told me, as though this was an area where either of us could exercise any choice. Lucetta might just as well have protested against popping up in my father's wedding-night dreams. My poor father – he is only a man like the rest of us; no wonder he could never be absolutely certain who his wife was: sometimes I have woken up next to Camilla and not known whether she was herself or my mother or my cousins or Sharon or the little girl whose head I split open on bonfire night, 1947, because her fireworks rose higher in the sky than mine.

And so, although Camilla happened to be the last and best, and although these are exclusively her haunts I try each day to track her down through, strictly speaking I walk this wild western shore, attired as if I'm on the way to a wine bar, for all of them.

That is not, of course, and I am the first to admit it, any kind of adequate explanation of how I came to have wound up here, washed up like that bit of exotic wreckage that was found on the rocks this morning – a splinter of a roulette table, the fishermen reckoned, from some capsized pleasure boat. And if I am ever to get away with a clear conscience and a clearer head – yes, that is my intention, despite the liquid looks I am getting from the local bean-eaters and other assorted fantasists I meet in the pubs and who want to tell me that they can see I have fallen fatally for the place as they have done – if I am going to escape, then I must follow Camilla's old advice to me and come clean. I don't expect it to be easy. It is not in the grain of my nature to

21

be candid and confessional. 'I'm an embroiderer,' I told Camilla, I don't know how many times. 'I'm interested in the filigree around the edges of the truth.' 'You mean you haven't got a straight bone in your body,' she used to reply.

Ours was, as I think I have already made plain, a very verbal, argumentative connection.

Well, I can't argue with you now, Camilla. But wherever you are, prepare to admit that you were wrong. Turn your fine stern eyes in this direction. Look at me. See how straight I'm growing. Watch how clean I'm coming.

Cleanish, anyway.

Part One

1

1

I'd be prepared to say that it was my own fault for tampering with the secret arts, except that that confers too much dignity on all parties. This isn't a Faustian story.

All I had done was act on some passing marital impulse, to please and pacify a wife and, while I was at it, confound a cheap and easy charlatan. And even though things had got a bit beyond me I would still have been all right – I had already convinced Sharon that continued conjugal harmony depended on her willingness to stop saying, 'But that's amazing!' – if only the local necromantic press, namely *The Finchley Zoist and Astral Traveller*, had not got hold of my story, or if only I had not got hold of it. I can still hear the noise it made – I'm referring to the actual noise of the actual paper, not publicity – as it came crashing, unsolicited – it goes without saying that I was not a regular subscriber – through my letter box. Rolled up so that it resembled the sort of weapon with which peasants revolt and delivered with enormous violence, it got three-quarters of the way into our hall and might have even made it up the stairs had it not collided with the telephone table and knocked the receiver off its cradle.

The racket caused Sharon to sit bolt upright in our bed and me to be forcibly propelled from those moist, dark places underneath her arms into which it was my custom, immediately upon waking, to bury myself. I mention this small domestic detail not to be indelicate but because it proves that although I had little time for immaterialism or popular metaphysics, and did not welcome periodicals of the tele- or the para-anything, I was not some rigid earth-bound rationalist, confined merely to the here, the palpable and the now. In my private life especially, in the matters of those mysterious intimacies between men and women which seemed to spawn, in these days, so many Acts of Parliament – this was 1967, that *annus mirabilis* for consenting adults – I considered myself to be unusually open to experience: an adventurer, a seeker, a wayfarer who knew that the way forward might also be the route back and that in order to come up it was sometimes necessary to go down. Sharon was not a woman who needed any encouragement to allow the hairs on her body to grow when and where they wanted, but I encouraged her anyway; a fanatic horticulturalist, I urged on wild profusions of growth, so that when I plunged nose first into them I could be back in the primaeval forest, listening again to the blatherings of the macaws, the faraway insistent beat of native drums, and the closer, the much closer screech of the baboons.

Ours was not, is what I'm trying to convey, a spiritually diffident household, but that didn't mean that I was pleased to find the current issue of *The Finchley Zoist and Astral Traveller* waiting for us amongst the wreckage of our hall furniture; still less that I was keen to read the article it contained concerning me.

Sharon was, though. She caught me on the point of feeding it down our mechanical sink tidy, took it from me and bore it back upstairs with her to the lavatory. It was also part of our relational intrepidity not to close doors, and I was able to hear her exclaiming 'But that's amazing!' at regular intervals. When she came down again she was still wearing her reading spectacles which I took to mean that she wanted to read to me aloud. But first she offered to soften me up with one of her famous calculations. 'Do you know,' she said, 'that if you add together all the numerals in today's date' – it was the 12th day of the 8th month in the year 1967 – 'and take away the number of pages in this paper' – there were 8 – 'plus the time it was delivered' – on the stroke of 8.00 – 'you will arrive at your age?' I was 27. I think you will find that the mathematics work. I never checked myself. I had a sort of stunned and absolute faith in Sharon's ability in the field of numerology.

Thinking about her now I feel a great nostalgia for her innocent almaniacal obsession with dates and numbers and coincidences, and I can see that it was nothing but the efflorescence of a good and hopeful nature. What she yearned for above all was a universal and perhaps even an inter-galactic certainty, and those little wonders of synchronicity she discerned were important to her because they were confirmations of coherence, and therefore causes for celebration. She was ready to crack a bottle of champagne every time something added up. After five years of marriage I suppose I must have been less responsive to this statistical optimism than I ought to have been, but I must confess that in the early days of our courtship I capitalized on it unscrupulously. I could get her to do anything for me provided that I justified it with a small sum. She would stay with me until whatever hour in the morning was equal to the addition of both her parents' birthdays divided by how many veins I could count on her forearm. She would kiss me in as many places as I could multiply the seconds we'd known each other by the minutes we hadn't. I always regretted that more of the means whereby men and women please one another were not referred to by numbers instead of names because I believed I could have totted her up into all of them As it was I gave myself a sounder mathematical grounding in her company than most modern boys, with their reliance on pocket calculators, can ever hope to equal.

But on this occasion, with everything totalling 27 and Sharon looking full of amazement, I didn't manage to be very graceful. 'Read it to me then, if you really have to,' is what I must have said, because read it to me she did; but I reckon I must have added some imprecations to my consent. I know I was most irritated with her.

This is what she read to me and if you wonder how I come to remember it so vividly I can at least tell you that it is not for want of trying to forget it.

MULTIPLE PERSONALITY, COSMIC MEMORY,
OR REINCARNATION?

The study of human immortality through hypnotic age regression moved one step closer to public recognition and acceptance three evenings ago when a number of local business people and literary luminaries crowded into Sharon Fugleman's bookshop in order to meet and listen to the distinguished London-based hypnotherapist, Harry Vilbert. After a characteristically lucid and modest introductory lecture, in the course of which he vigorously disassociated himself from those 'cocktail party illusionists' who bring the work of serious students of the paranormal into disrepute, Mr Vilbert proceeded to a demonstration of his remarkable gifts. As is often the case with first-time regression groups, where apprehension does not yet recognize itself as joyful expectancy, it took a little time for a volunteer to be found, but finally Mr Barney Fugleman, the husband of the bookshop's proprietress, stepped forward. He did not at first appear to be an ideal subject. His initial movements and responses suggested unwillingness and even suspicion, and when asked to relax he sat bolt upright in his chair, his fists clenched tightly on his knees, his eyes forced open to an unnatural degree. But Harry Vilbert proved to us once again that there is no recalcitrance which cannot be turned into quiescence. Only idiots cannot be hypnotized. Within a few minutes Mr Fugleman's head fell forward and he was taken with consummate ease through all the preliminary stages of hypnosis. Released from the constraints of his present personality and sent back to ransack the boundless immensities of time that preceded his birth for some vital memory or recollection, he dropped almost at once into a voice and style of diction not normally his own. What follows is given verbatim, and it can be seen that Harry Vilbert asked the most straightforward of questions and in no way coaxed or prompted the subject.

'Where are you?'

(Silence, but a rapid movement of the eyes and some moistening of the lips.)

'Where are you? Do you hear me?'

'Yes. Be quiet. I'm trying to see.'

'What is it that you are trying to see? What do you see?'

'I didn't come on purpose to look. I'm on an errand.'

'You didn't come on purpose to look at what?'

'The woman.'

'What is the woman doing?'

'I don't know . . . nothing . . . she is just swinging.'

'Do you know this woman?'

'I've read about her. Everyone has read about her.'

'Do you know her name?'

'How else could I have read about her? It's Martha . . . Martha Brown.'

'What kind of swing is she on?'

'She isn't on a swing. She is on a rope.'

'She's swinging on a rope?'

'Yes.'

'What is the rope attached to then? Is it tied to a tree?'

'No. (Laughter) It is tied to her.'

'Around her waist?'

'Around her neck.'

'Isn't that rather dangerous?'

'(More laughter) Not now it isn't.'

'Is she already dead then, this woman?'

'Just about.'

'Did you hang her?'

'I? No, I have too tender a heart. I am just here on an errand. Calcraft the hangman hanged her.'

'And you watched him?'

'I and thousands of others. It's a big crowd here . . . but I have a very good view.'

'Why do you want to watch?'

'She is a handsome woman. She makes a fine figure.'

'But isn't she covered?'

'They put a white cap over her face but it has become transparent in the rain. I can see her features quite clearly – even the parting of her lips.'

'What else is she wearing?'

'Only a black silk gown. It rustled when she was led past me, and you could hear it rustling when she first twisted half around and back again. But it is quiet now. The rain has made it cling to her body.'

'Is that why you are watching?'

'I can see all her shape.'

'How old are you?'

'I am sixteen.'

'Have you been to many hangings?'

'No. There hasn't been one for years. '

'What year is this, then?'

'1856.'

'I haven't yet asked you your name.'

'Tom . . . Tommy.'

'And your other name?'

'Ah . . . Thomas.'

'No, I meant your second name. Your family name.'

'Aaah . . . (A sudden switching of voices here) AAH.'

'What's the matter? Why don't you want to tell me your second name?'

'AAAH . . . AAAAAH.'

'What is it? Why are you frightened?'

'AAAAAH . . . AAAAAAAAAH.'

'It's all right Tommy. I just wanted to know how to address you if I needed to write to you. Tommy who? Thomas what?'

'AAAAAAH . . . AAAAAAAAAAAAAH.'

At this point Harry Vilbert hurriedly brought his subject, who was shaking violently, back to the present. He later explained to our reporter that he did not believe he could safely proceed any further with the regression as the reluctance to disclose the second name was not Tommy's but Barney's. The hostility felt by the present to the previous incumbent of Barney Fugleman's host body must have been very great, he went on, for there to have been an intervention, across time and consciousness, on this scale. It is not unusual, he said, for subjects to be dismayed and even disgusted by the unfamiliar personalities who have inexplicably usurped their accustomed functions; but he had never before witnessed such determined resistance: Tommy was so unwelcome to Barney Fugleman that he was not even allowed the most basic individualizing human right to name himself.

I stopped Sharon here. Apart from the suggestion that I had been behaving like a fascist towards my own unconscious or whatever part of me I had dredged that monstrous creation, Tommy, out of, all that Sharon read was familiar to me. It was only a few days since, to please Sharon, I had subjected myself to these indignities, and I still retained a sort of dull, anaesthetized recollection of the experience, much as if I had woken sooner and less oblivious than I would have liked on the morning after a drunken party. Only I knew I hadn't been to any party. 'I know all that,' I said, 'can I put it down the sink now?'

But Sharon wasn't dismayed by my lack of enthusiasm. 'You haven't heard the last paragraph yet,' she told me, launching straight into it.

Our researches have since established that on Saturday, August 9, 1856, a woman named Martha Brown was publicly hanged from a scaffold outside Dorchester prison. Her crime was the murder of her husband.

She wore for her execution a simple and light black silk gown. A crowd of several thousand people turned up, as the case had enjoyed much notoriety and there had not been a hanging here for many years. It was, as Tommy clearly remembered, a rainy day.

2

'Don't you think that that's amazing?'

I wasn't prepared to make even the pretence of considering it. 'No,' I said.

'Then how do you explain it?'

'Do I have to explain it? I can't explain how water comes up and waits for me in my pipes but that doesn't mean I have to be amazed every time I turn on the tap.'

Sharon might have been the one without the university degree but I could see she was not going to let me get away with *that*. 'Plumbing can be explained scientifically.'

'Not by me it can't, Sharon. By me nothing can be explained scientifically.' This wasn't rhetoric; for all that I consider myself to be a realist I have always possessed a very dim sense of how things operate. Perhaps it's Jewish. In the household I was brought up in you rang an electrical contractor when you wanted a plug fixing. So I wasn't exaggerating when I said to Sharon, 'I don't even understand how a mirror works.'

She helped me out. 'Refraction.'

For a numerologist she could be very literal. And I really did have a point that I wanted to make. 'Listen, Sharon,' I said to her, putting more than usual authority into my voice, 'my own body is a vast machinery of mysteries and minor miracles to me. Its every function astounds me. See, I can crook my little finger within an infinitesimal fraction of a second from the moment I decided I would like to crook it. If I want to stamp my foot, look, I can stamp my foot. How can this be? Sharon, if I were to put my mind to it – and putting one's mind to something is also a miraculous little activity – I would be filled with reverence for myself every time I moved a muscle.'

'Which isn't very often.'

'It might not be often, Sharon, but if we are going in for astonishment it is astonishing I can do it at all. Right now, even as I speak, thousands of tiny valves are opening and closing in obscure corners of me, without my even asking them to. So what am I supposed to do – consider myself to be a prodigy just because I work?'

'All right, stop shouting.'

'I'm not shouting.' I'm sure I wasn't shouting. 'Sharon, we're both approaching thirty; between us we're almost sixty. That's old enough to know that nothing is amazing because everything is.'

That was meant to be the end of it. Had we been a television programme the credits would have started to roll. But Sharon was dogged this morning. 'You don't want to know how you came to get Martha Brown's name right?'

I shook my head.

'You don't want to know how you were able to describe accurately the dress she was wearing?'

I shook my head.

'You're not curious about the date even?'

I poured myself some coffee.

'Do you realise that August 9th was the day on which Martha Brown was hung *and* you were hypnotized by Harry Vilbert?'

'A black day for both of us,' I replied. I couldn't stay silent all morning. 'But you can't make much of the coincidence, Sharon. Her August 9th was 1856, mine was 1967. If you could have managed an exact hundred years anniversary I might have been impressed, as it is – '

'As it is the difference is 111 years, and you don't need me to tell you that 111 is the devil's number.'

With which she rose from the breakfast table and left me, whereupon the credits, this time, really did begin to roll.

But in twenty minutes she was down again, dressed all in black and looking dangerous. 'By the way,' she said, 'we're not sixty between us, we're fifty-five and a half. Make what you like of that.'

God knows, I tried to.

We had enjoyed a similarly inconclusive exchange a couple of weeks earlier when Sharon had first proposed

Harry Vilbert (who lived in a basement bedsitter around the corner and did odd jobs for us) as a change from the usual blank versifiers and quaint antiquarians she invited every other Friday to address small audiences in her bookshop by West Finchley tube station. Because of its proximity to the tube, and because she had been twenty-one in 1960, and because there already was a Jules et Jim selling kitchen co-ordinates three doors down, Sharon had called her shop Zazie's dans le Metro. I had never been enthusiastic about the name, but then it was Sharon's constant complaint, particularly in conversations with her mother, that I wasn't enthusiastic about anything that I hadn't myself initiated. Such as Harry Vilbert.

But in fairness to me I must say that it wasn't because I hadn't thought of him first that I didn't want him. I have always had a strong aversion to people who want to swing pendulums before your eyes or tell you exactly how much change and how many sweets you're carrying in your trouser pockets or claim that they're receiving loving messages from your least favourite dead relation. The question of whether or not they're shysters hardly enters into it; it's the poor taste of their props and costumes that tells you all you need to know. The same irredeemable tawdriness that dogs stage magic dogs the spirit world. Materialism, I know, has its drawbacks, but disembodied souls lack the dignity even of the flesh. I have an unshakable conviction that human beings only approach divinity when they are upright, awake, a touch corpulent, and wholly sceptical. A God without a body is nothing but a trick of semantics.

This was why I was against Harry Vilbert. Not that he didn't have a body. He did – if anything too much of a one for my liking. He was one of those slight, wiry, ageing men whose earthly tabernacles seem to take a long time receiving from the brain the appropriate messages as to quiescence and decay. There was a grey pallor of death upon him, and yet one could see that there was still spring in his flesh, still a greedy respon-

34

siveness to sensation at the very surface of his skin. And his speciality – apart from doing odd jobs around the shop for us and selling copper charms and bangles on the Portobello Road – was conducting out-of-the-body experiments. This was why I was against him. 'Must we really have him?' I objected. 'Couldn't you try Ted Hughes again?'

'Too expensive for us. Anyway you poo-poohed him last time.'

'Ted Hughes?'

'Yes. You said you couldn't take one more fucking poem about a pike.'

It was true I wasn't a Ted Hughes fan. If he'd written plays I would almost certainly have walked out of them. But he was an attractive alternative to Harry Vilbert.

However, Sharon seemed to have made up her mind. 'I think I'll go ahead with Harry,' she said. 'He's very cheap' (it actually hadn't occurred to me until now that we were going to have to *pay* for Harry Vilbert) 'and we badly need someone to breathe life into our occult section – it's gone dead lately.'

That promptly silenced my opposition. How could I be anything but amenable to an argument which bore on stock? The shop was my livelihood as well as Sharon's, and it deserved to be treated as well as it had so far treated us. It was true that I had given precious hours of sweat and labour to the business, doing paper work, helping Sharon with the ordering, accompanying her to the Booksellers' Conference and so on, but it was also true that it gave me a blessed freedom from those sorts of drudgery – schoolteaching, probation work, writing drama criticism for the *Guardian* – that were sapping the energies of my friends. Time was what I had always insisted I wanted, time for the development and expression of my particular gift for analysis and dispute – poo-poohing as Sharon called it – and time had been given to me in plenty. I was only 27. Already I had published over a dozen articles in learned journals, including a blistering attack on the Powys brothers and, if I say so myself, the final word on Emily Brontë. I had a dislike for the English rural tradition. I didn't care for novels set primarily in the outside, on moors or under greenwood trees, especially if the outside they were set in was somehow also metaphorical, that's to say was really the inside of something else. My other pet dislike was for works that consisted of people asking Whether There Was Anyone Who Could Tell Them Who They Were. I was terribly intolerant of identity crises. Novels in which characters asked Whether There Was Anyone Who Could Tell Them Who They Were while standing in the outside that was really the inside were, naturally, anathema to me. I only mention this in order to give some idea of how many more articles I felt I had it in me to write, and how necessary it therefore was that Sharon's bookshop continue to prosper. I suppose you could say that I am justifying myself for having backed down on the issue of Harry Vilbert.

I didn't back down altogether, though. 'All right,' I said. 'Invite the hypnotist. But don't ask me to have anything to do with him.'

'I wouldn't dream of it,' Sharon assured me.

'As long as that's fully understood.'

'It's understood.'

But of course it wasn't. 'There is just one tiny thing you can help me out with,' she remembered. 'Apparently he likes to be certain that someone will volunteer to – '

'No. Definitely no. No. It wouldn't work with me anyway. I'm not suggestible enough. You volunteer.'

'I'll be taking round the cheese dip.'

'*I'll* take round the cheese dip.'

'All right.'

'You're more the sort of person he'd like to work with.'

'Because I'm more suggestible, you mean?'

I knew what I meant. 'Because you're more co-operative.'

'All right. I'll do it.'

'And anyway you'll enjoy it more than I would.'

'Barney, I've said I'll do it. You take round the dip. It suits me.'

She couldn't have been easier about it.

Which is what I have to admit I found unsettling. Wasn't she altogether too easy, too lacking in natural caution and reserve to be put into the hands of some crank hypnotist who might prove to be disreputable? An image of Sharon with her eyes closed, taking off her clothes in public, flashed into my brain and was thence transmitted in shock waves and impulses, not all of them unpleasant but none of them soothing, to those other parts of my body whose workings so astounded me. Everyone who knew Sharon knew what a terrific sport she was. I suppose that was one of the reasons why I'd married her. And she was the kind of sport, quite frankly, that only a girl with a very good figure – heavy Spanish and Portuguese breasts from her Sephardic mother, vertiginous limbs from her quarter-Scandinavian father, and high primitive buttocks from some African tribesperson lost in her family's past – could afford to be. She always conveyed the impression that she was grateful for all that she'd been given and wanted to give some of it back. She was a wild and one might even say careless dancer; she told jokes that were sometimes so outrageous I could only suppose she didn't really understand them; she needed no encouragement whatsoever to stand up in a pub and do her imitations of Sophie Tucker or Eartha Kitt; and when it came to charades her mimes of *Fanny by Gaslight* and *Tit Willow Tit Willow Tit Willow* left no one that I ever observed disappointed. I have no sympathy for men who deliberately marry mousy, retiring women and then spend the rest of their lives falling in love from a safe distance with glamorous, forward ones. But I am able to understand why they do it. A reserved wife in your bed might mean that you sleep more often at night but it also means that you sleep more soundly. For the whole time I had been with Sharon I had never once been able to enjoy the certainty, not for a single hour at a time, that she would not do something in public that would utterly disgrace and humiliate me. The fact that she never yet had was no guarantee that she never yet would. And what made my anxiety even keener now, notwithstanding that we had been five years married and added up, between us, to fifty-five and a half, was the way she had lately taken to dressing. Very short dresses made of filmy materials were the fashion this summer, and there was so much of Sharon compressed into so little that the threat of some sudden, palpable, and absolutely irrecoverable exposure made every social occasion a sort of hell for me. I watched with my heart in my mouth whenever she bent or stretched, and when she leaned forward I could actually hear the blood bubbling up in my temples.

So you can see that I wouldn't have been much of a husband had I left the Harry Vilbert conversation where it was. 'On further consideration,' I said, a little later, 'I think *you* should see to the dip and I'll take my clothes off.'

'You'll do *what*?'

'You know what I mean – I'll expose myself to Harry.'

She looked at me rather strangely, but she let it go at that. As she'd said, she really didn't give a fig who did what.

I, however – and this is a critical moment for my honesty – I, however, did. I'm not going to say that her prompt accession to my change of mind disgruntled me, but I will admit that I immediately experienced a drop of spirits akin to that of disappointment. I had been dreading for a long time what Sharon was going to do to me; could it be that I was also dreading that she wasn't going to do a blessed thing? It was right and proper that I protect her from herself and insist that she be the one to take around the dip. But I felt hollow inside. It might have been nice, that's to say exciting, that's to say frightening – it might have been *something* if she'd taken off her clothes under hypnosis and utterly disgraced me at last.

Along with the musk melon breasts and the tussock of glistering black hairs which curled up to her navel and which could, on a languorous day, be combed two-thirds of the way down to her knees, Sharon had inherited from her mother a taste for that Middle-Eastern Pastiche Baroque in domestic decoration which can be found, in Western Europe anyway, only in Manchester, North London, Solihull and Leeds. Even after five years of sleeping in it I was still not entirely free of the sensation, whenever I entered my bedroom, that I had strayed into a musical comedy stage-set for a pasha's pavilion; and it is the case that when the Finchley Amateur Operatic Society put on *The Desert Song* they asked if they could borrow some of Sharon's furniture. But it was nonetheless here, beneath a canopy padded, studded, and festooned, that the Fugleman marriage nightly reaffirmed its sacred vows and promises, and it was here, a few hours after I'd explained to Sharon why nothing was amazing, that I first began to shape the idea – the fear, the wish, the proposal and the prohibition, as yet the merest exhalation of dread-hope – that was ultimately to make of those vows and promises, in Sharon's words, 'a mockery', and in Sharon's mother's, 'a laughing stock'.

It was Sharon, however, as I clearly recall, who started it.

'When you were that Tommy or Thomas or whatever his name was,' she said, 'how excited were you by the woman you saw hanging?'

'Sharon!' It was not a question I could possibly have anticipated. 'I thought we'd agreed to close that subject.' I think I must have sounded quite prim. I might even have turned a little pink, to match the pillow cases.

'No, go on – tell me. It's fascinating. How excited were you?'

'How excited was *I*? *I* wasn't excited at all. The boy might have been, but I had nothing to do with it. I was as much on the outside as you were.'

'Yes, but you were also the boy, weren't you? You felt what he felt. So what I want to know is what you were doing enjoying looking at another woman?'

'Sharon, she was dead.'

'So you do admit you were looking?'

'The boy was looking.'

'With your eyes.'

'My eyes were closed.'

'Not while they were ogling Martha Brown they weren't. Faithless bastard. Why don't you admit you were excited?'

She was absurd and because absurd obscene and because obscene indomitable in a frilly bed-time play-suit the colour and the transparency of the drapes around the bed and dressing table. She was stretched out to her full length, enjoying her own superabundance, knowing that she had nothing to fear from the likes of Martha Brown, dead or otherwise, prone or suspended. Then she sat up, pulled her showgirl's nightdress over her head, and fell back again with her hands clasped behind her neck so that the moist hollows of her arm-pits glimmered black and mysterious like lost worlds. Starting from the very bottom I began the slow arduous climb to her summit. Once there I pressed my lips to her ear and was astonished myself to hear what they said. 'The only thing that excited me,' I listened to them whisper, 'was the thought that it might have been you.'

She didn't understand. 'The thought that *what* might have been me?'

I was confidential. Even husky. 'You know.'

'I don't.'

'That you might have been her.'

'That I might have been *who*?'

'The woman.'

'The woman on the gibbet? Thanks very much!'

'Forget the gibbet. I just meant you in front of all those people.'

'Swinging on the end of a rope with my neck broken and a muslin bag over my face, being stared at by weird adolescents?' She really hadn't got the hang of what I was trying to suggest.

'No, no, forget the rope, forget that she's dead, forget that it's a public execution. In fact,' I was suddenly totally dispirited, 'forget everything. I'm sorry I spoke. All I meant was that the idea of you with your dress plastered to your body being admired by three thousand people was mildly exciting to me. That's all. But let's by all means talk about something else.'

She was sitting upright now, irritated, drying with a corner of bed-sheet the ear into which I had attempted to deposit my poison. 'I can't work you out,' she said. 'One minute you're complaining that I let myself go too much in public, the next you want me to be a stripper.'

'Who said anything about being a stripper? Martha Brown wasn't exactly performing at a stag party, was she?'

'She might as well have been, given the kicks you and your creepy little Thomas friend quite obviously got from her.'

'Sharon, you amaze me – '

'*I* amaze you! Well that's something. This morning you told me that nothing amazes you. At least there's been some progress. Good night.'

I remained awake for a long time. I think I was just the smallest bit rattled. There were a few things I needed to be clear in my own mind about. I believed I wasn't exaggerating when I told Sharon that there was nothing that related to Tommy or to Martha Brown – neither the hypnotic experience itself, which occupied about the same position on the wow! scale as having a tooth extracted under gas, nor that morning's article, confirming my uncanny historical accuracy – which left me in the slightest bit curious. This might have been unimaginative and unadventurous of me, but what could I do? I held it as an article of faith that there were some events that simply did not merit curiosity. I felt exactly the same about members of one family falling out of bed simultaneously in different parts of the world, water-

41

divination, resurrections, omens, premonitions, polter-geists, psychokinesis ouija boards, Stonehenge. If a ghost had walked into my bedroom at that very moment – assuming there to be a ghost that could negotiate the orga-nized clutter and survive the chronological confusions of Sharon's domestic architecture – I would have been frightened right enough, but I would have gone about my business as usual in the morning and I would not have taken out a subscription to *The Finchley Zoist and Astral Traveller*. It was all a question, in the last resort, of self-respect and dignity. It didn't follow, just because the universe at times behaved absurdly, that I, Barney Fugleman, had to do the same. On the other hand – and this was what was keeping me awake so long – there was absolutely no point in my pretending that nothing had happened, that I didn't feel there'd been some subtle change in me, and that that prurient little Victorian rat-bag, Thomas Whosit, was not still hovering around in the shadows, filling my head with lewd and God-knows unbidden images, when, as my failed attempt to mutter foully in Sharon's ear plainly attested, something had, I did, and he was. I was not, though, inclined to blame myself for any of this. I felt that I was being trespassed upon. I had certainly not issued any invitations. As Harry Vilbert had testified, I had done everything in my power to make it clear to the morbid boy that he wasn't welcome. It struck me that if he wouldn't go away it was now up to Harry Vilbert, who had let him out, to lock him up again.

I looked at the innocent sleeping form of my wife beside me, and remembered how our two families had com-pletely filled the seats of the reform synagogue on the day we'd got married, and how many tears had been shed, and how many telegrams had been read out, and how many sets of sheets and pillow-cases, all of them bought whole-sale, we'd received as presents from relations we didn't know we had. A marriage, as the rabbi had said, was not merely a union of two; I owed it to more than just myself and Sharon that I see Harry Vilbert again as soon as pos-sible. Having arrived at which resolution I too fell asleep.

And very soon I was one of a seething mob, all male – all unmitigatedly male – who had gathered outside Dorchester Synagogue in the rain to watch Sharon Fugleman swinging from a rope in a sopping chiffon play-suit, doing her Sophie Tucker imitations. In front of me a group of farm labourers in dusty smocks were exchanging ribald comments.

'A beauty an' no mistake,' said one.

'An' willin' too, I'll be bound,' opined the other.

Sipping poison, I leaned towards them so as not to miss a single word.

When I awoke in the morning I could not at first remember what I had dreamt, but I could taste the poison still, warm and sweet upon my lips.

4

'You can't get rid of him altogether, then?'

Harry Vilbert was deprecating of his own powers. 'I'm not an exorcist,' he said. A trifle bitterly, I thought, as if he believed it was someone's fault that he wasn't.

I wasn't much pleased with his remark myself. 'I don't need an exorcist,' I said. 'I'm not possessed.'

Harry Vilbert looked out of the window of his basement flat at the ankles of the passing pedestrians. 'We're all possessed,' he said, after an interval.

I made a rapid decision not to fight with him. 'So I've got to have this person kicking around in my past whether I like it or not?' I asked, instead.

'If he's there, he's there.' He swept his long white hair out of his eyes. On both his wrists he wore beaten copper bangles, as around his neck he wore an amulet engraved with Celtic Trees of Life and triskeles and zoomorphics and Key patterns taken from the Nigg Stone, to ward off rheumatism and arthritis. He was a thwarted and a disappointed man and he had upon his skin that grey dye of suburban shiftiness and persecuted conviction which seems to be the spiritual and interplanetary traveller's bona fide, the equivalent to the more conventional tourist's Costa Brava sun-tan. 'The real question,' he went on, 'is why you're so against him. Why can't you accept him? What's wrong with him?'

I didn't feel that I could say that for a start he wasn't Jewish. That would only lead to Harry Vilbert asking how I knew and me having to reply that Jewish boys were not called Tom, not even in Dorchester in 1856, where they would not anyway have been, and that they in the main preferred their women living and on the ground. There was also the likelihood that he would have asked me why I cared, and I didn't want to get involved in that. How was I going to explain to the likes of Harry Vilbert, without giving offence, that Jews were particular in some areas; that they didn't eat pig or light fires on Saturday and that they preferred, if they had to be taken over by someone else's spirit, that it should at least be one of their own – one of *unserer*? I hadn't come here to discuss the ins and outs of *kashrut*. 'Maybe all that's wrong with him is his age,' I said, steering away from trouble. 'Sixteen isn't a good time for anybody. Perhaps if you could slide him along a bit – backwards or forwards, I don't care – to a period in his life when he's less fixated on female corpses. I think we'd both be grateful for that.'

'You and Tommy?' His ears pricked. I could see he believed he could detect some affection between us.

'Me and Sharon,' I disabused him. 'But you're right to remind me – Tommy's feelings have to be taken into account also. And surely he'd be pleased to be shot of Martha Brown and be given the chance to talk about his other interests.'

I smiled and winked and nodded, but the vitality of my conversation was lost on Harry Vilbert. Despite all his jingling talismanic paraphernalia (though I suppose things might have been even worse for him without it) he looked to be at death's door. Not knowing then that he was always like this, I wondered if I had chosen a bad time to call. Years later I was to meet him again, down here in this very village as chance would have it, and

44

there was no alteration that I could discern in his appearance. He still looked as if he had no more than another twenty minutes left in him. He had set up as a wart charmer and hung around the local museum of superstition exchanging stories of weird experiences with kids a quarter of his age. He used to come round to see us every now and then, mainly I think because he was smitten by Camilla, who was, of course, wartless, and he would tell us about the multiplying misfortunes of his life. He had been a sexual long before he'd been a spiritual pioneer, he explained, falling hopelessly in love with girls who were forbidden him on account of their extreme youth, outlandish colour, esoteric customs, or near-relatedness. In a stupor of rage and frustration he had sought vindication in popular anthropology. 'The ridiculous thing is that nobody would have turned a hair if I'd been a bushman or a pigmy,' he told us. I think he'd tried to tell his family the same. Then, after the parents of an eleven-year-old Kanaka girl, unhappily settled in Deptford, threatened trouble, he turned his back on human society and found the isolation he wanted in the deserted stands of minor counties' cricket clubs in summer and in the empty drizzling wind-swept grounds of fourth-division soon-to-be-relegated soccer teams in winter. Here, with no one around him to complain or appeal to, he fumed inwardly over the injustices perpetrated by the fallibility of referees and umpires. So scandalously unfair did all their decisions strike him that he was always astonished not to read in the newspapers the next day that they'd been overruled or rescinded. 'There'll be a major inquest into this one,' he muttered to himself as he left the ground. 'We've not heard the end of this – not by a long chalk.' But the score appeared unchanged and unremarked upon in the following morning's world press and humanity went its way unheeding. Fired by his passion for fairness he locked himself in his basement for two whole years, and using only the tools with which he fashioned the copper bracelets he made his paltry living selling on the Portobello Road, he

45

designed everything that was necessary to remove once and for all the arbitrary elements from sport. He built battery-operated cricket pads that buzzed when they were lbw and tennis balls that lit up when they were hit out of court. He designed a hand-held theodolite – accurate to a thousandth of a millimetre – for linesmen, and a heat-sensitive pedometer to measure the speed of spin of an ice skater's blade. He fashioned bleeping nets and talking shorts for fouled boxers and snooker balls that expostulated when they were pushed instead of struck. And then he constructed a rosewood sample case with brass handles to put them in and went calling on the authorities. He received the same answer from all of them. They couldn't see the need. They couldn't see what he saw. 'It will all be standard equipment after I'm dead, and somebody else will get the credit and the money,' he foretold, as crushed as Cassandra by the burden of futurity. He was in advance of his time. Therefore he turned himself around and concentrated on the past. That was how he got into hypnotic revivification. He was really searching for a better prior self.

If I had known any of this on the morning that I stood before him in his basement bedsitter, complaining about the poor moral quality of my previous incarnation, it is possible that I would have been less determinedly dazzling. I can see now that he really didn't have to take it from me. He hadn't even received his cheque from Sharon yet. He would have been quite within his rights to have shown me the door. But the habits of a lifetime of getting things wrong prevailed with him. His confidence was shot to pieces. He took my dissatisfaction with Tommy personally; it was further proof, if further proof were needed, that the cards were stacked against him.

'Fair enough,' he said. 'Point taken.'

I wasn't aware that I had made a point. 'Just put me back to sleep again,' I insisted. 'Only this time make a better job of it.'

He looked alarmed by my expectations. 'I'll do what I can for you,' he promised me, sepulchrally, 'but please remember that I can't change anything. I can only put you in touch with what's already there.'

'I think I understand,' I said, 'the limits of your capabilities. Let's get on with it.'

'Point taken,' he repeated, motioning me to sit. He didn't have an ounce of pride left. 'Now close your eyes. I want you to listen very carefully to what I'm saying. Your eyes are very heavy. You are floating out into the distance. Your limbs are very . . .'

'Yes, yes,' I interjected. 'I know all that.'

And that was how I came to be slumped in a hypnotist's chair once more, floating out into the distance, while that part of me I could no longer call my own was back haring about not my grandparents' Lodz or Lublin but Dorset – Victorian Dorset – of all God-forsaken places. Don't ask me what I was doing *there*: nowhere in the world interested me less. Conscious, I would not even have been able to locate it on a map.

What follows is a transcription from a tape that Harry Vilbert made at the time. His confidence might have been shot to ribbons but he was still sufficiently alert to the possibility of personal advantage to be bothered with fiddling with a tape recorder while I was comatose. I think he tried to interest the BBC in what he had recorded and I can only suppose they turned him down because they were sick of him: he had badgered them for years about using action-replays to prosecute referees in the courts for criminally wrongful decisions. Later on, when he was sweet on Camilla, he made her a present of the tape – I think to put her off me. That was how I came to get hold of it; and I reproduce it now interspersed with my own recollections of what took place. Throughout my ordeal – I don't think that is too strong a word – I retained a clear sense of who and where I was, and I never for a moment became unaware of Harry. It is possible that I was not as free then as I am now to speculate upon his motives and passions, but I am not going to begrudge myself the luxury of mingling present

47

thought with past experience. I don't respect verisimilitude enough, let alone Harry Vilbert, to make the sacrifice. That will teach him to have tried to put Camilla off me.

<h1 style="text-align:center">5</h1>

'Are you there, Thomas?' Harry's tape begins. 'It's me, Harry. I want you to go back to when you were a boy with your mother and those that loved you. I want you to remember a day when you were happy and secure. You have an excellent memory. You can remember everything. What are you doing?'

'I am sitting by the fire.'

'Are you happy?'

'Yes.'

'How old are you?'

'Eight.'

I ought to say that as I play all this back once more I am struck by the atrociousness of my Dorset accent; it is pure afternoon theatre West Country, that's to say it could come from anywhere from South Oxford to the Scilly Isles. But then that was about as accurate a description as I could have given of where Dorset was. The other thing I detect is the great relief in Harry Vilbert's voice. He was clearly very pleased with himself for finding Tommy young and happy and by the fire, in the full flush of cheerful, innocent boyhood. However, he was still cautious; he wasn't counting his chickens yet.

'Are you alone, Tommy?'

'No.'

'Who's with you?'

'My sister . . . and my mother.'

'What is your sister doing?'

'Playing.'

'And your mother?'

'Rocking.'

I don't know why, but there is a long pause on the tape

here. Rocking seems an innocuous enough occupation to me, but perhaps Harry was reminded of Martha Brown's swinging – that seemed to be fairly carefree initially, also. Anyway, Harry seemed to be full of alarm.

'How do you mean rocking, exactly, Tommy?'

'You know, backwards and forwards.'

'What on?'

'Her chair.'

'What kind of chair?' (I think Harry was chronologically confused and had visions of the electric.)

'Her rocking chair.' (Or *Psycho*.)

'Tommy, is your mother alive?'

'Of course she's alive. She wouldn't be rocking if she was dead, would she? We're all alive.'

Harry Vilbert fingered the amulet around his neck – it's perfectly audible on the tape – and gave a little prayer of thanks to the forces of benevolence. 'Good, I'm very pleased to hear that,' he said.

But he was a mite premature. 'All except Mr Rush, that is,' Tommy continued.

'Mr Rush? Who's Mr Rush?'

'Don't you know? Everybody knows who Mr Rush is. He shot people.'

'How do you know about him, Tommy?'

'My mother tells me. She is always telling us stories about murderers and witches and curses and the Bible.'

'And which is your favourite story, Tommy?'

'The one about Mr Rush. He was very brave, you see. On the night before he was executed he asked for roast pig and plenty of plum sauce for dinner. And in the morning he told them to tie the noose high and to take as much time as they wanted hanging him. He said he wasn't in any particular hurry.'

'I suppose he wasn't,' said Harry, dispiritedly.

'Mother says it was the governess who hanged him, but I don't see how a governess could be strong enough to hang a man, do you?'

Who can say what Harry saw? What I can tell you is that he sounded very low. He took failure personally.

49

And he had a shrewd idea that I was not going to consider the eight-year-old Tommy any more of a success than the one of sixteen. But he gave it a half-hearted try. 'Tommy,' he asked, 'what's your second name?'

'AAAAAH,' said Tommy in my voice.

'As I thought,' said Harry Vilbert, and he woke me up, needing a break to roll a cigarette himself.

A half an hour later – I'd taken the opportunity to go to the bathroom and plunge my head in cold water – I was back in the chair. It was Harry's idea to go forward in time, say seventy years, to see if Tommy had attained to the indifference and serenity of old age.

'Thomas, you are no longer young. It is the twentieth century. There has been a great war over Europe. Many things have changed. There are motor cars now and telephones. Do you recognize any of this, Thomas? Are you there? Do you hear me? Are you alive, Thomas?'

I must confess that I was very taken with Harry's quick sketch of the march of history, and if I could have called myself my own I would have applauded it. But already someone else was listening with my ears and speaking with my lips. Someone I didn't much care for, either, and who was at the same time vaguely and unpleasantly familiar. I'm not saying that I had been here, in this guise, once before – I wasn't having a bar of any of that spook stuff, even while it was happening – but something was dawning on me, some dim sensation of repetition, as if I was half way through a movie which I'd only just realized I'd already seen.

'Do you hear me, Thomas?' Harry Vilbert was droning on. 'Are you there?'

'Yes, of course I'm here,' it was time for me to say. 'There is no need for you to shout.'

'I'm sorry, Thomas, I wasn't certain you'd be there.'

'Where else am I going to be? You're as bad as Florence.'

'Who is Florence?' Harry Vilbert wasn't going to make the mistake of asking where she was, in case the answer turned out to be: Outside, swinging.

50

'Who, indeed! I can tell you she is not the Florence she was meant to be, or might have been but for another of God Almighty's mighty blunders.'

Poor Harry! He must have felt he had wandered into a minefield. But he went very cautiously. 'Is she your daughter?' he asked, giving the Almighty's blunder a wide berth.

'Daughter? There have been no daughters for me. Florence is my wife.'

'Have you been married long, Thomas?'

'Married? I have been married all my life! When haven't I been married?'

'So Florence is your childhood sweetheart?'

'She? No. The childhood sweethearts have all gone. Long gone. Florence is . . . *was* . . . a girl. Florence came later. She makes for continuity.'

'You are a lucky man, Thomas, to have a young wife.'

'I have never considered myself an especially fortunate or favoured man. It makes no difference, you know, young or old . . . it's all sweet for a space and then – lamentation. One is best left chasing the intangible essences, the aroma. But, yes, it helps to have young women around. I was talking to a rare beauty today. Lady Ilchester's daughter. A mere fifteen. Fair skin and a full mouth. A face of almost perfect classicality; Greek softened into English. I wonder who will marry her? I often wonder who marries these girls. Florence, of course, didn't like it.'

'Were you flirting?'

'I do not care for flirting. Too much cruelty in it. I was disinterestedly kind. As is her mother to me, and as are not *all* handsome women when they meet an honest man.'

'You say her name is *Lady* Ilchester? Do you know many members of the aristocracy?'

'Sir, I know them all. The Prince comes here to tea. I am descended, of course, from an old aristocratic line myself – half French; but it is extinct now. It was enfeebled and wore itself out.'

'Will you tell me what you were talking to Lady Ilchester's young daughter about?'

'Ha – so long as Florence doesn't catch me. She didn't approve. She cares about propriety. She comes from the town, you see. She watches over me to guard me from excess. And she pesters me to install her a bath. A modern woman. What did you ask me? Ah yes, what was I talking to the young beauty about – Mary Channing. Do you know her story?'

'I don't think I do.'

'Well, they said she had poisoned her husband – which she hadn't – and they burnt her in Maumbury Ring. Before they burnt them in those days – I'm going back two hundred years or more – they strangled them, you know. More humane. Only on this occasion they hadn't strangled her enough. So, just when the flames are enveloping her nicely and a good rich smell of burning flesh is filling every nostril, she opens her eyes, sees through the fire ten thousand faces agape, and begins to shriek. A kindly constable rushes forward and thrusts a swab in her mouth to silence her cries, but before he can get out of the way the milk squirts out of her bosoms – she had recently given birth to a child, you see – and hits him full in the face. Everyone at the front of the crowd jumps back for fear of being squirted likewise. And it is a long time before any one of them can relish the idea of a Sunday roast or a mug of warm milk again.'

'And was this the story you told to Lady Ilchester's sixteen-year-old daughter?'

'Fifteen she is. Yes, with embellishments, that's the story I told her. The poor girl turned quite white and nearly fainted clean away.'

'You don't say,' said Harry Vilbert.

He was very dejected. He'd been commissioned to find out something of Tommy's other interests; but what if Tommy didn't have any other interests? Whose fault was that?

Yes, yes – he knew.

'Go back to sleep, you old bastard,' he said. 'I'll give

you one more chance. You're going to wake up when you're fifty – that's my age.' It was probably the most vindictive thing he could think of doing. 'You're fifty now – the age of disappointment – and you can remember everything. Where are you, Thomas? What are you doing?'

'I am at my desk, writing.'

'Is Florence with you?'

'Who's Florence? I write alone.'

'What are you writing?'

'Another novel.'

'*Another* novel? Does that mean you have written several?'

'For my pains.'

'Are you a successful writer?' Harry Vilbert was always curious to know how other people were doing; even those who had been dead for fifty years. I suspect he was on the point of asking Thomas how much he made, per book.

'Successful? Not according to my critics, or my wife. But I have not sought worldly or social success. I do not care for loud acclaim.'

An odd thing happened to me here: I started shaking. Even at the time I grasped that I was riven by the enormity of the untruth I was telling. Not care for loud acclaim, eh? Not give a hoot that I could count Lady Ilchester and the Prince among my friends? My very knees, that's to say Barney Fugleman's knees, knocked together in rage and frustration; if I could have got my hands on the pathological liar that was opening and closing my mouth I would have strung him up, and you know outside which prison.

Harry Vilbert meanwhile, oblivious to this struggle, was nosing around the pains and privileges of popularity. 'Are the critics harsh about your work?' he wanted to know.

The question was meat and drink to the fraudulent old fibber. 'The reviewers – they scarely merit the cognomination, critic – are minor men whose minds lack all great power in judgement.' (Not that *he* cared! Not that anything they said could bother *him*!) 'They differ with an author's theology and claim the grounds for their antagonism to be a point of art itself. They'll yap at my heels like hounds when they read what I am writing now, and their objections, which they will cunningly disguise, will be entirely moral. I don't know, with all this public and domestic censure, why I continue.'

Harry Vilbert sighed sympathetically. He often wondered about the point of continuing himself. I think he was beginning to feel an affinity with this Thomas, who was, after all, his own age. I suppose he thought that there was every chance that I would find him more acceptable also. In which case a cheque from Sharon might be forthcoming.

'I can understand the way you feel,' he said. It must have been touch and go whether he added, 'Point taken.' Instead, he asked, 'Why doesn't your wife approve of what you write?'

'She thinks me irreligious. She had ambitions to be a writer herself. And she is a lady. There is no more to say.'

'But you are continuing with the present novel?'

'Oh yes. It is very nearly finished. But it might well be the last I do.'

'Will you tell me what you are writing about, Thomas?'

'Purity – though not as the world commonly knows and approves it. Purity, in the Natural sense, whose reward is popular ignominy.'

Popular ignominy eh? Harry was no stranger to that. Lost in the warp of time, he began to wonder when Thomas's novel would be finished and available. He was keen to read it. He made a mental note to order a copy from Sharon Fugleman. In the meantime he would like to hear a little more about it. 'Can you tell me something about the plot of your novel, Thomas?' he asked. He was respectful now, and even a bit obsequious. 'That is, unless it's secret.'

'I can tell you that at the very moment you interrupted me they were working on the tower for my heroine, measuring and sawing and nailing, to get the construction finished in time.'

'They?'

'Oh, the mere agents of the artificial ordinances of civilization.'

'I see,' said Harry Vilbert. 'Them.' But he was in need still of just the tiniest illumination. 'And what exactly is it then that they're constructing for her?'

'What else, in a pitiless universe – what else but the social machinery of an unsympathetic Will? The gallows, of course.'

'The gallows?'

'The gallows.'

Shit and bum, thought Harry Vilbert, the gallows!

He blamed himself. It was what came of asking too many questions. He should have shut the fifty-year-old Thomas up the moment he mentioned he was a novelist. That would have satisfied Barney Fugleman. Whereas now he would soon be wide awake and playing merry hell. A great weariness descended on Harry Vilbert. You can actually hear it falling on the tape. He suddenly felt very old and tired. He saw himself selling copper bracelets on the Portobello Road for the rest of what was left of his life. He didn't of course know that one day he'd be charming warts in Camilla's village. But he had one final question to ask of Thomas. 'Thomas,' he enquired, 'what's the name of this novel that you're writing?'

'Aaaaah. . .aaaaaaaaaaaah.'

'Thomas, what's this novel called?'

'Aaaaaaaaaaah. . .AAAAAAAAAAAH.'

'Thomas,' he was determined to try to get past me, just once, 'what's the title?'

'AAAAAAAAAAAAAAAAAAAAAAAAH.'

'Thomas . . .?'

But he didn't have a chance. I, by a massive effort of my unsympathetic Will, had shaken myself into consciousness. I was shivering and I was white. I might, for all the world, have seen a ghost. 'It's too horrible,' I can still listen to myself howling on Harry's tape. 'It's just too, too horrible!'

'What is?' asked Harry Vilbert. He was quite frightened. A subject was not supposed to be able to wake himself up from a hypnotic trance. It was not only dangerous for the subject, it was also a bit of a humiliation for the hypnotist. 'What is it?' he pressed me to tell him. 'What's the matter?'

I needed air and a glass of water and a long holiday as far away from Dorset as man could go. I also needed to get out of Harry's basement flat. But I didn't feel at all resentful of Harry. All my rage was against myself. 'I'll tell you what the matter is,' I said, as soon as I could collect myself. 'I've just finished writing *Tess of the Fucking D'Urbervilles!*' – but I didn't really expect him to have the wit to see what was so terrible about *that*.

6

From Sharon, though, I had looked for something better. 'So why is that so terrible?' she asked, when I got home. The woman I loved!

7

'You can ask *me* that?'

'You always said you wanted to be a writer.'

'Sharon, that's not funny.'

'You even wore Stendhal shirts when I first met you.'

'They were Byron shirts. You can't get Stendhal shirts in London. But what's that got to do with anything? I never wore Thomas Hardy shirts.' And my flesh crept, visibly, like Sue Bridehead's, at the thought of the propinquity.

'Well, you wouldn't have minded then if you'd discovered that you'd written *The White and The Blue.*'

'Sharon, I wouldn't mind it now. And it's *The Red and*

56

the Black – the white and the blue are the colours of the Israeli flag. But so what? There were never two men more unalike. Stendhal was generous, amusing, urbane, reckless. He wasn't a morbid superstitious little rustic who confused high peevishness with tragedy, niggardliness with humour, mean naturedness with melancholy, and put it on history, genealogy, blood, evolution and the Prime Mover that he couldn't get his end away.'

In the circumstances, considering what kind of a morning I'd had, I was reasonably pleased with this little speech. It wasn't my final word on Hardy – it was too mild for that – but it caught the flavour of my aversion. I was glad I had not descended to insults.

Sharon, however, believed she had caught me out in an impropriety. 'I thought you didn't approve of non-textual analyses,' she said, just as if she had been to university herself. 'I thought you objected to the importation of irrelevant biographical data.'

I shook my head at her. At another time I might have been filled with husbandly pride. 'Who's importing irrelevant biographical data?' I asked.

'You. You just said Hardy couldn't get his end away.'

'Sharon, that is a statement entirely about the art. It happened to be the only thing he ever wrote about.' And as *that* was not a statement that was meant to broaden the base of our discussion, I left her to do with it what she wanted and busied myself in the kitchen, preparing another wet towel to put over my eyes. I had a feeling that what I really needed was a poultice, but I was not sure what it was or how one made it.

I knew Sharon was not going to give in to me easily on this issue. Like all girls who had been good at English at school and had left when they were sixteen, she had not got beyond being taught to read a book as if it was only the thing it said it was. She had been sent out into the world of words quite unprepared, without any warnings about the wicked ways of writers; and consequently she would stop to take a sweet from any of them. 'Books are dangerous things,' I used to tell her. 'Selling them is one thing, but the minute you open a page you have to keep your wits about you.' 'Oh, I just read for pleasure,' she'd reply, as if a person might submit to assault and battery for the fun of it. In other words, she was in the perfect condition to fall for Thomas Hardy, and I knew that she turned to him whenever I was away from home or, as she thought, too preoccupied to notice. I also knew that she had gone off with her mother, only the other day and for the fifth time that year, to watch Alan Bates puncturing sheep and putting out fires and hanging on patiently for Julie Christie; and I had no reason to doubt that she had experienced Julie's dilemma no less keenly than on her four previous visits, when first Peter Finch fixed her with his demented stare and then Terence Stamp flashed her his sword in the hollow amid the ferns. Aflame to the very hollows of her feet? She should say so. Name a hollow, she was aflame there. I wasn't therefore totally surprised when I discovered, later that evening, that she had prepared us an elegant supper, dressed herself in something shorter than usual, and set the table for three.

'Who are we expecting?' I was nonetheless determined to ask.

'Nobody. We're all here.'

She had even chilled champagne.

I wasn't having it. 'Sharon,' I said, 'don't be an arsehole.'

She smiled longingly at me over her bubbling glass. I noticed that she was wearing her hair like Julie Christie's. 'Tommy wouldn't speak to me like that,' she said, already half-drunk on the mere smell of grapes. 'Tommy was mad about women.'

I became very angry. I've never been able to forgive women their complete inability to know who their friends are. Me, for example. And this was a pretty gross illustration of that erroneousness. 'You couldn't be more wrong, Sharon,' I assured her. 'He hated them. In his life and in his art. All his women characters are emanations of either guilt or grievance. He paid them out or he paid them back. The only women he ever cared about were dead ones and you don't need me to tell you that he only cared about them because he was hooked on the pain of missed opportunity.'

Instead of defending her position Sharon regarded me with unexpected archness. 'Do you suppose that's why he has come back?' she asked.

'I beg your pardon?'

'Do you think he has come back to pick up a missed opportunity?'

'Sharon, he hasn't come back.'

'And do you think I might be the one he wished he hadn't missed? Perhaps that's the reason he chose you – to have me!'

'Sharon, don't be preposterous.'

'I think it's enormously flattering. And I'm very proud – of both of you. Of course, Barney, I love only you, but I can't very well say no to one of your previous incarnations, can I?' Whereupon she rose from the table, filled up the third empty champagne glass, and clinked it with her own.

I was unaccountably irritated. 'Look, Sharon,' I said, 'I can see that you are having fun, and the last thing I want to be is a killjoy, but can we have it absolutely clear between us that there is no sense whatsoever in which I *was* Thomas Hardy or Thomas Hardy *is* me? I would like it to be agreed, here and now, that nothing in any way "amazing" has taken place.'

'So why are you so upset, then?'

'Who's upset? Do I look upset?' I even tossed down champagne to show how upset I wasn't. 'I'm simply a trifle disappointed in myself, Sharon, if you want to know, that something in the cellarage of my personality, something over which it appears I have no control, has latched on to Thomas Hardy and said, "This miserable thing of deviousness and darkness I acknowledge mine." I understand that you are nothing like as appalled for me as I am for myself. I am prepared to accept your completely misplaced enthusiasm; in return for which I would like you to accept my entirely justified repugnance. Now can we let the matter drop?'

'You won't hear another word about it from me, Barney,' said Sharon, 'if that's really what you want.' And she polished off the third glass of champagne, while I put another wet towel over my eyes.

But a couple of hours later, as I was kneading and nuzzling her breasts and imagining not that she was someone else but that I was, she felt the need to return fleetingly to the forbidden topic.

'Barney, you were born in 1940, weren't you?'

'I was, my love. You know I was. But I have never lived till now.'

'Mmmm.'

'What do you mean, "Mmmm"?' I stopped what I was doing and dried my lips on my forearm. 'Does that affect the way you feel about me? Do you want a younger man?'

Say yes, I found myself hoping, say yes and make my days and nights perpetual torment.

But despite the springy alacrity of her nipples, Sharon was not disposed to follow me into the tropic swamps of my imagination. 'No,' she replied, without even thinking about what I'd said, 'but I've just been reading a fascinating article on the effect of Spheres and Time Masses on the Creative Imagination. And did you know that people born in the first year of a new decade are likely to be unusually gifted?'

'I did not.'

'Well they are.'

'Well that's good to know.'

'The article mentions – ' she paused in order to gauge whether I was in a good enough mood for her to use the hated name.

'Thomas Hardy?' (I don't know if my mood was good, but I was always ready to trade.)

'Yes. Him. He's another example. Don't you think that's a coincidence?'

'Well, my love, it is only ten to one against being born in the first year of a new decade; there must be a lot of people going around with that advantage.'

'No, but Thomas Hardy was born at the beginning of the same decade as you – the forties. Only his birthday was 1840.'

I did what I could to rise to this little miracle of symmetry, to keep all irritation out of my voice, and even to sound a bit amazed, because I wanted Sharon to stay awake, because I had big plans for her tonight. 'I admit that that certainly makes one stop and think,' I said, 'but it is still only a hundred to one. If you were going to be born at all in the nineteenth century then the odds against your making it in 1840 were not staggeringly high.'

'But you've still not understood. Your birthday is in June, isn't it?'

'It is, my love.'

'June 2nd?'

'Sharon, you know that. You buy me cologne.'

'Well so was Thomas Hardy's. That means you were born exactly a hundred years apart – to the very month, to the very day, perhaps to the very minute.' She lifted herself up from the bed and rose above me, her cheeks flushed with excitement and vindication, her breasts swaying over my face, ready to put out my eyes. 'What do you reckon the odds are against *that*, Barney?'

2

1

This morning Lance Tourney caught me looking at him on the rocks and waved to me. I immediately went for a stiff walk. After that I came back here and put in a couple of hours going through more of Camilla's papers. Then – I suppose as a consequence of such obvious and potent associations (I don't just mean the cliffs and the wind oozing thin through the thorn from norward, I also mean the morning spent virtually spying) – I sat and leafed through some photographs of Hardy that Camilla had ripped from old copies of the novels and stapled together. This hadn't been a labour of love; Camilla, I ought to make it clear, hated Hardy even more thoroughly than I did. She once thrust these photographs under my nose and flicked them, in the way that children flick the pages of a book that have a moving cartoon character drawn on them, except that in this case, as I pointed out to Camilla, nothing moved. 'Precisely,' she said. 'That's what I'm showing you – inanimation.'

But she had another reason for collecting the photographs. 'What do you see?' she once asked me, as we looked at them together.

'I see a miserable old shit,' I said.

That sort of remark irritated Camilla. She had no time for detestations that were not grounded in keen observation. It was a point of fierce intellectual pride with her to know the objective causes of her antipathies. 'You can do better than that,' she said. 'Look at his face – what do you see in it?'

I mentioned the drooping moustaches and the weary eyes and the general sag of disappointment.

'Fancy dress,' said Camilla. 'Mere muscular imposturings. You're just describing the man's idea of himself. What you should be asking yourself is what that disappointment and those moustaches are there for. What are they hiding?'

I looked again. 'The lip?' I ventured.

'Of course the lip. That's the one real and uncontrolled feature on his face. The reason why of all the others. The soft, moist, plump, vulnerable vermilion lower lip. Can you imagine what it must have been like for him, having that as a permanent flashing beacon of his uncertain maleness? Not surprising, is it, that he duplicated its expression – "significant flexuousness", he called it – on every one of those less than masculine heroes of his. Look, look, even in his eighties it's still there, making a liar out of the tragic philosopher, a hot little protrusion of wet flesh, full of blood and girlish expectancy. So picture it in the heyday of his long delayed and long extended adolescence, while he waited and waited for his virility: how it must have glowed and throbbed, as fresh and as sweet as the skin behind a cherub's knee, as palpitating and as erubescent as a virgin's closest secret.'

'Jesus, Camilla,' I said, with a shudder, 'you almost make me feel sorry for the poor bastard. Is a man to be held responsible for his lip?'

'When it's in that condition he is,' she answered, without the slightest hesitation. She was just the person to be running a Thomas Hardy summer school.

The only pity is that she isn't running it now.

Of course I knew nothing of Camilla, had never even heard of her, at the time that Sharon was pressing home her advantage over me. I had to fight all my battles single handed then. And I was losing most of them. Sharon's impressive numerological revelations, what I can only call her rampant marvellings, had left me in a weakened state. I wasn't conceding or acknowledging anything, but my confidence in my old incuriosity was shaken and I had no practical resistance to offer as Sharon bombarded me daily with further coincidences and fresh corroborations.

It turned out that she had been sitting, all along and without either of us suspecting it, on a talent for research. She seemed to know how to dig things up; where to go, who to contact. Rare books and pamphlets and Xeroxed articles from obscure periodicals flooded into the house. Professors wrote to her. Visiting scholars dropped by. She held long, mysterious, and I suspected transatlantic conversations on the telephone. And because she knew I wasn't prepared to sit and listen to her latest findings, she left little pointed snippets of relevant Hardiana for me where I might come upon them accidentally: in my pockets, folded between bank notes in my wallet, underneath my pillow, sellotaped to the flex of my electric razor, wrapped around the handle of my toothbrush. As a consequence I moved about my personal belongings gingerly; I let myself go. I shaved and cleaned my teeth less frequently, I spent no money, and I grew lean. Quite frankly I couldn't crack an egg for fear of what I'd find inside.

One morning I woke up to the realization that there was a foreign object on my bed-side table. I have always been a creature of strict habit around the bed. I sleep better knowing what's waiting for me where, and that there will be no surprises when I wake. That was one of the reasons why I was only ever moderately unfaithful to Sharon (though I admit that it doesn't explain why I grew so keen that she should be unfaithful to me). But this morning when I reached for my watch I found myself fingering unfamiliar surfaces, and when I opened my eyes I was looking at something I had never seen before but which I knew at once was another of Sharon's impulsive purchases from the Burlington Arcade. It was a cloisonné photo-frame, all glowing pink enamels to match the bedroom décor – that was partly why she had to have it – and hinged in the middle, like a diptych, to take a pair of photographs. Only instead of the photographs being of her mummy and daddy or my mummy and daddy, or even her mummy with my daddy or my mummy with her daddy, they were of me and *him* – can you credit this? – me and you-know-who, in the same frame, as if we were family; me, looking gaunt and dealing with the sorrows of adolescence, and him at the same age, a hopeless fart of fifteen, with fluff on his face.

On the other side of the bed and glowing pink herself, Sharon was awake and grinning; her arms stretched out far above her head, her armpits, faintly dewy, waiting to receive me.

'I was struck by the resemblance,' she said, after I'd said nothing.

I trust I will be believed when I state that no two boys were ever less alike. I might not have been a handsome teenager, but I think there was a certain sinewy strength in my appearance for anyone who knew how to look for it, behind the pain a princely capacity to feel pain; whereas little T.H. in his photograph stood barely formed, scarce half made up – not much of an improvement on the infant who was all but tossed aside at birth (as Sharon had unwisely told me), so few of the usual signs had he exhibited that experienced midwives associate with life.

Struck by the resemblance, indeed! I think Sharon could count herself lucky that she wasn't there and then struck by something else. I have a feeling that I even went so far as to test the weight of the cloisonné photoframe. There certainly would have been trouble of some kind had a solitary sparkling crystal of perspiration not trickled, at that moment, down Sharon's side and sent me, oblivious to all else, prospecting for its source.

But later I returned to Hardy's picture. 'Not really surprising,' I said, 'when you look at him, that he pushed to the front of that crowd and stared his eyeballs out when Martha Brown did the decent thing and swung

half-way round and back again in the rain. Little beg-
gars can't be choosers. Who else, Sharon, was going to
grant such an unpromising lad such an uninterrupted
exhibition of herself?'

Sharon was sitting at her dressing table searching for
hairs in her chin – it was the one area from which we
agreed she could uproot. She shrugged her shoulders. 'A
mannequin for a mannikin,' she laughed. It was the kind
of crack I ought to have been making, and it shows how
far, when it came to the Martha Brown business, our
usual roles were reversed.

'A mannequin *in articulo mortis,* what's more,' I
reminded her, although I knew she hadn't forgotten.
Ever since I had whispered in Sharon's ear that it
excited me to think of her performing, thinly clad like
Martha Brown, before an audience of thousands, she
had steered clear of the subject. The Hardy that got his
kicks looking at suspended female corpses was simply
not the Hardy that Sharon insisted she was proud of me
for having been. And although I insisted in return that
any other Hardy was entirely of her own making, I happened secretly not to be too put out by that particular
instance of his morbidity. I am not saying that I liked it,
simply that I didn't see how I could pretend to a dainty
stomach when I didn't have one. It was altogether too
easy for me to remember the deprivations of my own
seemingly interminable adolescence, and the avidity
with which I seized upon anything that would help to
satisfy my curiosity about the female body: emergency
posters showing native women with elephantiasis and
distended bellies and skeletal babies at their breasts
(their breasts!), photographs of mutilated concentration
camp victims torn out of Monty Frankel's copy of *The
Scourge of the Swastika,* an epileptic girl who had dropped down in a dead faint in the school playground – you
took whatever you could get. You weren't in any position
to insist that what excited you should be living, let alone
in rude health. And to be fair to Martha Brown and all
who stared at her, she enjoyed at least two distinct

advantages over my staple stimulants: she was, by all accounts, good looking, and she moved.

Martha's movement, of course, her little half swing this way, her little half swing that, was not the merely technical bonus for Hardy that it would have been for me had one of those unfortunates from Belsen suddenly risen from the page and twitched. For movement, when a woman wore silks, meant sound, and it was the *sound* of a woman – being made to throb through the channel of the ear by her, as he himself contrived somewhere to put it – that Hardy loved best. What an extraordinary commotion they make, those heroines of his, in their rustling skirts and their trembling bodices! How they whistle and bristle and swish and whew! Who needs them naked when they go about in something more tactile and responsive than mere skin could ever be? Martha Brown uncovered, without her black silk dress on, without the creak and the squeak of her, would have been an event; but Martha Brown hung high and rustling, recalling the thrilling frou-frou of Julia Augusta Martin's four grey silk flounces when she used to bend over him as a boy and dangle him on her knee – there was an occasion!

Hardy wasn't the only person to turn out that morning to see Martha Brown hang. Three thousand others showed up as well. And they would all have had their separate reasons. Certainly Martha's chestnut curls and firm outline were well worth arriving early to get a good view of, silhouetted against the sky. And a woman in her forties in whom life still kicks so furiously that she not only takes a husband young enough to be her son but takes to him with an axe the moment he takes a little something of his own, will always tickle the public fancy. Throughout her trial, Martha Brown's composure had been remarkable. Even now she was placid and seemingly content, supported by some obscure but profound sense of right. The extravagance and grandeur of female justice – a life, both eyes, and anything else within hacking range, for a tooth – would not have been lost on someone who had it in him to write of the deadly and unceasing war between the sexes. What must a man initially inspire in a woman for his defection to be so devastating and her vengeance so without remorse? More especially, what had that young husband of twenty-six stirred up in a wife eighteen years his senior and the same age, just about exactly, as young Tommy's mum? The same age, come to that, as Mrs Martin.

Julia Augusta Martin, first lady of Puddletown, with money and a manor but alas no children of her own, had been wont to take the baby and the not-so-baby-Hardy in her arms and onto her lap, allowing him to breathe her perfume and listen in to the frou-frou of her silken flounces, confusing him as to deference and passion, as to sex and breeding, as to passivity and love, and thereby making of the child a too-soon too-willing gallant, of the mother an unforgiving rival, and of the man a chaser after shadows, a besotted lover of every woman and of none.

One mother is more than enough for any man. He does well if he can work out where she belongs and keep her there. God knows how many Hardy saw dangling on the end of that rope hoisted high above Dorset County Prison.

But there is a further and more fearful explanation of what Tommy was looking at in the rain, and that is to be found, I believe, in the very nature of voyeurism (or scopophilia, if you so prefer) itself. It seems to me – and I am not expecting any resistance to what I have to say – that the scopophiliac sets about his business reversing the usual *quid pro quo* contract of human relations. Put simply, it is as if he says, 'Now that you have shown me yours, be so good as to permit me to give you a glimpse of mine.' The voyeur, in other words, is scarcely more than an exhibitionist with small confidence and limited opportunities. That being the case, what Thomas Hardy was really staring at that Saturday morning, passive, helpless, humiliated, exposed to public shame and ridicule up there in the drizzle, was himself. Strung up, not by the judicature and its officers, but by the wondrous strength of some governess, not unlike the one who, according to his misunderstanding of his mother's observation, hung Mr Rush. He remembered that misunderstanding all his life. His mother had meant that the governess had led Rush, morally, to the rope. He had supposed that she had hoisted him up there, bodily, by brute female force. The word governess had that ring about it and the idea was not totally without foundation. There *were* women who could take a man in hand. Martha Brown had gone so far as to take an axe to hers. Julia Augusta Martin, thirty years Hardy's senior, had dangled him on her knee. A man can develop a taste for that sort of thing: why shouldn't he want to dangle some more?

I have to confess (since I am coming clean) that it is no mystery to me.

2

Whatever other advantages the 1950s enjoyed over the 1850s, they couldn't offer you, not in North London anyway, a public execution. I knew that – I say *I*, but you must picture me as I was then: vilely pubescent, all wispy down and flaming pustule, though a prince compared to the other boy in Sharon's frame – I knew about the lack of public executions not because I had enquired but because Monty Frankel told me. The date of the last open-air hanging in Great Britain, the name of the hangman, the age of the criminal, the nature of the crime – these were the sorts of facts that Monty had at the tips of his fingers. Whatever statistics of murder and destruction Monty didn't possess could not have been worth possessing. He knew the precise day and hour of every battle in both World Wars, the exact numbers killed and maimed on each side, and how many more were wiped out on the roads; he knew the names of all the commandants of all the concentration camps in

Europe, and which used gas and which used bullets, and how many tons of gold teeth were extracted from how many Jewish mouths, and where the deepest graves were dug and what their dimensions and capacities were. And he had countless tales to tell about women with names like Mad Olga who ripped open their uniforms and showed their breasts to their victims before castrating them. I dreamed about Mad Olga for years. Romantic dreams they were too, many of them. It was Monty Frankel, of course, who lent me his copy of *The Scourge of the Swastika*.

The Frankels were the poorest Jewish family I had ever seen. When they moved in next door to us the whole avenue supposed it would be only a matter of days before the garden was cleared and the outside of the house painted and the planning permission for extensions applied for. But months went by without a Frankel finger being raised. There was illness in the house. Monty's father crept out coughing before dawn to work in a bakery, Monty's mother choked with asthma and filled handkerchiefs with her blood. The For Sale sign put up by the previous owners continued to swing and was only removed from the front to the back garden at last when Monty discovered he could adapt the construction which bore it for use as his own private gallows. Every morning after that he was to be found standing beneath it on a stone, an old pyjama cord around his neck, his tongue hanging out, his eyes bulging, and his knitted yarmulkah – always his yarmulkah – on the back of his head. If I wanted to talk to him I had to meet him here, and mainly I just listened. He used to tell me how hanging worked, how long it normally took before the neck broke, and why it was an altogether inferior method of execution to the guillotine or the gas chamber. He knew of a few cases, for example, where the victim was still breathing when they cut him down; and that, he was prepared to assure me, never happened with the guillotine.

I knew that Monty would have preferred to own a

70

more efficient system himself and I had a pampered boy's sympathy (I was always given whatever I wanted) for someone who had to make do with second best. I also had a boy's optimism about the possibility of change though, and I often looked out of my window expecting to see a new construction in Monty's garden: a scaffold topped with a glistening blade, or a little brick hut with a tall chimney emitting a pall of black smoke.

One morning, before school, he gave me a nasty fright. 'Hello Monty, how's it going?' I had called.

He was in his usual place on the stone beneath his gallows, his tongue protruding, his head lolling onto one shoulder. Pretty much as ever. Only on this occasion he didn't answer.

'Monty, are you all right?' I asked.

There was still no answer.

I moved closer. 'Monty?'

Silence. Monty's tongue frothy white. Monty's head very still. Monty's eyes nowhere to be seen. Monty's yarmulkah – that was what really worried me – on the ground.

I panicked. 'Monty!' I shouted. 'Monty!'

I had no desire to touch a corpse, but I even began to shake him.

At last, and very slowly, one of Monty's eyes reappeared and flickered open. 'My name's not Monty,' he said. 'If you want me to answer you, you've got to call me Sam Hall from now on.'

'Sam Hall? Why Sam Hall?'

'Because he took no shit from anybody.'

'But who is he?'

'Who is he? Who's Sam Hall?' Monty looked at me in disgust. It's possible he was just sick of telling me things. Anyway, he wasn't going to give me a straight answer. He sang me a song instead.

'Oh my name it is Sam Hall, it is Sam Hall.
Oh my name it is Sam Hall, it is Sam Hall.
Oh my name it is Sam Hall and I hate you one and all,
Blast your eyes!'

I suppose he was trying for a lawless hillbilly accent. But to me, as he rocked to and fro on his gallows, his pyjama cord running up through his left sidelock, he sounded for all the world as though he were ravening, wishing boils and locusts and God knows what else on the Egyptians.

Nonetheless, he was known to all his friends as Sam Hall from that morning onwards; and even his asthmatic mother, dragging herself to the door to call him in for tea, shouted, 'Sam? Sam Hall? Your dinner.'

As for me at this period, I never really entered into Sam Hall's misanthropy or shared his interest in mortality. I had too much growing out of me to have any time to think about death. Life was my problem. I would go round occasionally to Sam's house – it was still unpainted and unfurnished – and while Mrs Frankel coughed and cried in the kitchen (I think it was the kitchen: it had a sink in it), I would join Sam and his brother Louis in throwing darts into the wall of what, since it had a table, must have been the dining room. And I would receive gratefully from Sam any concentration camp photograph in which a nipple, in which the faintest suggestion or implication of a nipple, in which what was not but just might in other circumstances have been a nipple, could be inferred. Apart from that, we went our separate ways. Sam Hall strung himself up for hours at a stretch while I seemed to spend no less of my time bent double behind my bedroom window watching our other neighbour, my mother's friend Rabika Flatman, doing her gardening or catching the sun. When she went indoors I would get up, fetch a book, and then resume my position. I had arrived, if indeed I had not come to something of a dead halt, at the pornographic prepositional stage of my reading; my eyes would race over the page in search of an *up* or an *in* or a *through* or an *under*, and although I had originally sought these out for what they promised of future action, what they offered as prepositions to position together, they had now assumed the character of all fetishes and become loved for themselves. Even now that I am a grown man I cannot read the word *between* without the flames beating up in my cheeks.

But then I cannot hear the words Rabika Flatman either, without the same thing happening.

If the Frankels were the poorest Jewish family I had so far come across, the Flatmans were the richest. They regularly went to Ostend for their holidays. Their children, two little tadpoles of girls aged somewhere between nought and ten, had their own paddling-pool in the garden (in 1953!); Mr Flatman drove around not in a round car with tiny windscreens but in a long sleek shooting-brake with space behind the passenger seat; and there was even a rumour that they were sending food-parcels, air mail, to their relations in America. Rabika Flatman was the first woman in the avenue and for all I knew in all North London to own what then passed as a bikini – shorts, I suppose they were, and a ruched top: a sort of *From Here To Eternity* number, modest in itself but the more suggestive, for that reason, of white surf and torrid encounters. And she would spend all her afternoons yawning and stretching and swinging in a bright orange garden-hammock set as far away as possible from the paddling-pool but in an absolutely ideal position for me to gaze down upon unnoticed from my station, bent double or even treble, at my bedroom window.

Rabika Flatman – Mrs Flatman, as it excited me to think of her – was one of those Jewish women who just miss out on looking African; she had broad nostrils and fleshy lips and an easy swaying nonchalance of gait, but no matter how much time she put in lying in the sun, she lacked the final finishing touch of colour. She was swarthy but she wasn't black. I didn't mind; the rippling mockery of her laughter was still sufficient to startle the elephants at a water-hole and cause the white men's wives to lie awake and worry under their mosquito nets. I blazed whenever she came near me, and she would throw her head back with gaiety, showing me the dusky

73

flare of her nostrils, and sending me on errands for her and giving me sixpence and ruffling my hair when I returned. Once, on a warm Sunday, the Flatmans invited the Fuglemans to a picnic and the two families squeezed together into the shooting-brake, the adults taking turns to put the children on their knees. On the way back, with only a couple of miles to go, I found myself (though I was neither child nor adult) on Mrs Flatman's. I could feel her thighs, not quite together, beneath me, giving off tremendous heat. Her fingers fluttered at my waist like drunken butterflies. Prepositions of the most brutal explicitness flooded into my brain. Suddenly, as she was attempting to adjust my weight, her left hand (the one with all the rings on, the one that made her Mrs) accidentally – accidentally? accidentally! – brushed my lap. On the instant, from hitherto small acorns, sprang the oak, the scarlet oak, the redwood, which now knew and was never to forget the climate and the terrain most propitious to its growth. The gold-ringed hand withdrew at great speed but the damage was done. *In*, I thought, *in*, *on*, *against*, *up*, *between*, *under*, oh *under*! And I was a long time waking up to the realization that the car had stopped, that we were home, and that there was a froth and bubble of laughter on Mrs Flatman's rubbery lips.

Thereafter, whenever the peal of her mockery reached me, clearly through my half-opened bedroom window, or muffled through the walls against which I pressed my best ear by the hour, I believed that I was its object. I was convinced that she told on me to her husband, to her friends, to the neighbours, to her little girls even; I was certain that there wasn't anybody who didn't know and hadn't laughed about what had happened to me under her hands. And I couldn't decide whether that was a source of pain to me, or a source of pleasure. But I took to staying indoors now far more than I used to, becoming unusually dreamy and bookish.

And then one hot afternoon, after a darts session at Sam Hall's had been brought to an end by Mrs Frankel's incessant coughing and retching, and Sam Hall himself, unable to bear it, had run from the house to the security and quiet of his gallows, I went up to my bedroom, automatically looked out of my bedroom window, and saw Rabika Flatman, not alone and prone and listless in the sun, as I would have expected her, but very much alive and energetic and cavorting with her best friend, Elkie Lisberg, in the children's paddling-pool – each of them, sweltering and frivolous, wearing only the bottom half of a bikini *and absolutely nothing else* and daring the other to pose for the sorts of photographs that I believed you could only ever hope to get your hands on if you knew a man who knew a man who'd been to Cairo.

It goes without saying that I couldn't believe my good fortune. I even felt warmly towards Mrs Frankel whose asthmatic attack I had to thank for my not being somewhere else. But I also knew that such fortune was precarious, that Mrs Lisberg might at any moment remember her laundry, that the sun might go in, that Mrs Flatman might look up. I kept very low and stayed very still beneath my window, and yet from this position and without missing so much as a millionth of a second of the action, I was somehow able to take off all my clothes. Don't ask me why I did this. I swear it was not with the intention of doing anything to my penis. I suppose I just felt better with it out. And indeed the only time I touched it was to slap it down after I had noticed that it had crept up above the window sill and was still rising of its own accord, as if charmed out of a basket, and threatening me with imminent exposure.

Please remember that these were the first living breasts, within recall, that I had seen. Sam Hall's collection of corpses had taught me what to expect in regard to shape but it had not prepared me for anything like so much movement. And those women were really throwing themselves around out there. Especially Mrs Flatman. In the whole time I had watched her I had never seen her do so much gardening. She ran the whole length of her lawn and back again behind the mower;

she stood on her toes and cut back roses; she sat in the wheelbarrow, she balanced on the roller, she put the watering can between her legs, she raked, she hoed, she scythed, she pruned, all the while shrieking with laughter and throwing back her head and saying 'Cheese!' as if it were a preposition, into Elkie Lisberg's clicking lens. Is it any wonder that I needed to let the air circulate around my normally muffled parts? Will it surprise you to learn that my eyes began to smoke with the speed of their own shutters as they clicked away like little cameras themselves, recording everything, storing up treasures – mementoes and memoranda – for penurious times?

But what was I doing bothering to store up anything? I was thirteen; I was seeing things I had never been privileged to see before; I should have been having the time of my life, not going shopping for souvenirs, not dying like a party of Japanese for the trip to be over so that I could be back home enjoying it in retrospect through my photographs. Wasn't the actuality good enough for me?

How can I say this? No, it wasn't.

Was there ever such a hopeless ingrate! Inches from my face Mrs Flatman was swinging from the crossbar of her hammock, her lips parted in mockery, her nipples, brown and mocking also, protruding like a chimp's – and I was complaining. Because I wasn't getting quite, because I wasn't getting exactly, because I wasn't getting *precisely* what I wanted. And did I know what that was? Oh yes – that Mrs Flatman and her best friend (but mainly Mrs Flatman) should look up and discover that I was there, that they should know whose red little eyes and whose even redder little putz that was, burning holes in the bottom left hand corner pane of glass. What, so that they could immediately scream and wrap towels around themselves and run fleet-footed like the startled worshippers of Diana into Mrs Flatman's kitchen? Or so that they could give me a special wave perhaps, and throw me kisses, and do handstands by the side of the children's paddling pool in my honour? No, I didn't want

76

either of these things to happen. What I needed to perfect my bliss was for Mrs Flatman and Mrs Lisberg to know that I was there and to take not the slightest bit of notice of me. I wanted them aware of me but indifferent; disrespectful, scornful, contemptuous of my presence. I wished for them to use me precisely as the Brobdingnagian Maids of Honour used the tiny Gulliver when his Nurse carried him to visit them at their Toylet, *without any Manner of Ceremony, like a Creature who had no Sort of Consequence.*

Oh, those giant women!

Observe the dangers of allowing unexpurgated works of literature to fall into the hands of children.

3

Naturally, I wasted no time procuring the photographs of Mrs Flatman that Mrs Lisberg had taken. It had never once occurred to me to doubt that they would, in due course, be developed, laughed over, and stashed away in those drawers which I was in the habit of regularly searching anyway, every time the Flatmans asked me round to baby-sit. In the course of the last year I had gone through the Flatmans' personal belongings with a toothcomb, and although there had been a few things worth lingering over – items of Rabika's underwear, the odd holiday snap, inexplicable bits of pink rubber tubing which I took to be part of the mystery of marriage – I never felt that my fervent anticipation had ever been properly repaid. But now I knew what I was looking for and I didn't expect to be disappointed. Even the search was part of the excitement. No sooner had the shooting-brake pulled out of the drive than I was down on my hands and knees turning up carpets and looking under mattresses. And if Mrs Flatman had come back early because she had forgotten something, and found me with my trousers round my ankles, and up to my elbows in her lingerie – well, that would have been part of the excitement also.

I suppose I must date from this period the growth of my affection for pornography. To this day I cannot walk into a newsagent's and see those rows of men's magazines without remembering the sweet furtive trance in which I went about for weeks, oblivious to all else, until I at last found Rabika's photographs. And whenever I hear the argument advanced that pornography degrades women I recall the moral condition to which this search reduced me. But don't think that you detect any grievance in my voice when I insist that pornography exists primarily to degrade the looker: I was getting what I wanted.

And of course the record was, once I had found it – Rabika frozen for ever on the crossbar of her hammock, Rabika dumped for all time in her garden wheelbarrow – more shocking than the actuality. From the context, those photographs isolated the gesture; from the meandering innocence of flux, they plucked the wicked promise of the moment; from the self-pleasing grace of a frolic, they stole the titillation of a pose. I had found what I wanted all right and I had come to know, already, the superior prurience of art over life.

But I had trouble getting Monty Frankel to see it my way.

'Well, what do you think?' I asked him, showing him the photograph of Mrs Flatman that I had at last decided, after much deliberation, to steal. I had a feeling I was sounding too eager for his verdict. His own style had always been more throwaway. 'Have a look at those,' he used to mumble, when he was feeling really expansive, as he thrust a page torn from *The Boy's Own Album of Torture and Humiliation* into my chest. He didn't care what I thought. He was simply doing me a favour. On the other hand, this was the first time I had been in a position to reciprocate his generosity; furthermore this was the first time that there had passed between us a picture not of some long dead central European refugee but of somebody we both knew. I thought that was quite a coup, myself.

I'd found him where he always was, making some fine adjustments to the knot in the rope around his neck. Only when he was comfortable, with his head dropped on to one shoulder and his tongue hanging out of his mouth, did he make any attempt to look at what I'd handed him.

'Not much,' he said.

'Not much?' I couldn't have been more insulted if he'd been talking about my mother.

'No, not much.'

'Why not?'

'Well for a start the tits are too fat.'

I was horrified. I hadn't expected bad language. 'They are not,' I said.

Sam Hall inspected the picture for another moment or two, as if to be quite fair to it, then he returned it to me. 'They are you know,' he said. 'And anyway she lives next door to you. Why do you want a picture of someone with fat tits who lives next door to you?'

I didn't know which part of this question to tackle first, I can tell you. 'But that's the whole point of it,' I returned, trying to tackle them all.

Sam shrugged, sending a tremor up his rope. He was a long way from understanding me. But he was curious to know how I'd come by the photograph.

'I nicked it,' I told him.

'Does she know?'

It was my turn to shrug.

'I bet she'd give you a thick ear if she found out,' he said.

I had one last go at making myself understood. 'That's also the point of it,' I explained.

He lifted his head and stretched it and shook it before letting it fall on his other shoulder. But he kept his eye on me all the while, as if I needed watching, like some pervert. 'What do you want her to give you a thick ear for?' he asked. 'You can always get your mother to give you that.'

He really was hopeless.

But I knew what his problem was. He was accustomed

79

to looking at photographs of women as victims. The idea of female fragility excited him. When he grew up he would be the sort of man who was transported by the image of Fay Wray in King Kong's fingers. If he'd been Gulliver he'd have stayed in Lilliput. Whereas I was made for those Brobdingnagians, those marvellous Maids of Honour who could strip a little chap *naked from Top to Toe* and lay him *at full Length in their Bosoms.*

'Do you know what I'd like Mrs Flatman to do to me if she caught me?' I asked, making one last effort to bridge our differences. 'I'd like her to sit me astride one of her nipples.'

It wasn't my idea, of course; I owed it to another of those resourceful Maids of Honour. But I was sincerely attached to it, as Sam Hall must have noticed. For he made a sudden desperate retching sound, clutched his stomach, and took off from his brick. For a fraction of a second he was actually in the air, some two or three inches from the ground, and foaming slightly at the corners of his mouth. I could even see his neck turning a deep purple. But he still had time to tell me what he thought of me. 'You're weird,' he said. 'You're completely weird.'

I watched him swinging on his pyjama cord, changing colour. 'Me?' I said 'Me weird? So what does that make you?'

But he wasn't listening. 'Weird!' he kept repeating. 'Weird!'

But I think we were both a bit hard on each other. We weren't really weird. We were just a couple of ordinary Jewish boys trying to make sense of things. As for me, all I wanted was a ride on Rabika Flatman's nipple.

3

1

From the moment that Sharon hit upon the happy idea of running a specialized rather than a general bookshop, and the even happier one of specializing in books by and about Thomas Hardy – 'Why shouldn't I, Barney? I've got all the contacts' – our business affairs took a not inconsiderable turn for the better. She moved premises from Finchley down the road to Hampstead, changed the name from Zazie's dans le Metro to Eustacia's on the Heath, and within a few short months was able to boast the largest and most comprehensive collection of Hardiana in the country. In response to the requests and enquiries which soon came in from as far afield as Lima and Osaka and by the bagful from Tasmania she sent out a friendly chatty newsletter, informing customers of fresh acquisitions, advising them as to pressing wants, and including tit bits of Hardy gossip culled from conversations in her showrooms with visiting Hardy cognoscenti.

There was no question in her own mind that all this activity gave a fillip both to her intellectual life and to her self-esteem as a woman. Whole days on end went by now, for example, without her remembering that she had never been to university. New acquaintances, completely unaware of my existence and never having known my wife when she was just good old sporty Sharon, called her softly by the name above her shopfront, and a leading women's magazine, in its Christmas issue, picked Eustacia Fugleman as one of the ten women in London under thirty most likely to go places in 1968. Sharon was especially thrilled by that prediction because of all the numbers in it.

But she was, withal, subject to one marring sadness: it pained her that she was not allowed to voice that retrospective wifely pride – that special connection she enjoyed with every volume on her shelves – which was so much more the reason for her success, she always maintained, than anything as humdrum as business acumen. I had extracted a vow of silence from her about all that, and difficult though she found it, she respected it.

'Can't I even tell my mother?' she asked me.

I shook my head.

'Never?'

I took my time replying. 'Not yet. Not until I find out.'

'But what more is there to find out?'

I took my time replying to this also. I had to go very carefully these days. On top of everything else I was having bad dreams. Only the night before I had stood in the darkness beneath the primeval yews and oaks and watched while Alec D'Urberville traced his coarse pattern on Tess's beautiful feminine tissue, as sensitive as gossamer, practically as blank as snow, only it wasn't Tess's tissue he traced it on but Sharon's. And on the night before that I had arrived out of breath at the schoolmaster's window in Marygreen just in time to catch the shadow of Sharon in Sue Bridehead's nightie as she submitted to Richard Phillotson's unspeakable embrace. As for the hollow amid the ferns, I knew every blade of grass in it, just as Sharon Everdene knew every thrust of Troy's scintillating weapon. So you can see why I felt I had to plan my sentences. I knew that if I wasn't careful I would find myself uttering something like, 'For pity's sake, Sharon, don't you understand? – I Have To Find Out Who I Am!'

In which event I really would have been in trouble.

What I finally said was, 'I have to find out what is going on,' but I said it very slowly, leaving plenty of space around each word.

Sharon smiled at me in a way I found offensive. It was one of those parental smiles suggesting a patience that was sweet but not infinite. She was wondering how much longer it was going to take me to catch her up.

'Look, Sharon,' I said, 'don't give me any more of that oriental ecstatic shit. You're a Jewish girl. Jews don't believe in reincarnation.'

She gave me that smile again, as if from the top of Pisgah. 'That's a common misconception of modern Jews, Barney. If you were more familiar with the Cabbala, in particular the theosophy of Isaac Luria, you would know how fundamental to Judaism are ideas of the re-integration and transmigration of the soul. Take the theory of *tikkun*, for example, which means the restoration of the Great Harmony which was shattered by the Breaking of the Vessels and later on by Adam's Sin – I'm sure you can see how that, implying salvation through restitution, making whole again,' she actually put her painted fingers together here, and made a perfect sphere for me with her hands, 'leads on to *gilgul*, which is the Hebrew word for transmigration. Once *tikkun* takes place, all those who have fulfilled the commandments become integrated once more into Adam's soul. And those souls which have not fulfilled their purpose – where do they go? Well, into stones and plants sometimes; but also into other bodies, for a second chance. *Gilgul*, you see, is both a humane and a retributive law.'

She paused and, I swear to God, she twinkled at me. You can imagine how I felt. I had known the girl for ten years. We had hardly been apart in that time. We had shared everything. I would have given her the food from my mouth if I had thought she wanted it. And now she was talking to me like this.

'Get fucked, Sharon,' I told her.

'There's one thing that I think will particularly interest you,' she went on, unperturbed. 'Some of the Cabbalists took a very special view of *gilgul* – they believed that reincarnation was a consequence only of offences of a sexual nature.'

I heard that, even though I'd stopped listening. But I wasn't going to evince curiosity. 'I'm going to bed,' I said, and I made my way upstairs where, no doubt, Damon Wildeve was waiting to put a certain proposition to my wife.

Down below, the wife in question was still calling after me. 'And another thing,' she shouted. 'If Jews don't believe in reincarnation why do they forbid cremation?'

'That's a different matter entirely,' I called back. 'They forbid cremation because it's an implicit denial of the resurrection.' It was one of the things I liked best about being Jewish – if you were going to rise, it would be looking the way you had always looked.

Sharon had come to the bottom of the stairs. 'So you at least concede that just because you're Jewish it doesn't mean that you don't have a future.'

'Sharon, I never . . .'

'Or a past?'

'Sharon . . .'

'And you at least admit that there are some things that you don't have the answers to?'

'Sharon, I have never claimed . . .'

'Then when can I tell my mother?'

If I'd had the answer to that I'd have given it to her.

2

As it happened, it wasn't her mother that got told. It was mine. And it was me that told her. I went to her to find out, among other things, whether there had been any irregularities in the family's immediate past, and she needed to know why I needed to know.

'Did any of my grandmothers or great-grandmothers spend any time in or around Dorset?' I had enquired.

It was a price my mother paid for living, imaginatively, at a very high level of personal drama, that the most innocent question would set going in her a train of the most horrible imaginings. 'My God, why do you ask?' she urged me to tell her.

And since the reality could only pale by the side of the foreboding, I told her.

I had arrived at the decision to do some poking around my own background only after exhausting the other possibilities. The most rational explanation of recent events – that I had simply retained a large body of knowledge and information about Thomas Hardy without consciously remembering that I had ever possessed it – was unsatisfactory to me for the following reasons: it didn't account for our shared anniversaries, for my bad dreams, for what I now wanted to do and have done to Sharon every night, and for my absolute conviction that I would never, under any circumstances or for any reason, have bothered to acquire a large body of knowledge and information about Thomas Hardy. I was similarly unimpressed by the usual psychoanalytical understanding of regression, namely that subjects invented new personalities out of repressed and largely unfulfilled desires. I wasn't going to have it that any desire to be this particular personality had ever been in me to repress. If I'd acted out the life of Attila the Hun or Errol Flynn or Henri Beyle otherwise known as Stendhal it might have been different. And as for reincarnation, as understood, say, in the Buddhist doctrine of Karma (I hadn't yet had time to digest *gilgul*), I can only state that I have always possessed a super-Western sense of individual goal and achievement and that any idea of life as an endless teeming continuity fills me with abhorrence. I roll my own rock up the mountain, and if that means I wake up desolate with futility each morning to find it has rolled the whole way back again while I slept, well, there are at least the compensating joys of arrogance and scorn to look forward to when I once more put my shoulder to the boulder. Go not guru-wards remains a general principle with me to this day, much to the dismay of those woolly-hatted bean-eaters I have mentioned, who meet and smile at me and play in Ceilidh bands in Camilla's old haunts and who, it often seems to me, have made the trek to this westernmost extremity of the country solely in order that they might then turn and face the East. No, it wasn't possible for me to accept that the unresolved cravings of another life were striving for expression through me. There was a modesty in this, for what, to look at it from the other point of view, could Thomas Hardy hope to resolve in the person of Barney Fugleman? Did he want to be a Jew? Did he want a Jewish wife? Or did he just want to make trouble? If that was the case then he was a dybbuk not a reincarnation, only I didn't believe in dybbuks either.

I did though, during my conscientious researches through Sharon's mystic library, come across a theory of rebirth that I found horribly feasible. It was held simultaneously, though with regional variations, by the Tlingit Indians of south eastern Alaska, the Pimbwe tribe of Tanzania, and the Yorubas of Nigeria, and without going into the small print I can tell you that they believed reincarnation was something kept strictly within the family, a sort of ancestral recurrence, like hereditary warts. No sooner had you got rid of grandpa than he was back again, squalling his little head off as his own great-grandson, trying to climb out of the cradle he had straw-plaited himself, ninety years before. This sounded to me exactly the sort of nasty trick that families would play on one another, and I found myself quickly relieved to remember that Hardy had died childless. No daughters for me, I remember him croaking, from the back of my throat, when Harry Vilbert had quizzed him about Florence; and there were no sons either, Sharon assured me. I breathed easier but I didn't feel altogether safe; there was always more than one line of descent – families branched out like Triffids. And so when, at about the same time I was discovering the Yorubas, I came upon the case of a man with no fingers who was able to regress, at the drop of a hat, into Artur Rubinstein – the very pianist his parents had always hoped a child of theirs would one day emulate; when, that's to say, I compounded my knowledge of the frightful atavistic habits of the Tlingits with the realization that a fellow might invent a new personality not to please himself but the little grey-haired couple whose dreams he'd dashed, then I thought the moment had perhaps arrived for me to put a few discreet questions to the senior Fugleman.

'Did granny ever come back flushed from a holiday in Dorchester?' was just the first of them.

There wasn't the slightest possibility, my mother assured me, there wasn't the faintest, the smallest, the remotest likelihood of anything of the kind I had intimated ever having befallen a single one of my forebears. She vouched, with extravagant confidence, for all of them. For a start she knew that none had ever been to Dorchester. My father's mother, it was true, had once spent a day in Bournemouth, but she was far too mean ever to have granted a stranger a sniff of her perfume let alone anything else. And my mother's own mother, as I knew, had been too timid ever to set foot outside the street. At the age of eighty she still hadn't got around to learning English even though she'd been born in Mill Hill. She never needed to, as my mother had often explained. She had the baker she could speak yiddish to on one side of her, she had the butcher she could speak yiddish to on the other, and she kept hens in her own backyard – so why should she worry? I could see that she shouldn't. As for my mother's mother's mother – she had arrived from Lodz in a wheelchair and had never been allowed out of her husband's sight; and my father's grandmother had not once left Lublin. How much further back did I want to go?

'That's far enough,' I said, 'though it still leaves you.'

'Me?' I have never seen a woman so shocked. But it didn't seem to be my sexual indelicacy that had shocked her. 'Since when do I ever have holidays?'

She gave me a long frank look, which meant that I had to give her a long frank look back. It wasn't easy. Looking at my mother, close up, has always been a disconcerting experience for me. We look so alike. It's as if I'm staring not just at my own reflection but into my very mystery, in drag. It makes my head spin. It makes me feel that I need to lie down. Which was how I handled it when I was a baby.

She got up to make tea, and I followed her into the kitchen. She still retained that uncouth Second World War habit of brewing tea directly in the strainer. The sight of the swelling tea leaves brought back acute memories of childhood when the pouring of the boiling water would be the only interruption to her storytelling. The melodramatic ferment in which she lived, the astonishment she reeled under when such a thing happened, the outrage she experienced when such a thing didn't, made her a spell binder. We literally sat at her feet by the hour, watching her eyes roll and the colour come flaming into her cheeks, marvelling that Auntie Lotte could actually have said *that*, scarcely able to believe that Uncle Melnick had *dared* to imply *this*. For wild incident and pure rage of passion, no Brontë novel could rival an average winter morning by the Fugleman fireside. But it did mean that our own lives, once the time came around for us to leave the house and lead them, were a bit of a let-down. Where was all that vehemence and exhilaration? Where were those acts of blackguardly treachery, followed by those sudden unaccountable explosions of apology? Where were the never-to-be-forgiven slights, the secret hopeless heartrending infatuations, the murderous wrongs, the never-dare-darken-my-door-again ruptures between cholesterol fathers and their good-time daughters? Suddenly, watching my mother pour more hot water into the strainer, I thought of the man with no fingers. 'Am I something of a disappointment to you?' I asked. But casually. As if it were a question she might take up or leave alone.

She stopped what she was doing. 'You?' She rolled her eyes. The colour flamed into her cheeks. 'Darling, I couldn't be more proud of you if' – if? if what? if I were somebody else? if I were her real child? – 'if you were President of the State of Israel.'

She'd said the first thing that came into her head but it was nonetheless a salutary reminder. Asked the same question, my father would have given the same answer. Of course that's who they would have wanted me to be, supposing them to have wanted me to be anybody. Standing on a jeep in the Negev, blessing the returning troops, not a no one in a crowd in Dorchester, looking up at a swinging *shikse*.

At no point during my visit did my mother express any surprise or consternation about what I had told her had been happening to me. Whenever I asked her a question she leapt out of her seat, but whenever I delivered an actual statement she received it placidly. I knew not to attach too much significance to this; it had always been so with her. As a boy I had only to ask her the meaning of the word tuberculosis or gangrene for her worst fears to be realized – within seconds an army of specialists was queuing in the drive; but if I'd come home from school with my head under my arm she would simply have tossed me an Elastoplast and gone on with what she was doing. She had no feeling for the bathos of factuality.

But one thing struck me as odd. When I told her that I was relieved we'd cleared a few things up because I'd been feeling a bit like an orphan for the past couple of weeks, not knowing where I'd come from, she visibly changed colour. Ten minutes later there were still two bright spots burning in her cheeks. And I hadn't even asked her a question.

My father came home, presently, looking satisfied with his day in his office overlooking the river. He seemed pleased to see me. 'Natalie Latterly, Byron Shortfoot, Malcolm Donalbain,' he said, tossing his coat to my mother and settling himself into his favourite chair. 'Mal Function, Ida Weekes-Grace, Rhodes Fellowes, Afrormosia Hardwood, Berndt Norton, Jocasta Motherwell, Aphasia Slurr, Inigo Knightley.' It was good seeing him in such good spirits.

Before I left, my mother referred to our earlier conversation. 'Barney's been wondering where he comes from,' she said.

'Isn't he a bit old to be wondering that?'

'No, not that way. He's been wondering if he's really who we say he is?'

'Who does he think he is instead?'

'Someone else.'

'Someone else's,' I intervened.

I thought for a moment that he looked hurt. Rejected. 'No such luck,' he said. 'You're stuck with being Barney Fugleman, son of Rebecca – '

'Rachel,' my mother corrected him.

'Son of Rachel and Benjamin. It's on your birth certificate, and if it's on your birth certificate it's yours for life. Ask Diddy Dunkit-Dayley.'

That was the only time I ever suspected him of fraud.

On the way out I ran into Rabika Flatman. She didn't live next door to my parents any more but she visited them regularly. She must have been getting on for fifty now and therefore, according to my sense of things, still some way off her prime. I have never shared Hardy's horror of ageing beauty. I suppose there must come a time when women's looks stop improving, but I can't trust a man who thinks that that time is around their eighteenth birthday. I'm not certain, either, that women ought to be the victims of the lunatic vagaries, the precariousness and the fragility, of male romanticism. Years after he had stopped gurgling into her silken flounces, when he was just tall enough to turn a door knob and just old enough to be given the vote, Hardy called on Mrs Martin in London and reeled from the shock. Her looks – my God, her looks! Ruined! What she thought of him, her fastidious child lover, standing stammering on her doorstep, with his lip out and his man's hat under his boy's arm, we can only surmise. But a thrashing wouldn't have gone amiss.

What Mrs Flatman thought of me (with whom a thrashing also wouldn't have gone amiss) I have no idea. I saw her no more than once or twice a year and I found even those infrequent meetings difficult. I could never be certain that she wasn't going to ask me for her photo back. That might have been why I reddened the moment she began to speak to me. That and of course the bubble of mockery on her lips. The impression she had always been able to convey that she knew something about me that even I didn't, was as strong still as it had ever been. But what was it that she knew? And when was she going to destroy me once and for all by telling me?

I could wait, but not forever.

'How's Sharon?' she asked me today.

'Very well,' I answered.

'No sign of any children yet?'

I went scarlet. This was a direct reference to my reproductive organs. 'Not yet,' I said.

'Well, I suppose you've got plenty of time.'

I misunderstood. I thought she wanted to keep me talking. 'I haven't,' I said, 'I'm in a hurry.'

'Where are you going? Somewhere nice?'

Where *was* I going? 'I've got to check my birth certificate,' I said. And if she looked startled, who could blame her.

3

It's a funny thing about families – sometimes you can go for months, years even, without having or needing to have the slightest contact with anyone bearing your name; but at others it seems that you can't run into a single relative, no matter how distant, without all the others suddenly descending upon you. It's like a contagion; be as foolish as to write to an uncle and you will immediately hear from all of your cousins; wave at an aunt and you will at once be dropped in on by people you've only ever seen at weddings. If you happen to like the warm smell of the litter, all well and good. But if you don't you are well advised to avoid all contact. At least that was Camilla's advice to me. That was one of the reasons she had marooned herself down here of course, in a cottage that was five sizes too small for her – to get as far away as she could from her crowd. 'I don't like myself enough to like my family,' she used to say. 'And I like myself even less when I see them.'

Well her words weren't wasted on me. I have never relished looking too hard at where I've come from. That visit home I've just described was uncharacteristic. It was the consequence of being under enormous pressure. And needless to say it didn't do me any good. I came back in a state resembling shell-shock. And what did I find when I returned but a message from my cousin Bernice, informing us that she was coming down from Liverpool for the weekend and wondering whether she might stay with us. See.

'All right with you, Sharon?' I asked. That wasn't meant to be a question that had much depth in it. It was simply basic domestic good manners. But I should have seen that Sharon was looking menacingly arch.

'I don't know,' she said, 'I really don't know.'

'Why don't you know? We'll put her in the spare room. You don't even have to talk to her. Leave her to me.'

'But that's just it. I'm not sure that I ought to leave you alone with her. Hardy couldn't keep his hands off *his* cousins.'

She was eyeing me cautiously as she spoke. She wasn't certain how I was going to take her little *jeu d'esprit*, or even whether that was what it was. She had a word for me when I was irate. It was *huffy*. She was wondering whether I was going to get huffy. But if she'd known where I'd spent the afternoon she wouldn't have worried. She was aware that visits to the scene of my incunabula took all the huff out of me.

'I don't think you need to worry about Bernice,' was all I mildly said. 'She's short and squat and ironical with a hooked nose and moustache.'

'Darling, so are you,' Sharon brightly returned. She was relieved to find me sparky. That was the word she used for when I wasn't huffy.

'All the more cause for you to trust us, my dear,' I said. 'As you well know, like to like has never been my bag. That's just another of the ways in which your friend and

92

I differ. What's more, I thought his cousins in fact turned out to be his sisters or his nieces or such like. I thought that was the subterranean reason he fell for them. Wasn't that why they had to keep pulling him off?'

'Pulling him off?'

'Dragging him away. Wasn't there an aunty or some-one who had to interpose herself bodily between young Thomas and anything faintly resembling a cousin, because they weren't cousins at all but illegitimate daughters of illegitimate sisters of illegitimate mothers and therefore in the Devil knows what relation to one another?'

'I don't think things were quite so confused as that,' Sharon corrected me. I got the impression that she didn't want to niggle; but only wanted to be fair. I detected just a touch of that exasperation in her that experts always feel towards critics. 'Accounts vary, of course, but it does look as though the one he was keenest on longest, Tryphena, might have been too closely related to him for them to marry.'

'*Might* have been? Sharon, you can bet your last far-thing on it. Do you think he would have stayed keen on her for long – he who only wanted what eluded him – if he hadn't recognized her to be a forbidden little fruit dangling from a rotten family tree?'

'Well it's true he found the type sympathetic.'

I waved away the word sympathetic. 'Sharon, she fed his deepest fantasies.'

'I don't know how you come to be so well informed,' Sharon said, before she realized that she shouldn't.

It was my turn to twinkle. 'Don't you?'

For a second or two she looked at me and I looked at her and we each wondered who was going to be the first to accuse the other of having it both ways.

But it was Sharon, finally, who said, 'Well so far not much evidence has come to light of what Hardy felt about Tryphena or of what Tryphena felt about Hardy or of what they did together. Beyond that they went boating in Weymouth Bay.'

'Boating my bum! I'll tell you what they did together. At the end of every evening she would put on her little bonnet, the one that made her look most like his mother and his grandmother and his aunties and his sisters, and she would strap him firmly – the more she hurt, the better – into that heavy trundling machinery of ancestral curses and family prohibitions and nameless atavistic horrors passed down through a deteriorating lineage, and she would slowly turn the wheel. Sharon, to a genealogical masochist like Thomas Hardy a cousin who was a little more than cousin and therefore less than kind must have been like a personal gift from the President of the Immortals himself.'

Sharon shook her head. 'Show me your evidence, Barney. There is nothing to suggest that he knew about the circumstances of her birth until the end. That was what broke them up.'

'And left him cursing fate for ever more?'

'Well, it would have been a terrible shock. I can see why he might have felt cruelly treated.'

'By fate?'

'By something over which he had no control.'

'Sharon, there's no such thing. There is no fate. There is only psychological necessity. He would have known what he was letting himself in for the moment he first clapped eyes on Tryphena. They always do, these obsessive backward-travelling voyagers to the sources of themselves. Do you think nothing stirred and twitched in Oedipus – nothing over and above, nothing extra – when he lifted the hem of that older lady's gown? Hardy knew all right. In that hot secret centre of his psychology, he knew.'

'And what, in the hot secret centre of *your* psychology, do *you* know?'

'In relation to what?'

'In relation to your relation.'

'Bernice? Well I know, or at least I think I know, that she is my cousin and not my mother's daughter's sister's something-else; and I know that even cousinship is consanguinity too much for my taste. I find I am not comfortable with women who in any way resemble me or remind me of my grandparents. I don't know where to look. Unlike Hardy I feel as if I come from luscious, not from etiolated stock; other members of my family are inclined to make me feel a little sick with surfeit at the best of times. There should never be more than one of us gathered in one room together.' This wasn't a very nice thing to be saying, considering where I'd spent the afternoon. You can see why I might feel guilty.

'So you're safe with Bernice, is what you're telling me?'

'Oh, as houses.'

But I wasn't, of course, if only as a consequence of this very conversation. I didn't say a wrong word to Bernice, naturally, over the weekend, and I didn't lay a wrong hand upon her either; but I felt that I at any time might, that I could, that I – how can I say this? – that I *should*. I felt it in my bones that it was just possible that she wouldn't repulse me, or that she would at the very least understand what I meant if I suddenly jumped her and whispered in her ear, 'Don't be alarmed, it's quite all right, it's only family.'

I didn't desire her at all – she was, as I had described her to Sharon, short with a moustache – and I don't think I even liked her very much, although she turned out to be good company, making us laugh with her imitations of the staff in the sociology faculty and forcing us to attend seriously when she described her uphill struggle to get herself elected as the first woman president of the University Jewish Society; but on the night after she left I stirred in a dream, I murmured and whimpered, I made low cooing noises in the back of my throat and straddled the soft pliant body next to me. With subtly charged finger tips I stroked hair and traced the outline of eye and cheek and nostril; but when I felt for the moustache and found only the smooth lip of Sharon I woke with a cry and was desolate.

* * *

'There's no point in ever beginning to put your mind to that sort of thing,' Camilla used to say. 'You've just got to face it – the minute your head hits the pillow, anything can happen.'

She had terrible nights herself. Most of the time she wouldn't tell me what had been going on. She would simply jump out of bed and plunge into a hot bath. It didn't make any difference if it was four in the morning. She'd even shampoo her hair. Occasionally, if I was awake, I would hear her muttering to herself between submersions. 'That bloody father of mine,' she would say. 'Jesus!'

As for me, I too tried never to be surprised by the promiscuity and fickleness of my unconscious. I was familiar with its ways; I knew how capable it was of picking up any old thing for the night and not even recognizing it in the street the following day. So Bernice was not a problem. A solitary swallow didn't make a summer, and it took more than one cousin to constitute a complex.

No, Bernice had nothing to answer for. And neither, come to that, had Tryphena Sparks. The real cause of the trouble – or let's rather say its precipitator, since there was already trouble about – was Horace Moule.

4

'It suggests here,' said Sharon one evening, emboldened by the success of her previous attempt to draw me out on her favourite subject, 'that he might have introduced his friend Horace Moule to Tryphena and that they might have had a relationship.'

'I thought we knew that they had a relationship.'

'No, not Tryphena and Hardy.'

'Horace Moule and Hardy?'

'No, Horace Moule and Tryphena. Apparently they were in London at about the same time. While Tryphena was at Stockwell Teachers' Training College in 1869, Horace Moule would have been in Chambers.'

I was not unfamiliar with the style of scholarship that Sharon was reading. It was of the sort that placed great reliance on the supposition that no two persons known intimately to a third and living in a city of some eight million inhabitants in roughly the same century could be so thoroughly unobliging as not to have met clandestinely on as many occasions as was consistent with the reasonable elucidation of an otherwise inexplicable poem. Especially as such a hot summer as was enjoyed that year – the hottest in living memory – was bound to bring them into collision in the park; just as the century's previous wettest of all winters had surely seen to it that they had taken shelter beneath each other's umbrellas.

But I wasn't looking to pick a fight with Sharon. She was extravagantly beautiful tonight, opulent and abundant in a tiny dress – a pearl richer than all my tribe. And the desire was hot upon me to give her away. So I went to the only part of the Moule–Tryphena theory that interested me. 'And what does it say that Hardy might have felt about that?' I asked.

'It says he might have been jealous.'

'It doesn't say that Hardy might have promoted the relationship for that very reason?'

'What very reason?'

'That he might feel jealous.'

'What kind of reason is that? What would he have wanted to feel jealous for?'

'Oh Sharon!'

'Don't "Oh Sharon!" me. What would he have wanted to feel jealous for?'

'For the same reason that everybody else does – pleasure.'

'Pleasure? I don't get any pleasure out of being jealous.'

'Yes you do. You just don't recognize the symptoms. You've been trained to call them something else.'

'Yes – pain.'

'That's right. But pain's just a word.'

'It's more than just a word, Barney. On those occasions

97

when you've dragged me off a dance floor at a party and called me slut and cut my lip, you were experiencing more than just a word.'

'Sure. I was experiencing a disreputable thrill.'

'I see. So Hardy introduced Tryphena to Horace Moule so that he could catch them smooching, cut her lip, and get a thrill?'

'Hang on. This is all hypothetical. We were talking mights, remember.'

'But that's what you would have done if you'd been Hardy?'

'I might.'

'And that's what you'd do now if you had a Horace Moule to introduce me to?'

'I might.'

'Well find one, Barney, and let's see just how much pleasure it gives you.'

'I might,' I threatened. 'I just might.'

I ought to say that menace has never really suited me. I'm good with scorn or derision, but I've never been at home with threats. And it's the same with anger. When I lose my temper, or try to, I feel that I also lose my stature. I seem to give way at the wrists and ankles. My head drops into my shoulders. Towards the end of this disagreement with Sharon I could actually feel myself shrinking by the metre. Whereas Sharon always rose on the back of her rage and flashed divine fire. Her bosom didn't so much swell as burgeon. Her hair hissed. And tonight she positively snarled, as no heroine had snarled for a hundred years – I swear she ejaculated, as no modern heroine would ever be allowed to ejaculate – 'Ha!'

Looking up at her from the little pile of myself on the floor, I recalled the night she swung from a rope outside Dorset County Prison doing her Sophie Tucker imitations for Joseph Poorgrass and Grandfer Cantle. Lacking language they had expressed their approbation in low grunts; but even those had made a wild music in my ear. How much the more so, then, was I eager to see

Sharon appraised, apprized, by one of Horace Moule's discernment and worth – a slightly older man of learning and refinement, the son of a good Christian family, a classical scholar, a mentor, a bringer on of the young, a reviewer yet.

'I might,' I repeated, long after there was any need to. 'I very well might.'

4

1

'Horace, my cousin Tryphena. Tryphena, this is my esteemed friend Horace. If you two must get together clandestinely in London while I'm slaving away for a better life in an architect's office in Weymouth – and I have to tell you that I do not consider the hottest summer in living memory to be a justifiable provocation – but if you *must*, then I trust that you will at least have the decency to report to me everything that happens in some detail.'

I tried this out, for fun, long after Sharon had given me the idea, on the retired annalists and archivists and on the wistful wives of bank managers and on the sundry spinsters of both sexes and on the visiting American post-graduates and the ordinary straightforward bad-tempered readers for pleasure who comprised, that year, Camilla's largest summer school intake ever. It was my contribution to Camilla's contribution to the festivities marking the centenary of the publication of *A Pair of Blue Eyes*, that early Hardy novel whose action, as everybody knows, takes place down here in the environs of Castle Boterel – scene also of Camilla's exile and latterly of mine. Just a little to the west of here, through dripping meadows, lies Endlestow, where Stephen Smith met and fell in love with Elfride Swancourt and made the mistake of telling her about his esteemed friend Henry Knight; and further on up the coast is the Cliff Without A Name to which Knight himself clung an unconscionable time, eyeball to eyeball with evolution, waiting for Miss Swancourt to tear her petticoats and save him. Windy Beak is hereabouts also, as is Dundagel and Parret Down and Camelton. And they were all alive this summer with allusion-crazy pilgrims. Not a seal flopped lazily in Targan Bay but a dozen cameras fitted the picture to the words.

It was a busy time for Camilla. Her school became the obvious focus for the celebrations, the base and meeting place and nerve centre. She arranged lectures and seminars and expeditions. She collected distinguished visitors from remote railway stations. She found beds and laid on guides and packed lunches. They even looked to her to organize the competition to find the bluest pair of eyes in Cornwall – won, incidentally, by a near-sighted clay worker from St Austell, much to the chagrin of the holidaying Germans, all of whom had entered and all of whose eyes, in truth, were bluer.

'You're going to have to help,' Camilla had warned me. 'You're going to have to take over some of my classes. But it shouldn't be too awful for you – they're nearly all women.'

'What do you want me to tell them?'

'Oh, anything. Just don't treat them badly.'

'I know,' I said. 'They're your bread and butter.'

She flashed me one of her fiercest looks, the kind that could split an oak. 'They're your bread and butter too,' she corrected me.

This was a reference to the deal we'd struck that I'd keep her company in the winter and keep the school clean in the summer if she'd keep me clothed all the year round. Camilla had shaken hands on that but accused me ever after of battening on her, even though I kept my part of the bargain and wasted the prime of my life on my hands and knees swabbing out toilets and trying to hold back the Cornish damp with coat upon coat of paint and artex and every anti-fungus solution on the market. It wouldn't have mattered if I'd never slept – she'd still have called me a bum. She badly needed a man to resent.

And on a daily basis. It was the only conventionality in her nature. That and the desire to wear a little gold engagement ring with a pretty diamond on her second finger. Every two or three years, despite the fierce independence of her character, she'd find another husband and accept another ring. In some remote corner of her there nestled a sweet prosaic wife and homemaker. She just wasn't happy unless she was unhappily married.

And as for me, I suppose I was getting what I wanted also. I accepted the unfairness of her treatment of me almost without demur. I was carrying a massive burden of guilt, remember . I had a lot of making up to do. I might not have been the thing Camilla accused me of being but I had been all sorts of other bad things in my time. It all evened out in the long run.

'I won't treat them badly,' I assured her. 'I'll give them a good time.'

'Yes, well don't give them too much of a good time,' she cautioned me. She could be very difficult to please.

So could the paying pupils of her summer school. I grew quite anxious when I saw two or three of them taking notes. They were writing down what Hardy had said to Horace and Tryphena. 'That's only speculation, of course,' I laughed. 'I mean there's no hard evidence that he ever did introduce his cousin to his friend. Indeed, if he was fascinated, in the way I have intimated, by what such an introduction could lead to, then he might well have decided it was best all round to keep the pair apart. After all, if he wanted that kind of excitement he didn't have to live it. He was a novelist. He could always write about it.'

What I was trying to get them to see was that that was precisely what Hardy had done in the novel they had all paid £125 for the week to come and study. (That included, by the way, accommodation and breakfast and three of Camilla's packed lunches, as well as tuition fees and a free flower press as a souvenir.) 'Don't forget,' I reminded them, 'that Elfride Swancourt is an amalgam of the essential qualities and circumstances of

102

Tryphena and Emma Lavinia – the woman Hardy had met almost on this very spot, when he came down here to work on the church which I believe Camilla is going to take you all to see tomorrow. The name Elfride, you will notice, doffs its hat ceremoniously to the new love – Emma Lavinia – while not turning its back too brutally on the old – Tryphena. Now it's no more certain that Hardy ever got around to introducing Moule to Emma Lavinia than that he allowed him to touch fingers with Tryphena, but with the invention of Elfride he was able to introduce him at a stroke, and as a rival lover, to them both. "Horace, Elfride. Elfride, this is Horace. Horace is the person I've been telling both you girls so much about." '

I paused and wondered what to do about the couple at the back who were taking notes again. I could see someone else looking troubled, leafing furiously through the novel in search of a character called Horace. And others, I could feel, were waiting for me to get on to the wild flowers and the local customs and, if I really had to, the question of indifferent fate.

'Look,' I said, 'what I'm suggesting is that complicity in your own cuckoldry is a recurring theme in Hardy.' That straightened a few old backs. 'Over twenty years and a dozen novels later his hero is still none the wiser and continues to make a present of his felicity on a handshake. "Richard Phillotson, I'd like you to make the acquaintance of my cousin Sue Bridehead." Only now it doesn't matter quite so much. Hardy is older. Moule and Tryphena have long gone. And no one is likely to take Emma Lavinia away from him, worse luck. So Phillotson isn't required to be a potent threat. True, there is the question of his extreme repugnance of person, that something-or-other vile about him that Sue jumps from the window rather than confront; but that is only Hardy rubbing at a spot that is no longer sore. "What is it you don't like in him?" the Widow Edlin enquires. "Did you ever tell Jude what it was?" "Never," Sue replies. Never? Since when was anyone in a Hardy novel delicate?

103

If there was ever going to be any meat in Phillotson's mystery Hardy would have clouted Jude over the ear with it, as a stimulus, just as Arabella, for a similar purpose, had pelted him with the pizzle of a pig. As it is – left dangling – the schoolmaster's secret is a gothic not a psychological horror. The structure of *Jude the Obscure* might be wholly prurient – has she yet? will she now? – but it lacks the grand conceptual salaciousness of earlier books.'

I stopped to spell salaciousness for a poor pensioner who had scraped together the last of her savings to get here. I also took the opportunity to light a cigarette but was asked by the class to extinguish it.

'By comparison,' I continued, 'the story of the rivalry between Stephen Smith and his erstwhile friend and patron Henry Knight is conceived in the very morning time of male trepidation, when one's own sex is all latent threat and odious comparison and the mysteries of the other stretch out before one as invitingly as a meadow laid with mines.'

I went on talking, all the while looking out of the window, not daring to meet the expressions on the faces of those who were bread and butter to Camilla. From where we were situated, in this once Methodistical church hall, high up in the old part of the village, I could just see a triangle of blue Atlantic and the cliffs describing their characteristic upward arc before they fell suddenly away. I liked the way there had never been any compact made here between land and sea. The water simply got in wherever it could and the cliffs looked the other way, poised apparently to soar skywards. But I hadn't been here as long then as I have been now, and I liked lots of things. I was even capable of finding the wind bracing. I hadn't yet acquired that appearance, native to local trees and shrubs and long-term inhabitants, of having been blown backwards at an angle of forty-five degrees to one's natural self by the unremitting blast.

Suddenly – I had been daydreaming even as I rattled

on – Camilla breezed in. The train bearing the famous Sri Lankan expert on West Country folklore in general and Hardy's place names in particular had arrived earlier than expected. She had brought him back and shown him to his room and left him to bore the locals with his explanations of what everything in their village really meant. And now here she was, looking harassed but bright, and wondering how we were getting on. I prepared her a watered down version of what I'd been saying, as she surveyed the care-worn faces ranged before her, and I warned myself not to be surprised if she sent me back, there and then, to scrape off more mould from the walls of the communal toilets.

'I have just been discussing with your charges,' I said, 'the way Elfride initially loves and then tires of Stephen's docility and gentleness, preferring at last to be led "like a colt in a halter" by the more forceful Knight who knows how to make a woman feel like a woman. I was just quoting the dreadful line – perhaps you remember it? – "Directly domineering ceases in the man – " '

' " – snubbing begins in the woman", of course. And I take it that you were also about to quote, "Decisive action is seen by appreciative minds to be frequently objectless, and sometimes fatal; but decision, however suicidal, has more charm for a woman than the most unequivocal Fabian success"?'

'Of course I was,' I said.

'And I take it that you were about to go on to explain that what lies behind this nonsense about the female craving submission is Hardy's pathological fear that women want nothing so much as to be tamed which is the same as his pathological certainty that he doesn't have what it takes so to tame them?'

'Of course I was,' I said.

'And that Hardy is not what you could call an active sadist; that his quaint notion of the sort of masculinity women pine for, where it is more than merely Victorian melodrama, is a projection from inadequacy not brutality?'

I nodded. 'I was on the point of saying that very thing,' I explained, 'when you came in.' Well I was. That might sound petulant, but it was quite upsetting to have a lecture lifted straight out of my hands. And to see the light of comprehension begin to shine in those previously unlit countenances. The annoying thing was that she was not a jot more lucid than I was, really – she just had a way of marching up and down in front of them, tossing chalk that she had no intention of using from one hand to another, and looking as if she would swing for her convictions – which made them think she was.

She had the natural tyrant's ability, also, to fix each person separately with her stare, so as to create an individual bond of loyalty based on fear. Within five minutes she had over thirty such individual bonds ratified in that room. The world, I was reminded, could never resist a despot. And I wasn't planning any revolutions myself.

'It is quiet men of private fears and perturbation,' she went on, 'who nourish the fantasy that women enjoy nothing better than a thrashing. The ordinarily outgoing brute who beats his wife doesn't suppose that he is thereby providing for her needs while he is satisfying his own. Thus the violence done on Hardy's heroines is always essentially vicarious, connived at by the author but inflicted in another's name. The daemon, you see, must be free to watch and feel the pain himself. The seduction of Bathsheba, the rape of Tess, the subjugation of Elfride, are all observed as by an injured third party, jealously. And the more assured the rival's mastery, that's to say the more complete the woman's surrender, then the more exquisite the sense of injury. In that sense Mr Fugleman is right' (that's what she said, the bitch!) 'to be drawing your attention to the possibility that Hardy was using his novels to have the women he loved, real or imaginary – it comes to the same thing – violated by proxy.'

She paused, in order to allow a question. 'That's p..r..o..x..y,' she replied.

Despite myself I was mad about her. She was so good at what she did. Our passions on this subject were just about equal; we suspected and mistrusted and saw through and wouldn't have and wouldn't wear and wholeheartedly disliked virtually in tandem. But my antagonism always got me embroiled, caused me to sweat and bluster, threw me back on brute force and calumny – I wanted to break the bastard's little back; whereas Camilla's burned pure white, instantly destroying everything it passed over like the spirit of Yahweh. I've seen newsreels of Japanese cities devastated by an atomic bomb. A hideous silence pervades and a few wisps of smoke ascend from the burned out shells of buildings. That was more or less the look of a terrain when Camilla had finished with it.

But she hadn't quite finished with this one yet. 'Notice,' she said, 'how it is precisely the language of masters and servants, the language of class transferred to sexuality, that assures Stephen Smith of a perfect humiliation when he spies on Elfride and Knight together, they in the light of the summer-house, he in the darkness without, and sees that she looks *up* to and adores his former patron from as great a distance as she had once looked *down* and smiled on him. And not just a perfect humiliation but also a double shame. For how much the more removed from that old friend and teacher must it leave him, that he was once the thrall of a woman who is now enthralled herself. You might wonder whether Elfride's role in all this, finally, is any more than functional. Could it be that her submission is a male luxury – call it Stephen's, call it Hardy's – not her own at all, and that she merely craves submission on behalf of someone else? Was it not Stephen that sought shelter under Knight's protection in the first place? They have strange needs, these men – watch them! Watch them especially when they offer to be merely satisfying the strange needs of women. Elfride takes the caning because, apparently, Elfride wants to take the caning, but it is Stephen Smith who revels in the afterglow.'

Ah, Camilla, Camilla!
The things you knew!

'Sharon, my wife – this is Rowland Fitzpiers. You must have heard me mention Rowland, Sharon, we were at school and university together.'

That was strictly but not really true; Rowland had been school captain when I was just a first-former, and he was well advanced with his research, was already very nearly Dr Fitzpiers, when I was a mere freshman. Together was not at all the word for what we'd been, notwithstanding the odd chat at the Union bar and the occasional tips about literature and life that he dispensed and the rather lordly postcard he wrote me when he came across my article slamming Miss Mitford's *Our Village* in a Mid-Western American University journal. But Harrods food hall, the scene of this surprise rencounter, was not the place to go into lengthy explanations.

Sharon extended an arm clinking with gold charms. 'I've heard all about you,' she laughed and lied, 'and if I'm not mistaken I used to sell a couple of your books.'

'Used to?' Rowland Fitzpiers, large and dark and affable, affected hurt and disappointment as if he'd never had any dealings with the real things. 'What, going from door to door?'

'Sharon had a bookshop,' I explained.

'Sharon still has a bookshop,' Sharon reminded me. 'Only it's a rather more specialized bookshop than the one in which I used to sell a couple of your books.'

Beneath his heavy black brows Rowland Fitzpiers's eyes twinkled, and from under his beard his lips twitched. 'You mean you no longer stock rubbish,' he said. 'Well I can't say I blame you.'

'On the contrary,' I said – for I too wanted to twinkle and shine – 'she only stocks books to do with Hardy.'

'Hardy? As in Laurel and?'

108

'No,' said Sharon. It was her shop. 'Nor as in Kiss Me. As in Thomas.'

'*Him*. Do they sell?'

'Like hot cakes.'

'Do they?' Dr Fitzpiers, critic and reviewer, became suddenly ruminative. 'Are there any gaps?' He had the air of a man who might just have the odd afternoon to spare to knock out a book on Hardy.

'I suppose there are,' said Sharon. She even appeared to stop and think where they might be. 'There must be.'

'Perhaps you could show them to me.' Rowland Fitzpiers's face was all mobility. I was struck by his ability to twitch his top and bottom lip in independence of each other, as if they were amused by different things.

Sharon threw her head back and laughed, showing her throat. 'I think you must find those for yourself,' she said.

'I wouldn't know where to begin.'

'That's hard to believe.'

'It's true. I lack initiative. I'm like one of those old family cars that runs well once it's going but needs a push start every morning.'

Sharon sparkled. She loved being out. She loved meeting people. And she loved Harrods food hall. 'Then you'd better come to my bookshop,' she said, 'and we'll see if we can get you started.'

'Yes, come to the bookshop,' I put in, just in case anybody cared what I thought.

I was pleased that we had run into Rowland while we were out shopping. It meant that Sharon was looking her very best. Shopping – proper social expeditionary shopping, not buying groceries – was Sharon's passion and she dressed for it with a wild extravagance as if it were a special occasion and not something that she in fact did every day. It was and always had been a compulsion with her. In the early days of our courtship we had loved and wooed each other exclusively in or between department stores; while other couples grew to mutual understanding by going to midday concerts and walking arm

109

in arm together through the National Gallery – systematically, some of them, comparing styles and schools and sympathies – Sharon and I were pounding the pavements of Regent Street, matching the tea trays and the oven gloves we would need when we were married. We bought and bought and bought, and when we ran out of money, we took back. There wasn't a memory or an association stored up for later life that wasn't charged with the history of our past transactions. Where other wives would remind their husbands of the time they fed the swans and strolled in sunlight through the Borghese Gardens, Sharon would run from the kitchen on a sudden thought and throw her arms round my neck and show me a potato peeler: 'Do you remember darling? The January sales, 1964! Selfridges!' I would have preferred it, in retrospect, if we had found the Cathedral on our honeymoon in Chartres instead of boots for Sharon, but I had followed her around obediently then for the same reason I followed her obediently now – because I liked to be seen with her. Especially I liked other men to see me with her.

And this was more the case than ever just lately, when skirts were getting shorter by the second and Sharon's skirts, as I am sure I have already mentioned, were always just that fraction in advance of fashion. It gave me enormous pleasure to discover that some man, some other woman's husband, was following us through cosmetics and haberdashery and bedding, at an even distance; it was a source of considerable husbandly pride to me that little gasps of admiration and astonishment could be heard behind us when we travelled on the escalators. I surprised Sharon by the amount of shopping I was prepared to do with her these days, and the frequency with which the very things I wanted to look at turned out to be situated on the top floor. She couldn't understand, either, why even when she was tired I forbade her to take the lift but insisted that she rode the escalator.

It was only some obscure instinct that it would be

better not to force the pace that prevented me from suggesting to Rowland Fitzpiers that we should all go up to look at Harrods garden furniture and that Sharon should lead the way. 'Coffee?' I suggested instead.

But even that accelerated things. 'Good idea,' said Fitzpiers, and looking straight at Sharon he added, 'You lead, we'll follow.'

Later, sitting over drinks – Fitzpiers drank strawberry milkshakes for some reason I couldn't fathom – we discussed Fitzpiers's career. He was doing less and less lecturing these days, he was pleased to say, and could very nearly see his way clear to doing none; he reckoned he had more than enough literary clout now to pick up sufficient reviews and articles and sundry commissions to support himself. It helped him, he was the first to admit, that his tastes were catholic. He loved westerns for example – the novels he meant, not the films, although he loved the films as well – and he had a contract in his pocket to edit an anthology of his favourites; he was mad on detective stories too, saw them as the most reliable pointers to social mores, and he was very keen on spy thrillers (the only genuinely political novels written), but his latest enthusiasm was for science fiction – if there was a future it was there.

'My colleagues don't exactly approve,' he explained to Sharon. 'Most of them think that literature is something that stops geographically at Dover (allowing for the odd day trip to Paris) and historically at Jane Austen.'

I looked guiltily into my coffee cup.

Sharon, though, screwed up her face in exquisite comprehension. She had taken off her fun-fur jacket. Underneath she wore a white cashmere cardigan. The contrast between the soft lamb-like woolliness of the garment and the parts of Sharon it contained had often brought the tears to my eyes. And it seemed to do the same to Fitzpiers. More than once, in his eagerness to talk and drink and not lose sight of Sharon, he had leaned forward to sip his milkshake and had impaled himself through the nose on the rainbow coloured straws. I marvelled at his willingness to take the pain rather than finish his sentences early. It was as a talker that I had most remembered him, certainly, but I had the feeling that he used to be rather more urbane, more physically composed, than he now appeared. Not that his clumsiness – he left bits of tissue sticking to his face, also, every time he wiped his mouth or dabbed at the mixture of blood and milkshake congealed in each nostril – looked like causing Sharon any distress. She even seemed to find it charming that there were tobacco stains on his front teeth, that he had grey hairs growing out of only one ear, and that his eyebrows met in the middle.

'I've never really read any science fiction,' she confessed. 'Though we used to have quite a big section in our first shop, didn't we, Barney?'

The sound of my name gave me a bit of a shock. I was surprised to discover I was still in the room. 'Yes,' I said.

Fitzpiers was appalled by Sharon's admission. 'You've never read any? Then you must. I'll write you out a list.' And on the spot he filled both sides of a serviette with writing, folded it and handed it to Sharon who put it in her bag. For all I saw of it it could have been a set of detailed instructions for getting to Fitzpiers's flat.

'In a hundred years from now,' he continued, 'this will be the literature the twentieth century is remembered by. The domestic novel will be forgotten. Who will care then about lovelessness and infidelity in Belsize Park?'

'Who cares now?' said Sharon. I could see that she was already half way towards being an SF addict.

'Precisely,' said Fitzpiers. 'Who cares now? That's not where we live any more. Science fiction has as its subject all the current threats and challenges to man: war, supersonic travel, television, metaphysical uncertainty, computers. It can make art out of the thrust or the waste, the dreams or the detritus of a technological civilization.'

I asked Rowland Fitzpiers if he wanted another milkshake. When I returned I ‘found him explaining to

Sharon that all the great nineteenth-century novels were in fact science fiction.

'Take *Dr Jekyll and Mr Hyde*. The first fictional attempt to explore the workings of the unconscious, under the pressure of contemporary scientific investigation. What's the most potent symbol in Dickens? The train. What's Heathcliff if not an alien, a visitor from another world, a child of the new scientific revolution? Even your own Thomas Hardy is as much upwardly mobile Darwinian as he is contented countryman. Everything struggles to survive in Hardy, precisely as the scientists said it does. Science fiction, you see. The central metaphor for Tess's confusions is the threshing-machine, superintended by one who has the appearance, you will remember, of a creature from Tophet, another world. Pure science fiction. If it was called *The Alien From Tophet* instead of *Tess of the D'Urbervilles* you wouldn't have the slightest resistance to the idea.'

Sharon was already not evincing much resistance, but I felt that I ought to demur, or at least put forward an amendment, if only for the look of the thing. 'Funny you should latch on to the threshing-machine,' I said, 'I think the Marxists do the same.' I wasn't, as you might say, pulling any punches. This was Harrods, don't forget.

But the imputation did not appear to hurt Fitzpiers. On the contrary, it seemed I was only furthering his case. 'Marx too,' he said, shrugging his shoulders and pulling a funny face – he didn't want to be blatant but there was no getting away from it – 'Marx too, though he wasn't exactly a fiction writer, could be classed as – '

'Oh come on,' I said.

But Sharon had another point to make. 'It looks like you've found your gap,' she said to Fitzpiers.

'My gap?'

'You remember, you wondered if there was room for another book on Hardy.'

'And you think I've proved there is?'

'Undoubtedly. *The Alien From Tophet*.'

'I see it. I see it. *A Study of Extra-Terrestrial Imagery and Lunar Aspirations in the Later Fiction of Thomas Hardy*, beginning with a chapter to be entitled "Did Men From Outer Space Construct Stonehenge To Get Tess Back?" You aren't taking the piss by any chance, are you?'

Sharon? She was just having the time of her life. She loved meeting people. By the time the afternoon was over she had got around to calling Dr Rowland Fitzpiers Fitz. It was all going exactly the way I wanted it to, in so far as I could be certain that I wanted it to.

3

'Well?' I asked.

'Well what?'

'Do you like him?'

'Fitz?'

'My friend Rowland, yes.'

'He isn't your friend. You hardly know him.'

'I see. This morning you'd never clapped eyes on him, tonight we're fighting about who knows him better.'

'I'm not fighting.'

'That's only because you think you've already won. '

'Won? Won what?'

'I hesitate to answer that, Sharon.'

'Good. Good night.'

'But answer it I will. The battle for my old friend Rowland's – or, if you prefer, your new friend Fitz's – affection.'

'Why don't you go to sleep?'

'I don't want to go to sleep. I want to talk this thing out.'

'What thing? There isn't any thing.'

'Oh but there is, Sharon. Are not you a Strumpet?'

Sharon rose in her bed and looked down at me. She knew that if I'd been seriously spoiling for a fight I would have been upright myself, wearing at least the top of my pyjamas and threatening her with the wildness of my

114

stare; but I was flat on my pillows tonight, with my eyes closed, blind like a mole, sniffing darkness.

'Barney,' she said, trying to get me to open my eyes.

'What, not a Whore?'

'Barney,' she asked, 'are you jealous?'

'Me?'

'You.'

'Jealous?'

'Jealous.

'Sharon, I don't know the meaning of the word.'

'Good. Then I can sleep contentedly. See you in the morning.'

'Don't go to sleep.'

'Why not?'

'I'm jealous.'

'Say it again.'

'I'm jealous.

'Barney, not so very long ago you told me that jealousy gave you pleasure.'

'I did. It does.'

'Then enjoy yourself. Good night.'

'No, no, don't turn away. I'll be awake all night in torment.'

'But that's what you want.'

'Not on my own. I need you to help me.'

'I thought I already had. I've made you jealous.'

'I want more.'

'All right, the next time I see your friend I won't just play footsie with him under the table. *Now*, can you go to sleep?'

'Sharon, what do you mean by next time you won't *just*? Are you trying to tell me that you already have?'

'Of course.'

'Today? In Harrods?'

'Barney, what did you think was happening this afternoon? I suppose you thought we were discussing science fiction.'

'I did actually, yes.'

'Ha!'

'You mean we weren't discussing science fiction?'

'*We* certainly weren't. I don't know what *you* were doing.'

'I was buying him bloody milkshakes, for God's sake.'

'And you know why he asked for milkshakes, don't you?'

'No, Sharon I don't. But my guess is that it's either because he's got ulcers or he likes sticking straws up his nose.'

'They take longer to prepare, that's why. And the more time you could be encouraged to spend at the counter, the more time Fitz and I could spend together.'

'I don't believe it.'

'Don't believe it.'

'All that ingenuity just so that you could play footsie under the table?'

'Oh no, we could do that while you were there. When you were away we did other things.'

'Under the table?'

'And over. And round the side.'

'What kind of other things?'

'You know. We took greater liberties.'

'I'd appreciate more candour, Sharon.'

'We went a little further.'

'In which direction, Sharon?'

'In every direction you can think of, Barney!'

I sat bolt upright in my bed and for the first time in what seemed like a small lifetime I opened both my eyes. With my left hand I unlaced the neck of her nightdress and with my right I fished out the nearest of her breasts. 'How could you?' I asked, bending over it. I expostulated directly with the nipple, not bothering with the formality of going through its owner. 'How could you?' I repeated, watching it grow and harden under the friction of my fingers, watching it bake and swelter in the furnace of my breath.

She did not, like Tess of the D'Urbervilles, whisper with a dry mouth, 'In the name of our love, forgive me!'

And therefore I could not, like Angel Clare, reply, 'O

116

Tess', or even 'O Sharon – forgiveness does not apply to the case. You were one person; now you are another. My God – how can forgiveness meet such a grotesque – prestidigitation as that!'

What she said instead, and rather crossly too, because this was Finchley and not Wessex, was 'Barney, I thought this was what you wanted.'

And what I replied, because I was Barney and not that other person, was 'It is, it is.'

'I can tell you it's not true if you want me to.'

'Tell me it's not true.'

'It's not – '

'Stop!'

'All right, then I can tell you that it *is* – '

'Don't tell me!'

'Barney,' said Sharon, taking her breast back and swinging out of bed, though she could very nearly have done that in the opposite order, 'I'm going downstairs to make myself a cup of tea. I'd appreciate it if you could be asleep when I get back.'

'While you're down there I'd like a strawberry milkshake,' I called after her, but she'd gone.

She returned in half an hour to find the bedroom lights off and me flat on my pillow once more, snoring lightly. She pottered about for a few minutes in the blackness, performing as by instinct her necessary bedtime tasks. Then she sighed and crept noiselessly under the blankets, where I was waiting for her. It wasn't an attack. I wasn't brutal. I simply nosed towards her, mole-small, mole-blind, and burrowed into her dark and secret places.

'Pretend it's him,' I whispered into them. 'Pretend I'm him.'

'Barney!'

'I'm not Barney, Sharon, I'm Fitz.'

'Barney, stop that!'

'Call me Fitz, Sharon.'

'I can't.'

'Of course you can. Say, "Fitz darling!" '

117

Sharon took a deep breath. Whatever else she could or couldn't say, she couldn't say her mother hadn't warned her. Unequivocally. At all times, Sharon, I promise you, and from all angles and for no reason. So Sharon said 'Fitz darling,' as if it were one word.

Which wasn't good enough for me. 'Jesus, Sharon,' I complained, 'could you put a bit of feeling into it!'

'Fitzdarling,' she said again.

'No, no. Look, it's not the name of an Irish settlement in the Australian outback. You're supposed to be addressing someone. Intimately.'

'I can't believe this. I'm being given drama and elocution lessons in my own bed at two o'clock in the morning. Barney, I'm tired.'

'Just try it one more time.'

'Fitz darling. Oh, Fitz darling!'

'That's much better. Now say, "Fuck me, Fitz!" '

'Barney, no!'

'Say it, Sharon.'

'Barney, why do you want this?'

I was very still. Whyever I wanted this, it wasn't for the exercise. And anyway, what did *my* wants have to do with anything? 'It's not me that wants it, Sharon,' I reproved her. 'It's you. You know you do.'

She could easily see where that was going to lead her. She swallowed hard. 'Fuck me, Fitz,' she said at last, for decency's sake.

4

But she lacked conviction. As an invitation it sounded about as enticing as 'Kiss me Hardy'.

5

1

Nor, I feel bound to add, did her acting ever get any better. And God knows she got the practice. I was a tireless, painstaking, meticulous director. I went for nights without sleep. I trebled our usual consumption of coffee. Sometimes I had to pinch Sharon's cheeks to keep her awake. But it seemed that she just couldn't simulate ecstasy to save her life. She whimpered woefully; she moaned as if she were in the last stages of a difficult labour; she couldn't manage the most perfunctory paroxysm without banging her head. She didn't even know, although I showed her and showed her, how to lash the pillows with her hair.

'I might just as well be married to Vanessa Redgrave,' I complained.

But she cautioned me against complacency. 'I could do it if you weren't watching over me,' she said, stifling a yawn. 'A rehearsal is one thing, your actual live performance is another. Just wait till opening night.'

Her natural verbal indelicacy kept me on the boil. Literally. I swear steam came out of my ears.

And I thought about nothing else. I stopped going for walks. I stopped watching television. I stopped dreaming (partly because I had stopped sleeping). And I learned to value the great orderliness that a thorough-going obsession can bring to your life; I was troubled by no misdirected energies, I was distracted by no fugitive desires – I was whole and harmonious, concentrated upon a single purpose, as if poured through a funnel. If Mrs Flatman had suddenly slid down my chimney and ripped open her shirt and said, 'Here, Barney – ride!' I would have buttoned her up with unshaking fingers and sent her back the way she came.

I think I can say that at no time since I'd known her had I been a better husband to Sharon.

Dr Rowland Fitzpiers, in the meantime, little knowing what liberties were being taken with his name and person after midnight, was fast becoming a regular visitor of ours during more conventional hours. Occasionally we visited him at his place, but that invariably meant that we had to make the acquaintance of whichever new lachrymose woman he had just taken up with; whereas if he came to us he could make his own decision as to whether she was fit to be met or was best left sobbing in his kitchen. In the main he chose the latter course, which suited us, and came on his own.

Despite the limit which such precautions imposed on our opportunities to meet them, it didn't take us more than a week or two to notice that Fitzpiers's girl-friends conformed to a rigid pattern: they were all thin and over thirty: they all had children who cried almost as much as their mothers did but whom Fitzpiers loved, on sight, as if they were his own; they were all the ex-wives or mistresses of SF writers whose success had come too early (or whose failure had gone on too long) for them to be reasonably expected to persist with domestic life; they all dressed, even while they merely sat and moped in Fitzpiers's kitchen, more or less in the fashion expected of the average get-up-and-go space-girl – that's to say they wore leather suits or thigh boots or satin tunics with wide shoulders and lacing up the sides; and they were all not just temporarily and circumstantially but forever and constitutionally, in the blood and genes and marrow, miserable.

'Considering how much time they spend sniffling,' I quipped to Sharon, 'you would think their husbands would have provided them with astro-hankies to match their suits.'

But Sharon didn't think I was all that smart. 'You don't suppose those outfits were their husbands' idea, do you?' I remember she was quite astonished by my naivety. 'I think you'll find that Fitz buys them those the minute he falls in love with them.'

'Fitz? But they're all dressed like that. You never see them looking any other way. Even the newest of them.'

'That's because he falls in love with them the minute that he meets them.'

I whistled through my teeth. 'It must cost him a fortune,' I said. But that wasn't what was really on my mind. What was really on my mind was how much better Sharon would look as a she-astronaut, how much more amusing a companion on a long inter-stellar voyage she would be, than the wan creatures with sore noses that Fitzpiers was vainly dressing to fit his fantasies. I had an idea that that was on Sharon's mind too. And on Fitz's.

'This is Suzi,' he announced one evening on our doorstep, presenting a hollow-eyed girl lost in the uniform of an air-hostess of the twenty-fifth century but carrying what seemed to be an ordinary contemporary baby at her breast.

Fitz had said he was coming to dinner on his own. However, he often changed his plans at the last minute and we had cooked enough for forty let alone for four. I mention this to make it clear that although we weren't expecting Suzi we were only too pleased that she had come. I know that I was all smiles and welcomes. 'Hello Suzi,' I said. 'I think Fitz has forgotten that we met you in his kitchen last week.'

'No, no,' said Fitzpiers quickly, 'that was Sarah. You haven't met Suzi before. We've only been going out together since this morning.'

'Hello anyway,' I said, doing what I could to conceal my irritation. It wasn't my fault that I couldn't tell one of Fitzpiers's girl-friends from another. I experienced a sudden aversion to him. And I wasn't softened any by the way he hovered devotedly over the baby as if he had known it since it was a little kicking foetus, instead of since breakfast.

The baby was in Sharon's thoughts too. She cooed over it and tickled its neck and rubbed its nose with hers. She even wondered whether he would like a little bowl of pasta. Suzi, close to tears, said that he wouldn't and that he was a she. Sharon went on to wonder whether they'd brought a carry cot or whether the baby would like to sleep in a big comfortable bed with an electric blanket and one of Sharon's own old teddy bears for company.

Fitzpiers looked anxiously at the woman he had loved selflessly for a full eleven hours. 'If it's all right with you,' she answered, 'I'd like to keep her with me. I believe that babies should be brought into adult life from as early an age as possible.' It was impossible to tell whether her small piping girlish voice was natural to her or whether she was learning (for Fitzpiers) to imitate the computerized lisp much favoured in the twenty-fifth century. But there was no doubting that she was not to be separated from her baby. She clasped it to the winged lapels of her glittering tunic and darted her eyes around the capsule nervously, alone and far from home and circumscribed by aliens.

Sharon wondered if the baby – it was called Tammy – if Tammy – short for Tamsin – if Tamsin would like anything to drink.

'I am her mother,' said Suzi. The word seemed to go through Fitzpiers like an electric shock. 'I have everything she needs.'

'Wine?' I asked.

'Thank you, but she doesn't – '

'I meant for you,' I explained.

'No thank you.' She wasn't having the distinction. She clung to Tamsin as if there were moves afoot to send them to different Galaxies. 'I'll drink Guinness. We've brought some with us. It's better for the milk.'

At the mention of milk – he had already been weak-ened by the mention of mother – Fitzpiers's eyes began to water. I believed that I caught him looking across at Sharon and wiping away a tear, as who should say, 'You, you are the most fascinating of women but she, *she* is lactescent.'

I began to feel distinctly uncomfortable. I knew where this was leading. I could recognize the tell-tale sounds and movements. Suzi's tunic was not zippered where it was only to make for ease of changing in weightless conditions. At any second it was going to be required of me to treat as perfectly commonplace and unremark-able the materialization of something I had wasted nearly half my life trying to get a look at. I suppose it's possible that my discomfort communicated itself to the others, but I don't think so. I believe my expression remained immobile. The trouble seemed to lie within Suzi herself. For some reason she couldn't finally bring herself to do it. Perhaps she hadn't known Fitzpiers long enough. Or perhaps she didn't want to enter a competi-tion with Sharon she could only lose. Anyway, something caused her to dither and look distraught. And the baby to cry.

Sharon wondered if there was anything she could do, if there was anything she could provide, if there was anywhere quiet that Suzi would like to go.

The girl rose and smiled and said thank-you and then suddenly changed her mind. Hitherto hidden lines appeared on her face. 'I am not used to visiting people who expect me to nurse in another room,' she said, in her quavering little voice. 'Or who hold back dinner on our behalf. Of course I understand that your child-lessness makes you prudish. And I am sorry for you. It's a great shame to miss out on the absolutely glorious aura of peace that babies bring.'

All the time she was speaking she was gathering together her things. Despite the glorious aura of peace in which she was bathed both her hands shook violently. Fitzpiers, like Sharon and like me, stood with his mouth open. Suzi was already at the front door when she delivered her final sentence. Nobody could be quite certain, afterwards, what it was that she'd said, but a rough guess, doing scant justice to the original, was 'You are not alone in a world that doesn't love its children.'

A moment later she was gone, and a moment after that Fitzpiers followed her, distraught, into the night.

I consoled myself, for the rest of the evening, with lasagne and chianti sufficient for four – there is more than one way of finding peace in this world – and by repeating, 'Prudish? Us? She ought to hear some of the things you've been saying you'd like to do to her boyfriend.'

But Sharon wasn't saying anything just now. Nor was she eating or drinking. She didn't even finish off Suzi's Guinness.

'Cheer up,' I told her, encouragingly. 'Who cares anyway?'

'I do,' she said. But she wouldn't say about what.

And she wouldn't join in our usual nightly rehearsal either – no matter what I threatened her with.

2

I lay awake a long time that night thinking about Sharon and Fitzpiers and Fitzpiers's passion for inter-galactic lactic nursing mothers, and all the while I nursed a little something of my own – the idea that Sharon was jealous. What else had she meant when she said she cared? She cared about Fitzpiers. She was jealous of Suzi. It was also possible, I realized, that she was jealous of that glorious aura of peace which went with motherhood, and that Fitzpiers wasn't the only small new thing she wanted at her breast. I knew that she had always had leanings in that direction and that she was, of late, beginning to panic slightly about her age. But I made a point of putting off all serious discussion of the subject; I wasn't ready even if she was; there was nothing about myself that I had so far discovered that I was expressly anxious to perpetuate. And naturally, what had happened to me in Harry Vilbert's chair disposed me even less to the principle of proliferation. There was too much chaos and carelessness abroad already; someone had to say, 'Hold! Enough!' and then and there husband his seed. So if it was Tamsin that Sharon envied Suzi for, there was nothing in all conscience that I could do for her; but if it was merely Dr Rowland Fitzpiers, well there was something that I could. I could stand aside. I could make way. I could make a present of each to the other. I was guided here, you will perceive, by motives that did not lack altruism. But they did not lack self interest either. I wasn't planning to stand too far away. I intended to watch them both unwrap their parcels. And having arrived at that decision – if it wasn't a decision, what was it? – I throbbed myself to sleep.

I awoke the next day late, still woozy with rough thoughts. I felt light in the stomach, as if I hadn't eaten for weeks, and dizzy, as if I had just come off the big dipper. By the time Fitzpiers rang to apologize for Suzi's behaviour, to explain that she had now gone back to her husband, and to suggest that he come round *that evening* to apologize to Sharon *in person*, I was so unsteady on my feet that I could have been blown over by one belch from Suzi's baby.

I did nothing all day. If I'd left the house I would certainly have got lost. When Sharon came home from the shop, full of news and gossip – guess how many *Desperate Remedies* she'd sold today? who did I think had been in looking for *The Hand of Ethelberta* this afternoon? – I merely stared at her across the kitchen table with dead eyes.

'What's the matter with you?' she asked. I could see that she had recovered from last night's despondency and was looking sparky.

'Nothing,' I replied. 'Fitz rang. He's coming round to say he's sorry.'

'When?'

Too hot, too hot.

'Eightish.' I looked at my watch. It was still only sixish.

Sharon sneaked up behind me and blew into my neck, pretty much as she had done with Tamsin. 'Well it's a good job he is,' she whispered, 'if you're just going to sit and stare. Because I feel like letting my hair down tonight.'

Given the completely combustible condition of my insides right now I wasn't safe from even the most inadvertent spark or friction, but a remark like that, hot in my ear, was as the application of the eternal torch to tinder. I went up in seconds. Although it was hours before Fitzpiers was due, I ran about drawing curtains and re-arranging furniture and altering the angles and the wattage of glaring lights. I put soft music on the record player and draped towels over the speakers to soften it some more; I lit joss sticks; I threw cushions on the carpets; I hid the telephone; I threw cushions on the cushions. Then I paced the floor and waited for Fitzpiers. I heard him coming from three streets away and met him at the door, before he could knock on it, with a tumblerful of gin. 'Hello! Here! Drink!' was all I could later remember saying. Then I poured a similar quantity for Sharon, topped up Fitzpiers, turned off the rest of the lights, and slipped away.

Forty minutes later I was still crouched at the top of the stairs, cold and motionless, trying to hear every word that was said, not wanting to miss a single syllable of the slide from sociability to venery. So far all that had floated up to me had been Fitzpiers's latest observations, punctuated by the odd laugh of agreement or surprise from Sharon, on the subject that was now apparently uppermost in his mind – Thomas Hardy as one of the founding fathers, along with Homer, Virgil, God and the Gilgamesh poet, of science fiction. Numb with loneliness, disappointment and critical outrage, I waited and waited, only shifting my position when it was necessary to change ears. But at last there came a break in conversation. I detected movement. If I wasn't mistaken someone rose. Someone walked to another part of the room. Something opened and rustled. And then there was Fitzpiers's voice.

'I'd very much like you to take a look at this,' it said.

Every last hair on the back of my neck rose and stood on end.

Sharon's laugh came rich and ribald and appreciative. 'Are you sure you'll be showing it to the right person?'

I put my knuckles into my mouth and bit them. They are scarred to this day. I remember that I tried to picture Sharon as she spoke. How she was sitting. The position of her hands and legs. And I wondered if that was mischief in her voice or pique. Was she letting Fitzpiers see that she was a trifle put out by all the other women who had been granted a prior peek at whatever he was about to show her?

His reply was confident and complimentary. 'I can't think of anybody else I'd rather show it to,' I swear I heard him say.

Sharon's laugh rang out again. I accepted that by now Fitzpiers must have seen her tonsils. I picked out the unmistakable sounds of a chair being pushed back, a footfall, the teeth of a zip slowly separating. And Sharon's voice, with laughter still in it, wickedly slangy: 'In that case you'd better bring it over here and give me a dekko.'

I clung swooning to the bannisters.

For a moment I thought I might have passed out, indeed lost an hour of my life, because the next thing I heard was the sound of turning pages and Sharon reading, as if from an essay or a lecture, 'Thermo-nuclear time, as perceived in extremity by any one of J.G. Ballard's isolated protagonists, can be paralleled in Thomas Hardy by the minute accretions of the past that go to form and determine the present for all of his tragically modern and therefore entirely un-free heroes; that scene where Henry Knight (literally benighted) clings to a Cornish cliff and stares into the mystery he shares with the merest fossil creates a frisson that is quintessentially Ballardian. . .' But then it dawned on me that this was only a blind, a ruse, a trespass on my credulity; that Sharon and Fitzpiers were faking an SF seminar, speaking words that had no meaning while they were all the time hideously entwined. Certainly there were one or two dreadful things that Sharon couldn't possibly be doing to Fitzpiers while she was reading aloud from his paper, but there was no limit to the number of dreadful things he could be doing to her. I felt let down. I wouldn't be exaggerating if I said I felt betrayed. It was absolutely against the spirit of the thing that I should be deceived. It wasn't necessary and it wasn't fair. There was supposed to be something in this for everybody.

I quit my position at the top of the stairs, paced the landing a few times to restore feeling to my limbs, then I headed for the bathroom. By climbing up on to the lavatory seat (a Jewish lavatory seat, so extravagantly fringed and furnished that it was a sin to sit let alone do what I was doing on it) and putting my head out of a tiny leaded window I could just look down over a side passage on to the flags on which the shadows of anyone in the living room were always thrown. It wouldn't be possible to see all the details, but you'd get the general idea. I heaved myself up and hung out. A huge yellow moon, indifferent but not incurious, looked down with me. For the second time in one evening I almost swooned – so far out of myself and Finchley did I seem to travel, so tiny a speck was I above the roof tops amid the peering stars. On such a night a centurion might have looked out from ancient ramparts and followed the direction of a swerving serving girl; with similarly beating hearts did the Reddleman and Gabriel Oak creep about moors and pastures, feeding on exclusion, harmonizing scopophilia with the great pulse of Nature.

As for the shadows – they were distinct and still and separate. They were not only not together, they were not even close.

Unable to determine whether it was relief that made me ill, or disappointment, I lowered myself and sat for a while among the deodorizers. Fields of flowers had been slaughtered to keep the air sweet in this little room where Sharon saw to it that there was always a choice of coloured tissues but that the waters always ran blue. The thought of Sharon as a homemaker overcame me with nostalgia and nausea mixed. And it reminded me that one of the likely reasons for those shadows keeping such a formal distance was Sharon's concern for the carpet. For a moment, Sharon and Fitzpiers figured in my imagination as a star-crossed pair of lovers who had no place, where they didn't have to worry about the furnishings, to go. I had left them to do whatever they wanted in the living room, forgetting that the living room, with its new anaglyptic wall coverings and its underlay the price of Qum, was the last place that Sharon would have wanted to do anything but dust. If I was going to be really good about this – and God knows I wanted to be good – then I was going to have to give them greater freedom. I was going to have to give them the run of the house. It didn't matter where I went. I could always sleep in the gutter.

I flushed the lavatory out of habit and leapt down the stairs, three at a time. I found Sharon and Fitzpiers sitting comfortably and at a respectable distance from each other, discussing Ballard. They both wondered where I'd been.

'Lying down,' I lied.

'Are you all right?' Sharon asked. But I didn't stop to answer. Once I had replenished their drinks I had to run into the kitchen to fetch a couple more glasses and pour them each a spare.

'You not drinking yourself?' enquired Fitzpiers.

'You all right?' asked Sharon again.

'A bit off-colour,' I explained to them. 'I think I'll take a walk around the block. Don't worry about me. I'll be away a long time.' And not daring to look at either of them, not wanting to see the joy on their faces and not wanting to miss it either, I removed myself from their presence.

*   *   *

I returned a couple of hours later and found the house quiet and the living room lights off. I listened outside, heard not a sound, then tip-toed into the kitchen. A sip of water, a hunk of dry bread, and I'd be off again. But I found Sharon at the sink, on her own, washing glasses.

'Fitz gone?'

'No, he's in the spare room, sleeping.'

'Sleeping?'

'Sleeping. Pissed as a rat. What did you put in his drink?'

'Gin.'

'Did you have to give him so much?'

'I wanted him to unwind.'

'Well he did that all right. He was sick on the carpet.'

'How long ago was that?'

'That's a peculiar question.'

'I just wondered.'

'Not long after you went out, if that's what you just wondered. He's been snoring his drunken head off for the last hour and a half. Where have you been anyway? You've been acting rather strangely tonight.'

I paced up and down, lost in my thoughts, not one of which, I confess, concerned the carpet.

'You know you can go to him if you want,' I said suddenly.

'What?'

'I said I don't mind if you go to him.' I remember that I was having trouble finding the appropriate vocabulary. I couldn't get past the Biblical-solemn. I came perilously close to suggesting that she ascend and uncover Fitz's nakedness and have knowledge of him. I suppose it was only to be expected: this was one of the sacraments of marriage that we were discussing.

Or at least that I was discussing. Sharon just stared at me as if I was mad.

'Why don't you?' I asked again, going over to her and taking the tea-towel off her shoulder and putting my hands on her underneath her apron where she was warm. 'Why don't you?'

130

She swung around. 'Barney, he's pissed out of his brain and he's covered in sick. Thank you for the offer, but no thank you.'

'Is that the only reason, because he's covered in sick? Does that mean that if he wasn't you would?'

'Barney, I'll leave you to finish drying up. After that, why don't you go to him? As for me, I'm going to bed – my bed. Good night.'

I stayed downstairs a little longer, pondering the wreckage of my schemes. I couldn't deny that it was good to feel my pulses beating evenly again, but I hadn't submitted myself to extreme physical discomfort all night and walked thirty times around the block in the freezing cold in order that I might feel calm, had I? I could feel calm any old time. I'd be calm, at the last, for much longer than I cared to think about. There were other things to do with a subtle nervous system meanwhile besides soothing it.

I turned off the kitchen light and went upstairs and knocked on the door behind which Fitzpiers was snoring soundly. When he didn't answer I let myself in.

'Fitz!' I shouted, standing over him. 'Fitz!' I bent across the bed and shook him by the shoulders. I even wondered about the advisability of slapping him a few times. 'Fitz!' I called again. 'It's me, Barney.'

He rolled over and moaned. Then very slowly and very painfully he opened one red eye. I think I can say he looked startled to see me.

'Fitz,' I asked, 'are you awake? Listen: Sharon wants you. I don't mind. I'll sleep here. She's waiting for you in her bedroom.'

Fitzpiers half opened another eye and wiped his mouth. 'You're pissed,' he said.

I shook my head violently. 'I'm not,' I assured him.

'In that case you're off your fucking head,' he just had time to say before he was sick again.

Michael Henchard, prior to involving himself in Casterbridge politics, priced his wife at five guineas and put
her up for auction, and thereafter experienced the ups
and downs of tragedy. But however great his remorse it
must have been an abiding comfort to him to know that
someone had wanted what he was selling, had accepted
his valuation (the child was thrown in gratis), and had
handed over the cash. Things would have gone a lot
worse for him, I contend, if he had failed to attract a
buyer. He certainly would have felt a bigger fool himself.
And his wife would have had a double insult to thank
him for. That's to say domestic anti-climax would have
claimed him instead of grandeur. Which proves that if
you want the pomp that comes with sin you've got to sin
efficiently. There's no point making tentative stabs at it.

I speak feelingly. Often as I revolved Fitzpiers's final
words in my mind, varied as were the interpretations I
put on them, I couldn't make them mean anything but
that I was an oaf. The more so as they reminded me of
what Monty Frankel had called me – his actual words
were, 'You're a fucking meshuggener' – a good ten
years earlier. So was there some inescapable pattern in
my behaviour? You see it wasn't just verbal similarity
that recalled Monty Frankel's charge – there was something reminiscent in the tone of it also, and indeed in the
circumstances; for then, as now, it was Sharon, or at
least my attitude to Sharon, my generosity to her and
about her, if you like my generosity *with* her, that was
the cause of the defamation; and then, as now, I was
mystified and hurt and, on Sharon's behalf, insulted by
it.

Not that it had been my intention to offer Sharon to
Monty Frankel in the way I had offered her – or rather
not stood in the way of her offering herself – to Rowland
Fitzpiers. No, all I had wanted was to show Monty a
photograph of my new girlfriend in much the same spirit
as I had once before shown him a photograph of Rabika

Flatman. Except perhaps that then I had made an offering from a position of weakness and inferiority whereas now I could give from a plentiful store. I was at university now and had found confidence and knowledge and, at a union dance, Sharon. I knew whereof I spoke. Poor Monty, on the other hand, had lost ground. At nineteen he had the prematurely aged look, the yellow skin and the shambling gait, the curved spine and the shaking head, of the fanatically orthodox. He had left school early because there had been no money to keep him there and he worked as a clerk on the Underground. No one in my family knew another Jew with such a job. We assumed that he had taken it for the same reason he had become orthodox – as an act of violence against himself, as part of a systematic and savage disregard of his comfort or appearance. He shuffled about in carpet slippers and a greasy yarmulkah, allowing the hair on his face to grow as it liked and the discoloured tassels of his tzitzits – the lunatic fringe – to hang out of his shirt. The house which he now had entirely to himself mouldered around him. You could smell it from the top of the street. In despair of his ever doing anything about it or of its falling down in time, some neighbours even moved out. It was considered a shameful thing in our neighbourhood for a Jewish boy to cause gentiles to leave the street. We liked to think it usually worked the other way.

Monty no longer kept a gallows in his back garden and he no longer insisted on being called Sam Hall. All that had changed in one brief three month period when he was just fifteen. It had been obvious for some time that Mrs Frankel was running out of the will and the energy necessary to drag her through each day's odyssey of pain and misery, but it was bad luck that she should finally have found herself without either one afternoon, when she was half in and half out of her bath, and there was no one at home to hear her or help her. It was even worse luck, for Monty, that he should have been the first person home, the first to wonder where she was and the first to find her, slung over the bath like a bundle of old

133

laundry. He threw a towel and a dressing gown and the bathroom curtains and whatever else he could find around his mother's now quite inconsequent nakedness and he waited with her in silence – all the while hugging her, he later told me – until his father and brother came home from work. Then there began a howling and a wailing such as I had never heard before and which did not let up for weeks. I was not a stranger to grief and mourning. The Jewish burial laws, forbidding women to attend funerals, meant that from time to time the street became the scene of wild and harrowing sorrow; wives flung themselves on coffins as they left the house, daughters hung on to the door handles and mud guards of slow moving hearses. And once or twice a year, for an hour or so, Finchley was not to be distinguished from Mecca or Benares. But there was something uncanny and far more desolating about the low persistent moan that issued night and day from those Frankel men; there seemed to be some grief they just could not get to the bottom of nor help one another with. Monty himself cried so hard and so long – for his mother's life, he told me, much more than for her death – that when, ten weeks later, he was the first one home again, the first one to wonder where his father was, and the first one to find him swinging, apparently weightlessly, from a beam in the cellar, only marginally less animated deceased than he had ever remembered him living, then Monty also discovered that he didn't have a tear left in him to shed. By the time his brother came home he had already cut down the body and cleaned it and put it to bed. He had even rung up the relevant authorities and the few uncles who might have been interested. It was all just a question of practice, he explained to me. He felt perfectly calm. He was getting the hang of it. But the next morning he went into the garden and dismantled his scaffold. I watched out of the window as it came down and instantly felt a pang of nostalgia for it. He did it, he told me, out of respect. But I felt that he also did it out of a sense of its superfluousness, because the time had come for him to put away childish things.

Lucky him.

Monty and I had never been particularly close friends and what friendship there was had been severely strained by our disagreement over Rabika Flatman's nipples and the uses to which they could legitimately be put. I was half tempted by the idea of a reconciliation founded on the extraordinary sympathy I would show him during his double bereavement; but when it came right down to it sympathy was not what he wanted and sympathy was not what I felt. I watched the goings-off and the carryings-on next door as if they were events upon another planet. I was affected by them all right, but they never struck me as bearing any relation to anything that might happen to me. Death would come to the Fugleman family someday, I knew, but it would not come like *that*. To tell the truth I actually blamed Monty for what befell him – not in the sense that I supposed him to be guilty of murdering his parents, but on account of its being impossible for me to see him as a victim, a merely passive recipient of terrible tidings, when it was so obvious that he had been implicated in his fortunes from the moment he was born. I had been brought up in a severe theology. My mother might have protested her amazement and her astonishment, her outrage and her disbelief daily, but in fact she discerned laws in the universe and held to the conviction that people by and large got what was coming. I was an apt pupil. I had no doubts at all that Monty was responsible for being Monty, and that being Monty what happened to him was bound to happen to him.

This line of reasoning was appealing to me because it helped me to see a rosier future for myself. Grief and tragedy might strike at any time, I knew – Hardy's wasn't the only mother to tell her son that a figure with an uplifted arm waited to throw him back from happy expectation – but at least I was free of the taint of the things. They were not mine. They belonged to Monty, not

135

to me. And sure enough *my* parents didn't die, *my* spine didn't curve, and I easily won myself that place at university that had been waiting for me from those first unmistakable signs of intelligence I had exhibited in my cradle. I liked having Monty Frankel living next door; the sight of his shaking head, his old yarmulkah, his wild sidelocks, even the swaying tassels of his tzitzits, had a soothing effect on me. The very house he lived in, unpainted, uncleaned, unaired, acted as a kind of talisman in reverse: it absorbed all the bad luck that was going.

And yet I was unable to impress him with my success. You would have thought that someone who lived as he lived and worked where he worked could not fail to have been envious of the grand vistas that were opening out for me. Yet he seemed completely indifferent. It might have been the case that all the major events of his physical life had now taken place, but he had an inner existence too and he was busy with that. He read apocalyptic books, books about the deaths of kings and the decline of empires and the ultimate destruction of mankind. He knew by heart all the dates that the great prophets had fixed for the final floods and famines. He didn't bother with stuff like *The Scourge of the Swastika* anymore; the Nazis and their concentration camps were just a small and passing phase of history, barely a ripple on the waters of the last cataclysm, only a trifle more significant than me, Barney Fugleman, with my new college scarf and my stories of student drinking parties. I could find no way to pierce his magisterial boredom towards me, and I suppose that that was partly why I insisted on showing him my photos of Sharon.

'Why do you want me to see them?' he asked.

'Because she's lovely.'

I remember that he scratched his face, a long raking movement, with his black nails. 'There are lots of lovely girls,' he said, and I wondered how he knew.

'But I'm going out with this one. I'm probably going to marry her.'

'All the more reason I don't want to see them,' he said. 'I don't like family photographs.'

But he needn't have worried – family photographs were the last thing Sharon's photographs were.

4

I had met Sharon a month or so earlier at a students' union dance. She was just nineteen. She wasn't a student herself but she went regularly to the union, partly because she liked dancing and partly because she liked to be close to learning. I couldn't believe my good fortune that I had found someone who looked Jewish enough to please my parents and Brobdingnagian enough to please me. And Sharon was enraptured by being with a boy who could recite literature as he undressed her. (Actually, 'undressed her' doesn't quite get it. It was more like an unveiling. I stood on a stool and pulled cords and clapped. If I'd bought champagne it would have been to smash against her side, not drink.) 'O, my America, my Newfoundland,' I declaimed, and she had to guess who I was quoting. We coupled, from the start, with Palgrave's *Golden Treasury* by our bedside, allusively. 'Earth has not anything to show more fair,' I said. 'Men may come and men may go,' Sharon told me, 'But I go on for ever.'

Our phone calls, often made a mere five minutes after we'd parted, were half spiritual adoration – the expression of ideal Platonic yearning – and half me wanting to put my – between her – , and her wanting to put her – around my – . And our letters were much the same. Some of them were so personal that they had to be put inside several envelopes and sent registered mail. Our communications were not limited only to language either; we had begun to post off parts of ourselves to each other also, clippings and cuttings taken from the most secret recesses of our persons. I spent a whole afternoon in the British Museum Reading Room once, writing Sharon a twelve-page description of what I

137

wished was where at that very moment, and then I put in another hour walking around Bloomsbury with the letter stuffed down my trousers. 'PS,' I concluded, 'can you guess where this has been?'

Sharon's reply came back with SWALC written on the back of the envelope. I knew she looked up to my superior learning so I corrected her when I next saw her.

'It should be a K not a C,' I told her.

'I know what I sealed it with,' she replied.

'I only wish I could paint,' I used to lament, when she stood in bedroom doorways for me with her arms in the air and the light behind her. So for our third anniversary – that's to say after we'd been together for three weeks – she bought me a Brownie camera with a flash attachment.

'I see what you mean about not being a painter,' she said, as I arranged her on the bed the way I liked her and put the camera to my burning eye. I suspect that she had imagined, from my love of the arts, that I would go for a subtler disposition of her limbs.

'My parents always wanted me to be a doctor,' I told her, as another bulb popped.

'You certainly have a flair in that direction,' she agreed.

She drew the line at some of my suggestions, more from a dislike of pain I think, than out of modesty; but she still wondered, once I'd finished the reel, whether I'd gone too far. 'How are you going to get them developed?' she asked.

I can't say that I had so far put my mind to that. I mopped my face with Sharon's feather boa. 'I guess I'll take them to Boots,' I said.

'Boots?'

'Or somewhere like that.'

'Barney, Boots is run by Quakers!'

How did she know things like that? I remember her once telling me that C & A was Dutch and that Tesco was named after Tessa Cohen. And yet she thought 'O, my America, my Newfoundland' was a quote from Captain Cook's journals. You can see why we were in love. We were such mysteries to each other.

In fact I took the spool of undeveloped film to a little place I'd sometimes whiled an idle hour away in at the Piccadilly end of Soho. I had planned to be quite casual about it – I wasn't asking for a service they weren't offering – but I confess I panicked the minute they wanted my name and address. What did they want those for? To give to the Vice Squad? So that they could send around the boys to beat the identity of my model out of me? The only name I could think of that wasn't mine was Humbert Humbert. 'Yes, that is e..r..t,' I said. 'Yes, e..r..t both times.' I couldn't believe what I was doing. I felt as if I had descended all at once and for ever into the ranks of the criminally insane. 'One hundred and eleven the Rue Morgue,' I said. 'Yes, that's g..u..e.'

I got out quick smart, clutching my little yellow receipt, and spent the next three days in agony, wondering whether I'd delivered Sharon into the hands of the Mafia. I fully expected, when I went back, to see her photographs on the cover of every magazine on the racks; and you won't be surprised to learn that I was even a trifle disappointed to see that they weren't. The transaction was not completed without one small hiccup, however. When I presented my receipt I was shown into the back of the shop where someone imitating Peter Ustinov imitating a mafioso delivered me a moral lecture – a homily I suppose you could call it – on the rights of women in the film processing industry not to have their sensibilities outraged. It seemed I hadn't warned them at the desk what I was bringing in, and Sharon's negatives had gone in one bag and not the other. I said I was sorry. Around the walls of this sanctum were ranged magazines promising scenes of even greater abandon and bestiality than were available in the front showrooms. My censor looked at me without smiling. I could see that he had sisters in convents all over Sicily whose honour he would cut me into tiny pieces to protect. He took a packet from his inside pocket and spilled the contents on to the table before us. Sharon! Sharon this way, Sharon that way, Sharon the other. 'Pretty diabolical,' he said, and he muttered something else that sounded like, *In vero disgustoso, ripugnante, stomachevole.*

I looked around the room again and then returned to the man's expression of pure distaste. Along with all the other things I felt, I felt a kind of pride. It wasn't everybody that could nauseate the Mafia.

But once I was out in the street I realized that I had felt another kind of pleasure also while Sharon's photographs were on the table. I wished we'd been able to talk about them in more detail; I'd like to have heard what he thought her fairest features were and which attitudes he thought suited her best. And if he'd been just that little bit indelicate about her, if he'd pointed with some exactness, if he'd called things by their coarsest names, why I wouldn't have minded that either, would I? For a moment I thought about going back into the shop. Then I considered stopping undesirables in the street and showing them what I was carrying in my breast pocket. Then I remembered Monty Frankel. You see I didn't just want to impress him – I wanted to share something with him. I was offering him a little pact.

So I wasn't at all prepared for the violence of his reaction when I finally forced him to take a look.

'So this is the girl you say you love?' he asked me, after a moment or two.

'Yes,' I said.

'Does she know you're showing these around?'

'I'm not showing them *around*, Monty.'

'Who else have you shown them to?'

'Nobody.'

'So why me?' I noticed for the first time that there was a break in his voice and that there were tears in his eyes.

I couldn't think of anything to say. I shrugged.

'So why me?' he repeated. He was yelling at me now.

'You think it's safe with me, do you? You think it doesn't count if I see them?'

I tried to explain that that wasn't it at all. But he couldn't hear me. He was cursing me in yiddish and he was crying. Then he threw the photographs at me – hard. And while I was on my knees collecting them he actually kicked me in the back.

Thereafter, whenever I met him he would shout 'Fucking meshuggener!' I began to avoid him but he would even shout it from the other side of the street. I had to stop taking the tube eventually because he would be waiting for me, in his ticket collector's uniform, and I knew from experience that he wouldn't think twice about showing a couple of hundred commuters what a fucking meshuggener looked like.

5

I wish to enter a plea for myself. I was young. I was ardent. And my only mistake really was to have chosen the wrong medium in which to work. If I had written a short story about Sharon (I could have made it as intimate as I liked) and published it in the student newspaper or the London Magazine, I would have found the very satisfaction I was searching for and earned myself some extra pocket money to boot. Who knows – I might even have made a bit of a name for myself. Look at Thomas Hardy. He was twice my age and had titled ladies making a fuss of him when he stripped Paula Power down to her pink tights and doublet and swung her from the rope in her gymnasium – in 'absolute abandonment of herself to every muscular whim that could take possession of such a subtle form'. The fact that nobody reads A Laodicean is not a cause to congratulate Hardy on his decorum – he didn't know that nobody was going to read it. And he certainly did whatever he could inside the novel to give as many people as possible a look at Paula 'bending, wheeling and undulating', even going so far as to have her spied upon through a hole in the

141

wooden wall of her private fitness centre. That way we can all get a peek, heroes, villains (especially villains), readers, author. Especially author. You can see why he didn't need to take photographs.

Not that we can be sure it never crossed his mind. Photography, as it happens, has a role to play in *A Laodicean*. The diabolic Dare – he's the one who instigates the invasion of Paula's privacy and actually makes the hole in the wall for Captain de Stancy to peer through – is himself a dab hand with a camera. And that can be no mere concidence. No coincidence is ever merely mere in Hardy. As Rowland Fitzpiers was later to notice in a well-received paper on the subject, there is a profound connection between Dare's scientific expertise – he has patented a photographic process of his own, especially effective in dim indoor lights – and the darkness (if you like, the dark*room*) of his moral nature. More to the point, the vision of Paula that he procures for Captain de Stancy belongs to the convention of more than one kind of art. 'What was the captain seeing?' Hardy pauses to ask. Well he wasn't going to say, 'The same thing the butler saw,' was he? What was the captain seeing? Why, 'A sort of optical poem.'

I'll never forget the time Camilla first came across that phrase. We were sitting on the cliffs in the warm early morning, reading. Around us the waked birds preened. Below us the seals . . . you know all that. Suddenly there was an explosion of violent mirth from Camilla – it shook the cliffs, I'll tell you; it was a good job that no one from the National Trust was there to spot fine us. And then there was the sound of the New Wessex Edition of *A Laodicean* spinning through the thin air and falling into the Atlantic spume. 'Christ!' Camilla exclaimed. 'I hate the little rat. Optical poem indeed. He'd use any word but the true one. I suppose he called his prick a telespectroscope.'

To this day a round blue Greater London Council plaque commemorates the London house where peeping Tom Hardy resided for three years and shaped the notion of inviting everyone round to Paula's gym for a secret session (secret to Paula) of prose photos. Take a number 19 bus from Piccadilly and get off the stop after Wandsworth Common, or better still take the tube to Tooting Bec and walk up Trinity Road, and you will find it – Hardy's house that is, not Paula's gym. I did, years later. I stood on the pavement opposite for half an hour and looked for shadows on the blinds and wondered if the place stirred any memories. This was after I'd received another shock to my confidence about who I was. But at nineteen I had other things to occupy my mind. At nineteen I was literal and urgent; I wanted immediate returns; it would never have occurred to me to sit down quietly at my desk and compose ophthalmic poetry. That is why no round blue plaque commemorates the spot in which I foisted photographs of the girl I loved on that ungrateful *frumkeh*, Monty Frankel.

Nor that wherein, some ten years later and apparently not much changed, I tried to make a present of the girl herself to the equally ungrateful critic and reviewer, Rowland Fitzpiers.

6

Weeks passed and we heard nothing from Fitzpiers. Not a phone call, not a postcard, not a whisper – nothing. Naturally I put myself through every refinement of suffering. Sometimes I blamed him, sometimes I wished to make it up to him. Sometimes I thought I'd maybe heard him wrong, sometimes I was relieved I'd heard him right. One day I would miss my jealousy terribly, and would really long to be tormented again by his desire for Sharon; on another day I would find the idea that he didn't desire her even more stimulating than the idea that he did. For some reason the thought of sexual discourtesy to Sharon was especially rousing. But those were deep waters. And I had already foundered in shallower. I reminded myself that there was Sharon, too, for me to feel bad about.

And I did feel bad about her. When I thought of all the insults I had subjected her to over the years, when I thought of Monty Frankel and Peter Ustinov's double, let alone Fitzpiers, I was shot through with guilt. I dreaded her asking me if I had any light to shed on Fitz's continuing absence, but she never showed the slightest sign of concern. It was me finally, unable to bear the tension, who blundered into questions about his whereabouts, and it was Sharon who said, 'Oh, he'll be busy with his girlfriends at this time of the year. He'll ring us when he feels like it.' At which demonstration of her unsuspiciousness and easy nature I was prostrate with remorse.

I tried to mend my ways. I showered her with tenderness and solicitude. I let her talk to me about Thomas Hardy. I agreed that I might go back soon to Harry Vilbert to see if I could produce Hardy's signature under hypnosis. It would increase the value of some of the volumes on her shelves no end, if they were signed by Thomas Hardy. And I even helped her out in the shop in the run up to Christmas, and once, in her hearing, recommended *The Dynasts* to a customer.

On Christmas morning I brought her champagne in bed and watched as she opened all the presents I had bought her. Normally, that is to say in the bad old days, when I had changed from the one who was all to her, I gave her scarlet nighties and sequinned underwear for Christmas, but this year my theme was demureness. I believed I had misused her body. Yes, she was my wife and my helpmeet, flesh of my flesh, but she was not mine to do with as I wished. Her body was the tabernacle of the Lord. I looked on, as she buttoned herself up in her new quilted bed-jacket, with watering eyes; and it might have been a time for the making of babies had the phone not then rung.

It was Rowland Fitzpiers. He had been playing Father Christmas all morning, he explained, distributing presents to the children of all his ex-girlfriends. It had been quite a morning. He had also been taking a celebratory brandy with all the ex-husbands of his ex-girlfriends. But that wasn't the purpose of his call. 'Do you remember our last conversation?' he asked me. 'The last thing you said to me, the last time I saw you? Well, I've been thinking it over . . .'

My heart crashed into my stomach like a meteor. I smelt sulphur. 'Get round here right away,' I told him, tasting lava.

6

1

It turned out to be a much more commonplace event than I could ever have anticipated. Sharon had insisted that as it was Christmas it was to be communal or it was to be nothing, and so here we were, all three of us, sitting up in bed in broad daylight, with Sharon in the middle, eating Christmas chocolates and mince pies. All we lacked was a tree.

'Mint?' I enquired, leaning across Sharon and handing Fitzpiers the open box.

'Mmmm,' said Fitzpiers, 'I think I'll try an orangey one. Thank you.'

Naturally, we hadn't gone straight into the chocolates. There had been an hour of feverish activity during which I was granted every one of my most secret wishes, some of them twice over; and there had been moments, sure enough, when I could scarcely trust the veracity of my own eyes – as, for example, when Sharon dropped to her knees and drew back Fitzpiers's foreskin (how did she know what to do with a foreskin?) or when Fitzpiers dropped to his knees and drew back *her* – but no! I might have promised to come clean, but not *that* clean. Suffice it to say that things were done in my sight that might have turned the brain of a more fastidious man. And yet, after the first shocks and incongruities, after a brief introductory period of horror, shame and mortification, I discovered – insane ingrate that I was – that what I was suffering from most was disappointment. In a remarkably short time a feeling of familiarity, even familiality, had taken possession of me – as if we had all three of us got together like this, on festivals and holy days, a dozen times before. I had fallen prey to that sensation of hollow anti-climax that waits for all men who try too hard to sin. No one had tried harder than I had, God knows. I was sin's martyr. And therefore I felt cheated, balked of my pain.

I ascribed this dissatisfaction, partly, to the open good naturedness with which Sharon and Fitzpiers went about enjoying themselves. They gave themselves up to rapture all right, they were roused when it was right to be roused and transported when it would have been improper to be anything else, but there remained something incorrigibly convivial and companionable about them. They paused for cigarettes and jokes and conversation, and when they started up again they were painstakingly considerate of me. If I had had to put my disappointment in a nutshell I think I would have said that they were not adulterous enough.

I would have been getting more the thing I was after if words of love or desperation had been wrung out of Sharon in her ecstasies. Phrases such as, 'Never leave me, Fitz!' or 'I want it only from you, Fitzpiers!' would have done the trick, but if they crossed Sharon's mind they never escaped her lips. Once in a while I tried to coach her, coming at her from the other side to Fitzpiers, and whispering in her ear instructions for her to follow. 'Implore him to kiss your breasts,' I suggested.

'What?'

If I whispered any louder Fitz would hear. 'Beg him to kiss your breasts,' I repeated, stressing the beg.

But it was no use. 'Barney wants me to ask you to kiss my tits,' she announced.

Mind you, once we had all become a little weary I was grateful for the prevailing mood of simple companionableness. I didn't really want my wife to be in love with my friend, and in fact I must confess to feeling quite

147

peeved on a couple of occasions during the aftermath of passion when Sharon took liberties with Fitzpiers, even though the liberties she took were as child's play to what she'd taken a half an hour before. It concerned me that Sharon seemed unaware of the unspoken rules that govern the before and after. I believe that I am not and never have been an oaf or a brute in this regard. I knew that one had no right to disown when one was spent what one had longed for when one was eager. Sadness after the event, for example, had never seemed to me to confer any privileges. And I never turned on women as Thomas Hardy the novelist did. But I was a confirmed and compulsive fantasist, and I understood in all its refinements the etiquette of make-believe.

Sharon, it appeared, from the way she ran her fingers through the hairs on Fitzpiers's chest, didn't.

This isn't a complaint, but nothing seemed to be happening, for me, in the order in which I wanted it to. Take the incident over the plum pudding. There were no plans for all three of us to sit down, like a regular Christian family, to a regular Christian dinner. Our Jewishness – Sharon's and mine – might not have got in the way of our buying each other Christmas presents or polishing off boxes of chocolate liqueurs, but it did rule out, on the grounds of cultural nationalism and self-respect, such things as the singing of carols or the hanging of mistletoe, just as surely as it ruled out going to midnight mass. A plum pudding, on the other hand, was something else again; a plum pudding, according to my reckoning, was sufficiently free of associations with virgins and wise men and infant saviours to be eaten by my wife and myself at any time with impunity. As for Fitzpiers, he had spent the morning dashing from one SF widow to another, crying over their babies and helping them to baste and stuff and sample turkey; he'd already had a terrific Christmas, the best he could remember – plum pudding with brandy butter would round it off perfectly.

It had been steaming on the stove for hours. I'd popped downstairs I don't know how many times to

148

check the water. At three-thirty it was ready and at three-thirty-seven we were sitting up in bed eating it. But I was not enjoying mine as much as I usually did, or as much as I believed I had a right to. I was put off and put out. In the seven minutes I'd been away in the kitchen, untying the cellophane and being careful not to splash any water and measuring out three equal portions (equal to the last crumb!), Sharon and Fitzpiers had sneaked one in – I could tell it from the queer look on their faces and the three little beads of fresh perspiration between Sharon's breasts – *without me.* An hour ago I would have given up my share of pudding gladly for the sweet pang that such an act of silent complicity would have caused me; the little secret something that Sharon and Fitzpiers now had together was the very element that had all along been missing from my excitement. But it belonged to then, not now. Its place was in the dream, not the reality. Sharon, of course, was the one I blamed. Yet again she was guilty of a breach of that etiquette whose principles were the only things that stood between civilized life and barbarism.

2

'It's a pity Hardy didn't write Christmas stories like Dickens,' Sharon said idly, much later in the afternoon, when it was quite dark ouside and we had all woken up together after dozing fitfully. I can't remember now whether it was snowing but I feel as if it must have been; in my memory it was a soft silent day, eerily free of the usual clamour of London, in which every infrequent footfall was as on a carpet.

I lay flat on my back and looked up at the ceiling. The fingers of Sharon's left hand drummed companionably on the inside of my right thigh just as, for all I knew, the fingers of her right drummed companionably on Fitz's left. 'I have to say that I am glad he didn't write any more than he did,' I said. 'As you know, I'm something of a reactionary when it comes to Thomas Hardy. I

149

subscribe to the doctrine that more must mean worse.'

Fitzpiers rolled over onto one elbow and addressed me over my wife. 'Ah, but that's a value judgement,' he said. He had bits of bed stuck in his beard, which oddly pleased me. And bits of Sharon stuck between his teeth, which oddly didn't. 'Whereas I thought I detected a regret more commercial than aesthetic in Sharon's words.'

Can I say that what I thought I detected was that Fitzpiers was already explaining my wife to me?

'Oh commercial, most certainly,' Sharon confirmed. Indeed, her remark had been prompted by the vicissitudes of Christmas trade which, while it had been fast for Eustacia's On The Heath, had by no means been furious. She wasn't complaining; business, touch wood, could have been a lot worse. But she did feel that her specialized stock was always bound to let her down at this time of the year; that it of necessity lacked the festive element. *Life's Little Ironies*, she explained, gift-wrapped with ribbons and a rosette, made a pretty enough present, but as a seasonal seller it couldn't hold a candle to *A Christmas Carol*.

'In which case,' said Fitzpiers, 'it's not a question of more meaning worse but more meaning richer.' In all fairness to him I don't think he intended that as a gibe at our Jewishness. I don't think he intended it as a criticism at all. As I was soon to find out with a vengeance, he was all for making a good living out of literature himself.

I meanwhile was more concerned with value judgements than my livelihood – they released more tension. 'I think Hardy was wise to stay away from the genre,' I persisted. 'He had none of the necessary feeling for food and drink.' I was rather disappointed with the way that sounded; if I'd been in better spirits I'm sure it would have come out more sybaritic.

'Well I can't argue with you there,' said Fitzpiers. 'A happy Hardy Christmas party is certainly difficult to imagine. Think of the fuss there'd be, for a start, over the killing of the dinner. You wouldn't want to leave it to Jude and whatsername.'

'Arabella,' Sharon helped out.

'That's right, Arabella. Arabella Donn – she of the rank passions and the latent hungry sensuousness and the ample. . .' But here Fitzpiers was guilty of the unpardonable sin of explicitness, for he lowered his eyes in mid-sentence and allowed them to range referentially over Sharon's uncovered breasts. The action irritated me not because it was libidinous and even possessive but because it was overt – it *alluded*, it brought into the realms of the spoken what belonged properly to the understood; it confused the darkness with the daylight. What's more I didn't want Sharon associated, even by implication, with Arabella. I had nothing against Arabella – apart from her passing interest in Jude – but I remembered how much Hardy hated her because she was passionate and buxom, and the bad faith of the novelist's impaired sexuality was suddenly with me, like an ill omen, in the bed.

I felt queasy, as if I'd perceived in myself the old symptoms of an old sickness.

Sharon was still at the impossible Hardy Christmas party. 'Of course all the presents would go astray,' she said.

'Or go to the wrong people,' Fitzpiers came back.

'Yes, yes, they would,' she agreed. 'And later on in the evening, when the mummers had gone home, all the men could get drunk and auction their wives.'

At this I looked hard into Sharon's eyes, but they were limpid. If there was a woman anywhere freer of intention I would like to have seen her. 'And then all the wives could get up a skimmity ride,' I suggested, just to keep it equal.

Fitz had an even brighter idea. 'What about the mottoes inside the Christmas crackers? Imagine the kiddies' smiling faces when they unfold the riddle in the party-hat and find, *Question: Which do we live on – a splendid or a blighted planet? Answer: A blighted one. Ha! Ha! Ha!*'

I had one too. 'How about, *All laughing comes from*

misapprehension. Rightly looked at there is no laughable thing under the sun.'

'Yours wins,' laughed Fitzpiers.

'It's beginning to look,' said Sharon, after another ten minutes of this kind of jollification, 'as though we don't take the idea of a Hardy Christmas story very seriously.'

We didn't.

'And it's also beginning to look,' she went on, 'as though there's no point in my asking you to knock me a couple out for next Christmas.' She fixed me with a long stare which I recognized to mean that she considered that I owed her.

'A couple?' I wasn't arguing with the obligation, I just wasn't certain what she wanted me to pay with.

'One then.'

'Sharon, are you proposing that I write you a Christmas story that you can pass off as being by Thomas Hardy?'

She sat up and drew the bed clothes up to her neck. I got the impression that she was drawing a line below which she would never again do me any favours. 'Forget it,' she said.

I was staggered. 'Sharon,' I said, 'what makes you think that I am capable of writing a Christmas story that I or you or both of us together could foist upon an astonished world as Thomas Hardy's?'

'You're always saying he wrote trash.'

'That doesn't mean that I can duplicate it.'

'Just hang on a minute,' said Fitzpiers. He hadn't been able to follow very much of this, but if Sharon knew some way of making money by counterfeiting Thomas Hardy he would be in on it if I wouldn't. He considered himself to be a gifted copyist, and, as he later told Sharon, he had always secretly preferred parodies to their originals anyway. One of his major points about science fiction was that it was essentially a pastiche of all other narrative forms. 'Just hang on here. Surely the three of us could in fact put our heads together and come up with a pretty passable imitation, particularly as we're talking about a genre that we've all agreed he never could have mastered. We don't need to do too good a job – in fact the clumsier we make it the more authentic it will feel.'

I marvelled at his ingenuity. I confess that there was a boyish, sanguine quality about Fitzpiers that I always liked. But I was not disposed to give him any encouragement in this enterprise. It might have been Christmas but I had already given him enough today. 'Forget it,' I said. 'Faking Hardy doesn't just carry a heavy term of imprisonment. You'd be lynch-mobbed. The English are very sensitive about their primitives. A boy at my old school was sent to borstal for drawing a moustache on a photograph of Emily Brontë in the public library. His parents had to leave the district.'

I could tell that Fitzpiers thought I was hopelessly negative. And Sharon was even more contemptuous of me still. It clearly helped her to have some moral support. 'Who's talking about *faking* Hardy anyway?' she wanted to know. She almost spat the question at me.

'Then just what are you talking about, Sharon?' I asked. She wasn't the only one who could spit.

'I'm talking about you going back to Harry Vilbert with a pencil and a piece of paper in your hand, if you want to know,' she said. 'And don't tell me that it doesn't work – I've just been reading about a woman who composes Beethoven sonatas that way.'

I couldn't believe what I was hearing. The name Harry Vilbert – brought up in Fitz's presence. It was against everything that we'd agreed. It was an abrogation of all her promises. 'That'll do, Sharon,' I ordered.

'Who's Harry Vilbert?' asked Fitzpiers.

'Nobody,' I told him.

'A hypnotist,' said Sharon.

'I love hypnotists,' said Fitzpiers. 'I went to one once, to stop me smoking. He smoked like a train himself. He wore a buttoned cardigan and carpet slippers and he smelt of sprouts. What do you go to yours for? To help

153

you write? Or to remove some other kind of blockage?'

'I don't *go* to him,' I said.

'He *went* to him' said Sharon.

'That's not true either. I fell into his clutches.'

'How wonderful!' said Fitzpiers. 'What did he do – turn you into an opera singer? Or did he get you to procure small boys for him?'

'He did neither,' said Sharon. 'He regressed him.'

'Sharon!'

Fitzpiers just wanted to make sure he had heard that right. 'He regressed him?'

And I wanted to make sure that he had not. 'Sharon,' I boomed, 'that's enough!'

'Yes. He regressed him. Twice.'

'Sharon!'

Fitzpiers sat up in bed. You couldn't hope to see a man having a better time. I think we all knew that he would never again experience a happier Christmas. But he was also taking a scientific interest in what he was being told. He wanted to be clear about the details. 'Do you mean he regressed him back to his own childhood?' he asked. 'Or did he take him back even further?' It didn't at all help my temper that in Fitzpiers's fidgety excitement his penis had become visible from under the bedclothes.

Myself, I leapt from the bed and issued an ultimatum to my wife. 'Not another word Sharon, I warn you.'

But she rose on her pillows, a pink circle of recklessness glowing on each cheek. Her breasts were uncovered again and the nipples also seemed to flush and start, as if alive to her temerity. She addressed Fitzpiers. 'Oh, well beyond his childhood,' she confided. 'He went back a hundred years.'

'A hundred years!' All the disparate elements of Fitzpiers's face expressed astonishment. I'd never seen him so unified. 'And who did Barney discover that he'd been?' he asked. 'A footsoldier in Her Majesty's expeditionary forces or a private secretary to Disraeli?'

'Somebody more notable than either,' said Sharon. It

was odd that she should be so vindictive towards me as I was and yet so proud of who I'd been. 'Why don't you try and guess?' she dared Fitzpiers.

That was enough for me. I was already well into my clothes when Fitz started rattling off names. 'Florence Nightingale? Holman Hunt? The Mahdi? Cardinal Newman? Prince Albert? Mrs Trollope? Lord Balfour? Friedrich Nietzsche? Christina Rossetti?' And I didn't stay to hear Sharon saying, 'Warmer, warmer, no, now you're cold again.'

I was at the foot of the stairs by the time Fitzpiers had been given enough clues and exhausted enough notables to be able to announce, 'Of course – him!' And I was at the front door, buttoning up my overcoat, when I heard Sharon explaining how extraordinary were the coincidences she'd unearthed and how exact were the details she'd confirmed and how everything was amazing and pointed in only one direction.

Before I had to listen to a single further infraction of confidence and good form – not that there was anything much left of either for either to infract – I opened the door and let myself out on to the deserted Christmas streets.

3

Which is where, for respite and the recovery of some little dignity, I would leave myself – were it not that I have promised to sacrifice truth to nothing, not even cadence. Life, as must already have been observed, is not so discreet as the reticent spaces between chapters sometimes pretend. It was all very well my getting myself out on to those deserted Christmas streets but once out on them I had to do something. It was cold and I was big with sorrow and I had nowhere to go. And don't think that any ironies were lost on me, either.

If there had been a single hamburger or kebab joint open in Finchley I would have gone and sat in it. If I'd known where the nearest Salvation Army soup kitchen was I'd have gone and sat in that. As it was, the only places with any lights on were the pubs, and from those there issued the impossible sounds of festive couples. I walked around for hours in the hope of seeing something that would lighten my burden – a meteorite crashing on Hampstead or a rascal beadle lashing a whore or a Russian peasant maltreating a mare. But I was out of luck. Then, as I happened to be close, I stumbled round to my parents' house and discovered that they were throwing a party. They hadn't told me. I don't think I need to explain how I felt.

'Thanks for the invitation,' I said to my mother who was sequinned and excessively *décolleté*.

'Darling, I imagined you'd have other things to be doing tonight. I didn't think for one moment' – she could make one moment sound like an eternity – 'that you'd want to come to this. It's just for oldies.'

Oldies! You should have seen them. Or at least you should have seen Rabika Flatman. She'd just come back from a couple of weeks in Honolulu without her husband and she was even blacker than she used to be when she was wont to swing in her garden hammock and I was wont to watch her from a bent position at my bedroom window. She was still twinkling from the good time she'd had. I guessed that she had frolicked on the beaches in just the bottom half of her bikini, and that she had scampered laughing up the trunks of palm trees pursued by native boys. She looked as though she'd eaten well, too, while she'd been away. Guavas and mangoes and paw-paws. There was a little sway (I won't say sag) of surplus flesh – burnt flesh – on her upper arms, that I couldn't take my eyes off as I talked to her. And her calves, pushed up and out by her silver strappy high-heeled sandals, were a touch plumper than usual also. If she'd been a guava herself she'd have been declared a touch over-ripe – that's to say perfect.

'No Sharon?' she asked me.

'Out of sorts,' I said.

'What, too much of the hard stuff?'

156

I wondered how she knew. 'That more or less gets it,' I said.

'Well my old man will be disappointed. He always likes to see her. He thinks she's a corker.'

'Sharon?'

'Oh yes, he's mad about her.'

My mind raced to the possibility of organizing a swap before it remembered to race back again to the possibility that I had nothing left to swap with. It was just my luck. Why hadn't she mentioned her husband's infatuation the last time that I saw her? In the days before Fitzpiers.

However, I wasn't going to let that prevent me from showing some gallantry. 'That makes two of us,' I said.

'Well, I should hope you are mad about your wife,' said Mrs Flatman.

She hadn't understood. 'I mean if he's mad about mine, I'm mad about his,' I corrected her.

She still hadn't quite perceived me. 'His what?' she asked. As my mother used to tell us, Rabika Flatman was not Marghanita Laski exactly. Not that that had ever worried me. I'd never seen Marghanita Laski swinging from the crossbar of her hammock.

But I'm prepared to admit that she might have been an easier person to pay a compliment to. I persevered with Rabika Flatman though. 'Mrs Flatman,' I said – I had never in all the years I'd known her had the courage, or come to that the desire, to call her Rabika – 'Mrs Flatman, whatever Mr Flatman thinks of Sharon is nothing to what I think of you. I've been crazy about you ever since I was a little boy.'

Perhaps I could have put it better. But I was still taken aback when she responded to what I was trying to tell her by sticking her tongue out at me. It wasn't an aggressive poke exactly, it was more a sort of slow squeeze, the gradual appearance of a third lip between the other two. Now, whenever I see a nature programme on television about volcanic activity in Rotorua, and there are slow motion shots of hot mud springs erupting, I am reminded of what took place on Mrs Flatman's face that night. At the time I was electrified by it. Childish as her gesture was, it also reminded me of her seniority. It dated her precisely. I wasn't in possession of all the relevant social history but I was sure that sticking your tongue out was a highly lubricious act in the 1940s. Hadn't English girls driven G.I.s wild doing that? I wasn't in any doubt, at any rate, that the young Rabika Flatman had.

And that the old Rabika Flatman hadn't forgotten the trick. It certainly worked with me. I was instantly hot and hers. I followed her around all night paying her gross compliments. God knows what my parents thought. Or Mr Flatman, who couldn't have been so engrossed in that simple noisy card game in which you had to collect sets that he didn't notice. But I was careless of opinion or publicity. And I forgot completely about Sharon and Fitzpiers. All I was interested in was getting Mrs Flatman to show me once again the pink tip of her tongue, and then after that all I was interested in was getting her to pass the wet bubble of her mockery from her lips to mine. I wasn't seeking a transfer of power, I simply wanted her to taste the full extent of her own. I swear I had nothing else in mind when I at last caught her coming out of the bathroom onto an empty landing and pushed her back again and turned the lock on us. I bent her over the sink and went in search of what I wanted. And for a moment, as she relaxed beneath my weight and laughed Pimms No 1 into my face, I believed I had found it. There seemed to be no end to her old fashionedness. She lifted one foot, she pressed one of her knees between mine, she trembled. Back, back she took me. And sweet, sweet was the sensation of wrongness – the confusion of time and needs and persons. But it was also brief. 'No,' she said, breaking from me, 'no, no, this is terrible!' And she was out of that door and down those stairs as if what we'd done had the primal eldest curse upon it.

Later, as the party was coming to an end and people

158

were going home, I saw her in earnest conversation with my father. I couldn't believe she was telling him what had happened but I thought she looked distressed. In fact I thought they both did. If they were discussing our kiss it seemed to me they were discussing it with unnecessary seriousness.

Once everyone had gone my father went around emptying ash trays and I shared a cigarette with my mother. She had put something glittering in her hair, particles of which had fallen onto her bare shoulders. Light flashed from her eyes also. She looked rather fine and fierce I thought, like one of those avenging Greek mothers. But she was insisting she'd had a good night – or rather, since she did nothing by halves, that she'd had one of the best nights of her life. 'Everybody said they'd never been to a happier party,' she told me. She said the same on the day I married Sharon: 'I haven't spoken to a single person that's ever seen a more beautiful ceremony.'

My father joined us for a moment before retiring. 'Well I'm off,' he said. 'Good night, Barney. I'll see you up there, Rabika,' he said to my mother.

'It's Rachel,' she reminded him.

'Yes, well I'll still see you up there,' he said. He was short with her. I knew he believed that I was a bad influence on her, that I brought out the pedantic side of her nature.

We sat silent for ten minutes, listening to him pottering about upstairs. Then, when we heard him snoring, she said, 'I'm concerned about your father.'

I raised an eyebrow.

'I think there's something between them,' she continued.

I didn't seem to need any prompting. 'Dad and Mrs Flatman?'

She nodded. A great tragic movement of the head, her eyes full of wild scorn.

But I was sorrier for me than for her. It was just a question of a husband and a best friend for her – a trite tale; whereas for me, if indeed there was something between them, unspeakable conflicts raged, between blood and passion, between pride and shame, between selfishness and duty, pitting loyalty against loyalty, pitting the son against the lover, ploughing up the green fields of my past, ravaging my settled sense of who was who in the drama of my life. And I wasn't even thinking about Sharon and Fitzpiers sitting up in my bed finishing off what was left of the plum pudding.

'How long have you suspected this?' I asked.

She gave me one of her immoderate stares – the kind that usually accompanied the description of some arcane abstruse insult. 'Twenty-eight years,' she said.

Looking back on it now, I accept that I should have expressed a bit of sympathy; twenty-eight years is a long time to be harbouring a suspicion. But it was also a period of time that had a special significance for me. I was twenty-seven; if my father and Mrs Flatman had been giving my mother cause for concern a year before I was born then all sorts of other eventualities sprang into life. Such as, for instance, that my father wasn't my father. Was it not possible that my mother, in a fit of pique after discovering them together in an air-raid shelter when there wasn't an air-raid, had offered herself to some other man – some army officer billeted next door, some old friend returned legless from the front, some German airman shot down over Hendon and concealed by my mother in her cellar for the duration of the war? In strife-torn Europe such things were not unheard of. Alternatively she might have been evacuated to the country where she could have made the odd gift of her honour to the odd basic farm-hand, some simple sturdy wight too illiterate to be trusted with a gun. There'd be plenty of those – wouldn't there? – out *Dorchester* way. You see I hadn't forgotten how she had evaded my questions on the day I had quizzed her about the peregrinations of my forebears. She'd been firm enough about their movements, but she'd been decidedly slippery about her own. And a little red spot had glowed inordinately in

160

each of her normally pale cheeks when I had voiced some passing doubts as to my parentage.

But there was another and far more terrible interpretation of those signs. For was it not conceivable that a woman who could keep her suspicions to herself for a full twenty-eight years was capable of even greater wifely magnanimity and had taken to her own bosom the fruit of another's guilty love? And could it not therefore be conceived that *I* was so conceived, not by she I called mother but by she I called Mrs Flatman? (The very she I had bent over the bathroom sink a mere hour or so before?) It was all horribly plausible. To save the young Rabika's honour, to show her brave loyalty to her own erring husband, to try to get him to remember her name at last, she I called mother had progressively padded herself with cushions for six months while she I called Mrs Flatman had been secreted somewhere in the country. She wouldn't have been the first Jewish girl to vanish for a while before turning up again looking well-cared for but thinner. There was a nursing home out there somewhere, probably under the supervision of Beth Din, that specialized in those sorts of breaks. Which one of them dangled me on her knee for the first months of my life and fed me – I don't mean with strained peaches – I didn't want to investigate. But I didn't have to look far to find the person who removed all traces of Rabika from my birth certificate.

Yes, such a version of my distant past was possible and explained far more than I had ever wanted explaining. It didn't tally only with the words in which my mother, that's to say Mrs Fugleman, had voiced her concern about my father and my other mother. 'I think there's something between them' she had said, and that surely was not the way a woman naturally given to hyperbole and who had sacrificed the best years of her life to the rearing of their love-child would have put it. I took that as my consolation and went to bed on it in my old bedroom, the one from whose window I used to watch Mrs Flatman – that's to say she I had never been

161

able to call Rabika – frolic in her garden.

But not before I had done something to soothe my father's wife. I bent over her and kissed her on the neck, like a good son. 'Don't jump to hasty conclusions,' I told her. 'And don't concern yourself either way. Sexual fidelity is only a small favour between people. You have to be very pernickety to insist on it. As long as he gives you money and makes you laugh you don't have anything to complain about.'

'He doesn't make me laugh.'

'Ah, then it's serious,' I said.

I spent the next day – Boxing Day – on my own, wandering bareheaded in the rain on Hampstead Heath. More than one person would have seen me standing in exposed places, looking skywards, a fly to wanton boys, demanding to know Whether There Was Anyone Who Could Tell Me Whose I Was. But no one offered me any help.

I went home in the early evening, hungry and hoping not to find Fitzpiers, having rejected most of the more lurid explanations of my birth. I believed that I could very nearly have been Rabika's – that it was a close thing – but that I wasn't quite. I didn't look like her. I didn't have her rubbery lips or her bold eyes or her expression of easy confidence. I looked like my mother. We had the same heavy slightly saturnine countenance. And I didn't believe she could have given me that just by bringing me up as hers.

I decided similarly against the German airman and the legless bombardier and the unconscripted Dorsetshire yokel. After all, I had my father's lack of concentration. His selective memory. And his soft spot for Rabika Flatman. But nothing was dead certain. Doubt had entered my soul. I was relieved to remember, at least, that Thomas Hardy had died childless.

7

1

I was never able to forgive Sharon for giving away my
secret and Sharon was never able to forgive me for
giving away her.

'I don't know how you could have told him,' I said.
'And in our bed.'

'I don't know how you could have allowed him *into* our
bed,' she replied.

'Sharon, I didn't see *you* objecting,' I said.

'Me? Why should *I* have objected when *you* didn't?'
she always concluded.

She accused me of a threefold dishonesty: of lacking
the courage to admit that I no longer loved her, because
if I loved her I could never have etc etc; of manoeuvring
her into a position where she couldn't complain when I
brought home strange women; and of being a latent
homosexual – that's to say employing her as a proxy to
have done to her by Fitzpiers what I really wanted Fitzpiers to do to me. I answered the first charge by
explaining that it was precisely because I loved her that
I wanted her to hurt me, and that if she couldn't follow
that she didn't deserve my love; I answered the second
by asking where they all were then, these women I was
bringing home, and by assuring her that her infidelity
was much more exciting to me than my own could ever
be; and I countered the final calumny by laughing at it.
Homosexual? Me? Ha! Latency charges are, of course,
notoriously difficult to refute; the more you say you

aren't, the more latent you therefore are. But I believed that the evidence of the afternoon I'd spent in bed with Fitz, each of us on either side of Sharon, was in my favour. There had never been the faintest suggestion of any impropriety between us. We had divided Sharon up and worked in close but formal proximity, like a couple of eminent surgeons hitherto unknown to each other except by reputation. On the rare occasions we accidentally touched we apologized extravagantly; at moments of culmination or of crisis for one, the other looked away. We comported ourselves, at all times, impeccably. Only once, that I was aware of, had I confused a bit of Fitzpiers for a not dissimilar bit of Sharon, and I had leapt from the contact as if it had been leprous.

Camilla would not have been at all satisfied with that account of my lack of interest in Fitzpiers's person. 'You don't have to think you like it to want it,' she told me more than once. 'It's the horror that would get you in, every time.' But this was Sharon not Camilla. And I could prove Sharon wrong on all three counts.

The odd thing was, however, that although Sharon resented me for giving her to Fitzpiers, she didn't resent Fitzpiers. What's more, she continued to invite him over and she continued to compound the sin she could not forgive me for initiating. I drew this anomaly to her attention.

'But you say you don't mind,' she reminded me.

'But you say you want me to mind.'

'Yes, but you don't.'

'And what if I did?'

'You'd say it if you did.'

'And would you stop seeing him if I said it?'

'Say it and find out.'

I wasn't going to be taken in by that one. I knew a trap when I saw it. 'Why is it dependent on me?' I asked. 'Stopping seeing him should be *your* decision.'

I had seen the trap but I had missed the snare. 'Precisely,' she said.

*　　*　　*

164

I suppose it's possible, as I look back upon it now, that this situation, whatever its small inconsistencies, could have gone its humdrum way for some considerable time. Most marriages not in their first flush have a third person hovering close, to take the strain, to absorb surplus energies, to act as a kind of referee and Vice-regent and au pair all at once. But Sharon and I didn't just have a third person at our shoulder, we had a fourth – Thomas Hardy. And it was as much Thomas Hardy as Rowland Fitzpiers that brought the Fugleman marriage to its final bloody close.

2

It was clear to me that Rowland Fitzpiers had been unable to take his mind off the story Sharon had told him about me and Harry Vilbert. I caught him on several occasions reading books about regressive hypnotism and I knew from brief conversations with him, as we crossed and re-crossed at the bedroom door, that he neither believed nor disbelieved the astounding evidence produced. Those were the sorts of distinctions he had long since ceased to make. He spent so much of his time now inhabiting that marshy border country between the science and the fiction of SF, armed with the most up-to-the-minute technological data but on the look-out for demons and hobgoblins, in possession of the expertise to fly himself to the moon and back but held fast in the mud of allegory and symbolism, that he had lost that sure sense of the difference between the actual and the unlikely that torments the mind of ordinary sceptical man. All things were equally likely and impossible to Fitzpiers. Take, for example, his adventure with us. Someone else might have rubbed his eyes and said it wasn't happening. Not Fitz. He went along with it almost absently. If it wasn't happening what did it matter, so long as he was enjoying it? Sharon might, for all he knew, have been a metaphor for something else, but he took her on all her levels of signification and unmeaning.

He was totally and irresponsibly and sentimentally hedonistic – committed with every bone in his body and every tear duct in his eye to the high ideal – he made it seem like a high ideal – of pleasure. And so he strictly speaking had no thoughts whatsoever about my relation to Thomas Hardy – if I was a reincarnation I was a reincarnation, no big deal – beyond feeling that something advantageous could be made out of it. Not advantageous only to him; Fitzpiers's opportunism, I must say, was not without its philanthropic side: when there was a sniff of gain in the air he nosed it out, in a general way, for anybody who cared to benefit. If he'd struck oil in his own garden he wouldn't have rung you up to tell you – not unless you were a woman with a baby – but he wouldn't have kept it from you if you'd called round. In this case he just happened to be the first on the spot, the first to understand that what I needed above all else was someone to realize my potential, some sort of business manager or agent, someone who combined entrepreneurial flair with the proper literary tact. And Fitzpiers happened to know just the person.

'No,' I said. 'Absolutely no.'

'But you haven't given yourself a chance to think about it.'

'I've just thought about it,' I said. 'No.'

Fitzpiers had had the decency – and it wasn't lost on me – to put his proposition to me in person rather than to go through Sharon. But it didn't help his cause. I was determined. I was not going to be hypnotized on stage across America; I was not going to address historical associations on the actualities of life as I had lived it in rural Dorset in the 1850s, nor would I take to the university circuit with the truth and nothing but the truth about the prototype of Tess. I was not willing to appear on television as my present and then, after the adverts, as my former self, and I was not prepared to help Fitzpiers, who knew people in films, script my predicament, along the lines of *Dr Jekyll and Mr Hyde*, for Alan

Bates and Dustin Hoffman. Fitzpiers improved the deal: 'Dustin Hoffman could play Hardy,' he compromised. But I still wasn't having it. 'Not even if it was Jimmy Durante and Clark Gable,' I told him. And I also warned him, while I was at it, that I would do everything in my power to stop Sharon selling the story of her crazy mixed-up life with two husbands – meaning Hardy and me, not me and Fitzpiers – to whichever Sunday paper bid the highest.

'I can't understand you,' said Fitzpiers. And he really couldn't. He scratched his face raw under his beard, so perplexed was he. 'It's a golden opportunity. Aren't you the slightest bit tempted?'

I shook my head. I was, of course. I would have enjoyed a lecture tour across America, the money, the fuss, the food, the girls – yes, Sharon had correctly predicted it, I *was* beginning to feel I had some rights in that direction, a few special treats owing. But the conditions were all wrong. I would be taking pleasures under false pretences. I would be up there on the stage but it would be Thomas Hardy they were turning up to see. I was then, as indeed I still am, scrupulous and egoistic; I wanted to be loved and lauded for myself.

'Not the slightest bit,' I lied.

'And nothing I can possibly do will make you change your mind?'

'Nothing.'

Fitzpiers sighed. For a moment he looked a broken man. I could see that he couldn't believe he had come so close to the pot of gold but was not a jot the richer. I think that if his cheeks had not been covered in black hair I would have seen rivulets of tears on them. As it was, Sharon had to cradle his head in her arms and rock him gently to sleep that night. And the pair of them kept me awake for hours, she with her lullabies and he with his whimpering.

A couple of weeks later he invited us to an informal little get-together at his place – nothing much, just a few friends, for wine and cheese and amiable chat. Sharon

167

attended to her toilet, on the night, with great particularity considering the casualness of the occasion, and she even fussed and quibbled over mine, sending me back to my wardrobe twice to make a better job of matching my tie to my sweater and my sweater to my socks. Herself, she wore her breasts and shoulders largely out but expensively accoutred, in that style designed to draw attention as much to the man who can afford to own them as to themselves. 'Jesus, Sharon,' I remarked when she was ready, 'you look as though I run a string of racehorses. Who are we expecting to meet tonight – Lord Longford's daughters?'

'I don't know who we're going to meet,' she said, and I would have noticed guilt in her expression had I not been transfixed by what happened to her shoulders when she shrugged them.

As it turned out there were no titled ladies that I could identify at Fitzpiers's party, but there did appear to be rather more guests who were knowledgeable and keen to talk about Thomas Hardy than one might have expected to find in any random group. There was a Hardy Professor of Modern Literature whom I knew by sight and a hack Hardy biographer whom I recognized through his sentences. There was a president of a Hardy moorland preservation society and a treasurer of a Hardy anti-vivisectionist association and three members of a Hardy hiking club. Add to these a pair of Hardy topographers arguing over boundaries in a corner, the curator of a Hardy museum, four Hardy editors with their research assistants, and a hatful of assorted Hardy fellows, memorabiliasts and amateur enthusiasts, and it is possible to understand why I became progressively alarmed.

'I don't like it,' I challenged Sharon. 'I don't like it one little bit.'

'It's just a coincidence,' she assured me. She was standing against a wall, not talking to anybody but looking obscurely proud. 'Fitz knows all kinds of people. Go and mingle.'

I mingled with a nervous woman who'd been either smiling or grimacing at me for some time.

'What are you researching into?' I asked.

'Thomas . . .'

'Yes, I realize that. I mean what aspect.'

'The juvenilia.'

'The juvenilia? Really? That wouldn't be leaving much for anybody else to research into, would it?'

I also tried to mingle with a girl who was taller, stronger, more confident, and if anything better featured and proportioned – though less amenably beautiful and on display – than Sharon. Sharon was dark and lustrous and seemed to yield the promise of infinite understanding. Nobody could see Sharon and not want her to kiss some part of himself better. The stranger, on the other hand, possessed Valkyrie looks and appeared to be as sympathetic as a razor blade. I was especially taken with her teeth which were big and white and pointed, apparently sharpened daily on raw flesh.

'What's your bag?' I asked her, looking up.

The girl regarded me with distant curiosity, as if surprised (but only for want of other occupation) that something such as I should have a voice. 'Gertrude Bugler,' she told me.

I remember that I shook my head and pondered the strange and cruel distribution of God's gifts – a fine creature such as this, apparently finished and perfect, to be hard of hearing! Tragic.

'I asked you what your *bag* was,' I tried again, taking great care to mouth my words carefully this time, so that she could read my lips, 'not your *name*. I just wondered which bit of Hardy you were into.'

'Gertrude Bugler,' she repeated.

It was heart-rending. The contrast between her beauty and her affliction brought a lump to my throat. 'I love you,' I told her, without any hope of being understood. 'I love you and I'd like to take you somewhere far away from here where we could be alone together and not mind the silence and the misunderstandings forever.'

And I kept smiling so that she would know it was all all right.

She looked at me placidly. Then she looked into her empty glass for a moment before she said, 'I can't see that wife of yours approving such a plan. She is yours, isn't she, the one with the stupendous tits? You look like a tit man. I think you ought to get back to her. She looks too pretty to be left on her own. I need to get myself another slug of gin.'

'Met anybody interesting?' asked Sharon, shortly afterwards.

'Gertrude Bugler,' I immediately confessed. 'I don't know whether she's interesting but she's certainly unusual. She pretends she can't hear what you're saying. But at least she's not an authority on Hardy.'

'Gertrude Bugler? Isn't that the name of the actress that Hardy fell in love with when he was eighty? The one that played Tess on the stage?'

'Don't ask me,' I said. 'I wouldn't know.'

But of course I didn't doubt that Sharon was right. I felt foolish and I felt threatened. The girl was an authority on Hardy like the rest of them.

So what was Fitz up to? This was supposed to be an informal gathering of friends not a conference. Could it be that he was whetting my social appetite with this little foretaste of the kind of company I could be keeping if I only yielded to his suggestions and let him manage me? If that was so then he was wasting good wine and cheese. I looked around the room; with the exception of the murderous Valkyrie who had gone in search of gin (I'd supposed she'd meant the drink but she might have meant the instrument of torture), and Fitzpiers who was at the front door welcoming a latecomer, and Sharon who was at my side, and of course myself, this was an abysmal gathering. I considered myself to be something of an expert on experts. I'd met a lot of them. I'd been taught by them. I submitted articles to them. I came upon them browsing in Sharon's shop, looking for information that no one else possessed. And I knew that they were all, *a posteriori*, anal retentives. There was no other explanation for why they wanted to know more about something than anybody else, and for why they hoarded knowledge, like loose change, in case the good times never came again. I wasn't being metaphorical when I called them anal retentives; they walked about the room with their buttocks clenched and their faces stiff with the strain of literally hanging on to their stools. Years later their like would surface – not as experts on Hardy but on other comparable kinds of tightness – in the great potty-conscious Conservative governments of Margaret Thatcher; and that air of triumphant niggardliness wedded to that waddle of extreme physical discomfort would become a *sine qua non* for the retention of government office. A sound principle was in operation: it was presumed that if you could hang on to one thing you could hang on to another.

But I wasn't thinking politics on this occasion. I was wondering how Fitzpiers could have possibly hoped to woo me with company such as this. And I was still wondering it when Fitzpiers approached me, his hair wild, his colour high, propelling before him, as someone else that I should meet, whoever it was that had arrived late. Even now, when I look back upon it, I feel convinced that I recognized the newcomer immediately; but I suppose the truth must be that I registered him at the time in a series of abrupt ocular shocks. First the loose but precisely creased Levis, then the cricket sweater worn, to suggest youthfulness, next to the skin, then the hammered cross around the neck, then the jiggle of copper bangles warding off rheumatism, and finally the familiar befuddled face, still at death's door but artificially tanned for the party, in sunglasses. Out of place, painfully uncomfortable, but bent on a purpose and already advancing on his victim was Harry Vilbert – inventor, anarchist, public speaker, coppersmith and hypnotherapist.

Hypnotherapy, if I read the situation aright – and it certainly seemed to be confirmed by the intense direct

171

look in Harry Vilbert's eyes when he took off his sunglasses, and by my own sudden drowsiness – was already underway. Harry's hand was outstretched but I knew that I would be asleep before I could shake it. In the few seconds that were left to me to stay Barney Fugleman I understood the beginning and the end of Rowland Fitzpiers's plan. He was going to have me Hardy again whether I liked it or not, and the distinguished experts and enthusiasts were there to guarantee scientific good faith, to witness, to judge, to verify, and all being well – all being well for Fitzpiers, that was – to enthuse. And Sharon – my Sharon – had been in on it from the start, had cooked it up with Fitzpiers, had even put the original suggestion to him, for all I knew; that was why she was dressed like the wife of someone famous and had seen to it that I was wearing socks that matched my sweater and a sweater that matched my tie. She wanted me to look good in the chair.

3

I don't think there can be any doubt that I took my resentment of Sharon's collusion with me into my hypnotic trance. For I regressed very badly. If it's not a good idea to eat cheese immediately before bed then I can vouch for its being even less of a one to hate your wife immediately before hypnosis. The effects can be similarly turbulent. I closed my eyes as I was told all right, but thereafter I was totally self-willed. I disregarded Harry Vilbert's instructions. I hung loose in time. When I finally found myself somewhere I wanted to be I paid no attention to Harry's enquiries. Was I there, Tommy? I was damned if I was going to respond to questions like that. I stormed and raged instead, waving my arms about and knocking things over; and when I did put together coherent sentences they were in a form of French that those who knew anything about it described as formal, stilted, much out-of-date and quite obscene. I can remember some of them still.

'O filles voluptueuses,' I exclaimed, addressing the three unmarried sisters I had met earlier, whose proud boast it was that they had cycled together to every part of Wessex mentioned in Hardy's novels, 'livrez-vous donc vos corps tant que vous le pourrez! Foutez, divertissez-vous, voilà l'essentiel; mais fuyez avec soin l'amour. Fuck for all you are worth,' I told them, 'but never be guided by your heart.'

Then I turned to Sharon. 'Ah triple foutredieu!' I said, 'cette charmante fille m'a sucé comme un ange.' And when she looked distressed I struck her across the mouth and I swear I danced for joy when the blood came. 'Ah foutre! Voilà la bougresse en sang. Je bande, je bande.'

'Are you there Tommy?' I heard Harry Vilbert asking, as Fitzpiers rushed to Sharon's aid.

But I wasn't finished with her yet. 'Double gueuse, je t'étranglerais si je n'en voulais laisser le plaisir aux autres,' I said, before I struck her again. And again I revelled as she fell backwards with a cry into Fitzpiers's arms. 'Je bande,' I told them all again. 'Mon sperme coule ... ah foutre! foutre! c'est fini ... je n'en puis plus. Pourquoi faut-il que le faiblesse succède à des passions de vive?'

I don't remember anyone offering any answers to that. But I know that Fitzpiers was bending over Sharon who was weeping, and that he was demanding that Harry Vilbert either wake me immediately or he would call the police.

The police? I shrugged my shoulders. You only called the police when there'd been a crime, 'Et les crimes sont impossibles à l'homme,' I told him. 'Pour moi, mon ami, je ne mange jamais mieux, je ne dors jamais plus en paix que quand je me suis suffisamment souillé dans le jour de ce que les sots appellent des crimes.'

'You're going back to sleep now, Tommy,' said Harry Vilbert in his most defeated voice, and I'm sure I only agreed to it because I was sorry for him. I certainly couldn't think of any other reason to stop hitting Sharon.

And I felt that I had plenty of filthy French left in me yet.

So I closed my eyes and opened them a few moments later and said 'Where am I? What's happening?' But I wasn't at all disconcerted or dismayed to see Sharon bruised and sobbing softly on the floor, her breasts all but out of her dress, and Fitzpiers with his arms round her, white and shaking.

Many years afterwards, long after Sharon and I had severed all connections with each other, she sent me a postcard from Paris where she was attending a book-fair. 'Just stumbled on an interesting addition to your genealogy,' it said. 'B. Fugleman born June 2 1940; T. Hardy born June 2 1840 – as you are aware. But did you know M. de Sade born June 2 1740? Thought you'd like to. Sharon.'

It was thoughtful of her. But in fact by then her news was stale. Very stale. Because only about a week after Fitz's party I received substantially the same information, also, as it happened, on the back of a postcard. Except that in this case the postcard was not illustrated with one of Goya's war atrocity sketches, and the writer was more interested in tracing the sources of my French invective than in assembling amazingly coincidental data. The writer was evidently not out to cause me any pain either, since the communication concluded with a cheerful congratulation and the words, 'What larks!' What's more – and this is a pretty big more – it was signed Gertrude Bugler.

Strange to relate, it was the signature that interested me far more than the message. Or perhaps that isn't strange at all. Men who have supped full of horrors must end up losing interest in their own natures. One hears of mass murderers rushing back upstairs from the abat-toirs at the bottom of their garden to engross themselves in television. First things first. I had supped full of rev-elation and coincidence. I suddenly couldn't care less who I'd been. Instead of marvelling that I was now con-nected in some unfathomable way not just with a little

English rustic novelist but with the Divine Marquis himself, I couldn't get my mind off the problem of how Gertrude Bugler (I still didn't know her real name) had discovered *my* date of birth. That seemed to me a profounder mystery and one susceptible of far more stimulating interpretations. It appeared to suggest, for one thing, that her apparent indifference to me at Fitz's party had been either feigned or had undergone some startling transformation in the course of my regression. Perhaps she had been impressed by my French. It was even possible that my violence excited her. But whatever the reason, she had been making enquiries about me, finding out who I was and where I lived and when I was born. I would have found that thrilling no matter what she looked like, but when I recalled her marauding beauty I gave at the knees. Bugger de Sade, I had thoughts only for Miss Bugler.

Who said blood was thicker than water?

4

Events moved very quickly on the day of that postcard, and although its message therefore became forgotten and obscured, I have to admit that it must itself have been an active element in the precipitation of those events. Perhaps I'm still not being as truthful as I should be. Let me say it and have done then: I would probably not have left Sharon that very afternoon if I had not felt that I had established some tenuous connection with Gertrude Bugler that very morning. But then again – I'm damned if I'm going to *martyr* myself to truthfulness – I might have.

Because the unfamiliar garment that I found hanging in Sharon's side of the wardrobe would have annoyed me whatever the circumstances.

'What's this?' I asked her, holding it up so that she could see its reflection in the mirror before which she sat for long periods at a time now, trying to repair the damage I had done to her face at Fitz's party.

175

'What's what?' she asked. She was rubbing oils into the skin around her eyes and couldn't see.

'Let me describe it to you,' I said. 'It resembles an ice-skater's tunic, except that it has wide padded shoulders, lacing down the sides, is made of white leather, and appears to offer more freedom of movement and exposure of the limbs than the ordinary olympic ice-skater would – '

'Oh, *that*. That's my space suit, what do you think it is?'

I didn't answer. Instead I tossed the garment on to the bed where it fell, suggestively, in the shape of Sharon. I paced the bedroom floor, in the manner I knew she didn't like, wearing out the carpet. Then I asked, 'Have you had it long?'

She hesitated fractionally, 'About a week.'

It was as I thought: Fitz had bought it for her after the terrible scene at his place, to make it up to her, to fly her to the stars. But I wanted to hear her say it. 'Would it be altogether too literal-minded of me to ask you what you want it for?' I asked her.

Sharon's lips were still a touch swollen, but she could move them all right. 'Would it be altogether too simple minded of me to say to wear?' she let them answer.

'To wear for what, Sharon?'

'To wear for going out in, Barney.'

'Sharon, correct me if I'm wrong, but this doesn't look to me like the sort of thing that even you with your much remarked on flair for the outlandish would go to Sainsbury's or your accountants or the Calcutta Book Fair in. Isn't a space suit specifically designed for space travel? I am still your husband – I think you ought to tell me if you're planning a long trip.'

Sharon sighed at the mirror and wiped her hands on a tissue. I remember being struck by the action; it had a decisive air about it. 'It's for parties, Barney,' she said.

I didn't expect to hear any mention of parties in this house for some time, and I wouldn't have dreamed of using the word myself, but she started it. 'I wouldn't have thought that you and I will be going to many more of those,' I said.

'We won't. It's for going to parties with Fitz in.'

She was brutal. And she upset me. Even though I was carrying around a postcard from Gertrude Bugler, she upset me. 'Well I hope you'll be a sensation in it,' I said.

'I'm sure I will be. I was the last time.'

That was a dare. And I accepted it. 'The last time?'

'Mmm,' she said. 'The last time.'

I started pacing the room again. How could she have already worn it? She'd said she'd only had it a week and I knew for a fact that she'd stayed in every evening since Fitz's party – the one I'd been at – attending to her face. I put that to her. But tactfully. I didn't want her to think I was checking up on her.

'Who said anything about going out in the evening?' she asked. But she was no more accusatory than she was defensive. If anything she was rather blankly neutral. 'It was a daytime party I wore it at.'

'A daytime party?' I don't know why that stung me as much as it did. I don't suppose I would have liked it had I discovered that Sharon was slipping out of bed after midnight and stealing away for assignations in piano bars and casinos the minute I began to snore; but the idea of her tootling off in her space suit in broad daylight, in the middle of the afternoon, struck me as far more sinister. 'Who the hell goes to daytime parties?' I asked, and I instantly wished that I hadn't. I was absolutely certain that I didn't want to know the answer.

But it was too late. 'SF people mainly. You know – friends of Fitz's.'

'I see,' I said.

'Not the kind of people you would like,' she assured me.

'I guess not,' I said.

'They talk about SF classics.'

'Like the *Odyssey*,' I suggested.

'That's right, and they watch old SF movies.'

'Like *The Battleship Potemkin*.'

'That's right. And they swap wives.'

177

I swear that I snapped my head up so abruptly at this that I have suffered ever since from some of the side effects (not excluding the indignity) of whiplash. 'They *what*?' I demanded to be told again.

Sharon couldn't have been more matter of fact. She was even dipping the tip of her little finger in her jars again and rubbing soothing balms into her skin. 'They swap wives,' she said, 'but you wouldn't like any of them – they're all SF wives. Well, almost all.'

My heart was pounding at my ribs, hammering to get out. But how was I to ask what I wanted (wanted? – I was consumed by the need) to know? 'Sharon,' I said, 'am I to assume that you're trying to tell me that you – '

'Took part? Of course. Why else would I go? You know I don't like old movies.'

I didn't know what to ask next. There were so many things I did and didn't want to find out. I sat down on a corner of the bed, stood up, and sat down again. Something made me cast my eye over Sharon's space suit. I expect I was looking for signs of carousal: knife slashes or sooty fingerprints or hairs from the beard of Fitz-piers's SF friends. But the suit was spotless except for a minuscule orange stain on the skirt, and a suggestion of an indentation – indications, both, that Sharon had sat for God knows how long on an object resembling the pip of a satsuma. I can't tell you why but I found that detail horrific; it somehow implied bestial engrossment and oblivion. In which case I knew what I needed to know. 'I take it you got something out of this,' I enquired in a rather unsteady voice.

I might have been mistaken but I thought Sharon laughed. 'Naturally,' she said. 'But I hope you're not going to pump me for details.'

Details? What else was there but details? 'Is the number of times you were swapped a detail?' I asked.

She stopped what she was doing and turned around to face me. 'Are you asking me for the number of different men, or do you want me to count repeats?'

178

'Whichever you feel you can talk most cheerfully about.'

'Well that's neither. It really is my affair, you know. You oughtn't to expect me to give you a blow by blow account.'

I didn't care for her choice of words and I didn't like her attitude. Which meant that I was now where it was safest for me to be, aggrieved, at the nub of the thing. 'Look Sharon,' I said, raising my voice, 'don't tell me what I ought or ought not to expect. You're my wife – if anyone takes you to a wife-swapping party it ought to be me.'

'I see,' said Sharon without any surprise – I've always hated that in women: their assumption of my predictability – 'so that's why you're stung – because he took me and you didn't.'

'So what's wrong with that?' I suspect that by this time I was shouting. 'Haven't I provided enough diversions for the snivelling little prick?'

'*You* haven't provided anything. And he isn't little. He's bigger than you are.'

'He's little in the soul, Sharon. He's a worm. He's the worm that flies in the night. That's the only way he knows how to travel. And if that's the direction you like to be approached from – so be it. That, as you say, is your affair. But there is one right that remains to me – I won't have him taking you to wife swapping parties while you're still married to me. Do you hear me, Sharon? *You're not his to swap.*'

I knew, the minute I heard myself say this, what was coming. 'I'm not yours to swap either, Barney,' Sharon said, and there was still a year to go before the publication of *Sexual Politics* and *The Female Eunuch*.

Of course I accepted that she was right semantically, if we were going to quibble over words, but I was damned if I was going to argue with her about the nature of possession at a time like this, when the great tragic themes were hereabouts. I hurled myself across the bed in the direction of the telephone and dialled Fitzpiers's number. It was part of the science of his life that he should possess a telephone answering machine, just as it was part of the fiction that he should suppose he needed one. But it served him well today. 'This is a recorded announcement,' his voice said. 'After the bleep would you please leave your name and a brief message.' 'This is Thomas Hardy,' I answered, after the bleep. 'Here is my brief message: Swap your own fucking wife.'

It's possible that I was still nothing like as angry as I would have liked to be. At any rate I hadn't frightened Sharon. 'What are you whipping yourself up for?' she asked me. 'You don't care that much. You're just suffering from mild pique. You always said you wouldn't care. You were right.'

'Sharon, I'll show you how much I care. Before this day is over I'll be out of the house.'

'Why, because you feel humiliated? I thought you liked to be humiliated.'

Me? 'There are humiliations and there are humiliations,' I explained to her, so that she wouldn't confuse them ever again.

'No there aren't,' she said. She had risen from her dressing table stool and had come over to where I stood. She pressed her full weight against me and wrapped her arms about my neck. 'They're all the same. I bet I could persuade you to stay if I promised to tell you everything I did at that party, if I gave you all the tiniest details.' She brought my face close to hers and put her lips to my ear. Only the words that came out were not those I expected and, yes, yes, wanted to hear. 'I'm pregnant,' she told me, instead of who had done what to her how many times and where.

The news enabled me, at least, to pull away. 'I see,' I said. 'And because you were so busy while all the other wives were watching *The Battleship Potemkin* you don't know who the father is?'

'I'm more than five days pregnant,' she assured me.

'That narrows the field, does it?'

'There is no field, it's yours.'

'How do you know it's not Fitz's?'

Sharon shrugged. 'I just know,' she said. I had to accept that there were some things that women just *knew*. And there was something else that I had to accept also. 'I've told Fitz,' she added.

'Why did you tell him if it's mine?'

'Barney, Fitz noticed.' She patted her stomach. I was meant to understand that she'd put on twenty stone. 'He asked.'

'And what does he say?'

'He's very pleased for me. He wants me to have it.'

'That's nice of him. Does he know that it might be mine.'

'Yes, of course.'

'Of course of course. That would make it even better for him, wouldn't it? I'd forgotten how he hankers after other men's offspring. I suppose it would break his heart if it turned out to be his own. I'm assuming that he's offered to stand by you if I proposed that we abort it or sell it or just give it away.'

Sharon looked at me stonily without saying anything. She struck me as having a maternal air. Already I was feeling nostalgic, missing the good old days when she used to get about in a little leather space-suit and would roll around the floor with strange men, oblivious to the discomfort of the satsuma pips beneath her. There was something in that for me. But there was nothing that I cared for in the idea of her as a mother. 'And I suppose you'll call it Tommy if it's a boy,' I said, mirthlessly.

We were neither of us much amused. I could see that Sharon felt that I had failed some crucial test. As for me, the idea of competing with Fitzpiers over fatherhood filled me with distaste. My only strong desire now was to pull out and leave the pair of them – correction, the three of them – to their devices. Fitzpiers had already tapped my unconscious and swapped my wife, I couldn't see any good reason why he shouldn't go on to slap my baby. A delicious sensation of languor, as sensuous as sleep and as sweet as corruption, overtook me at the thought of giving everything to someone else. Hadn't I been trying to give Sharon away from the moment that I'd met her? It felt like a fulfilment. The reason I'd been put on earth.

And the sight of me packing my bags seemed to fill Sharon with a quiet and melancholy calm also. She clearly believed that I'd had my chance and turned it down and therefore ought to go. But at the last moment, as I sat on the edge of the bed in which I'd always felt a stranger, and told her that I didn't want anything from her, that she could keep whatever we owned, that it was all much more hers than mine anyway, she attacked me with everything she could find. She threw shoes at me and coat hangers and a shaving mirror and the hair dryer, all the personal and pointless things we had bought together over the years rained down on me, and I fended them off, I ducked and sheltered, until she caught me decisively on the temple with the Swedish bathroom scales. The sight of my blood made her the more determined. She seized back the scales and using both her hands she crashed them against the side of my face. For a moment I thought she had taken my ear off – gone for it deliberately, in order to rob me of my obscenest organ – for I was bleeding copiously, I could hear with an unfamiliar roaring loudness as if an impediment had been removed at last, and I felt an unaccustomed flap of skin against my neck. I was in a dreadful panic. My body, as I had once before explained to Sharon, was a mystery to me whole; how much the more so, then, was I bewildered by it dismembered. I covered myself with both hands when she came for me again, and I knew that she wouldn't stop of her own accord, that she would certainly kill me if she possibly could.

I was surprised to discover that I was sobbing, but whether it was for my own ringing pain or for Sharon or for both of us, I couldn't tell. I feared for her though, almost as much as I feared for myself, and quite suddenly I saw, as vividly as if she were in the room with us, the figure of Martha Brown, wheeling slowly half round and back again just as she had in the misty morning rain in Dorchester, her black silk gown wet on her body, the hood cold on her face, but withal perfected, as if in the murder of her husband she had attained to the consummation of her purpose. Sharon would swing likewise, gladly, if she could finish me off as comprehensively as Martha had finished off Mr Brown. Between men and women – or at least between husbands and wives – there was, after all, a long standing conflict of interests. It wasn't for me to sort out the rights and the wrongs of it just now. But it did seem that it wasn't in the best interest of either of us that I should let Sharon complete her work. I summoned up what was left of my strength therefore, and shielded myself as best I could with my arms and my elbows; then I ran like a blind thing into the worst that Sharon could do to me, pushed past her, and got out of the house.

5

I am not exaggerating when I say that at no time during this fight, and at no time for several weeks after it, did I give a thought to the contents of Gertrude Bugler's post-card. Gertrude Bugler herself flitted before my eyes briefly, while I cowered beneath Sharon's blows, as a desirable alternative to present company, but there-after I let her go. And I let Monsieur de Sade go with her. I possess a gift, in extremis, which I hope will never desert me, of being able to allow my mind to empty and then drop, like a cataleptic's jaw. An assessment of all that had happened must have been taking place in some part of me – in my liver, or my kidneys, or wherever my immortal soul was situated – but it certainly wasn't taking place in my intelligence. That corner of myself was clear, given over to long luxurious bouts of nothingness interrupted only by passionless anticipations of physical needs. It was not unlike being a teenager again. I recall that I was even able to satisfy my small sexual requirements during this period without having to conjure up a single image of womanhood. This was not an

183

entirely retrograde step for a person whose past performances as a giver and a taker of ecstasy had relied so heavily on a plentiful supply of mental pictures. But all I wanted from a woman now was ministration and I didn't have to look beyond my mother for that.

Naturally she was pleased to have me back under her care. I created a diversion, for one thing, from her agonizing suspicions about my father and Mrs Flatman, now entering – her suspicions that is, not my father and Mrs Flatman – their twenty-ninth year. And for another she was pleased to be given the opportunity to build me up after my long lean years in exile. She was no different from all other mothers (how could she be?) in that while she wanted me, in a general way, to be married, she didn't want me, in a specific way, to have a wife. Every time a son leaves the woman he has married – the details of the dispute are immaterial – he makes a decision in favour of his mother. What's a marriage for a man anyway, but Mum's brave little champion carrying the fight into the very territory of the enemy? Mine looked ten years younger the minute she opened the door and found me bleeding on the doorstep. 'I wish you and Sharon didn't have such serious disagreements,' she remarked. 'One of these days one of you is going to really get hurt.' But she wasn't in the slightest bit concerned about the dents in my skull or the ear that hung on a thread from the side of my face. I honestly think that the first thought to cross her mind was how long it would take her to ring all her friends and get them over for a party.

And why not? I'm all for parties. (Providing Harry Vilbert doesn't get an invite.) And her victory was bound to be a brief one. I was only resting up. There were thousands of other potential wives out there, waiting to whisk me away the minute I was ready for something other than ministration. My return home, when all is said and done, was just a little sentimental re-run of an ironical drama whose denouement was well known to both of us. And sure enough, no sooner did I begin to gain in strength under my mother's grandiloquent care, no sooner did the perfect body she had once weighed and washed (and now could only discreetly sponge) show signs of full recovery and promise to suffer no permanent mutilation, than my mind began to look out-ward again, and through the throng of opportunity Gertrude Bugler's features became once more distinct. I sat up in my old bed, propped up on a dozen pillows and surrounded by hot water-bottles, drinking Lucozade and doing jig-saw puzzles (the biggest of which, the one with the most sky, was sent to me – I didn't at the time know why – by *Mr*, not *Mrs*, Flatman). And I wondered how I was ever going to discover where Gertrude Bugler lived. There had been no address on the postcard, not even a legible postmark, and the only person that I knew who could tell me her real name was Fitzpiers. Naturally I had no intention of consulting him.

I didn't think much about Sharon, not even when I was well and up and about again. I didn't write to her or ring her, nor did she ring or write to me. Solicitors would eventually do our chatting for us. But images of her came back to me sometimes, whether I wanted them or not. It was the sound of her that I think I missed most – her singing and splashing in the shower, her wildly excessive laughter when I told her an amusing story. The noise of Sharon I would remember, often with great sadness, all my life. But I never once thought of making it up with her. For there was nothing further that I wanted from her. She had done her worst, and I don't just mean with the bathroom scales. I had tested out my fears on her and I had survived. There was nothing more she could do to me. Whereas Gertrude Bugler filled me with forbodings; I believed there was no end to the trou-ble she could cause me. And if being in love isn't being terrified I don't know what is.

Gertrude Bugler scared the living daylights out of me.

But meanwhile how was I to find out who and where she was? Fitzpiers, as I have said, was out. So was

Sharon's bookshop. I thought of putting an advertisement in the *Thomas Hardy Yearbook* but I was afraid that Sharon and Fitzpiers would come across it and enjoy a shared joke at my expense. When I recovered my strength I went to libraries and searched bibliographies of Hardy to see who had written anything – a book, an article, a passing paragraph, anything – on the actress Gertrude Bugler; but I found nothing that could have been by the fierce unforgiving girl I remembered. I quizzed librarians: was there anything forthcoming? I wrote to societies. I scanned publishers' lists. But all to no avail. Gertrude Bugler was a neglected area.

I was not, however, downhearted. The search was exhilarating. The longer it went on the more desirable and mythological the object became. She certainly put on a couple of inches in height and grew longer teeth. And all the time my health returned. I took a small flat in Notting Hill Gate and commuted four days a week to Oxford where I taught in a language school and tried to persuade Danish girls that naturalness was an enemy to fun. I was no longer morbid. I no longer wondered who I was. If I might so put it, I felt like my old self again. But my old self with a new future. Everything pointed forwards. I didn't have a care for the past. And then I came upon some alarming information that undid all this good. I had put myself on a mailing list to receive news of every fresh addition to the Hardy canon – it didn't matter how trivial or seemingly unimportant – for that way I would be on to Gertrude Bugler the moment that she surfaced. I wasn't in any hurry, but I didn't want to miss out on her. And it was through this channel that I came to hear about the sensational findings that were rocking the world of Hardy scholarship to its core. Someone had unearthed a photograph of a mysterious boy and was arguing that he had been born in the early summer of 1868 to Tryphena Sparks and her cousin/uncle/brother, Thomas. The argument was plumped out with the usual biographical and meteorological authentication – why wasn't Tryphena showing up for work that week? what else could a couple do in such a long late hot autumn but make babies? – and it was even accompanied by confirmatory interviews with ancient members of the family. I didn't look too closely into any of that. The photograph was enough for me. It showed a familiar woe-begone countenance and an unmistakably full wet lip. There was no evading it. It was all in the saga. The miserable basket had not died childless after all. He had kept the lines of communication back to him open. It was therefore possible he had a great-great-grandson still living, somewhere, in pain.

Predictably, a letter from Sharon's solicitors reached me first post the following morning. It told me what I had learnt already and added another fact that I might find instructive.

'Our client informs us that you intend to disown your son – our client entertains no uncertainty as to the sex of the child she is carrying – just as Mr Hardy disowned his. We draw your attention to the presumption of law that all children born in wedlock are the legitimate offspring of the husband, which presumption is not rebutted by the fact in itself of the wife's adultery, in this case connived at and condoned by yourself. Our client is particularly concerned that you learn that your boy was conceived early in '67 also, exactly one hundred years after Mr Hardy's. She understands that you do not find anything amazing, but she wishes us to convey to you that on top of everything else, she thinks that *that* is.'

I immediately grasped something about the past (not just mine, anyone's): it lacked dignity. Parents, family, skeletons in cupboards, hereditary diseases, curses, Atrean atrocities, fatal weaknesses of the line – it was all the stuff of low farce, not tragedy. The last person to have any right to self-respect was Adam; even Eve was compromised by a demeaning antecedence.

I tore up the letter from Sharon's solicitors. Then I tore what had been sent to me the day before, including the photograph of Hardy's despondent child. Then I tore

Gertrude Bugler's postcard which had simultaneously tied me up with de Sade and promised me the illusion of a fresh start. And only then did I fall to tearing the hair I couldn't call my own.

Part Two

. . . a subtlist in emotions, he cultivated as under glasses strange and mournful pleasures that he would not willingly let die just at present . . . To be the vassal of her sweet will for a time – he demanded no more, and found solace in the contemplation of the soft miseries she caused him.

Thomas Hardy, *The Woodlanders*

1

I

'I wired a room for us at the Temperance Hotel,' Jude told Sue Bridehead, after he'd given up his job and she'd given up her husband, and they were together at last on the 18.52 train from Melchester, due in at Aldbrickham at 21.59.

'One?'

'Yes – one.'

Sue bent her forehead against the corner of the compartment. 'O Jude! I thought you might do it – but I didn't mean *that*!'

'So what, for fuck's sake, *did* you mean?' Hardy decided against letting him reply. (It was an unnecessary scruple in the event – the book got him into trouble anyway.)

'Well!' was all Jude was allowed to say instead. But he did get to say it twice. 'Well!' he said again. And then he stared, stultified, at the opposite and presumably vacant seat.

Sue drew away from him and looked out into the darkness. Whatever she saw it couldn't have been the hill, unless the train was well off course, where the gibbet of their common ancestor had stood. It wasn't often that they did anything without the gibbet symbolically looming up behind them. So this journey at least had the merit of variety.

'I resolved to trust you to set my wishes above your gratification,' she reproached him. 'Don't be a greedy boy.'

This stultified him once more. But his response – 'This is a queer elopement!' – showed admirable restraint. He might have been forgiven, in the circumstances and with his history, pulling the communication cord there and then.

So might, in another version of a strikingly similar story, Florence Henniker, the apparently emancipated and promising society woman with whom, at the very time that he was writing *Jude*, Hardy took an abortive train trip of the heart to Winchester, and who, whatever it was she'd promised or that Hardy thought she'd promised, found herself, like Sue Bridehead, having to explain the whys and the wherefores of non-delivery in that perfect setting for disappointment, that place from which everything seems possible but nothing much happens in, a railway carriage. The metaphor of the train as an inexorable engine of non-consummation had been a favourite of Hardy's long before he'd failed himself to run away in one with Mrs Henniker. Stephen Smith and Elfride Swancourt, fleeing Castle Boterel (the lucky blighters), have their passions rocked and cooled on the Plymouth to Paddington express some twenty years in advance – and when the trains were that much slower – of Jude and Hardy having theirs. This might seem another intriguing example of the faculty of prophecy in novelists their uncanny knack of being able to describe in their early fiction what they are going to do in their later lives; but in fact it's no more than rudimentary self-knowledge. One has a pretty good idea at thirteen, let alone at thirty, what sort of fool one's going to be; one might as well get in first with the fable and steal a march on fate. That's the only advantage over it one is ever going to enjoy.

But even if Hardy had been a dab hand at queer elopements all his life, the connection between Jude's with Sue and his own with Florence Henniker doesn't look fortuitous. He's been hurt by a woman's prevarication afresh, and Jude made to look an oaf is a reproach to Mrs Henniker, a prick, if ever there was one, to her Christian conscience; just as the sepulchral humour of the scene is a go at putting a brave face on mortification.

And why not? Mistaking the intentions of the other sex is never much fun, and all the evidence suggests that Hardy mistook Mrs Henniker's, eyeball to eyeball in that compartment, on a scale. Part of the trouble, of course, was class. By which I don't mean that Hardy couldn't afford to travel first. Florence Henniker was the daughter of an aristocrat; and the daughters in the Hardy family were not always dead certain whose they were. That in itself didn't stand in the way of friendship and needn't have been a bar to romance; but a woman at home in society, accomplished in all the conversational arts, of which flirtation – especially literary flirtation – would of necessity have been one, such a woman could not have supposed, merely because she sent a fifty-three-year-old novelist photographs of herself in average *décolletage* and translations, done in her own hand, of only moderately doubtful French poets, that she was thereby embarking upon a desperate passion. The point is not that she was unaware of the way things worked in Dorset; what she could never have known was that the novelist fell in love with every woman he met, fell in love with her instantly and irremediably and on the spot, and all the more ardently if her spot was at some remove from his, that's to say on the far side of a busy street or on the opposite bank of a wide swirling river, espied from the top of turning omnibuses or through the windows of fast moving trains. As long as she was walking in the opposite direction or was too far away for him to catch, he needed no further encouragement. He left home and changed his life for her, imaginatively, there and then. Which was a lot of fun for Mrs Hardy. Fifty years on he would remember in fine detail the features of a girl who had flitted past him while he was in a florist's and he would ache for the happiness with her that he'd missed. But if it was distance that did the trick, if he sought the contrivance of some impediment or barrier, it didn't have to be material. Glass was good. Class was better.

So Florence Henniker, sister of the Viceroy of Ireland, daughter of the literary Lord Houghton, who entertained famously and owned a notorious collection of erotica – erotica! who collected erotica in Puddletown? – Mrs Henniker could be construed as leading Hardy on just by being alive.

As for being alive where he could see her – that was nothing short of coquetry. And she piled it on. She smiled at him and shook his hand. They conversed and corresponded. He wrote to her about church architecture and she, throwing prudence to the wind, replied. She accompanied him to the theatre to see Ibsen – Ibsen! And finally she agreed to take a train ride with him to Winchester. It must have felt to him like a betrothal.

No wonder he was disappointed. Men far less susceptible might have pinned their hopes on Winchester. It's not only for convenience and privacy that Henry James's most intensely adulterous couple go off to plight their infidelity in

Gloucester. There's something in the air of cathedral cities.

Just as there's something in the movement of a railway carriage, which was where, alas, it was all decided, long before they got to Winchester. No. No. She shook her head. She was sorry. She wasn't as free a thinker as he thought she was. She hadn't meant *that*.

'Well!' he might have been excused exclaiming, in the circumstances and given his history. 'Well! This is a queer elopement!'

But it's unlikely that he would have enjoyed himself with her in Winchester whatever she'd said. He was, above all things else, the poet of the disappointment of the actual moment. A successful afternoon with Mrs Henniker would have left his creative sensibility in ruins. You can't throw yourself into writing *Life's Little Ironies* or *Time's Laughing-stocks*, if you've got a warm aristocrat snuggled into your shoulder. Those whom the Muses love must go without. *Ecce signum!* –

> And we were left alone
> As Love's own pair;
> Yet never the love-light shone
> Between us there!
> But that which chilled the breath
> Of afternoon,
> And palsied unto death
> The pane-fly's tune

– he got the thing he wanted after all.

But since they were in town, not doing what he thought they were going to do and therefore doing something even better, he had the opportunity to take her to look at the milestone where, impelled by a force which seemed to overrule their will, Angel Clare and 'Liza-lu had stopped, turned, waited in paralyzed suspense, and seen the black flag signifying Tess's successful execution move slowly up the mast. Florence Henniker, as an admirer of his prose, would not have needed pressing to see such a distinguished landmark. And Hardy himself was never loth to imagine or re-imagine the hanging of a woman – particularly, perhaps, in these circumstances, one whose death made it possible for Angel Clare to get a second bite of the cherry and toddle off up the hill hand in

194

hand with 'Liza-Lu, as he, Thomas Hardy, was not destined to toddle off anywhere with Mrs Henniker. Which is not to say that Mrs Hardy was the only obstacle, any more than it is to say that he would have taken active steps to remove her if she were. A wife is an absolutely essential possession to those pathological romancers who see a shimmering new future in every woman they meet but are congenitally parsimonious with their seed. She saves them from their own timidity. She serves as a bulkhead against which they can knock their skulls, a moral impediment in the name of which they can curse the fates, and thus she confers a tragic grandeur on a small disability. It's difficult to imagine Hardy taking the chance of laying a single part of himself on any woman, let alone, as current speculation would have it, being careless, or giving enough, to get Tryphena Sparks with child. As for Florence Henniker, think of it like this: if he had really hoped to hear her call him hers, he would surely have chosen a different place to hear her call him hers in – he had known all his life to expect nothing good from public transport.

2

I found the above only this morning, along with other painful documents, amongst Camilla's papers. And I was surprised by the effect it had upon me. I like to think that I am sufficiently accustomed to going through her belongings now – I do an hour or two each day – not to be hurt by anything I find; but in fact I am still disconcerted by photographs of her with other men and by the letters – largely illiterate incidentally (she had a taste for unverbal brutes, Camilla) – that they sent her. They are not stab wounds to me any more, but they do pierce me. Like little pin pricks to the heart. Her piece on Hardy, Mrs Henniker and trains, however, is painful to me in another way. It reminds me of when I first read it in its published form with acknowledgments and footnotes and the swearing left out, as a pamphlet bearing the imprint of the Alternative Centre for Thomas Hardy Studies, Fore Street, Castle Boterel, from which address further information could be obtained about other specialized publications and residential courses for individ-

195

uals or parties. I picked it up from Blackwell's on my way from the language school to the railway station, and I read it over and over again on the train back to London. If the train had gone to Bratislava I wouldn't have minded – I probably wouldn't have even noticed, I was so engrossed. Camilla's pamphlet, you must understand, didn't just amuse me – it cheered me up, it freed me, it lightened my load, in a manner of speaking it cleared my name. Because if Thomas Hardy could never have been a father then he could never have fathered anyone who could have fathered me. I took Camilla's word for that completely; it didn't at all matter to me that what was put forward as proof was but three-quarters supposition; as far as I was concerned no blood test could have been more conclusive. Camilla's argument had the unmistakable ring of truth: it was witty and acerbic and misanthropic and disdainful. And if you can't trust acerbity and wit backed up by misanthropy and disdain, what can you trust?

The train not in fact going to Bratislava, I wrote to the author of the pamphlet the minute I got home to Notting Hill Gate. I had never heard of Camilla Marteline before, but I noticed that she was sole director of the Alternative Centre so I wrote to her there, at Castle Boterel – on the off-chance that it had a postal system – expressing my appreciation and gratitude, venturing to differ ever so slightly with one or two of her judgements, just for the look of the thing, and asking her if she would be so good as to send me whatever else she had written on the small but significant subject of Thomas Hardy's virility. I signed myself a fellow thresher in the cornfield of inflated reputations and enclosed what seemed to me an appropriately sized self-addressed envelope.

I wish to make it clear that I am not one of those people who regularly write to writers. I have a friend (or rather *had* a friend, since I see almost nobody I used to know now) who travels the world taking up invitations sent to him by famous authors in response to the fan letters he sends to them. He claims a ninety-five per cent success rate. It seems that only five out of every hundred successful writers are not so flattered by a letter from an unknown admirer that they are able to resist writing back immediately offering him a bed. He came down to see Camilla and me a couple of years ago when he was in these parts – I think he'd mistimed a visit to John Fowles and found Le Carré out – but Camilla wouldn't even let him sleep in the bath. 'He has a disgusting compulsion to adopt the prone position in the houses of people whose intelligence he fears,' she whispered to me. 'I'm not having him supine under this roof.' I couldn't be as hard on him as Camilla. Partly because he was my friend, and partly because I'm more susceptible to ingratiation; I don't mind it if someone wants to lie down close to me. So I let him sleep in the outside toilet – we were living in another of Camilla's dream cottages at the time – and I even secretly lent him Camilla's sleeping bag. I suspect he would have preferred sleeping in mine if I'd had one, but at least he didn't go away entirely empty handed. I mention my friend only to demonstrate that I know what motivates people to write to writers and that I was not similarly driven when I wrote to Camilla Marteline. I simply felt that here was a case in which I had special rights and interests, that was all. Reviewers are always talking about the way books change their lives – they undergo a major existential convulsion a week, some of them; well, I'm a touch less responsive to the written word myself, but Camilla's pamphlet certainly changed something for me, if only in the sense that it restored me some antecedent pride, or at least, if that's going too far, lightened the burden of antecedent shame. I wrote thanking her for what she'd done for me in the hope that she could do still more. Perhaps it made a difference that she was a woman, I don't know. I am convinced that I would have communicated with the author of *Hardy's Jaunt With Mrs Henniker: or the Duffer in the Puffer* even if it had been a man, but I am prepared to admit that I might have waited for the reply with less impatience.

I had another reason too, if any other reason were needed, to be taken by Camilla's pamphlet: I was provoked by what it had to say about railway travel. As I remember – I don't have the pamphlet itself in front of me, only Camilla's original notes – it bore a Freudian tag relating the erotic significance of trains to the sexual excitation caused by the mechanical agitation of the body; but if Camilla was a dedicated Freudian (as how could she not be, as I was later to understand, with a father like hers?) she was at once more metaphysical and more unforgiving than Freud also. And she had a more developed intuition for the principle of unpleasure. Anyway I believed she was right not to ascribe merely to the sensation of rocking and the incidence of tunnels that emotional turbulence, that yearning for violent change in transient circumstances, which is forever associated with locomotives. It wasn't just Hardy and Mrs Henniker that she put me in mind of, it was also Lawrence's heroes pressed up against erect soldiers with dumb coarsely-beautiful hands on the journey from Charing Cross to Westerham, and Anna and Vronsky caught in a raging tempest within and without, actual and metaphorical, but ostensibly on a platform somewhere between Moscow and St Petersburg, and Tolstoy himself stopped in flight in ardent and destructive old age at Astapovo station. And above all she put me in mind of me, commuting from London to Oxford daily, a railway freak, unable to buy a ticket without wanting to fall in love, incapable of setting foot on a train without having at once to go in search of the someone it contained who could make it all better brighter newer for a lifetime or an hour or as long as it took to get from Paddington to High Wycombe.

The only journey I can remember making in which I stayed in my seat the whole time and kept my eyelids lowered, was the one that was taken up by my reading of Camilla's pamphlet on Hardy's queer elopements. Is it any wonder that I wrote to her?

In the meantime, between pacing the platforms and corridors of British Rail, waiting for Camilla Marteline's reply, and wondering if I would ever run into Gertrude Bugler, something happened that compelled me to ask myself yet again whose – since it looked as though I wasn't Thomas Hardy's – whose on earth I was then.

A hysterical telephone call from my mother started it off. She wasn't going to tell me what the matter was, not when some operator who might know us could be listening, but she wanted me round there right away. She understood as well as any mother that I had my own life to lead and she would lie bleeding in the gutter rather than disturb me, but this was urgent. Actually she didn't use the word urgent, she used the word strange. 'Something very strange is going on here,' she said, so I rushed round immediately expecting to see the dining-room table floating a foot above the carpet.

The front door was opened for me by Mr Flatman, which in truth was strange enough. 'Your mother's quite distressed,' he told me. 'I'm glad you've come.'

I'd never paid much attention to Mr Flatman. It hadn't even occurred to me that he could be an obstacle to my passion for Mrs Flatman. He was one of those nondescript Jewish businessmen, bald-headed, bespectacled, with a little silver moustache, who allow their wives to dominate their social lives while they burrow away in the background, buying and selling blocks of real estate and keeping docile mistresses. They are capable of great sentimentality in the secret hinterland of their lives, these commercial city Jews, often giving their hearts and a fair proportion of their fortunes to wasted widows or paraplegics or mortally struck asbestos victims. It seems to be necessary for them to find some soothing contrast to the blooming health of their wives and daughters. Whether Mr Flatman spent his private life crying in a cancer ward I didn't know. All I knew about him, and I got this from my parents, was that he owed his success to a phenomenal gift for mental arithmetic. 'If I could keep in my head one-tenth of what he keeps in his,' I recall my father once saying, 'I wouldn't still be slaving over television licences.' 'You're slaving over birth certificates,' my mother reminded him.

Since Mr Flatman had never demonstrated his remarkable facility to me I'd had no opportunity to marvel over it, but he certainly remembered who I was, treated me with kindness, and seemed genuinely concerned about my mother. I hadn't forgotten either, come to that, the giant jig-saw he'd bought me while I lay in bed mindlessly convalescing from my marriage to Sharon. So I was in the main predisposed towards him, even though I wasn't certain that he was the right person to be letting me into my parents' house and telling me he was glad I'd come.

I found my mother in her bedroom, propped up with cushions in a high-backed white and gold boudoir chair and dressed as if for the opera – a tragic opera, that is, whichever one has got Medea, Dido, Ariadne and the Trojan Women in it. I have said that she was hysterical on the telephone but I ought to explain that hysteria in my mother's case never issues in common tears. It is marked, the rather, by a heightening of colour and diction, by an extravagance of vocabulary and gesture, and by a triumphant air of vindicated fatalism. She slowly turned her head towards me on my entrance and with a great roll of her eyes gave me an intimation of her woe. When I say she was dressed for the opera I don't mean that she was dressed to go to one.

'For myself I don't care *that* much,' she said, snapping her ringed fingers above her head. 'In so far as the only one to suffer might be me, it doesn't concern me *that* far.' She blew imaginary dust from her grand brocaded bosom, sending an aroma of scent and powder – the aroma of my childhood – into my nostrils. 'I have never expected happiness or sought it, so why should I complain that it has eluded me?'

I was surprised to discover that Mr Flatman was in my mother's bedroom with me. 'Rachel,' he said – he had followed me up the stairs and was continuing to show off his phenomenal memory for names as well as figures – 'Rachel, don't talk like that. You've got your whole life ahead of you.'

She waved away his interruption, but I noticed that she didn't wave away him. 'I'm not what's important,' she went on. 'What happens to me is not worth – ' I could see that she was looking for some other part of herself to snap or cuff so that I should be given further proof of the low esteem in which she held her own life and person. It was only when she couldn't find any that she allowed one round, perfect, opalescent tear to appear in the corner of her eye.

'Mother,' I asked, 'what's the matter?'

Mr Flatman was pacing the floor. He had an altogether coarser conception of agitation. 'What's the matter?' he repeated. 'What *isn't* the matter?'

My mother beckoned me to her. A gesture of infinite sadness. She put her hands on my face and looked into my eyes. I felt a sudden spasm of discomfort and even distaste. I've always been like that; if I get close to a member of my family – physically close, eye to eye or cheek to cheek – I instantly lose all sense of who either of us is. I go into a kind of swoon. It's like being unravelled or unborn. Perhaps that's the real thrill of incest. A plunge not into the heat of consanguinity but into oblivion. And perhaps that was what Hardy was after from his cousins: the sensation of an even greater ghostliness than he already knew.

Who on earth is this person? I found myself thinking, as my mother kept up her stare into my face. It's possible she was wondering the same about me. Or would have been if her grief had not got in her way. It certainly seemed to be the only thing on her mind. 'What I can't forgive,' she said, 'is what this is going to do to you.'

'*Mamzarim*,' Mr Flatman muttered.

'What's *what* going to do to me?'

201

She looked at the ceiling. Mr Flatman looked at the floor. '*Chazerim*,' I heard him curse. '*Zey beyde pishen in der zelber grib. A klug af* the pair of them!'

I might have been slow, but for the first time it occurred to me to wonder why my father wasn't here to share this family sorrow, whatever it was. 'Where's Dad?' I asked.

Something clicked in my mother's throat. I was close enough to her to hear it plainly. When she spoke again her voice had changed. But she hadn't just lowered her range, she had descended in an instant from the empyrean of *opera seria* to the bare boards of *opera buffa*. 'He's done a bunk,' she said.

'Hopped it,' added Mr Flatman. He was now standing at my mother's window, looking out into the night. 'Vamoosed, skedaddled, gone aroys.'

I didn't have to ask with whom.

An hour later though, propped up with cushions in the chair my mother vacated – I was now the one with the livid colouring and the rolling eyes – I did allow myself to be drawn into the crude farce of explicitness. 'How?' I demanded to be told. 'When? Where? *Why*?' The answers themselves – by taxi, first thing this morning, to the other end of London, because they're *mamzarim* that's why – were not in the slightest bit interesting to me; what I was greedy for was not information but the relief that comes with the articulation of amazement. 'What!' I said. 'No! Never! *Really*!' The more I marvelled the better I felt. And they, who had been over the same ground a thousand times and had, what's more, been expecting it for almost thirty years, they were just as eager to use dramatic punctuation as I was. We shared a little confederacy of exclamatory resentment that night, my mother, Rabika Flatman's husband, and I. After all, we'd all been betrayed, hadn't we, all three of us? She'd been made a fool of (!), he'd been made a fool of (!), and I – I was a poor fatherless child! (!!)

But when I rang up my mother a dozen times the next

day and got no answer, and when a postcard from Positano arrived through my letterbox a few days after that, hoping I was not still taking it too hard and signed Mum and Menashe, and when I put it to myself that if I could ever find her again I would, after all was said and done, prefer to be slashed to ribbons by Gertrude Bugler than kneed in the groin like a GI with a crewcut by Rabika Flatman, then the massed rights of grievance and jealousy began to break up and disperse. In fact we were all all right. I was less all right than they all were but I was all right too. In truth I was proud of my father and wished him well. I hoped for his sake that Mrs Flatman was still athletic enough to swing from something high for him, wearing only her bikini bottoms. I would even have gone to see them both in their love nest in Tooting – they had actually taken rooms in the very house that Hardy had lived in when he wrote *A Laodicean* and thought he was dying – were it not that a phrase of my mother's kept going round and round in my head and eventually prevailed over my instinctive generosity. 'I wouldn't dream of saying a word against him to you, his own flesh and blood,' she had assured me towards the end of that dreadful night, after she and I and Menashe Flatman had got thoroughly and miserably drunk together. 'And the last thing I want is to sour the love you feel for him with my bitterness. But you ought to know this before you go: your father is a sadist!'

Such an accusation, I maintain, dragged out of a wife only by the acuteness of her shame and delivered against a backdrop of such domestic dereliction as was ours, would have come as a shock to any son. But for me, made sensitive by recent events, my mother's words carried an extra charge. Drunk as I was, I thrilled to my very finger tips. I asked her to tell me what on earth she meant, but she refused to elaborate. I begged her for some clue then, some small yet all revealing intimation, but she shook her head very slowly, as if it were heavy with memories of unspeakable acts, destined to remain unspoken. 'Between a husband and a wife,' she reminded me, 'some things are sacred.'

'Even when the husband is a sadist,' put in Mr Flatman.

Filial loyalty – to him not her – rose in my chest. I longed for specificities. But how was I to get them? This had been a night for unexpected revelations sure enough, and unprecedented candour also – as I had been warned over the telephone, something very strange was going on – but that didn't mean that the primitive decencies were not still operating. I couldn't very well strike my own mother in her bedroom and demand that she explain to me, down to the last weal and minor laceration, what she had in mind when she said my father was sadistic. I looked to Mr Flatman to see if he would help. I petitioned him with my eyes. Tell me what he did to her, I mutely pleaded. Did he simply strike her with his hands, or did he use the belts and latterly the braces which she bought him religiously every year on his birthday and for chanucah? Did he force other women on her, women whose names he could not remember – Lucetta, say, or Helga, or even Golda? And is that what *your* wife found irresistible about him? Is he at this very moment roping Rabika to a rented bed in Tooting? Does he compel her literally to piss with him in *der zelber grib* – in the selfsame pit?

Menashe Flatman read my mute but burning inquisitiveness impatiently. He looked at me as if I were a boy still. He made a sweeping gesture with his hand, designed to take in the boudoir and its broken promises, and the three of us and our unbearable suffering. 'This,' he said, and his voice was so unsteady that he might have been standing on a hill overlooking Auschwitz. 'This. Isn't *this* the work of a sadist!'

Well, it might have been, but I was frankly disappointed. I would have welcomed more tangible proofs of my father's depravity than just the three of us getting tipsy. A blood stained sheet or a collection of specimen bottles or a folio of sworn affidavits from violated secretaries in the birth certificates offices of Somerset House would have done more to restore my faith in my family connections. I might have had a lot on my mind but I hadn't forgotten how much I'd enjoyed speaking virulent French and beating up Sharon at Fitzpiers's party, and I hadn't forgotton whose virulent French it was that Gertrude Bugler reckoned I'd been enjoying speaking. What larks! she had written on the bottom of her postcard. And what larks if it turned out that my old man and his old man before him had been enjoying themselves likewise. It was difficult for me, as I have already made abundantly plain, to show much forbearance to my forebears; my instincts were all for cursing my precursors. I hated being beholden to anybody. But if I had to make a choice – if it positively had to be the one or the other – then better the Marquis than the mason, any time. Any time.

So why did my mother's denunciation of my father make me hesitant about going to see him? Why wasn't I, by my own logic, hot-footing it across the river down to Hardy's old place on Trinity Road, Tooting, and looking for signs of bruising on Rabika Flatman's body? Why wasn't I shaking my father warmly by the hand and asking him if he could try to remember, just once, for me, if there were any virulent Frenchmen in the annals of our family? Why? – because I wasn't certain I was up to it. Because suddenly I wasn't so sure that I was a deserving case. It was one thing to be ashamed of one's genealogy, but what if it turned out that one's genealogy had reason to be ashamed of one? I wasn't being unnecessarily self-effacing; at the same time that my father was setting up house with Mrs Flatman and subjecting her, in between re-plastering the walls and ceilings and choosing tiles for the kitchen, to the most extreme forms of degradation that either of them could think up (Oh, Mrs Flatman – up!), I was involved in an incident that enabled me to take a long look at myself as a chip off the old block, as an example of Sadeian manhood – and I wasn't much impressed by what I saw.

205

4

'Harder!'

'Harder?'

'Harder – ouch – yes,harder!'

'But I am already doing it harder.'

'Use your shoe.'

'My shoe? I couldn't. It would hurt you.'

'That's the whole idea, boy.'

Boy? I knew that I oughtn't to take offence. 'Boy', I reminded myself, was just a Welsh way of putting it, a mere tic of the patois for Melpomene who, despite her Caribbean colour and coconut smell, had been born in Maesteg, to the west of Swansea, where she had grown up wild among the choir boys and the prop forwards. 'Boy' wasn't personal.

But it might just as well have been. I was, frankly, at my wits' end. Ever since she had unclipped her skirt and assumed this aggressive posture of submission across my knees, issuing me with the most precise and detailed instructions for her chastisement, I had been belting away at her, first with my palms open, then with them closed, then with the skin drawn tight over my knuckles, then with my fingernails hooked like claws, but I had not once come even close to giving her what she wanted. I had succeeded only in tiring myself. My hands were sore. I had broken a couple of nails. Something had even gone in my back. If her flesh had been white I might at lease have taken some consolation in seeing the marks I'd made, but that too was denied me. No matter what I did to them Melpomene's buttocks sat up firm and shone back at me like polished aubergines. At best I could claim to have buffed up their patina.

My own buttocks were pressed into a painful and possibly permanent lattice design by the little wicker hotel chair in which I was trapped, and my penis, on the tip of which, when Melpomene first bent over me without her skirt, I could have balanced not just her but the whole of Maesteg rugby football club, was now vanished. It wasn't just Melpomene who could no longer feel it throbbing against her belly, I myself couldn't locate it anywhere. It was to all intents and purposes, gone; and my balls, if I was not mistaken, were shrinking by the second also. Some evolutionary process – Nature shedding what it had no further use for – had speeded up in me.

Part of the trouble – I'm not making excuses – was undoubtedly the extreme earliness of the hour. Melpomene and I had been forming an acquaintance at Paddington Station for weeks. Every Monday morning at around about eight thirty-four she stepped off the express bringing her from Swansea, which was around about the time that I stepped off the tube from Ladbroke Grove, looking for something to happen to me on my way to the train for Oxford. Sometimes we were just able to snatch a cup of coffee together, at others our encounter was so brief as to allow only an exchange of hopeless smiles. This Monday morning, maddened by platform changes and late alterations to timetables, we turned our backs on the whole system – porters, ticket collectors, the public address system, the lot – and made straight for a hotel. We were in our room, undressing, before some of the more conventional guests had taken breakfast. Even now, as Melpomene rapped out orders and I rummaged for my lost penis, the sound of cutlery and the smell of bacon wafted up the stairs and under our door. A greater man than I might not have been ready to do his worst at such an hour.

But Melpomene seemed to have no understanding of the inappropriateness of the time and the conditions to the deed. There was a quality of impatience in her voice, a growing irritation in her pleas not to be spared, that told me she was blaming failure on me. Me! I was becoming so angry myself that if it hadn't been my inability to beat the shit out of her that had made her that way, I would have beaten the shit out of her.

I still wasn't going to use my shoe, though. I have always been a bit of a puritan when it comes to the introduction of foreign bodies as aids to intimacy. Instead, in desperation,

I dipped my head forward, like a feeding parrot, and I sank my teeth into her rump.

'Ow!' she cried. 'Oh! Ow! Ouch! Jesus!' Her voice ringing with the music of the valleys, her backside bucking on my knee.

Because I owed her, because I had failed her when I'd flailed her, I held on with my teeth. Think about it: it was the very least that I could do.

'Ouch! Jesus!' she cried again, as I bit deeper, up to my gums in her. 'Jesus! No! No!'

Looking back, I can't say that I got any discrete pleasure out of biting Melpomene's bum – the taste was an acceptable one, no more, of burning rubber and shredded coconut with a distant tang, I think, of wild limes – but I was pleased that she was pleased. I didn't want her to feel that she had completely wasted a Monday morning. So I was quite taken aback when, the moment I loosened my jaw to draw breath, she rolled off me sobbing and cursing. 'You stupid shit,' I was astonished to hear her say. 'That bloody hurt!'

I stayed where I was in the wicker chair, dumbfounded, offering nothing in my own defence. She dressed at lightning speed – perhaps hoping still to be at work by nine – taking time only to rub the pain and insult me some more. 'Not much of a man that's got to bite a girl,' was her final summation of my character, as she opened the door and then slammed it on me, giving me the strongest whiff yet of bacon and sausage and fried tomato.

I didn't move for ten minutes, then I prised myself out of the chair and took a look in the wardrobe mirror. Melpomene was right. I wasn't much of a man. Where was the sacred terror? Where was the insolent assumption of cruel male will? A little less than half-way up my body my penis was beginning to surface again, was looking around to see if the coast was clear, like the periscope of a cowardly U-boat, unaware that the war was over ages ago. No, I didn't have what it took to be a sadist. I lacked the application. I lacked the stamina. I lacked the natural aptitude. Above all I lacked the seriousness of purpose.

Not that this came as any surprise to me. I had always nursed a softer spot – in so far as it came down to an out and out choice – for the Chevalier von Sacher-Masoch. 'I can only be the anvil or the hammer; I want to be the anvil,' he had said, and if I had understood him only imperfectly before, after Melpomene I grasped his meaning fully.

So I was relieved to meet Dawn, the ironic shot-putter from Brisbane whose rucksack I offered to carry off the train at Oxford. 'You must be joking,' she had said, looking me over and laughing; and she had enjoyed the joke so much that she took me to meet her friends from Surfers' Paradise who had a holiday squat in Summertown.

'Meet a friendly Pom I found,' she announced. 'His name's Barney.'

'What's Barney short for?' one of them asked, still marvelling at all things English. 'Barnold?'

I told them that it wasn't short for anything; that it was my full name.

They all agreed they couldn't call me by my full name.

'What about Banjo?' Dawn suggested, and nobody demurred.

But I wasn't entirely happy with it. And later, alone with Dawn on the straw mattress, I voiced a query: 'Isn't a Banjo a little round thing that you put on your knee and play with?'

'It sure is,' said Dawn.

She had a name for everything. 'That's called a Boston Strangle,' she explained as she tied her breasts around my neck. And what she was doing when she swung them just out of reach of my lips and then lashed me across the cheeks, first with the left and then with the right, was known as the Wodonga Whip.

I suspected that she made these titles up as she went along. 'And what do you call that?' I challenged her, after she had sat on my face for a full five minutes and left me squashed and purple, but by no means unhappy.

'That?' She didn't hesitate. She was astonished that I needed to ask. 'That was an Ayers Rock. But now I'm going to give you a Filipino Flick for being untrusting.'

I didn't mind. You wouldn't have heard me complaining, as they say. I loved Filipino Flicks.

In truth there was nothing that Dawn did to me that I could think up any stringent objections to, and my only complaint finally was that she failed to understand the solemnly ritualistic needs of the sexuality she herself inspired in me, and responded to them at all times with indefatigable boisterousness. There were moments, for example, especially after a prolonged St Kilda Smother, when I wanted nothing so much as to submit my whole being to her, to offer myself up in one supreme act of self-annihilation and love; if I could have undergone some molecular transformation and been compressed into the iron shot I had seen her practise with in the garden, tucking it under her chin and rolling it round and round until she had it just where she wanted it, it would have been my perfect consummation – she could have putt me as far and as often as she cared to. The trouble was that this desire of mine not just to cease upon the final expulsion of my seed but to become actually inanimate, her *thing*, did not find any echo or correspondence in her. She couldn't treat it, therefore, with the appropriate seriousness. Even as I twitched and throbbed on her straw mattress, even before the last liquid promise of future life had left my body, leaving me mainly mineral with just a vestige of vegetable, she was reaching for her beach towel and telling me her favourite jokes about lonely sheep-shearers.

'You can do anything you like with me,' I kept trying to make her understand, as I lay back spent, tasting the blood that ran in a trickle from one or other of my nostrils and from the re-opened cuts below both my eyes. 'I belong entirely to you. Destroy me.'

210

But her response was always the same. 'Shit, Banjo!' she would say, letting me go. 'Don't be a fuckwit!'

The masochistic pleasures, I discovered, were no easier of attainment than the sadistic ones. I could see why the Chevalier and the Marquis had ended their days without too many friends or comforts in provincial lunatic asylums. Other people are incorrigibly unco-operative when it comes to ministering to specific needs; it's a lonely, hopeless, heartbreaking business trying to get someone to give you the precise thing you require.

But I got lucky. The Gods – notorious degenerates themselves – must have been watching over me. Just about the time that I was growing sick of Dawn's good nature I received the package of pamphlets I'd been waiting for, together with an invitation to look in on her if ever I was passing – passing Castle Boterel? – from Camilla Marteline. And that seemed to promise me assurance that I was not destined to spend the second half of my life alone and crazed, with no one to beat me or be beaten by me, in a home for the criminally ungratified. You see I recognized the handwriting. (Hadn't I, in some hidden corner of myself, always known that I would?) Camilla Marteline was none other than Gertrude Bugler – or rather, to get them in their proper order of appearance, Gertrude Bugler was none other than Camilla Marteline.

And both of them – even now I still think of Camilla as a pair – remembered me. 'Still harping on the good little Thomas Hardy,' they were surprised to notice. 'Does that mean you've disowned the filthy Frenchman? Pity. We're short of well-connected continentals down here. Look me up though, if ever you're passing, in any of your incarnations.'

Look her up? She even seemed to possess an instinctive understanding of my taste in prepositions.

Hope, indistinguishable from panic, fluttered at my heart. Love, inseparable from terror, bobbed like a coracle in my stomach. If I'd been able to hold my hand steady I would have made out a will. I had nothing to leave, but that still didn't stop me wanting to leave it to Camilla.

It should be plain by now why I didn't choose to visit my father. We were travelling in different directions. He was taking life by the scruff of the neck these days, whereas I – well let's just say that I wasn't. And I didn't want his eye on me. He had always thought I was a bit on the indulgent side with women as it was. I know for a fact that he had never been able to understand why I had returned home after my last fight with Sharon with no money and my ear hanging off. 'So just how badly hurt is she?' he kept asking me. True, he was now a lover himself, but I was convinced that he was the hammer not the anvil, and that it was Rabika Flatman who was black and blue. It was even possible that he had already taken to muttering other women's names in his sleep, prior to forgetting hers entirely. Who knows? – he might have been addressing her as Rachel for weeks. Such ironies lurk in acts of supersession. Was it not the fate of Hardy's second wife to watch in misery as the aged poet crawled across the landscape in crazed obeisance to the memory of the first? Well, no one was going to suffer in that fashion at my hands; there was no chance of my forgetting for one minute of the day who Camilla Marteline was, or Gertrude Bugler come to that.

I rang my father, instead of paying him a visit, and got Rabika Flatman. 'Why don't you come and see us?' she asked.

'I'd love to,' I said, 'but I'm going away for a while. Are you happy?'

'Deliriously.'

I'll bet, I thought. But I merely asked if they were comfortable.

'Oh very. It's not what we're used to, of course.'

'Have you got a garden?'

She seemed taken aback by my question. 'A small one, yes.'

'Has it got a hammock in it?'

'A hammock? No. As a matter of fact it hasn't. Why?'

'I'll come and see you when I get back,' I said. I was pleased they were going without a hammock. I didn't want my father to have it all his own way. I liked the idea that there was something Rabika Flatman had done for me that she would never do for him. I don't think that was unreasonably Oedipal of me.

I wasted no time buying myself a train ticket. There was never any question of my travelling any other way. 'Make it a single,' I insisted, despite the booking clerk's assurances that a return was infinitely cheaper. 'Who's planning on returning?' I just stopped myself from adding into the steamed up layers of antiseptic glass. That's what happens when banality and melodrama once enter your life: they race through the blood like a contagion. Not so very long ago I had been leading a quiet, sedentary existence, propounding my final solution to the Brontë problem in the pages of American college journals and in between times combing out the hair that sprouted by the minute from the hottest places of the best of wives. Now that same wife was shaving for another man, getting rounder and rounder in micro-maternity smocks, and from what I'd heard, making the same sorts of raids on the stock of Mothercare in the company of Fitzpiers as she'd once made with me on the matching serviette and place-mat counters of Harrods and Bloomingdales and Galeries Lafayette. My father and Mrs Flatman were living in sin in Hardy's old place, without a hammock. My mother and Mr Flatman were consoling each other with pasta in Positano. And very soon I would be standing on cliffs, wind-lashed, spray-splashed, admiring the power of the foam-fingered sea.

And this was peace time!

Be warned.

2

1

We approached our fates by different routes, Thomas
Hardy and I. When he set out for Lyonnesse it was
impossibly early in the morning and he had to change
trains more times than he changed cousins to get from
Bockhampton to Launceston – 'a sort of cross jump-
journey, like a chess-knight's move,' as Emma Gifford
put it in her recollections – before driving the final sixteen miles over the dreary poetical hills in a hired trap,
via Halworthy, Otterham, and Tresparret Posts, as the
world well knows. I sped to my destiny with much less
mythological ado at the time, and, as I expect, much less
publicity in the future, arriving at Bodmin Road from
Paddington direct and completing the journey in a taxi.
Nonetheless, the places from which we returned with
magic in our eyes (not that I've returned yet) were
scarcely more than a couple of miles apart. His was a
touch more inland than mine, that was all. Emma Gifford
was up at the rectory, listening in to the silence, waiting
for the head man from Crickmay's of Weymouth (Hardy,
altering her recollections after her death, changed
'head man' to 'assistant architect') to come and start
work on the restoration of the old church tower;
whereas Camilla Marteline was out at sea, with the
fishermen, not waiting for anybody. Why should she
have been? I hadn't told her I was coming. Drop in if you
are ever passing, she had written on the bottom of the
invoice she had sent me for her monographs, and as I

214

happened to be passing I dropped in. The keynote was informality. The three suitcases were not significant. I simply didn't own a rucksack.

The Alternative Centre for Thomas Hardy Studies was not open when I arrived at it; neither was its souvenir and coffee shop. Local people I quizzed were ironical when I asked if they knew the whereabouts of the proprietor or when the doors of her establishment were due to be unbolted. I gathered she was notorious not just for keeping irregular hours but for keeping no hours whatsoever. If the day was at all fine she would be off in her two-seater sports car or out in the harbour fishing, regardless of the number of people queuing outside for cream teas and engraved replicas of the tiny picnic-tumbler that Thomas and Emma lost, while they were courting, between boulders in the Valency river. Later, when I knew her better, I came to understand that staying closed was more than just a convenience for her – it was a satisfaction in itself, an unassociated pleasure, an act of pure disinterested violence against the public. Sometimes I have seen her sitting at a desk inside her locked premises, clearly visible, with all the lights on, while disbelieving visitors hammered at her doors. The expression on her face, on those occasions, can only be described as beatific. Locals didn't know what to think. In so far as those I conversed with could be said to have an attitude it was one of bemused and grudging admiration; they didn't like high-handedness, especially in a woman, but then they didn't like visitors either. They were squeezed on every side, like all inhabitants of remote places, by their conflicting prejudices; and this was nowhere more evident than in their responses to the famous episode of the coachload of mature Japanese students from Osaka who, arriving early one morning at the Centre for a week's tuition – booked and paid for months in advance – and finding it shut up and unattended, no messages or apologies or directions left, sat on their cases in the porch and waited without a word of complaint until sunset. Such a sight could not fail to stimulate the nationalism inherent in rustic ribaldry, yet it at the same time quickened resentment of Camilla. She wasn't offering a very good example of country hospitality was she? – leaving all those Nips parched and starving in the lane. Especially as, according to all accounts, she was not in the slightest bit nonplussed when she returned to find them waiting for her. 'And so ends day one of your course,' she apparently told them, bronzed and tired herself and carrying a plastic bag full of writhing mackerel over her shoulder. 'Now you know something of the adversity, the frustration of expectation in a harsh terrain, suffered by Hardy's tragic protagonists. Tomorrow, if the weather holds, we'll do indifference and neglect.'

Not wanting to sit and wait on my cases myself I persuaded the village postmaster to look after them for me. It wasn't easy. He was rancid with bitterness and inexplicable rage like all village postmasters I have met since, and he was from Birmingham to boot. I later learnt that he resented Camilla because she bought a hundred pounds' worth of stamps from him at a time – he took such profligacy as a personal insult – but he resented everyone else in the village also, and often with slimmer justification. He hates me to this day – though he no longer runs the post office – because I once emptied him out of manilla envelopes, and I suppose because I asked him to mind my cases. Having got rid of them I walked down the hill, past the white cob cottages, ancient and huddled and slightly tipsy looking, all of them bearing names culled from a never-never land of eternal pastoral innocence and nautical high spirits – 'Tinker Bell', 'Lucky Pixie', 'Halcyon Days', 'Smugglers' Cove', 'Tall Ships'. In a few minutes I was out in the harbour. I had never been to Cornwall before. As I've intimated already, Jews don't in the main make for the West Country. Hammersmith is far enough in that direction for most of us. And we certainly don't holiday in villages – not English villages anyway. So it was all new to me and surprising. I don't really know what I expected. Violent seas, I suppose, and villagers in striped bandanas and hooped earrings stripping down the recent wreckage of some Portuguese man of war that they'd lured on to the rocks. It was therefore strange to me to see holiday-makers perambulating aimlessly, staring into shop windows, deciphering simple menus, loathing their children, and stuffing ice-creams and candy-floss into their faces, for all the world as if they were in Blackpool or Brighton. Don't mistake me: I wasn't then and I am not now censorious. I have always borne a determinedly tolerant good-will towards the more basic forms of tourism. You won't catch me complaining about crowds. I won't have it that you must carry a blackthorn stick and wear thick red socks rolled down over your boots before you can rightly claim the countryside is yours to spoil. I abhor the snobbery of rambling and the feudal politics of conservation. And I have always enjoyed a runny ice-cream in noisy company myself. What I couldn't comprehend in those who treated Castle Boterel as if it were Blackpool or Brighton was why they weren't in Blackpool or Brighton, since, according to any rational definition of seeing and doing and enjoying, there was so much more to see and do and enjoy there. Sharon wouldn't have stayed in such a place as this above ten minutes; there were no department stores, and no deck chairs. And she would never have kept her footing on the sea-sprayed slate. I had trouble enough keeping mine, and I wasn't wearing six-inch heels – not quite. I even went right over on my back once, lacerating my hands on thorn and rock, and entertaining otherwise thoroughly bored children.

However, I wasn't blind to natural grandeur where I found it. I acknowledged the wild beauty of the snaking S-bending harbour, and the graceful curve of the old harbour wall, and the fierce enfolding cliffs guarding the mouth, in the shape of icthyosauri snoozing. The effect, from where I had at last found some stable ground to stand upon, was of a vast marine amphitheatre, the perfect playhouse for extravagant natural

217

melodramas, whose acoustics would be remarkable, I was able to imagine, when the wind was right. Even now, on a still day, I could hear as if they'd been amplified the words of carolling families a couple of hundred yards away, on the other side of the water, across the slender waist of the S. Thanks to such tricks of air and stone I have since, from a similar position, listened in to Lance Tourney's grunts as he stretched and bent himself in readiness for the call of destiny. And I have heard Camilla too, far away from me, laughing in the night at the jokes of other men, just as I heard her on this day, way way below me, even over the chug of the little fishing boat that was bringing her in.

Don't ask me how I knew it was her. I had only met her once at Fitzpiers's party and she hadn't come close to laughing then. (Who had?) But there are some things you just know. Sharon knew whose baby she was carrying, I knew from whose chest that laughter came. I scrambled down the slate escarpment, which did my shoes no good, and I waited for her at the top of the stone steps that were built into the harbour walls. I couldn't boast much familiarity with the logistics of boats and harbours but I reckoned that if she ever was going to come up out of the water it would be by means of those steps. You can't keep a smart Jewish city boy down: I hadn't been in the village above two hours and already I was getting the hang of the way things worked here. Who was to say that they wouldn't be electing me mayor, or beglerberg, or hetman, before the week was over?

Out of breath, as much from apprehension as from exercise – like Cortez (forget the stout) on the penulti-mate ridge – I watched for Camilla and her crew to snake into sight.

The boat she loomed in burned on the water. If the poop was not beaten gold I don't know what it was; but I can't tell you if there were sails or oars, or how many pretty smiling fishermen dimpled on each side of her. I saw only Camilla. As did the holiday-makers who had thronged the wharfs to watch her come in, drawn not by her strange invisible perfume – Camilla was theatrical, not meretricious – but by the hundreds of white squalling gulls, seemingly lured from the whole stretch of coast, which wheeled and swooped and dipped around her as she towered in the boat, her arms outstretched, her silken hair streaming, her laughter mingling with their desolate cries. I was astonished that she didn't fear for her eyes, so close did they come to her, some of them brushing her shoulders, others hovering fractionally in flight to pause on her palms and forearms. Later she explained that she had been gutting the catch at sea (in accordance with the wishes of the fishermen, by the by; she herself believed in bringing the fish in whole) and that the gulls were simply feeding from her, on the heads and tails and innards of mackerel. It was a little miracle, she told me, how infinitesimally accurate with their bills such large birds could be, how they could swoop and take what they wanted from her hands and not injure her in the slightest. Such accuracy, I was to discover, was also expected of me when it was my turn to approach Camilla with my bill. Grand and generous as were the expanses of her body, she was quickened only in minute and hidden recesses which it was my task to find with prompt and intuitive precision, much as if I were a great bird in flight myself. And Camilla had no patience for clumsiness or approximations; one millimetre to the left or right, one centigramme too little pressure (or too much), and that could be a whole summer's happiness down the drain. But I knew nothing of any of this as Camilla's boat came nearer to me, and I certainly didn't think of the gulls as creatures who cared only for their stomachs; even now they still figure in my imagination, as they wheeled around Camilla's imperious head, as animistic worshippers, bacchantes in some pantheistic ritual, acknowledging Camilla's divinity, protecting her, revering her, and of course longing for her. There was no mistaking the hopeless yearning melancholy of their cry, that desolate call from their genetic incarceration, victims of the cruel caprices of the incontestable Gods – I knew exactly, standing overdressed on that jetty in the heat, how they felt.

I did what I could not to look too out of place as Camilla's fishermen friends tied up below me. On the other hand I wanted to look sufficiently distinct to be noticed. I leaned against the old wall and loosened my tie. I tapped my foot on a stump of weathered timber as if I knew every grain and knot of it, as if it had been me or one of my forebears who had hewn and tarred it moons ago. It's not even entirely out of the question that I whistled shanties. But although Camilla looked in my direction a couple of times – she was abandoned by the gulls now that she had run out of offal, and was doing something expert but I reckoned unnecessary with coils of rope – she did not appear to recognize me. It had been altogether different for Hardy. The moment he rang at the rectory door Emma Gifford was arrested by his familiar (her first word was homely) appearance – as though she had already seen him in a dream. He was what she was waiting for. Whereas Camilla didn't seem to be waiting for anything, unless it was a beer with the boys. But then Emma Gifford must have been growing a touch jumpy in the social seclusion in which she'd been placed and must have been wondering, at thirty, if her great moment had passed; and Hardy was as we know him always to have been, his nether lip pumping blood, the manuscript of an unfinished poem poking out of his pocket. They were both, that's to say, in a more susceptible state than we were, or at least than Camilla was and I should have been – given my contention that romance was no less a deliberate act of the will, a measured response to the pressures of the market, than going fishing.

I decided that I couldn't wait for ever to be recognized. 'Ahoy there!' I shouted, recalling the seafaring literature of my youth; but Camilla and her myrmidons looked so startled that I was glad I had hung back on 'Me hearties!'

'Gertrude Bugler, if I'm not mistaken,' I said instead, which wasn't just me being droll – I was possessed by a sudden and not entirely honourable need to remind her of the intellectual threads that bound her to me, and not those deep water fisherfolk.

She stopped what she was doing and examined me from head to toe (no great distance, her gaze implied) exactly as she had done on the night of Fitzpiers's party, except that this time she had a sharp knife in her left hand and not a stiff gin. She wasn't wearing a party dress either, naturally enough, but old jeans rolled up to her knees and a slight sleeveless tee-shirt that clung to her breasts like a lover but also gave freedom to her arms, still wet and faintly reddened where the webbed feet of the God-sent gulls had rested. I still couldn't be certain that she knew who I was. I was just on the point of putting paid to the suspense by formally introducing myself – of course, if I'd had any presence of mind I'd have leapt from the jetty into her boat crying, 'Why stand you so amazed? It is I, Donatien Alphonse Francois de Sade!' – when she said, 'Well, well, well, if it isn't the Mayor of Casterbridge.'

That wasn't exactly the mayorality I had been imagining the grateful villagers pressing on me a moment or two before, nor did I at once understand the full force of the reference. (I honestly didn't.) 'I think you've got the wrong person,' I replied. 'I've never given away alcohol.'

She didn't hesitate. 'I hear you've given away just about everything else,' she said.

I suppose that was the moment that was granted me to be master of my fate. I could have turned my back on her and walked up the hill the way I'd come, collected my suitcases from the rancid postmaster, and kicked the seaweed of Castle Boterel from off my shoes for ever. Alternatively there was still time for me to leap snarling and unbuttoned into her boat, bend her over the gun-whale, and take her illegally before a single one of her flabbergasted fisher-friends could raise a rod. As it was I did neither. I simply stood my ground and flushed scarlet. I didn't even remember to be flattered that she knew so much about me, so taken aback was I by the easy

221

scorn with which she appeared to judge my conduct. This was the first time it had been brought home to me that my abandonment of Sharon to Fitzpiers, along with the house, the shop, the electrical appliances, the insurance policies, the co-ordinated kitchenware, my books, my trivial fond records, and my baby (that's if it was my baby), could be construed as weakness. Until now I had seen it as an act of a free and generous spirit – not existential bravery exactly, but something along those lines. I had given, I had disencumbered, I had – a little high-handedly perhaps – dispensed. I was not good but I was grand. Camilla, however, did not appear to see it that way at all. Unless, that is, calling somebody the Mayor of Casterbridge was her idea of a compliment. I didn't think so. There wasn't anything obviously complimentary in her manner. It was the *schmuck* who couldn't organize a garden party, who couldn't keep the affections of his friends and lovers, who gave dead birds for wedding presents and asked that no flours be planted on his grave – even de Sade asked for acorns and knew how to spell – it was *that* Mayor of Casterbridge that she seemed to have in mind, not some saturnine heroic figure striding the moors alone. There's more than one way of looking at grandeur. I might have been a starved goldfinch myself, the way Camilla looked at me.

'So what brings you here anyway?' she asked at last, pointing her knife in my direction, not so much sorry for my discomfiture as plain bored by it.

I wondered. So did her friends the fishermen. So even, it seemed to me, did the aimless holiday-makers who would stand and stare at anything (I *said* they should have been in Brighton) and who had not dispersed with any of the prompt tact and restless self-interest of the seagulls. All of them clearly knew the whole history of my moral capitulations so far and were only curious now to discover what I was going to relinquish next. 'You,' I therefore said in answer to Camilla's question.

These days, if it's a rumbustious evening you are looking for – a drunken sing-song extending well into closing time, a noisy altercation in a brutish tongue, a spot of social danger, what's called local colour – The Jolly Wreckers is your place. Then, when I first arrived in the village and stood disconcerted – my rose flush coming and going – in the picturesque harbour, a mere yard or two from the point of Camilla's gutting knife, The Spattered Sofa was the pub to go to. And in between times The Sour Grape and The Tight Fist have alternately enjoyed and forfeited favour. Whose turn it will be next there's no knowing. That will depend on the usual village pub imponderables: the social habits of new arrivals, the death of old loyal drinkers, the state of the landlords' marriages, the supersession of real by ever realer ale, and above all on the operation of that system of expulsions and rustications known in Castle Boterel as the Ban. Scarcely a night goes by down here, scarcely a night has gone by since I moved here all those years ago, without someone being Banned from some bar somewhere in the village. Essentially the Ban is internecine – to be used by locals on locals. When they invented it there *were* only locals; and no one has a better grasp than they of its original needfulness. But as the autochthonous population has become watered down by Londoners and Midlanders (and a solitary Jew) so the Ban has become popularized and even – dare I say? – vulgarized. No landlord not actually born in Castle Boterel or thereabouts can hope to remove someone from his bar with the wild spite, the inexplicable explosion of pique of the true-born native – centuries of neglect, isolation, damp and bad diet are needed for that – but what man, let him be howsoever dedicated to the principle of hospitality, does not need to turf somebody out on his arse sometimes? And since the Ban is there, it is a kind of profligacy not to apply it. I swear that I have seen the friendliest of foreign visitors, the most genially anglophile of Germans, sent packing from a pub with instructions not to return for anything up to the life of the current European Parliament as a consequence of some infinitesimal confusion of currency or mispronunciation of a flavour of potato crisps. I myself was once Banned from the bar of The Crushed Emmet for asking the landlord if Camilla had been in before me. 'I'm not having outsiders squabbling in my pub,' he told me. 'You're Banned.' 'How long for?' I asked him. I knew better, by then, than to argue. 'Life,' he told me.

Where there is no resident police force, some such method of applying sanctions is of course necessary. And it can sometimes attain to an exquisite justice. Two or three years ago, on a hot night, the village butcher found himself unable to keep his hands off the local trout farmer's wife. 'I'd like to tickle you out of his stream,' he kept telling her. A fight followed, naturally, the two combatants rolling over and over each other on the slate tiled floor of The Sour Grape and falling apart only when the trout farmer, finding the village butcher's nose between his teeth, took a great bite out of it and spat the end into the empty fire grate. Now although it was the butcher who began it, it was the trout farmer who was banned. After all, the trout farmer could enjoy his handiwork – the butcher's bandages were on for months – every time he bought a pound of mince; so it was only fair that the butcher should keep his place at the bar. In due course he would lose it over another misdemeanour and join up with the trout farmer in another pub at the top of the village. Thus a kind of democracy of censure and commerce works itself out in rural communities.

Camilla, I found out on my first night, had been shown the door of every pub in the village in her time, and at one period stood Banned from all five of them at once.

'What did you do?' I asked, because I could see that she valued social connections.

'I dragged everyone round to my place,' she laughed. 'I was soon asked back.' I was meant to be amused by the image of five totally deserted hotels bitterly ruing their Ban while crowds of boozy merry-makers spilled out of the doors and windows of Camilla's place, but I was already jealously possessive of Camilla's place even though I had not yet seen or stepped foot in it myself, and the only thing I could think about was who the last person had been to leave and whether he had left at all.

The lunacy of love! The dullard it makes of the imagination! I don't know how many good jokes of Camilla's I must have missed over the years, or how many excellent stories my concentration has drifted away from, because of some dark menacing figure I believe I have glimpsed stalking their peripheries.

Yes, I steamed that first night in The Spattered Sofa. Heat whistled out of my ears. I smoked through my nose like a gelding. And all because a young woman I didn't know, who hadn't, strictly speaking, invited me, was good enough to take me out and show me a good time. Naturally it was her having such a thing as a good time to show me that I resented her for. Though naturally that wasn't how I put it to myself. I was an intellectual as well as a lover; I wanted to pin with some precision exactly what it was I didn't like.

'These songs,' I whispered to Camilla during a break in the revelry – she'd been joining in many of them herself and even had some well established solo routines going – 'they're not all genuinely Cornish are they?'

'Oh no, they'll sing anything that takes their fancy here.'

I was glad Camilla was not trying to protect them, because I was pretty certain that I'd heard mention of fair Dublin and Skye and Botany Bay alongside the Lamornas and the Camborne Hills. I didn't believe there was an Ilkley Moor in the west country either. 'They grab their sentimentality where they find it, you mean,' I rejoined, lightly.

Just as The Bell or The Toby Jug often have a bell or a toby jug in a prominent position, so The Spattered Sofa had a spattered sofa. Designed to be low when it was first built it was even lower now with all its springs gone. It was on to this that Camilla invited me to collapse when we first arrived while she herself sat upon a high bar stool. And it was from here, with my head below my knees, that I shaped my nice discernments. 'There's something about these ersatz folk songs, that kind of nasal male maritime bravado wedded to maudlin sentiment,' I went on, 'that I cannot abide. I suppose it's just routine Celtic mendacity.'

Camilla regarded me from her bar stool eminence without any trace of maudlin sentiment. 'Why don't you get up and stretch your legs,' she said (she seemed to mean that literally) 'and while you're at it fetch me another drink.' She watched me with a distant curiosity as I thrashed about on the sofa, trying to bring myself upright, then she offered me one of her strong brown hands. 'Here,' she said, 'let me help you.'

I wandered off to the bar, braving the hostile inquisitiveness, the quizzing aloofness that I was to grow to know as typically Cornish, and ordered Camilla what she wanted. When I returned she was standing singing, her arms around men's shoulders, her voice a fine soprano, surprisingly sweet, powerful, her accent ever so slightly burred to make the song belong to here and nowhere else.

'Once I had a bunch of thyme,'

she sang;

'I thought it never would decay.
Until a saucy fiddler he chanced to pass my way,
And stole away my bonnie bunch of thyme.'

I felt suddenly and unaccountably sick. If I had not been carrying drinks I might have doubled up with pain. To this day I can locate with my fingers the place where a hole seemed to open up in my stomach. It is still sore. And what caused it was not Camilla's immersion in the life of the village, making her remote from me – I soon learned anyway that she was as determinedly estranged

226

as I was; nor was it her familiarity with the local men who patted her back and stroked her arms as if they knew from memory every bend and turn and hollow of her. No, though these things all hurt me, ludicrously, what opened me up in the middle was the sad mocking fatalism of that song and Camilla's submission to its truths. There and then she provided me with an image of menace and impermanence and careless theft that has never left me: the saucy fiddler. I had always believed, even though I had not stopped to slug it out with Rowland Fitzpiers, that I could make myself as dazzling as any man to a woman if the situation required it. I was even prepared to take on Norman Mailer, remember, when Camilla posed him as a possible threat. But I knew my limits. I couldn't handle fleet-footed impishness. I couldn't hope to defeat the saucy fiddler. I had no answer, from the start, to the melancholy sexual jaunti-ness, irresistible to even the best of women because it knew the sources of woman's unchanging weakness, of the Celt. Don't get me wrong: I didn't suppose for one moment that such a thing actually existed, any more than I shared its insolent pastoral certainties about female fraility. What scooped out a great hole in my insides was the realization that Camilla did.

3

If Camilla were here she wouldn't let me get away with that.

'The saucy fiddler stalks the peripheries of your dread, not mine,' she would tell me. Only she wouldn't use those exact words. Peripheries of dread was my sort of language, not hers.

'But Camilla, I'm only frightened of what he could do to you because *you're* frightened of what he could do to you.'

'Frightened? Who's frightened? I'm not frightened!' She had a buccaneering, ready-for-anything look, which she would almost certainly have shown me at this point.

And which wouldn't have offered me much in the way of consolation. 'That's what I mean. That's why *I'm* frightened.'

'And what do you fear he'd do to me, this saucy fiddler?'

Camilla could make the idea of anyone doing anything *to* her seem pretty far-fetched.

But nothing is impossible to the imagination of a dotard. 'Steal you away, for a start.'

'And then what?'

'God, Camilla, isn't that *enough*?'

'Not for you it isn't, no. But listen to me, Barney, and I'll tell you something. I've never met a man yet who possesses the softness of tread, the easy stealth, the musical genius, and above all the social confidence, to beguile any rational woman of her senses. Men don't come as impressive as that, more's the pity.' (This is supposed to make me feel better?) 'The idea that they do, the fear that they might, lives only in other men's brains. The saucy fiddler is a figure from male mythology. Just like Hardy's flashing Sergeant. You're all hot to know the secret of one another's potency, you men. The woman is merely incidental – she simply serves as the post box you communicate through. In fact, you're all just flashing and fiddling amongst yourselves. You're queens, Barney, the whole pack of you. But especially you and Thomas Hardy. At least de Sade admitted that a loose woman was just a prelude to a tight boy.'

Yes, if Camilla were here she would say such things to me, and more. She always knew how to butter me up.

But Camilla isn't here. To my great grief.

4

She took me back that night, since I had nowhere to stay and my cases were still in the post office, to her place. She didn't live behind or above her school as I supposed she would but in a hamlet a mile or two from the village. As we drove into it I thought I recognized its name.

Hadn't you-know-who done something throbbingly unforgettable there?

'No, that's Trethis.'

'What's this then?'

'This? This is Trethat.'

The cottage was much too small for her. I don't just mean for her needs and her comfort; it was too small for her morally and psychologically and spiritually. It made her look clumsy. It asserted the rights of prettiness and daintiness and quaintness over her stark super-abundance. It mocked her grandeur. And that, I learned later, was why she chose to live there. It was an act of aggression against herself. Part of her general rebellion. She needed to wage war on everything that had been given to her, and that included the composition and arrangement of her own genes and molecules. Long afterwards, when we used to go house hunting together – like having babies it was either that or break up – we would fight furiously because I aspired to a rambling Victorian Villa on a cliff top and Camilla declined to derelict cowsheds in dripping valleys. She wouldn't look at anything that had space or elevation. And she was never happier than when we found a one-storey one-room converted sheep-pen constructed of mud and straddling an ancient running ford. We lived there for one whole wet summer, sleeping in shifts – there wasn't room for two to lie down simultaneously – in wellington boots and urinating through the rotting window frames – there were no windows – into the very stream from which we drew our water. 'Don't you just love it here?' she used to ask me, in a small sweet voice, pouring me afternoon tea in doll's house china cups which I would empty back into the walls when she wasn't looking.

But tonight, in her place, we didn't achieve that sort of intimacy. She was tired from her day at sea and her evening singing, and she didn't want to talk. She didn't want to kiss or in any other way get to know me better either. 'You can sleep down here,' she told me, leaving me in the little prettily beamed and sanded parlour. She didn't add that she was pleased I'd come or that she hoped I'd stay or that she trusted I'd sleep well. She simply turned abruptly from me, went upstairs, and a moment later tossed me down a sleeping bag.

I took this to be a discouraging sign. In more ways than one. I'd never been camping before, not even indoors. And I'm not ashamed to say that this was the first sleeping bag I had ever seen. By and large Jews don't bother with them; there is something needlessly spartan, to the Jewish mind, about the idea of putting yourself in a bag at bedtime. We prefer to retire with more ceremony. How we managed during those forty years in the desert I don't know, but I cherish an image of richly festooned marquees, not unlike Sharon's bedroom, in which the wandering tribes rested their stiff necks on self-ventilating orthopaedic mattresses set on pocket-sprung divans. Comfort, however, wasn't the only point at issue here. When I say that it is un-Judaic to climb into a sleeping bag I am referring to one's *own* sleeping bag; what had been unceremoniously thrown down the stairs to me was *someone else's*. I didn't need to check what the Talmud had to say about that; I possessed in full measure the race's instinctive dread of those places where other people's bodies had been and where alien germs were therefore bound to congregate. And I possessed it in the usual illogical form. I would press my lips to absolutely any part of some girl I'd known for five minutes – in my bachelor days it was my boast that, orally speaking, there wasn't anywhere I hadn't been and wouldn't gladly go again – but I'd invent every kind of fantastic excuse rather than lay my head upon her pillow or slide my unclothed body in between her sheets. Witness, then, against what a background of abhorrence, trepidation, and impiety, I ritualistically undressed, opened Camilla's sleeping bag, stretched myself out inside it, and slowly drew up the zipper. But don't even attempt to imagine the bliss of infamy and the languor of betrayal which overcame me as I closed my

eyes and waited for them to come and bite me –
Camilla's germs.

'Well?'

It took me some time to know who I was, and where,
and why, let alone to recognize the voice of someone who
wasn't me. Only the unfamiliar compression of my
limbs, their unaccustomed heat and itchiness, told me
that I wasn't in my flat in Notting Hill Gate; and only the
sound of the close encroachments of the sea told me that
I wasn't back in Finchley, being woken up by Sharon.
When at last I came round I saw Camilla standing over
me. She was wearing a man's shirt (whose? *whose*?)
which didn't entirely conceal, not from where I was
lying anyway, the thick undergrowth of her sex. I have
already said something about the way a woman's bodily
hairs affect me first thing in the morning, and I was at
once ready, with the sleep still in my eyes, for another
supreme act of self-immolation, of burial and obliteration.

But anyone who has tried to be demonstrative in a
sleeping bag will understand something of my plight. I
could no more rise this morning from the floor of
Camilla's fairy-tale cottage than I had been able to
spring unaided the night before from the settle of The
Spattered Sofa. And this time Camilla wasn't even offering me her arm. 'Well?' she enquired again, as I
thrashed around on the floor like a forsaken merman,
and if I thought I detected impatience in her voice I was
right. For the next thing I knew she was actually
prodding me – I will not say she was kicking me – with
her foot.

Of course, if I'd known anything about sleeping bags
I'd have kept calm, sat up, found the zip, and set myself
free. As it was it took Camilla to find it for me. 'For God's
sake stay still, will you,' she ordered, and taking the
zipper between her big toe and its neighbour – believe
me, that neighbour would have been a big toe on anybody else – in one smooth deft movement she unseamed
me.

'Come on,' she said. 'It's never any good the first time, so let's get it over with.'

This challenge would have been provoking to any man under any circumstances, but I had special reasons for rising to it as I did. Thomas Hardy, she had written, belonged to that class of men who are ungenerous with their affections and timid in their caresses and niggardly with their seed. They seem to promise everything but part with nothing. And they cause great circles of black unhappiness to appear around the eyes of the women they undermine. It was these words of Camilla's that had brought me down here. I wanted to hear more of them, too. Only I wanted to hear them from a position of unquestioned strength. I sought confirmation of what I wasn't and never had been and stood in no danger of ever being. And I was anxious to refute that charge of moral gaucherie that hung over me also, that accusation that I no more knew how to hold on to what was rightly mine than Michael Henchard, one time Mayor of Casterbridge. So I was rich and giving with *my* affections, and I was expansive – you've never seen such expansion – with *my* caresses, and I was prodigal – I positively threw it around – of *my* seed. I promised everything and I gave much more. I drove it home, too, that I knew the difference between giving and giving away. And since I was driving I didn't rest until I had driven every line of care and hopelessness from Camilla's face.

But she still seemed relieved to have it over with. 'Good,' she said, without putting any adjectival fervour into the word, 'now what would you like for breakfast?' She pulled her shirt back over her head just as impersonally as she had originally pulled it off.

I must say that I would have preferred a warmer demonstration of appreciation, but I didn't feel entirely deflated; I wasn't being prodded with her foot any more, for one thing, and for another I quickly grasped something about this business-like attitude she adopted to our first naked encounter. She assumed an air of briskness and rationality about her body because in fact, when it came right down to bodies, she wasn't in the slightest bit calm or self-possessed. Sharon had been able to luxuriate cheerfully in her own nudity because her body struck her as a pleasant and amenable object in her life. She was on free and easy terms with it. It gave her extreme pleasure and excitement all right but always of an overt and even sociable kind. Think of how readily she accepted Fitzpiers's presence in our bed for example, how unshocking she invariably found it. Camilla's body, on the other hand, and all it could do and have done to it, showed her a clear route down to hell. For all its familiarity to her, for all that she soaped and sponged it every day, she was still overpowered by the obscenity of the structure that was her. You might say that in despite of time and experience she had retained some essential characteristic of original childhood sinfulness. Like me she had never been seduced by the twin imps of naturalness and health. We had both of us not come even close to losing our first profane innocence.

And I reckon that we knew that about each other as we wrestled in the sleeping bag on the floor in sight and sound of the sea. It was our first and our last blind coupling. Hereafter we would look upon every inroad that the one made into the other – every swollen inch that I travelled into her, every finger's length of her invasion of me – with wide eyes and gasps of appalled complicity. Whenever I think back upon our lovemaking now the image that most frequently returns to me is of Camilla below me, always below me, but trying to sit up, craning her neck so as not to miss a single detail of the outrageous drama of penetration.

All of this, however, was before us. At the time the important thing for me was that I felt strong and confident enough to get the request I had come down with off my chest. 'I would like to hear you expound your views,' I said as I drank my coffee, 'on the question of Thomas Hardy's virility.' I recall that there wasn't so much as a tremor in my voice. My curiosity could not have been more academic. But since I'd started there was no reason for me not to finish. 'I was very taken by what you wrote in your pamphlets on the unlikeliness of his ever having had the necessary whatever to sire offspring.'

Camilla brought me toast to the table and subjected me to a long slow smile of recognition. The obscene tangle of her pubic hair, still visible beneath her shirt but less tightly curled than it had been when she stood over me and prodded me with her foot – a touch dewier now and more straggly – was on a level with my eyes. She stood dead still so that I could breathe in her aroma and see the cleft fleshy swell of her, and she actually followed my gaze with her own, so that for a short while the pair of us were united in one single act of shameless contemplation. 'For all the commanding authority of my personality,' she appeared to be inviting me to notice, 'for all my stature and assurance and contempt, look in what a primitive and vulnerable spot even *my* forces must muster, behold the soft pink quiver of even *my* mystery. Isn't the contrast *lewd*?'

This moment should have been the crown and consummation of all my sexual hopes and aspirations. I had been trying to get other people to see the lewdness of the human body all my life. I had been baulked at every turn by jollity, blank incomprehension, lyricism, or sheer bloodyminded wholesomeness. Now here I was, being granted everything I had ever wanted – do you know, Camilla and I were so undivided in our scrutiny of her mystery, so one-eyed as it were, that our faces were actually touching, we were actually forehead to forehead, indistinguishable in almost every regard from a pair of fond parents peering into a crib and waiting for the first gurgle (now that's what I *call* obscenity) – and what did I do? In what manner did I give thanks to the Gods for twinning me with a kindred soul at last, when Camilla turned our attentions from what was lewdly stirring under her shirt to what was lewdly materializing under mine, glued our foreheads once more together, and said, 'Alors, tu bandes, tu bandes, mon propre sale seigneur?'

Well, must I really divulge what I did? Let me hide my shame in brackets. (I returned to the subject of Thomas Hardy – ill-fated undeserving lunatic that I was.).

But it wasn't entirely my fault. You see, although I am now able to reproduce, having had a few years to think about it, what Camilla said to me, at the time I couldn't decipher it at all. I've always been a preternaturally poor linguist. My ear just refuses to pick up un-English sounds. Even when I'm abroad and expecting them, foreign words take me entirely by surprise. And at home, when I'm unprepared, the simplest unfamiliar vowel throws me completely. I don't care to think how many lively discussions I've brought to an end by asking someone who has made a noise like *weltanschauung* or *vichyssoise* if he'd be so kind as to come again. But I couldn't ask Camilla to do that. You don't ask a woman who is paying a compliment to your penis (I understood that much) to repeat herself. I might not have been to public school but I had grasped the rudiments of etiquette between the sexes. And besides, I didn't want her to know how bad my French was. Some things she was bound eventually to find out. But not yet. So I kept my head close to hers, I continued to share her absorption in my engorged and glowing organ, and I sighed a sigh of profound experience and even sadness, as if whatever she'd said touched chords that were best left to throb in silence; and when I felt safe from the folly of inconsequence I hurried quickly, to escape further French conversation, to the shelter of my previous request. 'I really am very keen to discuss his potency with you, you know,' was what I said. Only I did my best to empty my voice of all urgency as to Hardy, and at the same time to retain all fervour as to Camilla. I wanted it to sound as though we were a couple of madly-in-love botanists who still had things to say to each other about the reproductive habits of the mollusc.

Camilla, though, reacted badly. She pulled my shirt down, pulled her own shirt down, and moved away from me to the window. I realize now that she was disappointed, that she had hoped for de Sade and been lumbered with the other chap; but I wasn't to know that at the time. I simply thought she was getting ready to love me for myself and was gazing out of her window only because she found a metaphor for her burgeoning passion in the irresistible tumult of the sea.

'Fucking Thomas Hardy,' I was therefore not prepared to hear her murmur.

Then, before I'd made up my mind whether I ought to get her to repeat that, she turned around somewhat wearily, all traces of lewdness vanished, and asked me how long I'd got.

'How long have I got for what?'

'To hear what I have to say about Thomas Hardy's virility.'

I shrugged my shoulders. 'All the time in the world,' I said. I thought it best not to mention that I'd come down on a one-way ticket though.

'Well it won't take that long. But why don't you come to the class I'm giving this morning on *Our Exploits at West Poley*?'

'*Our* what?'

'It's a children's story that Hardy wrote for an American family magazine. It was lost for years. Someone's just dug it up.'

I wondered if that someone was Rowland Fitzpiers. It even crossed my mind that Sharon might have got him to do the forgery that I wouldn't. But Camilla was in no doubt as to its authenticity. 'Oh, it's his,' she assured me. 'There's no mistaking the dead hand of the master.'

'And it's a children's story, you say?'

Camilla could hear me winding up my little *jeu d'esprit*. 'Yes, yes, I know,' she said. 'All his stories are children's stories. But this one has a special interest, because where all the others are meant to be for adults and aren't, this one isn't meant to be for adults but is.'

'You mean it's really about virility?' I wondered.

Camilla looked at me. She'd clearly had a lot of experience of dealing with people who thought she was fanciful because she was serious. She seemed sombre, impenetrable. Once again it was hard to believe that there was any part of her that was pink and soft. 'It's a story about caves and potholes,' she said. 'It's about going underground. When a novelist who has always more of himself concealed than an iceberg decides, literally, on a subterranean action, then one must lower oneself down with him. The plot centres, by the way, on the damming of rivers.'

She was, as I have said elsewhere, a committed Freudian. And I was becoming a committed Camillarite. I opened my eyes wide. I seemed suddenly to know more than I'd ever known I'd known on the significance of damming rivers. 'In that case,' I said, 'I can't wait to go to your lecture.' And I rose from the table and went over to where Camilla now stood and I set off in search of her moist and vulnerable areas. But she didn't have any. I'd blown my chance. She was thinking of Thomas Hardy now and she was hard and closed to all men.

3

I

Our Exploits at West Poley concerns two cousins with
deceptively uncharged names – Steve, tall, masterful
and headstrong and not near the Author's conscience,
and Leonard, delicate, nervous and acquiescent and the
I that grows to tell the tale – who go exploring in the
Mendip Caves and accidentally discover that they are
able to alter the course of the stream that runs through
the local parish, diverting it from West to East Poley and
back again, and thus influencing the domestic and commercial well-being of the parishioners in each. The story
affects a gently homiletic air, not exactly that of mere
precept, but a healthy tone, as Hardy himself put it,
suitable to intelligent youth of both sexes, alternating
action with comments on the difficulty of discriminating
between one community's rights and desserts and
another's, and pressing the superior claims of discre-
tion over adventure. In the background but never far
away hovers the mythic figure of the Man who had
Failed, enabled (and indeed ennobled) by that very failure (he had failed through want of energy and not want
of sense) to make the wisest decisions and speak the
truest words. 'Quiet perseverance in clearly defined
courses is, as a rule,' he tells Steve who needs to be told,
'better than the erratic exploits that may do much harm.'

'Okay,' said Camilla to her class. 'What's this story
really about?'

It always makes a melancholy spectacle, adults

penned in children's tiny desks, straining their eyes towards a teacher just as they did a half a lifetime before, still without any answers to someone else's questions. And the matrons who sat in rows before Camilla this morning – all members of a vigorous local women's group – were especially touching. Tyrannical instructresses in their own homes, empresses and undisputed law-givers there in all matters great and small, they were cramped and even cowed here, mere vassals in the grip of another's imperious will. Worse for them, too, they had been set the conundrum most bewildering and insulting to the domestic and maternal mind: they had been asked to consider the possibility that a thing was not the thing it said it was but another thing entirely. Motherhood is necessarily inimical to philosophy; the close proximity of a baby fills a mother's head with the inescapable poignancy of the real, and long after the baby has grown up and gone she is still fiercely protective of hard facts and actualities. And so they were angry with Camilla who didn't look as if she had ever kept a child or a kitchen clean, and their anger made them wilfully obtuse, wedded them to their obtuseness, bound them in an intense ideological attachment to it. 'It's just a story,' they said. 'It's about two little boys who go into a cave and get up to mischief. Little boys are like that, you know.'

'Go on,' said Camilla. 'What else is it about?'

'It's about why boys should learn to look before they leap, and to leave things as they find them.'

'Yes, go on,' said Camilla.

'It's about not altering what already works. Not being too ambitious. Not letting other little boys have too much influence over you.'

'Go on,' said Camilla.

'It's about why you shouldn't make comparisons. Why you shouldn't go into caves. Why you should listen to the advice of your elders.'

'Yes, yes, so what is it *really* about?' asked Camilla. She seemed to imply that they were on the brink of it now and needed to make only one more little leap of the mind.

But she had wearied them. She searched the rows of closed faces in vain. I was sitting at the back, lying low and keeping quiet, but I felt that even I had let her down.

'Let me give you a clue,' she said. 'Thomas Hardy was forty-three when he wrote this story, which means that he had been married for almost ten years. He was becoming famous and meeting other women. And as we know, not a woman could alight from an omnibus in sight of Thomas Hardy without suggesting to him another turn that his life might take.' Camilla looked hard at me as she said this, but whether I was meant to see myself as Hardy or the girl getting off the omnibus I couldn't decide. But there was terror in it for me either way.

'And here we find him writing,' she went on, 'ostensibly for children, about the damming and diversion of streams, about the small obstacles which hold back the mighty roll of the seas, about the excitement of watching the water change direction, about the havoc it causes, and about the final inadvisability, for spurious parishional reasons, of altering the directional flow of a single solitary drop.' She paused and smiled – what a marvellous public smile she had – at an image that had formed itself in her mind. 'Let me put it another way. The climax of this story is reached when the two pre-pubescent males find themselves lost and drowning in the cave, itself screened and fringed by bushes, with nothing to help them but a small supply of inadequate guttering candles.' She threw back her head and laughed one of those ravening piratical laughs of hers. 'Now tell me that you don't know what's going on in West Poley,' she dared us all.

There were still pockets of resistance to her, but the small guttering candle lit a common recognition amongst the women. There were some smiles, there was even some laughter, and more than one curious face swung around to see how I was taking all this, alone and masculine on the back row. They needn't have bothered. It wasn't necessary. I had already sputtered and gone out.

Camilla was now at the blackboard, with an assortment of coloured chalks between her fingers, drawing a picture. In her free hand she held a copy of *Our Exploits* and she consulted it as she spoke and drew as if it were an instruction manual. 'You will remember,' she told us, 'that the reason the boys play with the water in the first place is because they want to turn it out of their way so that they can get to that delightful recess in the crystallized stone work of the cave which is shaped like the apse of a Gothic church.' We watched as Camilla carefully drew the apse of a Gothic church. 'It is Steve, the headstrong one, who almost pays for his impetuosity with his life, who is most delighted by this beautiful glistening niche. "How tantalizing!" he says. "If it were not for this trickling riband of water, we could get over and climb into that arched nook, and sit there like kings on a crystal throne!" And what is it that Leonard says in reply? "Perhaps it would not look so wonderful if we got close to it." The soul of Thomas Hardy is distilled into that line – that is all you need to know to understand the bitter dejection of his wives.' Camilla's chalk squeaked on the blackboard. Pink dust flew like sparks from under her fingers. 'Because what is that niche that Leonard fears to approach, that beckons so alluringly to one and threatens so much anti-climax to the other, and is finally blown up with dynamite and sealed for ever? What is it that is described as having the colour of flesh, ornamentations resembling the skin of geese after plucking, or the wattles of turkeys' – on to the board went the wattles of turkeys – 'and is decorated withal with water crystals – what is it if it isn't this?'

Camilla stayed where she was for another half minute, engrossed in the minutiae of art, then, with a theatrical flourish, she tossed the chalks into their tin and strode from the blackboard, allowing us all to admire the giant yawning vulva which she had sketched with such faithful attention to texture and tincture from its early origins as the apse of a mediaeval church. *Our Exploits at West Poley* she tossed to me, high over the

241

heads of the intervening women. It landed open on my desk. 'I think you'll agree that I've stuck closely to the text,' she said.

Well, she was a shock tactician. They would never have granted her tenure at most English universities. But she knew how to send a current through me. Her drawing galvanized me. I sat at my desk with my hair erect and light coming out of my fingers. If I needed further proof that my ties with Thomas Hardy were not familic, then here it was; not I, nor anybody else for that matter, could be connected to him through *that* channel – not I, nor anybody else living or dead, could claim kinship with him via *that* organ of transmission, emblazoned on the blackboard in shocking technicolor pink. But that wasn't the only reason for my soaring temperature and the odour that I must have been giving off, to anyone in the row in front of me, of charred fingernails and singed flesh. Don't forget that these were the second pudenda I had looked into in one morning, and that Camilla had had, so to speak, a hand in each of them. It was impossible for me to avoid the conclusion that without in any way deviating from Hardy's detailed instructions Camilla had drawn herself for me. In public! Can you take the full measure of what that meant? I couldn't. I was rapidly losing all sense of distinction between reality and art. It required all my powers of restraint not to leap from my desk and mount that blackboard. And years afterwards, stirred by some fugitive association, I would rummage between Camilla's legs in search of the smell and the taste of schoolroom chalk.

Is it any wonder that I am consumed by loss? Do you think I don't know how unlikely it is that I will ever again find a woman who will do for me what Camilla did?

The ladies, naturally, were not as carried away by Camilla's demonstration as I was. I wasn't paying them an awful lot of attention but I had the impression that they were thawing out a bit. And I do remember that one of their number actually found the courage to applaud. But of this I am confident: they'd recognize aggressive

242

misogynistic timidity when they next saw it, and they'd know what they were reading about when they next came across the crystallized wattles of turkeys in a so-called children's book.

'You can now see the significance of the role of the Man who had Failed,' Camilla concluded. 'The Failure he proudly wears, like a badge, is a failure, in Hardy's words, of energy. He is a not uncommon figure in Hardy's works. He represents the superior moral worth of enervation. He is the apotheosis of impotence. What a humiliation it must have been for Emma Hardy to have lived with a man who yearned every day of their life together to channel his stream into another bed but lacked the force to do so and called his inertia sagacity. A faithless husband is a shame to a wife but a husband who is ineffectively adulterous, who wants but lacks the courage to take, dishonours her ineradicably. After Emma's death Thomas Hardy found amongst her papers a mass of diary entries gathered together under the title, "What I think of my Husband". You won't be surprised to learn that he destroyed them. His remorse for his wife is famous, but it wasn't strong enough to allow her to have her say. People have often speculated as to the contents of those diaries. It isn't necessary. *I* know what she wrote. *I* know what She thought of her Husband.'

2

Later that day I took the step of deciding to stay in Castle Boterel. Camilla made it easier for me by driving me a few miles out of the village so that we could talk and drink together far from the farmers and fishermen and the saucy fiddlers whose familiarity with her troubled me so much. As indeed it troubled her. 'It's good to get away,' she said.

I thought I recognized our whereabouts from the signpost. 'Isn't this where he felt bad about feeling good that he had made a rival jealous?' I asked.

'No, that was Trewill.'

243

'What's this then?'

'This? This is Trewont.'

We ate chips and pasties out of a basket, and at Camilla's insistence swilled them down with champagne in celebration of the deal we'd struck. I'd clean out the toilets at the school and make sure there was fresh soap in the wash bowls and paint the window frames and help out with the paper work – I now see that it was not unlike the arrangement I had arrived at with Sharon – in return for which she would keep me happy and sheltered and warm until boredom set in on either side.

'Do I stay in the sleeping bag?' I asked.

Camilla thought about it. 'Not all the time,' she said at last. And to mark the bounteousness of her concession she got me to fetch her more champagne.

I don't expect that I will ever again meet a person who drank champagne in such quantities as Camilla. She guzzled it. And it wasn't as though she was a connoisseur. She couldn't tell one champagne from another. It was even possible, when funds were low, to palm her off with cheap sparkling wines from Portugal. She wasn't an alcoholic either. And she certainly wasn't a romantic. I think she drank it quite simply because she needed the sensation of bubbles going off inside her mouth. It made her feel that existence was not totally without excitement; that there were things exploding somewhere in her life. There was a gaudy streak in her. She would have made a marvellous wartime mistress, alternately thrashing and sobbing on a broken bed in the glare of searchlights, waiting for the Gestapo to knock.

So why had she settled like a moth of peace in Castle Boterel, where people came on pilgrimages to ashen melancholy, to walk their pets and boil lentils and expire?

'I fell in love with the idea of an idyll,' she told me. 'I came on a sort of working holiday, to continue my researches into Emma Hardy in the daytime – there were descendants of her family I wanted to interview, and relations of a young farmer who courted her before Hardy did – and to get drunk at night. I was working on a book about Hardy's women then, hence Gertrude Bugler' – we looked deep into each other's eyes at the mention of this name – 'and had other places to visit. I didn't plan to stay here. But I made the old mistake of confusing a holiday with life. I loved the beauty of the harbour and the valley, and I loved getting drunk here. I fished, I swam, I sang in the pubs, *and* I was on a grant from the Arts Council. It was like paradise. I suppose too that I wouldn't have been so willing to stay if I'd had anything better to go back to.'

I didn't seek to plumb this mystery there and then; I knew I would hear it all eventually. I still was not thirty years of age, remember; I could still luxuriate in the length of time it took to get to know another person. I still wanted to take into myself, slowly, as a precious possession, someone else's past.

Now if a woman wants to tell me about herself and her adventures – not that I meet many women down here – I stop her mouth, it doesn't matter with what, with food or kisses or French wine. That's one thing I can thank Camilla for: she gave me my fill of the sweets of female narrative. Hers still hangs around my heart like a fatality.

'And I *was* excited by the village,' she went on. 'At first. Or at least the village was excited by me, which amounts to the same thing. I took on the role they gave me, that of a dangerous and exotic visitor from another world, elusive, mysterious, hard to hold, and soon to be gone. I'd catch the village boys looking up at me with black eyes. The first fisherman I kissed' – I'd come back to that; Oh, I'd strip the flesh off that one – 'trembled in my arms. He shook like a baby. He couldn't believe his good fortune. He would stare at me and rub his eyes as if he thought I might at any moment vanish, like a mermaid. And all I wanted was to go out fishing with him.' (Liar, Camilla. Liar.) 'He wouldn't leave me alone. He insisted that I take his arm whenever we were in the harbour, in sight of his pals. He offered me everything he owned to go and live with him, even his boat. His wife wasn't too pleased with me.'

'And did you go?' I asked. I couldn't wait after all.

Camilla shook her head. She seemed to be still regretting the boat. 'No,' she said. 'I married a farm labourer instead. He was much younger than me. He was just a boy. I only stayed with him one night. His mother and sisters sang hymns of joy when I left.'

She didn't fail to notice my stupefaction. There was a total collapse of my facial musculature. My mouth actually did fall open.

'Well,' she said, with a wan smile, as if her nature had surprised her once, also, 'he used to take me on his tractor.'

It wasn't just the fisherman's wife and the farm boy's mother and sisters who didn't like Camilla. None of the village women did.

'In an earlier age they'd have hung me for a witch,' she told me. 'As it was they were perfectly capable of making life uncomfortable for me in other ways. They murmured when they passed me in the village streets. They actually made a growling sound in the backs of their throats. Some of the shopkeepers refused to serve me. They accused me of strange and pointless crimes: stealing and poisoning their pets, making anonymous phone calls, scratching their cars, intercepting their mail. I can't tell you how many times the police came round to question me.'

'And all this because they suspected you of sleeping with their husbands?' I ventured. I had hoped to get away with asking that question without any hint of throatiness in my voice, but I hadn't succeeded.

Camilla threw me a stern look. She wasn't having any backward glancing possessiveness. 'What do you think? The men in this village would lie down with dogs; of course they'd have taken me if they'd had the chance. But the fact is I had nothing to do with any of them – apart, that is, from the peck I gave the fisherman and the night I spent in his caravan with the farm boy. And *he*, don't forget, was my lawful wedded husband.'

I must have shown some sign of relief or complacency or some other satisfaction that Camilla believed I had no right to feel, because she instantly recalled that what she had just said was not entirely the truth. 'I suppose I oughtn't to leave out the black Mormon choir who came to perform down here and stayed in the village one weekend,' she corrected herself.

'You . . . er . . .?' I knew I shouldn't have asked. A hand as big as God's was trying to clamp my mouth shut. And a booming voice was telling me to get up from the table, take a turn in the evening air, and return with a bottle of champagne. But I've never welcomed outside interference in my affairs; and I've always been poor at perceiving my own best interests. 'You . . . er . . . went out with one of them?' I enquired.

Camilla, on the other hand, unlike me, never failed to press home an advantage. 'Barney,' she laughed, and I think it was the first time she had addressed me directly by my name, 'Barney, I fucked every man jack of them. Or rather, they fucked me. I just lay back and sang spirituals.'

3

There's one folly I don't have to reproach myself for. I never then or at any time subsequently sought to discover from Camilla or from anybody else how many Mormons it takes to make a Mormon choir.

But I am still not able to listen to a rendering of *All God's Child'n* with any equanimity.

4

If I say that we spent the next two or three months in this fashion – Camilla swilling champagne and me taking in the details of each of her suddenly-remembered lapses from continence – I don't want it to sound as though that was all we did. We also went out. Took walks. Picked wild flowers. Climbed stiles. Hung over precipices and peered dizzily into waterfalls. Sailed up the coast to look at caves and colonies of Cornish choughs and corn-crakes in Lionel Turnbull alias Lance Tourney's boat. Two pounds an hour it cost us for Lionel's services, but Camilla considered his expertise was worth every penny. He knew where to take us. Camilla couldn't believe how little I knew about the creatures with whom I shared the miracle of existence. 'What's that?' she would ask me, grabbing me by the arm and pointing at something twitching in the sky.

'A bird,' I would say, proudly.

'Barney, it's a sparrow-hawk. And that one there, bobbing in the water, is a guillemot.'

I followed her finger, conscientiously enough, God knows, but all I could see was some duck.

It was high season. Parties of enrolled students were arriving at Camilla's school by the hour. Visitors drop-ped by to ask for prospectuses and while they were at it any other scraps of information to which they felt they were entitled: what time the buses ran, where the castle was (there wasn't one), whether the harbour was at the top of the hill or the bottom. So Camilla had a double reason for closing her doors and taking me off on whole day excursions. 'I'm going to show you where you live,' she used to say, dragging me through the crowds of furi-ous souvenir hunters and thwarted Hardy enthusiasts who were hammering at her windows.

She led me down the sides of sheered off cliffs to lonely rocky beaches where she taught me to tell a gastropod from a bivalve. She introduced me to gribbles. She drove me out onto the mist shrouded moors, where Arthur's sword was dropped, and made me study bell heather and cloudberry and common gorse. She took me for long hikes into the tinkling valleys and out again on to the perpendicular meadows, where she would set me little tests. 'I'm going to sit here,' she would say, 'and you're going to pick me a bunch of bluebells.' And if I returned with anything approximating the size and colour of bluebells – it was enough, initially, that I knew she was referring to flowers and didn't come back holding up a bunch of worms – Camilla's eyes would light up with pride, much as if she were the mother of a child afflicted with Down's syndrome who had just put together his first sentence. I can still see her, in the grass, her lovely strong brown knees drawn up to her chin, her shoulders gone golden in the sun, her face aflame with merriment under the shadow of the black broadbrimmed hat she wore on hot days, and which made her look like one of those tall blonde Spanish women who come from Malaga and own riding schools in men's imaginations.

As she got to know me better, Camilla evolved a system of encouragements and rewards which might have struck some as unacceptably Pavlovian but which was guaranteed to bring on my rural education by leaps and bounds. 'If your heart is set on fellatio tonight,' she said to me – it was, it was; set rigid – 'you'll have to collect me some flax, some fleabane, and some fritillary. You've got five minutes.' 'What's cunnilingus worth?' I used to ask, and within seconds I had identified a curlew, a cuttlefish, and was back with armfuls of columbine and bloody cranesbill and lesser celandine.

Sometimes, if the sun was too strong and the tides were favourable, we stayed in the village and went swimming in the harbour – that's to say Camilla went swimming in the harbour while I paced the walls and jetties with a book and watched her disappear. Whatever else she had been able to lure me into learning Camilla had not yet got me into the water. I had to dig my heels in over something, if I was to remain recognizable to myself, so I dug my heels in – I wouldn't know if the metaphor is mixed – over that. She was a strong swimmer herself, capable of diving from any height and holding her own against the most wayward currents, but she had never yet made it out to the Mazzard, the black rock that

249

loured in all weathers at a tantalizing distance from the harbour mouth and was named after its uncanny resemblance to a skull. 'I could do it if I had flippers and goggles,' she assured me. 'When you next feel like buying me a present, buy me those.' But I never did. When she finally got them they were from someone else. 'I'll get there yet,' she promised herself meanwhile, breathing heavily from her last effort, dripping water on my book, while I seethed with jealousy of the black rock that was more challenging and less attainable than me.

I came to know something of the animate nature in the village also in these first months. The hostility which had greeted Camilla when she had first moved in and driven seasoned salts to offer her shares in their boats had not passed exactly – it takes half a hundred years for the Cornish to think about relaxing their suspicions – but she had been resident long enough to have lost some of her first dangerousness. Most husbands were still with their wives, and those that had left had left with someone else. And because holiday idylls are not, after all, uncommon, Jaimie wasn't the only farm boy hereabouts who got drunk every night and slept in a ditch, unable to resolve the mystery of whether he had in fact possessed a worldly bride for a day or had dreamt it. So there were no more pins stuck in her effigy in crumbling cob cottages, no more polythene bags of chicken giblets left on her front step, and no more talk of her being drummed out of the village by the local women, gathering in the lanes and hammering their pans and kettles with wooden spoons. She was still subject to withering looks from some of the older inhabitants, but she could buy provisions without inconvenience now, she could pat the village dogs, she could turn up at fêtes and carnivals, and she could even get herself elected a parish councillor to sit alongside the plumber, the electrician, the malevolent gardener, the ladies' hairdresser, the retired angling correspondent, and the deep-voiced village sculptress. I wasn't a nobody therefore when I strolled about on Camilla's arm and was introduced to the local doctor and the local vet – both of them from up-country, far gone in the eccentricity of professional boredom, and indistinguishable, one from the other, even to themselves (though it was said the vet was better qualified); the potter and the slate painter, Ken Stinsford; the Restaurateur (his capital letter) from West Bromwich who was going to teach the Cornish how to Eat; the sad-eyed proprietor of the rock and ice-cream shop who held us in urgent conversation about recent developments in the French *nouveau roman* as he twisted interminable threads of sugar into candy floss; and any number of Camilla's favourite musical codgers and sentimental blatherers from the pubs and fields and wharves. The vicar said good morning to me, which had never happened in Finchley. The families from the remotest farms, who came in once a month to shop and who had interbred so resolutely that the baby looked older than the grandma and in all probability was, smiled at us in the streets and touched their hats. I was so much not a nobody in fact that I actually grew to be on nodding terms – though the confession shames me – with the area representatives of the National Trust who drove around in Land Rovers and hacking jackets and brandished sticks like officers of an occupying army. Which in a sense they were.

But all the time I knew that I was in Camilla's world and that I didn't choose to make it mine. Hers were the antecedents here, hers the history, hers the friends. I was out on a limb, a new shoot on an old stem, and for some reason I wanted to stay that way. I enjoyed the fragility of my position. I relished not knowing what each new day was going to bring – what threat to my stability, what fresh revelation, what whim that would exclude me. I woke up every morning sick in the stomach. Was this the day that Camilla would finally be bored? Was this the day that she would disclose to me the real nature of her relations to the village plumber? Was this the day that she would at last swim out to that black rock she seemed to need to reach and sit on far more than she seemed to need to reach and sit on me?

Unutterably sweet was the sickness of my uncertainty as I hung retching over the wash basin in the morning, not wanting to wake Camilla but not wanting her to stay asleep either, hoping that she had stirred of her own volition and opened her eyes and was at this very moment spreading herself for me like a forbidden banquet.

Of Camilla as a banquet I will have more to say.

So: although the rocky and populous outside world was an apparent break from the intense mental activity of our investigations of each other's pasts, for me it offered no real refreshment. It merely served to fan the flames. Pity the poor Jew. Let him gentrify and ruralize himself all he likes, let him surround himself with acres of goyische greenery, he will never know what it is like to take a turn around a garden. For all that I stood on cliff tops and breathed the sea air, for all that I rambled and marvelled and meandered, espied seals and puffins and paddled in crystal streams, I never once left Camilla's mind.

So pity poor Camilla also.

'Tell me,' must have been the two words most often on my lips. 'Tell me, tell me.' For just as children pass the parcel or the apple, tucking it from under one chin to another, so I wanted Camilla to pass the poison of her experience from her head into mine. 'Tell me what you did then. Tell me what he said. Tell me how you felt. Tell me, tell me.'

And Camilla, who was wary of my avidity (and weary of it, too, at last) but who was also amused and understanding initially, and ascendant and therefore punitive, and naturally not unwilling to recall the past pleasures of her life – Camilla told me.

About the boys and the youths and the young men and the old men and the women (yes, yes, the *women*) and the piano tuners and the violin teachers and the professors and the safe breakers and the circus dwarfs and the security guards and the pop stars and the fan extraction engineer and the cucumbers and the Coke bottles and the aubergines and the Lithuanian and his brother and the Maltese and his wife and the three Yemeni diplomats (Camilla! Arabs!) in full regalia and the five French-Canadian pole vaulters and the gas masks and the rubber gloves and the pulleys and the harnesses and the wet suits and the parachute silks and the anonymous toes under the table and the ownerless thumbs in the Tube and the nameless ones and the faceless ones and the legless ones (no, no, Camilla; yes, yes, Barney) and the priests and the nuns (need I say that Camilla was a Catholic?) and the Ibo lawyer and the steel band from Grenada and . . .

Enough already?

Who? Me? Never.

Or at least not until I had broken the back of every hand and operative in the semen factory that had once been my body. Only then, when I was literally a spent force, did I yield to pressure from the unions. 'All right,' I would say, 'I think that will do for the time being.' And then I looked for soft soothing words and disclaimers. 'I take it that you're speaking figuratively,' I would show Camilla that I understood, flat on my back on her bed, looking up at the beams of her pretty other-worldly cottage, while outside the sea clawed its way back into the land. 'I take it that there wasn't *actually* a Scottish caber-tossing team.'

Camilla was always matter of fact. 'Of course there was. I wouldn't lie to you, Barney. I've got no interest in elaborating fantasies.'

'And no need either,' I said bitterly.

'No, no need at all.'

She wasn't kidding. What has to be understood about Camilla is that she was a puritan. She was fixated on truth. She would neither embellish it nor censor it. It was up to me, since I'd asked, to deal with what she told me as best I could. And detumescent, I dealt badly. I suffered. Oh, how I suffered! For I was the lonely one in that excruciating triangle which linked me, Camilla, and veracity. The other two had each other, lay locked in an indissoluble embrace, while I groaned vulnerable and flaccid, yearning for denials, but unable to find any refuge from the relentless honesty of Camilla's narrative. On and on she would go, leaving out nothing, not altering an action or a word, not willing to change the length or colour of a single hair, and all with precisely the same degree of artless intimacy and amusement that had aroused me when I'd been armed and helmeted to ride into the very eye of her storm – only now I was defenceless and in a foreign field, without a kingdom or a horse.

Of course, nobody is a compulsive truth-teller for no reason. Truth doesn't insist that you keep talking. He (she?) can't possibly feel betrayed by occasional bouts of judicious silence. So I wasn't in much doubt that Camilla was garrulous over and above the call of verisimilitude; that she was paying me back for trying to assert my will over her past, for supposing that her erotic history and imagination should be at my beck and call. 'Don't think you can transcribe my tunes for your organ,' she once told me.

As it happened I was at that moment hot for her. (At *that* moment? – at what moment wasn't I?) 'Which other instruments do you want them to be played on then?' I demanded to be told, as I penned her in a corner and ground my ear into her lips.

Two hours later she was still going through the orchestra while I lay whimpering on the carpet.

But Camilla had another grudge, too, for which she punished me with truth. And that was my lack of it. For unlike her I *did* tinker with my history, I *did* leave out a little something here, remove a little nothing there, confuse, conceal, conflate. I didn't add on anything, notice, I simply took away. I clipped and pruned my past life more ruthlessly than if I'd been the monstrous moral

254

housewife – the Birmingham Ripper – let loose in the cutting room for an hour. So that in return for Camilla's epic sagas I had only milk and water fairy stories to relate, impossibly lame adventures into which I'd been dragged kicking, affairs of the heart that were not near my heart, passions that barely quickened my pulses, encounters in which I wasn't there to be encountered. I even tried to convince Camilla for a while that my penis had never truly risen except for her. 'So how did you ever effect an entry?' she enquired. I thought about saying that I never had. 'Either by bending it double and pressing with my thumbs,' I decided to explain instead. 'Or by using my index fingers as splints. It's not comfortable but it's better than nothing. There's a lot more of that sort of thing going on than most women realize.' 'I see,' she said. She didn't believe a word I told her.

So why did I go on lying? Why? – that's easy to answer. Because I didn't want to hurt her. (Hurt *her*? *Camilla*? Yes, yes, I know – but old habits die hard.) Because I didn't want to threaten her with who I'd been. Because I wanted to clear my decks (while keeping hers full); and because I wanted her to understand that if ever any beauty I'd desired, and got – 'twas but a dream of her. That was an insult for which she never forgave me.

But what was I to do? I had been brought up – or at least I had brought myself up – to spare women. I had been accustomed to viewing the grossest distortion of truth as the subtlest form of tenderness. I produced a lie as another man might have produced a spray of flowers, as a mark of devotion, from the heart. I would never have dreamed of causing Sharon pain, for example, with accounts of what I'd done behind her back, and similarly I saw no reason for making other women miserable with the truth of my feelings for my wife. You see I felt that I owed them all something. Even in my blithest days with Sharon, when my heart rose as high as her skirts, I couldn't bear to punish all the others with her. I denied her for their sakes. I'd be happier with you, my eyes would say as I passed a stranger in the streets; and if that improved her day and Sharon was none the wiser, what then? Barney Fugleman, the spreader of underhand universal joy!

Camilla understood the implications of my constitutional incapacity for truth in these matters, from the start. 'If you can't come clean to me about your relations with other women, how are you ever going to come clean to your other women about your relations with me?'

I found that a difficult sentence to unravel but I believed I had the gist of it. 'There aren't any other women,' I assured her. 'There never will be any other women.'

'There you go again.'

'I'm sparing you,' I explained to her.

'What from?'

What from? I shrugged. How should I know what from? I was the liar in the house. I was the last one to ask. If she'd pressed me I might have said something like, 'From the chaos of the affections that causes my father to confuse names.' Which would have turned out to be a bit of a joke, considering that it was the chaos of Camilla's affections that finally confounded me. But she didn't press me to say it.

'Don't spare me, thanks,' she warned me instead.

But of course I did.

And of course I still do. I make my daily expiatory expeditions. I haunt the village and the weird shoreline, up the cliff, down, till I'm – well, till I'm what I want to be. I guard the rights of my remorse jealously. I can't be expected to give up everything that makes me a man.

4

1

I must be feeling better. Or at least I must be looking better. This morning, for the first time in months, Lance Tourney actually stopped and engaged me in conversation. Ever since I have been on my own, ever since Camilla has been known to be ... elsewhere, he has respected the privacy of my grief and simply nodded whenever we have come face to face. He has enjoyed the spectacle of me with my back bent and my eyes hollow, naturally – they all have – but he has not shown it except in the little extra pep he has put into his early morning exertion. He stretches just that bit higher these days, it seems to me, and he is just that touch more demonstrative and playful in his relations with the seals. It was the same throughout the winter months when the sea was too cold even for him to swim in and he would come flying past me in his running shorts, flapping his wrists by way of greeting and hurling himself into the wind – was I mistaken, or did I detect a more than usual resolution in him to master the air, just as surely as he'd mastered most other elements, in order to point the contrast with my leaden footedness? Far be it from me to suspect Lionel of anything, least of all of peeling off his shorts, layer after layer of them, just for me; but I do think that he gets down to his white satin posing pouch more quickly now as a consequence of his knowing that I'm out there limping and stooping amongst the crags.

This morning though – a lovely faintly stirring morning of early spring – I must have appeared more robust, because he found it necessary to accost me and get me to talk about him. I was scampering down the rocks, after a brisk guilt-laden but pleasantly un-muddy trek to Targan Bay and back, and Lionel was on a lower path, presumably making for his boat. There was absolutely no necessity for us to talk. A wave would have done the trick. But he called up to me, without any preliminary greeting, 'How am I looking?'

Looks are important to Lionel, even though I'm sure his own mother would agree he doesn't have any. They are given a whole section to themselves in *Lad of Destiny*, from which one sentence in particular has for some reason lodged itself in my mind. 'Vanity is a weakness, but so is self-neglect; remember to tense the buttocks hard whenever you are on the telephone or standing in a queue or otherwise not using the body.' I remember, too, Camilla's description of the one time she got to see inside his house. He lives in a prefabricated chalet, neighbourless and without electricity, at the very edge of Windy Beak. Here he keeps himself warm and fed by burning driftwood and cooking up bones begged from the village widows whom he charms, or wrenched from the jaws of the village dogs whom he terrifies. He isn't renowned for hospitality. Camilla had gone to see him to arrange boat trips up the coast for her students – if she could pack them off for an afternoon with Lionel she wouldn't have to talk to them herself – but he would only let her in on the understanding that there was to be nothing between them. 'I won't sleep with you unless I fall in love with you,' he told her, 'and there isn't much likelihood of that.' Camilla offered to shake hands on it but he wouldn't chance the contact. He was thinking of *her*. 'He's got an iron bar and a mirror over every doorway,' she swore to me, 'so that he can raise himself by his arms and see how he looks every time he passes from one room to the next.' I snorted. 'Don't laugh,' she said. 'Living in the country can do that to you. And at least he's not Cornish.'

I tried to recall Camilla's words this morning, as I gazed down on Lionel's sun-baked baldness. He was wearing his white walking shorts, which meant that there were four more pairs to go, and his matted primatial chest was bare. 'At least he's not Cornish,' I said to myself. And that helped me to say, 'You're looking fine, Lionel' to him.

'Someone just told me I was looking pale.'

'That's a calumny, Lionel.'

'You don't think I'm overdoing it?' Lionel has a habit of peppering you with questions about himself and then staring out to sea while you reply. Even when he has initiated the conversation he has a knack of making you feel that you're keeping him from where he'd rather be – from the three natural sources of his strength. Of course he could have utilized the time I was stealing from him this morning by clenching and unclenching his buttocks – unless that was the very thing he feared he might be overdoing.

'Overdoing what?' I asked.

He gave a wild laugh. 'Good question.' He made as if to leave me, brushing back the hair he didn't have. But then he turned back, as on an afterthought. 'How's your writing going?'

I shrugged. I had made the foolish mistake, when I first arrived in the village, of letting it be known that I was a contributor to learned journals, even though I hadn't contributed a single word since the day Sharon had me hypnotized. I don't know why I told anybody this; I can only suppose I didn't want to be thought of as Camilla's cleaner and nothing else. Since then the village has given me no peace. 'How's your writing going?' everyone wants to know, hoping to catch me out in a lie. 'What writing?' I am meant to be tricked into blurting out. Inhabitants of remote rural places don't believe that anybody that they know does anything that they don't. It hasn't endeared them to me that in my case they happen to be right.

It wasn't quite like that with Lionel, though. As Camilla had pointed out, he was his own man. He had a pen name himself. And he claimed that he had once come across a slashing piece of mine on the Brontës – not just the sisters but the whole family, great aunts, second cousins, the lot – in Plymouth reference library. So we might reasonably have had an author to author conversation out there on the rocks. Except that I have an aversion to that sort of thing.

'How's yours?' I enquired, without feeling.

'Ask me about sales.'

'How are sales?'

'Down.'

'I'm sorry.' I was, too. *Lad of Destiny* had been on sale for a few pence in every shop in the village – even the grocer sold it – ever since I could remember. It had gone into countless editions. If Lionel's sales were down then nothing could be accounted stable.

'Of course I used to do best at Camilla's place,' he said. 'Have you got any plans to re-open that?'

I shook my head. I must have been looking better all right. No one had mentioned Camilla's name in my hearing for months. And it was especially unexpected on Lionel Turnbull's lips. Because he'd been in a measure involved; he'd been there, or thereabouts when Camilla had . . . when it had happened.

'No, no plans,' I said. I remembered that I had a grievance against him and I was now pleased that sales were down. I hoped I could keep them that way.

'Pity. Well, I must be off. Are you sure you don't think I look as if I've been overdoing it?'

'Overdoing what, Lionel?'

He didn't stop to answer. 'Don't spend too much time with other people,' is the advice he gives to young boys in the final chapter of his guide to Health and Confidence. 'Because that's when you are most likely to lose control.' And besides, the healthful rays of the sun, the life-giving properties of the water, were beckoning. 'You've already asked me that,' he called back over his shoulder. 'You shouldn't keep repeating yourself.'

*   *   *

As if that wasn't enough to undo all the good work I'd put in on myself on the cliffs this morning, I no sooner got on to flat land and into the harbour approaches than I walked straight into Harry Vilbert, lounging against the wall of the Off Wessex Museum of Nugatory Spells and Superstitions. Harry too, as a testimony to my improved appearance, chose today to break our tacit vow of silence. He extended to me with difficulty a hand weighed down with copper bracelets – as he gets closer to sixty his battle against rheumatism and arthritis is hotting up – and when I offered him mine he slapped it as though we were a pair of black brothers meeting in the streets of Harlem. Only it wasn't the excitement of the city and our natural volatility that united us, it was Castle Boterel and melancholy. 'I know what you're going through,' it had been killing him not to say to me all these months. 'I'm going through it too.'

Harry first turned up here about four years ago. Needless to say, it had nothing to do with me. The Off Wessex Museum had advertised wherever such museums advertise – in the *Finchley Zoist and Astral Traveller*, I suppose – for a resident wart charmer, chiromancer, ticket collector, and general thaumaturgical dogsbody, and Harry had stolen the job, according to all accounts, from under the noses of some very strong candidates. Strange things have happened down here over the years – and I don't just mean strange in my mother's sense, that's to say involving my father and other women, but strange as in *really* strange – as a consequence of which many seasoned observers of the *really* strange have made the area their home. The queer white light that never left the sky on the night horses ate one another on Bodmin Moor, for example, doubled the rentable value of every derelict moorland cottage at a stroke. The bleeding stone in St Launce's churchyard, and the white parrot that was found on Parrett Down and could answer questions on the life and times of Queen Guinevere, had similar effects. There were a lot of experienced people in for the same job as Harry. Nonetheless, against all this stiff and, more significantly, *local* competition, he came through. In his own words, he interviewed like a man possessed and bloody well needed to. This was the last throw of the dice. He was in deep trouble. It was Castle Boterel or nowhere. On the occasion he told me that, he looked at me in a very knowing and personal way, as if I was supremely qualified to understand what he meant.

'What's wrong with Finchley?' I asked.

His eyes didn't leave mine for a second. I was struck by the terrible thought that he was intending to put me to sleep again. But in fact he wanted me wide awake. 'You should know,' he said. 'I left for the same reason you did.'

I honestly couldn't guess what he was hinting at. 'And what was that?' I wondered.

His eyes relaxed their hold on me and roamed over Camilla. She and I had been sitting in a corner of The Jolly Wreckers, arguing, when Harry had wandered in and recognized me. Camilla he didn't recognize. 'Women trouble,' he said.

I suddenly began to feel anxious. I couldn't remember what lies I'd tried to persuade Camilla to swallow about Sharon and Finchley and Fitzpiers. I'd sworn to her a thousand times that until I met her I'd never had women troubles, that I hadn't cared for any woman enough to be troubled by her. Sharon, she had to understand, was just a youthful error. Yes, all right, a youthful error with big tits, but still an error. Camilla didn't believe a word I said to her – by the time we'd known each other this long I couldn't even get her to trust me when I told her the time – but that still didn't mean that I could feel comfortable having Harry Vilbert at our table blurting out his version of my past.

'Well I don't know what troubles you've left in Finchley,' I said, coldly, 'but mine had nothing to do with women.'

Fortunately he was more interested in his life than he was in mine. 'Oh, I haven't left my troubles behind me,' he explained. I thought I caught the signs on his face of one of those implosions of idolatrous pride to which erotomaniacal men (erotoleptics, Hardy called them) are subject – especially when they are of advanced years and their teeth are going. We were at that stage where, if Harry *had* left his troubles in Finchley, we would have been compelled to look at photographs; as it was, since he'd brought them with him, I guessed correctly that we were about to be invited to meet them in the flesh.

'She'd be grateful for a visit,' he said. 'She hasn't been out since we got here. We're just up the hill in Myrtle Cottage. Will you come?'

Camilla would not be removed from a pub until a good two hours after closing time. 'Why don't you bring her here?' she suggested.

He gave us both a wild stare. 'I can't,' he said. I will never forget the way he managed to look defeated and defiant, crumpled and contemptuous, all at once. He pushed his face close to ours and somehow managed to get us huddled like conspirators. 'I daren't,' he whispered, when he was certain that no one else could hear.

Camilla and I exchanged glances. Each of us waiting for the other to do the decent indecent thing. 'Why?' we both asked together.

By this time Harry was in a state of high excitement. He was fingering the Nigg Stone at his neck. Sweat ran down the deep furrows in his cheeks. Even his grey hair, swept up and back now in the style of the more old-fashioned of the two Everly Brothers, glistened with perspiration. I don't think I've ever seen a person more in his element. Fire flashed at us from each of his old red eyes. But it was Camilla he was looking at. It was Camilla he wanted to inflame with his secret. 'She's under age,' he told her, in a voice rich with phlegm.

Actually, Harry wasn't involved in quite so much criminality as he wanted us to believe. Avice was only marginally younger than she ought to have been, and in another two and a half years would be able to accom-

263

pany Harry to the pub with impunity. As for the trouble
he was in, well it was true that Avice's parents had
kicked up a bit of a stink when Harry had first started
paying her serious attentions – she was thirteen and a
day then – but they had got used to him, and since Avice
was not making much progress at school they could
think of no really positive reasons why Harry shouldn't
carry her off to Castle Boterel. The thorough unpleas-
antness of her personality might have contributed to
their open-mindedness also. It certainly contributed to
that of the community of spell-casters into which, once
Harry felt relaxed about letting her out of the house, she
was thrown. Nothing could have been more touching
than the sweetness which those nicely brought up girls
in their painstaking plaits and vegetable-dyed cardigans
showed to Harry's under-age girlfriend as she ran
through all their menfolk, disrupting their rural quiet,
entirely misconstruing their principles of hospitality
and sharing. 'It's simply that she's in too much of
a hurry,' I remember Clemency Fanshawe saying to
Camilla and me, as she sat, beatific, with her loom
between her knees. 'Once she understands that everything she wants will be here for a long time, that no one
is going to take it away from her, then I'm sure she'll be
all right.' 'Perhaps she just wants to be with some
younger men,' I suggested. I promise, on the Bible, that I
wasn't offering that as a criticism of anybody, least of
all Harry. I knew what one could and couldn't say in
Clemency's company. But apparently I'd gone too far.
'Nobody is younger than Harry,' she reproved me.

Avice and I must have been two of a kind. She didn't
think there was nobody younger than Harry either. But I
still wouldn't have done what she did. I wouldn't have
spent the whole weekend (not the *whole* weekend) with
Clemency Fanshawe's acupuncturist husband, Priam,
and returned home to Harry on Monday morning with a
thousand tiny pin pricks on my body. I wouldn't have
been quite so trusting with Tarquin the tattooist either, I
wouldn't have permitted him so much scope and freedom

of artistic expression, so much licence, in his trans-mogrification of me into the great turning wheel of the Zodiac. And I certainly wouldn't have chosen my sixteenth birthday, the very day I was legal and entitled to buy my own cigarettes, to run away, back to Finchley of all places, with the headmaster of the local compre-hensive school at which Harry had enrolled me, in the evenings, to re-take my CSEs.

It hasn't been one of the village's prettier sights, over the last year or so, Harry Vilbert trudging up the hill to Myrtle Cottage on his own, a pathetically empty shop-ping bag hanging at his side. And don't think it hasn't crossed my mind that that's how I look every morning heading off towards Dundagel or the Cliff without a Name. Why do you think I've kept out of his way? Why do you think I was so displeased to run into him today when my guard was down? Until now I've been able to hold him at bay. Even on those mornings when we've been out on the cliffs together, him on one side of the harbour, me on the other, each of us perched on the skulls of those slumbering icthyosauri, looking out to sea, with nobody else awake except Lionel Turnbull, naked below us, reminding us of our common origins in rock and water – even then I've managed to avoid any kind of recognition or acknowledgement. I've been only too aware of what he was storing up to say to me the minute I showed any sign of being well enough to hear it, the minute I relaxed my vigilance and looked his way. 'Let's have a drink together one night. I know what it's like. I've been through it. The pain never goes away, but talking about it helps. Come round and see me. I'm always in. Where else am I going to be? We've got a lot in common, you and I. I knew that when I first regressed you. Do you remember that? It seems a lifetime ago, doesn't it?'

And that's exactly what he did say to me, a couple of hours ago, word for word – except for some stuff about the depth and dignity of a man's love and the intrinsic harlotry of women, which I don't choose to repeat.

To complete my morning's misadventures the phone was ringing when I got in, and when I picked it up I heard my mother saying, 'Hello darling, you're sounding much better today.'

So it looks as though I must accept the opinions of witnesses who are unlikely to have conferred: I *am* getting better.

My mother, of course, although she was exquisitely tactful and understanding and even (by her standards) reticent initially, is now actively willing me on to good health. I can detect a sort of preternaturally positive cheer-leader quality in her voice, whenever I speak to her, as if, over the air waves, she is rallying my genes or corpuscles or whatever it is that can make me strong again. She hasn't liked my grieving over Camilla. It isn't personal – she didn't get on with Camilla on the one occasion they met, that's true – but she wouldn't have liked me grieving over any woman. 'You've sacrificed the best years of your life to girls,' she stung me by saying on the phone only last week. 'You're a big disappointment to us,' she even tried, during the same conversation.

I didn't ask who 'us' meant. The environs of the personal pronoun are pretty treacherous territory up in Finchley just at this moment. My parents' and the Flatmans' divorces are now through, but there are occasional ruptures of the new alliances, followed by abrupt and baffling restorations of the old, and in between times complete outsiders, total strangers as far as I can see, briefly assume positions of importance. The clearest picture I can get is that Mr Flatman is, in the main, a regular companion of my mother's now – they had a week in Ibiza together only recently, and they've been back to Positano countless times – but he isn't always the other half of what she means by 'we'. It referred for a while, for example, to herself and a visiting American rabbi who was already married to someone else. 'Can rabbis do that?' I asked. I was genuinely surprised. There was a long silence on the other end of the phone. I could hear my mother trying to decide whether she had enough credibility left as a matron to deliver the line, 'Do *what*, Barney?' I think I must have waited a full five minutes before I heard her say, 'He's a reform rabbi, Barney', instead.

It's not likely, therefore, that I was a disappointment to *him*; reform rabbis, from what I've heard, don't bruise easily. Just who it is, then, that I am a disappointment to, remains in some doubt. Unless it is Asimova.

It was Asimova, as usual, that my mother wanted to talk to me about today. 'You should see her,' she said, as part of the same sentence in which she told me how much better I was sounding.'You should see how big she is now.'

Asimova, as I'm sure it is not necessary for me to explain, is the child Sharon was carrying when our marriage broke up. Sharon's confidence, as expressed to me through her lawyers, that she was, Tryphena-like, carrying a boy (a Hardy boy), turned out to be unfounded. Asimova – Asimova Wollstonecraft Ursula, to be exact – is a little girl, and not so little these days either, if my mother's astonishment at the rate of her growth is anything to go by. Though why she thinks that her size will somehow endear her to me I don't know. Towards Asimova I have, naturally, no feelings, except in so far as I am relieved for her sake that her mother was wrong and that she wasn't a boy. Arthur C Ballard Pohl Fitzpiers – and that's generously assuming that they'd resisted Moorcock – is not a blight I'd have wished on anyone, no, not even on Fitz and Sharon's offspring.

That last phrase is not meant to be contentious. I am simply unable to think of Asimova as in any way belonging or connected to me. Sharon had assured me, as she has since forcibly assured my mother, that the child was mine; she just knew, she said – 'A woman just knows these things.' But she had claimed a similar mystic knowledge about the embryo's sex, where she had a one in two chance of being right, and she hadn't put up a good showing there. So there was no reason for me to trust her on the question of paternity where, on account of those SF wife-swapping parties, the odds were that much longer. My own bet was that the child was Fitz's. Don't ask me why – a man just knows these things. It's true that Fitz's first love was for other people's babies, but he had so much else of mine already that I believed he was prepared to sacrifice his first passion to his second, that's to say the supplanting of others to the perpetuation of himself. Indeed he was so keen for himself to continue, ad infinitum, in those last months the three of us spent together, that I think he would have impregnated me if it had been possible and if he could have been certain that I'd have let him see the baby.

But let's say that Asimova was mine biologically, let's say that she had my looks and my brain and my good nature, let's even say that she lacked linguistic aptitude, disliked going outside the house, and wanted to give all her toys away – was that any reason for me to be proudly and paternally possessive? Surely, for someone who found all family resemblance the painful trial that I did, the opposite had to be the case. If we are to be logical and consistent about this, wouldn't she have stood a better chance of winning my affection if she had resembled Rowland Fitzpiers? What did I want with a child that had me as a father?

Not that Sharon and Fitzpiers – let there be absolutely no mistake about this – were pressing me to take Asimova from them. A more doting pair of parents, according to every report that came my way, could not be found. I'm sure that Fitzpiers would have fought me with his fists if I'd dared to come near the child, let alone suggest that she might spend a summer fishing with me in Castle Boterel. So what were they up to? Why did a new photograph of the growing Asimova arrive through my letter box – through Camilla's letter box, rather – every fortnight? And why, once a year, did Sharon's solicitors write to remind me of the presumption of legitimacy law and Asimova's birthday? I can only suppose that what they wanted was a cheque. To help defray the cost of their rapture. It seemed to burn a hole in Sharon's brain that Asimova hadn't cost me anything. 'Why should he get off scot-free?' she asked every one who knew me. We appear to share a basic assumption after all, Sharon and I, even though our vocabularies differ: we both agree that propagation ought to hurt.

As for my mother, her interest in the subject isn't difficult to fathom. For a start she is hurt. My lack of enthusiasm for what comes after she takes as a slur on what went before. In fact she is no more in love with her own image than reason – notwithstanding Mr Flatman – tells her she should be; but the other side of self-dislike is self-assertion – if you can't join them, beat them – the practical consequence of which is that she wants her likeness (my likeness, our likeness, it's all one) stamped far and wide on generation after hungry generation. The ideology of proliferation is native to all oppressed peoples. Thus my indifference to Asimova was not just unnatural, it was bad politics.

'You should see her – she's almost up to my shoulder,' my mother informed me this morning.

Well, she'd chosen a bad time to ring. 'Mother, so is Menashe Flatman,' I told her. 'And I don't want to hear anything about him either.'

With which I put the phone down on her.

More guilt.

3

And Camilla? Did she not encourage me to send little pink woolly bootees and musical nursery mobiles up to Finchley, on the off-chance that it was in fact one lone long-swimming spermatozoon of mine that was the cause of all the loving care and consternation which day and night shook the Sharon-Fitzpiers ménage?

Did Camilla not stay my hand as I was about to toss the latest of the fortnightly photographs into the bin, and

269

urge me to position it instead alongside all the other memoranda of the heart that filled our mantelpiece?

Did she not whisper in my ear, as we lay without our clothes beneath the waterfall or in a field beside a tree in Parret Down, 'A father's love is even more sacred yet, my dear,' and get me, trouserless, to write the little one a hefty cheque?

No.

4

In order to discover whether I had it in me to deliver a straight sentence Camilla deliberately refused to remember who Asimova was.

'Who's this Assimovna person?' she would ask me, when the name, perchance, arose.

For me that was like being asked to give the plot of all three parts of the *Oresteia* in one sentence. And I had to censor it too, don't forget. Camilla had to be spared as well as enlightened. 'You remember Sharon,' I would say. 'Well she claimed . . .'

Camilla always stopped me here. 'You mean this Akimono is your daughter?'

'It's not as simple as that,' I was at pains to explain. 'You have to remember that relations between Sharon and . . .'

'Yes, yes, so she's *not* your daughter.'

That didn't seem to me quite to get it either. 'Things are not so black and . . .'

'Yes they are. It's only with you that they're not. But I'll tell you what: if you ever do work out your relations to this – what's her name again? Quasimodo? – write them down so that we can both remember.'

I never failed to get angry at this point. It didn't matter where we were. We could be sitting in the grass in the valley at sunset, with squirrels running over our feet. 'I know precisely what my relations to Asimova are,' I would thunder. Most women would have quaked, believe me.

Camilla, though, didn't turn a hair or bat an eyelid.

270

'Barney, *you* don't know what your relations are to your own prick,' she would tell me.

But she was wrong there: I knew a state of grovelling subservience when I saw one.

Taken all round, relations – the actual people themselves as well as the abstract idea – were not our best subject. And that wasn't only because Camilla wasn't keen on mine – 'I only wasn't keen because you weren't clear,' I can hear her objecting – but anyway, whatever she was to mine she was positively barbarous towards her own.

'Good!' I remember hearing her exclaim when she received the news that her brother had turned his sports car over (I think he drove a Triumph Stag) at a busy intersection.

'Pity!' I remember her saying to herself when she learnt that he was only scratched.

I met Camilla's brother just once. He boycotted our relationship for some reason best known to himself – 'Don't investigate it,' Camilla advised me – but came down here to see her when his fourth or fifth marriage broke up. He drove straight from the divorce court, without stopping for so much as a cup of tea, and claimed a new world land-speed record. I had no means of checking that, but his wheels smoked for two hours after he arrived. I had no means of checking the number of children (all boys) who stared out of the passenger windows either, every one of whom, Camilla assured me, was his. Like many aggressively suicidal men he was consumed by the need to duplicate and reduplicate himself. In a fairer world my mother would have had him for a son.

'I see you're still looking petite,' he said to Camilla the moment they met.

'And I see you're still overpopulating the globe with little fat versions of yourself,' she replied, opening the car doors and allowing her swarming nephews to roll into the village street.

'There are some you haven't met. Hank, Simeon, Victor, Rocky, Vidor, Zed, come here. Jason, show your

271

Aunty Camilla your muscles.'

'I'm pleased you're still concentrating your fatherly energies on bringing them up to be sweet-natured.'

'Just like their Aunty. But what about you? Not able to have any yourself?'

'Not choosing to. One of us has to do something about stamping us out.'

'Why don't you get fucked?' he asked, kissing her on both cheeks.

'He seems a nice kind of person,' I remarked to Camilla after he'd left.

She sat and shook for twenty minutes before she said, 'My earliest memory of my brother is of him trying to choke me with my pillows. My next memory is of him kicking me all the way to school and all the way back home again. If he found me in the playground he would pull my hair and tear up my books. At weekends he stole my pocket money. He also threw my violin out of the window and poisoned my fish. I have a bruise on my back today where he hit me with his cricket bat. When I got a little older he charged his friends a penny each to spy on me in the bath. Though as soon as I started my periods he let them watch me free. The drop in my value was related entirely to his psychology. My periods sickened him. He complained that I smelt. He wouldn't let me touch him; he plastered himself against walls when I passed. He invented a nickname for me – the Camel. When I brought my first boy friend home he told him that my underwear wasn't clean. Tell me what kind of sisterly regard I ought to show him.'

I shook my head. I didn't know. Christian families were a mystery to me. 'Why didn't your parents restrain him?' was the best I could think of saying.

'My mother was too busy trying to work out what had gone wrong with her own life to notice.'

'And your father?'

Camilla looked at me wearily. 'On whose behalf do you think my brother was acting?'

I wasn't having that. 'Come off it, Camilla. You're

272

not saying your brother was your father's psychic emissary?'

'I'm saying my father set a tone in our household that was conducive to such behaviour as my brother's. My father was contemptuous of both of us, but especially of me. I was a "no-hoper" every time I lifted a finger; I was a "bloody idiot" every time I opened my mouth. That was until I won an essay prize, a violin award, a swimming race, and my breasts shot out – all in one day. Suddenly there was this thing called paternal pride in the house. I was appalled by it. I caught him looking me over one morning, his eyes glistening with love and admiration. I shot him a glance that was so witheringly disdainful that he has never dared to look at me since.'

I sighed. Partly for Camilla. Partly for her father.

'What are you making that noise for? Do you think I should be more affectionate? Tell me how affectionate you feel towards yours.'

'I haven't seen any of my family for some time,' I reminded her. 'I'm a bit far from home.'

'Aren't you ever! And why do you suppose that is?'

I sighed again. Entirely for myself.

But Camilla wouldn't let me off. 'Come on – tell me how affectionate you feel every time your mother rings you up and informs you how big Haji Baba's growing. Come on – come clean – tell me how you handle it.'

'There's nothing to handle,' I explained. 'We've never gone in for the sort of violence that . . .'

'You mean you all love one another?'

'Not exactly, but . . .'

'Not exactly? Barney, you're hopeless. You couldn't tell the truth if your life depended on it.'

5

I think it's time I set the record straight about my reputation for dishonesty. I was nothing like so big a liar as Camilla said I was, or indeed as I allowed her to say I was. I don't know whether the fact that I lied about my

273

lying means that I was more honest than I pretended to be, or less, but the truth is that I encouraged Camilla not to trust me in order to make myself more interesting to her. I wanted to frighten her with duplicity – that's to say with the double-deception of my duplicity – in exact proportion as she frightened me with truth. One can only fight with the weapons that one has; the truth of Camilla's life – her teeming past (of which she spared me not a solitary gasp or shudder), the volatility of her present (the ever beckoning black rock, the saucy fiddling fishermen, the never-absent threat that I might be banished to the sleeping bag) – quite simply riveted me; the truth of my life was therefore simply that: I was riveted. Remember the hammer and the anvil? I had gone one better – I was the rivet in between. I was put in my place, beaten, hammered, heated, and secured. And I liked it. I thrilled to every thwack. I got up in the morning, hung over the sink, returned to find the banquet of Camilla either spread or not spread for me, put in eight hours fighting back the damp that rose up the walls of the Alternative Centre for Thomas Hardy Studies, and came home at night and waited for the blow to fall. If the English language had never so far needed the word uxoriating, it needed it then, because that was what I was doing, long before I was a husband – luxuriating in the supremacy of a wife. I was an uxoromaniac, a luxoriator, a disenfranchised subject under close house arrest of the despotic state of Luxorembourg. Which was fine for me but not so good – I wasn't a fool – for Camilla. Nothing bores a despot quicker than a vassal. Why else are they always restless and sad-eyed? I knew full well that I didn't dare look the thing I was. So I lied a bit. I let it look as though I was somethng else entirely. I affected the air of a man who kept secrets. I ran downstairs early to collect the mail and made frantic rustling sounds and stuffed innocuous circulars into my back pockets. 'What are you hiding?' Camilla would demand to know, as I did a perfect imitation of dripping guilt. And sometimes, just to add starch and leavening to my performance, I would slip away and do the thing I wasn't really lying when I said I had no stomach for. I didn't dare get caught, of course, with my hands on the hips of Trixie Trewarmett who pulled pints behind the bar of The Unwelcome Traveller and called me 'Me 'andsome', but I equally didn't dare be believed when I swore I would never dream of doing such a thing. If Camilla had once got wind that I was telling the truth – that's when I *was* telling the truth – then it would have been all up with us. On those rare occasions that I slipped away to give myself something actual to lie about, I was doing it for her – and that *is* the truth.

5

I

I expected it to take a lot longer myself, given everything that's happened, but it really does look as though I'm on the mend. Today, for example, I have not only been through two whole drawers of Camilla's private papers *plus* a shoebox of letters without shedding more than a thimbleful of tears, I have also ventured at last into that tea chest marked 'Matrimonial' which I have for so long sedulously avoided. In fact, thanks to Camilla's comprehensive candour about her past, I didn't discover anything I didn't know already; but knowing that Camilla had once been married to a Polish seaman who looked like her brother, a septuagenarian opium pusher with dead book-keeper's eyes, just like her father's, as well as Jaimie the tractor driver and an Irish pedlar called Dinny (yes, she had been Camilla O'Meara for a whole fortnight) and a convicted multiple arsonist of whom the Kray twins were said to be in awe, was not the same as seeing photographs of them in their suits with carnations in their buttonholes. I breathed heavily, I can tell you, when I came to the set taken outside Parkhurst, which showed Camilla looking radiant in her white straw hat (she always married in the same hat, for luck) alongside her fire-crazed groom, a couple of smiling watchful warders, and, if I'm not mistaken, one or other of the twins evincing the sort of entrepreneurial concern that goes with being best man.

I breathed heavily but I didn't break up. I flicked

through all the old marriage certificates. I held up to the light the assorted unreturned rings – wedding and engagement and eternity – which Camilla had tied together with a piece of pink ribbon, the romantic. And I respected the instinct that had led her to assemble a little album of tangible memories – a sprig of Irish heather, some dried pressed blackthorn, the wrapper from a stick of Polish sausage, a letter of rejection from the parole board, and an envelope of dope. I didn't harm anything, is what I'm saying, least of all myself. Which can only mean that I am much more robust than I was. A month ago I wouldn't have been able to stop myself flinging the photograph of the arsonist into the fire.

And since I am feeling better, I am going to chance tackling a subject long owing to me as a special treat and one without reference to which no explanation of what kept and still keeps me in Castle Boterel can be complete.

I am referring, of course, to Camilla as a banquet.

Here's hoping that I have not been premature and that my health is indeed up to it.

For all the depth and range of her experience, for all the decorations she'd earned and all the despatches she'd been mentioned in, Camilla was not what even her most ardent admirers would have called a busy lover. She bore no resemblance, for example, to those gadfly women who tear from one end of a man's body to another in a fever of ambition and virtuosity, like a circus plate-spinner, pledged to the tremendous feat of keeping everything up and whirring at the same time – and who, by the by, I lied to Camilla that I had never found particularly satisfactory myself. She did not belong either to that gentler but more rhapsodic band who seek to extract strange worshipful music from the male, the xylorimbists or tympanists or flute players. Essentially – although she was the one who had quite literally kicked us off, prodded me with her big toe while I lay unconscious on her floor, and zipped me clean out

277

of her sleeping bag – essentially she was receptive rather than dynamic. She spread herself each morning as if she were a banquet, succulent, sumptuous, formal (she was always a black tie affair, Camilla), and therefore – since it is not in the nature of banquets that they sit up and bite you back – passive.

.That's not meant to sound in any way like a complaint. I did not begrudge Camilla her passivity. I was, as I approached my thirtieth year, a different person from the boy who spied on Rabika Flatman as she swung from the crossbar of her hammock and hoped that she would hoist him up on to her nipple as a punishment. I was nearing maturity. With the help of Dawn from Brisbane I now knew what I reasonably could and couldn't expect a woman to do to me. In a sense it was Dawn who sounded the knell over the hopeless optimism of my youth. She was my last fling with the idea of athletic womanhood. Camilla, it's true, was irresistibly bellicose; I knew when I came down here that I might never get back. Why else did I spurn the booking-clerk's offer of a cheap period return? But I never imagined for one moment – I didn't dare – that she went in for hand-to-hand combat. Camilla was an intellectual: she did for you with ideas. So I am not saying that I was in the least surprised or disappointed by the absence in her of erotogenic attack. In so far as I had a complaint, it was no more than this: not satisfied with just being a banquet, Camilla insisted on doubling also as her own doorman, major domo, and chief butler, and each of those was determined to out-stickle the others for the punctilios of ceremony. I simply wasn't allowed to gourmandize in peace. A firm hand guided me – I mean that literally – through all the fine points of etiquette and precedence. I was in trouble if my manners were sloppy, I was bawled out if I rushed or missed a course. Not since I was a boy on a raised chair at the barber's could I remember my head being so forcibly twisted from one uncomfortable position to another. I must say that I never came away from Camilla's creaking board

278

hungry, but I never came away without severe external bruising of the pericranium either.

This, however, is mere cavilling. The real misery I suffered, chose to go on suffering, and still suffer willingly today – the real *glory* of my wretchedness was not caused by this or that physical disappointment or discomfort, it was brought about by the painful, thrilling, irrefragable truth inherent in the very spectacle itself, of the woman I loved laid out as for a ceremonial banquet: CEREMONIAL BANQUETS ARE NOT NORMALLY LAID FOR *ONE*.

It was unmistakable from the lavishness of Camilla's spread – a blind vegetarian could not have missed it – that she regarded herself not merely as a morsel for a monarch but as nourishment for a whole line of kings, that she believed her natural abundance obliged her, even against the dictates of her anti-egalitarian politics, to feed the five thousand. And that the five thousand, by the same natural law, owed her something in return. She convinced me of that, utterly, without having to advance a single line of argument. Time and again, as I approached her and looked on the profusion of her flesh – it was a remarkable detail, never lost on me, that her breasts retained their full rotundity, didn't in the slightest bit subside or spill, when she lay stretched out on her back, and that the springing hairs of her sex (my health can take one more remarkable detail) scorned the usual triangular arrangement favoured by conventional women, climbing instead the slopes of her belly, straggling the soft downs of her thighs, like uncultivated vines – time and again, I say, when I feasted on all this, I felt pity for her, that I was only me, and shame for myself, that I wasn't a crowd. Naturally I didn't let on. I wasn't such a fool as to blubber out an apology. I didn't drop to my knees (I was usually already on them anyway) and cry, 'Forgive me, I'm afraid I've come on my own again.' But I knew in my heart, and I suspect Camilla knew I knew, that I was a poor substitute for a party.

Whatever else I loved Camilla for, whatever miraculous conjunction of spirit, word, and flesh, had found its way into my soul, I loved her most intensely for her incontestable right to be loved by others – or to put that another way, for her capacity to loose the devils of rivalry against me. She didn't even need to whisper in my ear; she had only to stretch herself out to her full length on the bed, precisely as I have just stretched her, for me to feel that adversaries past and present, ghostly and imminent, were coming at me from everywhere. I could hear them thumping up Camilla's fourteenth-century staircase. I could see them prising out the panes from Camilla's tiny leaded windows. It was with an exquisite sensation of inadequacy that I drew my weapon afresh each time, certain of nothing but comprehensive defeat. Barney Fugleman – love's warrior – alone and lightly armed in the continuum.

Against the charge that I was seeing phantoms and defending myself unnecessarily, I will not unnecessarily defend myself. This is love I'm describing, not reason. And my subject is Camilla as a banquet. Would that the whole camp, foot soldiers and all, had tasted her sweet body, love puts it into Othello's mind half to dread, half to hope; but nobody leaps onto the stage to complain that Desdemona is too diminutive to go round. And Desdemona wouldn't have been half Camilla's size. I have seen men in thrall to anorexic midgets, similarly wracked, their lives made a perpetual torment by the belief that a press of hungry rivals cannot wait to sink its teeth into the lean meat of their felicity. What does one do? Tell them that they're imagining things? How will they be able to keep their own appetites keen then? Competition – fierce, unhealthy competition – is as necessary to possessive love as guilt and jealousy are to good adultery. Consider, without going into the usual politics of how they got there, the last couple left on earth: what better reason for cherishing a mutual passion would they have (ruling out philanthropy) than the first? Adam's and Eve's is no one's idea of a moving love story, and if it ever can be said to develop erotic interest, it is only when they prick their ears to a third party, rustling in the grass. For one obvious reason neither the Garden of Eden nor the Plain of Armageddon provides the right environment for romance – each lacks the necessary piquancy of populousness.

Romantic lovers: Thank the snake.

Oh, and ban the Bomb.

2

'One day,' I said to Camilla as we were walking along the beach at Stratleigh, she with her jeans rolled up, despite the cold, enjoying the water on her legs, me in a less harmonious frame of mind, tossing pebbles back into the sea – 'One day, someone, and preferably not another Shakespeare (we know what he thinks), should tell the story of what would have happened to Othello if he'd had his dread/wish granted.' I didn't need to explain to Camilla what I meant; we knew each other's thoughts well now, and she had heard me before on the subject of feeding the love of one's life to one's troops.

'Yes,' she said, without even stopping to think about it, 'from Desdemona's point of view.'

I smelt trouble instantly. 'What's the difference?' I wanted to know. 'Wouldn't they all be getting roughly the same thing out of it?'

'No, Barney, not necessarily. Contrary to your idea of what all women are busting to do if only men as magnanimous as you would let them, it's just possible that Desdemona wouldn't get anything out of it at all. It's also possible that she'd resent the pressure.'

'Pressure?'

'Pressure.'

'Well there's gratitude.'

Camilla answered that with only a look. Albeit a pretty murderous look. We were fighting, as might be gathered. What about? Pressure, I suppose. Pressure from me. But I'll come to that.

281

I stayed where I was, at the water's edge, trying to get just one of the smooth stones I'd collected to skim lightly across the surface. My failure to do this was irritating Camilla. 'Are you trying to kill fish, or what?' she asked me.

I was glad when she left me alone and went to sit on a cluster of rocks with her book. She was having to re-read *Tess of the D'Urbervilles* for a new course she was giving, and I ascribed much of her ill-temper to that. She was unapproachable when she read Hardy, more difficult to get along with even than when she was expecting, enduring, or recovering from a period. I'd had to get out of the cottage for a whole week-end when she re-read *Jude the Obscure*. That, in fact, was the week-end that had put each of us seriously out of sorts with the other. I'd borrowed her car and driven up to Finchley to see how things were going with my delin-quent parents, both of whom, but separately, were lob-bying me intensely on behalf of the Flatmans – both of whom, but separately, were anxious for me to prove that my long exile was not because of them. It turned out to be an unusual week-end.

I had read about tug-of-love children in the newspap-ers, but I had never supposed that at the age of thirty I would be one of them. 'You really must stay with us,' my father and Rabika insisted. 'What do you want to stay there for?' my mother and Menashe demanded. 'Do you want them to think you're condoning what they've done? Your old bed's made up here.'

On the Saturday my father and Rabika took me shop-ping. Rabika chose me a tie and my father, who wasn't certain what my interests were, offered to buy me a pair of boxing gloves in one shop and a waterproof watch for deep-sea divers in another. He couldn't believe it when I turned down a judo outfit. Finally, since I didn't want trouble, I accepted motoring gloves and all the ice creams there were going. If it had been the right time of the year they'd have paid for me to go into Selfridge's grotto and sit on Father Christmas's knee. I'm certain I could have got a whole electric train set out of them if I'd asked. My mother and Menashe were no less lavish. When I went round there on the Sunday morning (in order to remain impartial and to give Camilla something to think about I hadn't stayed at either establishment), I found a breakfast table laden with my favourite Finchley foods – slightly burnt bagels, gafelbeiters, sweet and sour cucumbers, smetana and kes, blintzes – all the little delicacies, as my mother pointed out, that I couldn't get in Castle Boterel or Tooting. In the afternoon they took me to Regent's Park Zoo, watched me watching the monkeys, and bought me even more ice creams than I'd been bought the day before. All in all, it really would have been difficult for me, supposing I'd been forced to make a choice, to decide which pair of parents I loved the most.

But later that second afternoon, after I'd come round from a snooze of surfeit on the sofa and found my mother and Menashe hovering over me with concerned looks and expensive bottles of spirits bought duty free in Positano, I caught them out in an act of near unpardonable duplicity. 'Why don't you go up to your old bedroom and see what's waiting for you in your old wardrobe?' my mother suggested, once we'd had a drink or two, toasting one another, certain absent friends (but not certain others), and the State of Israel. Given Menashe's generosity to me in the past, to say nothing of his glistening attentiveness to me right now, I expected to find nothing less than a 30,000 piece jig-saw and a big bundle of twenty pound notes waiting for me where I used to hang my school blazer. (And where, incidentally, it still hangs.) Imagine how I felt then, when in the very nick of time, just as I was about to turn the knob of my old wardrobe, the smothered cries of an infant warned me that what was waiting for me was nothing other than Asimova, growing by the minute and borrowed for the afternoon (I didn't believe Sharon was in there with her) in order to soften the conscience and break the heart of the man who would not let her call him daddy. I didn't stop to wonder how long she'd been in the wardrobe. I was down those stairs, into that car, and on to that motorway, quicker than if I'd been Camilla's brother.

I drove home – was not Castle Boterel my only home now? – at breakneck speed, thankful at least for my new motoring gloves and trying to calculate as I went Camilla's likely progress with Jude, the obscure boy who had got me into this. I didn't think it would be all over with him by the time I got back – the letter killeth, but not that quickly – but I reckoned, computing at a generous number of pages to the mile, that it would be close, that with a bit of luck she would be round about the place, give or take a groan, where the dying Jude interweaves the words of Job with the cheers of the naturally unfeeling Oxford undergraduates. But instead of finding her almost finished when I came screeching into the driveway and honked my horn, instead of finding her hunched over her desk, bleary eyed but pleased to see me back safe and early, I found the book tossed into a corner, open at page three, and her, Camilla, out.

Let the day perish wherein I was born, I came pretty close to saying. I hate coming home to an empty house at the best of times, but when I'm hungry and tired, when I've been driving for five hours without a stop, when I have been subjected to gross family indelicacy, and when the house I've come home to is in fact a converted cow-shed with deserted fields to its rear and the blank sea in front – well, *Why died I not from the Womb?*

3

I don't know what time it was when she got home – I'd gone to bed already myself – but I judged from the smell of alcohol that came in with her that it must have been late. Camilla staggering was an awesome sight. It was also dangerous if you happened to be anywhere near anything she might stagger into. The bed, as I knew from experience, was the worst place, because although she couldn't locate the rest of her furniture she would make for that out of brute instinct. I got out quickly and helped her to fall in. The other disgusting thing about Camilla when she was drunk was that she instantly became sentimental about her family. I have seen her in a heap on the floor, hiccoughing and choking, unable to keep a pen between her fingers, trying to write a letter of reconciliation to her father at four in the morning. Tonight, in the pitch black and not much earlier, she wanted to telephone her brother. 'We're so like each other,' I think she said. But I wouldn't swear to it. I wasn't really listening. The words I wanted to hear – 'Hello, darling, I've missed you terribly, let me make you some supper even though I'm thoroughly pissed which I know I have no right to be, and apologize for' – were not forthcoming, and I wasn't interested in any others. I didn't think having my nose pinched and being called a humourless prick was particularly amusing either. And I didn't want to get into an argument about whether or not that proved I was a humourless prick. So I left her to search for the holes in the dial of the telephone without me, collected the sleeping bag from the bottom of the airing cupboard, and felt my way downstairs – where I was surprised to find a person I had never seen before making himself toast in Camilla's kitchen.

'Hi, I'm Tarquin,' he announced, seemingly quite unperturbed to be discovered. A year or so later he was to become the best known vegetable dye tattooist in the area, thanks largely to the work he did on Harry Vilbert's under-age girlfriend, Avice; but at this stage in his career he was still travelling from place to place, trying to find himself, and enjoying no reputation to speak of.

I just stared at him.

'I'm really hungry,' he continued, accompanying his words with that slightly simple smile and nod of the head, much favoured as a sign of shared artlessness and brotherhood by peace-and nature-loving peoples the world over.

I must confess to nursing a resistance to that sort of

smile. I don't like being dragged into brotherhood willy-nilly. Camilla, on the other hand, had no trouble with it. She was a patrician by nature but she got on well with the alternative culture and shared its interest in beans and rice. I had no doubt, for example, that she had found Tarquin in a pub, liked the look of him, bought him drinks all night, and finally invited him back, as her guest, to help himself to toast. It wasn't a puzzle to me that he had called out what was altruistic in her. He had a sweet, lost face. Behind all the hair he had soft, brown eyes. I wanted to do something for him myself. But I wanted to do something *to* him more. Not for the first time in the company of someone who had studiedly turned himself into a waif, I felt a violent polarity of instincts in me: I was half Jesus Christ, wanting to give him food and shelter and unforgettably pithy advice, and I was half Raskolnikov, believing that to such a person, who seemed to hold himself of so little account in the world, I could – and should – do whatever I wanted.

It's unlikely that he knew what I was thinking. He believed we were all brothers under the skin. But I hadn't spoken to him yet and he must have thought I needed reassuring that he wasn't a burglar. 'Hey, it's okay,' he said. 'I've cleared it with your chick.'

I still didn't say anything.

'She *is* your chick, isn't she?'

The idea of my Camilla as a *chick*, the idea that she could be seen in such a light by this hopeless hairy boy with patches on his jeans, affected me powerfully. It will save time and spare me some painful recollections if I say that I felt precisely as I had on that famous afternoon in Soho when that pillar of Sicilian respectability fingered my photographs of Sharon, scrutinizing them from this angle and from that. Now, as then, something old and sweet rose to the back of my throat. Now, as then, the solid ground of my passion – pride, possession, fondness, respect – fell away from under me. Chaos had come again to the life of the affections. Only this time – I was mature now, don't forget – I knew what to do. I had

286

a brown-eyed hungry visitor on my hands – fine. Above me a drunken banquet was laid out, going to waste. Also fine. I didn't have to choose between being Jesus Christ or Raskolnikov, did I – I could be both.

Gently, but firmly, I pushed Tarquin in the direction of the stairs.

I won't go into the details of our negotiations. I would rather not remember my words, and apart from really and hassle and hey, I can't remember his. The only thing I will mention is that when he was half-way up the staircase he stopped, looked down over his shoulder at me, smiled that stupid smile of universal solidarity in simple-mindedness, and said, 'Wow!'

To this day I remain in ignorance of what, thereafter, took place. I had given Tarquin five minutes to disappear from sight and stop his head from shaking, before slipping out of the cottage myself. I had made a decision in favour of the ocular over the auricular, as Hardy might have said, and planned to sit on the garden gate and watch from there. In fact the cottage was so low that it was possible to see into the bedroom window just by standing on a small stone. But I wanted to be comfortable and I didn't want to miss anything. The only trouble was that there was nothing to see. The curtains were closed (I'd forgotten that I'd drawn them myself when I got home, to spite Camilla who preferred them open), all the lights were off, and there was not a movement of a shadow or a silhouette to be discerned. Outside, the night was black and cold. The same hugely indifferent moon that had looked down on me when I hung out of the lavatory window at Finchley, straining for a view of Sharon and Fitzpiers, looked down on me again. From where she was – the moon was definitely a 'she' tonight, seductive behind wisps of gauze-like cloud – Finchley and Castle Boterel must have seemed quite close. In the distance the Lundy lighthouse winked at me at approximately seven second intervals. The insane sea boomed away, frightening no one. The great lyers-low and watchers-over – Oak and Winterbourne and the Reddleman – were out there somewhere, silently waiting their turn. Not a sound issued from Camilla's bedroom. I decided to give up and go back inside, but when I came to try the door it was securely locked against me. So was the back entrance. So were all the windows. I thought about waking up the house – raising the alarm, as it's called in adventure novels, where things are easier – then I thought better of it. If I hadn't been afraid of bats and snakes I would have tried to get some rest in the outside toilet, where my friend who liked to adopt the prone position under the roofs of the eminently articulate had once spent the night. But he'd at least had a sleeping bag whereas mine – that's to say Camilla's – was locked inside the cottage along with Tarquin.

I took a turn around the garden, not knowing what to do. I felt poignantly towards myself. Back in Tooting I had found my father and Mrs Flatman more than ever mutually engrossed. I had noticed that Rabika had bites on her neck and carried her arm in a sling and walked with a slight limp. 'We've just bought a hammock,' she had informed me, while my father was paying for my motoring gloves. I tried to imagine Camilla on her bed, with her toes erect, and wondered how far apart, at this very moment, the left toes were from the right. Finally, too tired for prepositions, I went back into the lane and passed the second half of the night exactly as I'd passed the first, in the front seat of Camilla's draughty old MG.

Camilla didn't address a single word to me for three days. On the fourth she delivered me a simple warning. 'Don't ever do that again!' Something in her voice told me that she wasn't referring to my having spent the night in her sports car.

I know very well that I ought to have been grateful that she had decided to speak to me at all. I know – I would be a fool if I didn't – that I ought to have been relieved to have got off so lightly, with so little in the way of recrimination and reprisal. It could, after all, very easily have been a week in the polyester bag for me. And I recognize that even if I was lost to diplomacy, good taste should have prevailed upon me to lie low and say nothing for a while. But what's gratitude and relief, what's diplomacy, what's good taste for Christ's sake, when curiosity will have its way? It was all very well for me to be told what I'd better not do again, but if we were going to enter into a discussion about doing, then what about her – what had *she* done? I hadn't seen Tarquin since he had turned and smiled at me on the stairs, but even if I had I wouldn't have asked him. It was from Camilla that I wanted to hear it. And preferably in the dark. 'Tell me,' I dared her over breakfast. 'Tell me,' my eyes implored her whenever we passed, even in the corridors of her school. 'Tell me,' I begged her in the kitchen and in the garden and in the bed. But she invariably shook her head and went on with whatever she was doing. One morning I contrived to surprise her by leaving the cottage when she wasn't looking and ringing her from the village phone box – the one whose colour the National Trust was thinking about changing, so that it shouldn't be so conspicuous. 'Tell me,' I said in an assumed voice when she lifted the receiver, but she simply told me I had the wrong number and hung up. I made one final effort to change my intonation, to rid my plea of its terrible urgency. 'I wondered if you'd be prepared to tell me,' I whispered into her ear in the dead of night, casually and just by the by, as if I wished to sound out her views on late Kierkegaard. 'Bugger off, Barney,' she whispered back, still fast asleep.

But at least she remembered who I was.

4

This – my curiosity, my insistence to be told – was partly what Camilla had in mind when she complained about 'pressure' on the beach at Stratleigh. But as I've said, she was re-reading *Tess of the D'Urbervilles* and that alone was enough to account for her filthy mood. All kinds of noises of loathing and contempt came from the little knoll of rocks on which she sat and suffered, while I frolicked in my own fashion at the water's edge. In the usual way of couples, my spirits lightened as hers grew more depressed. By the time Angel Clare had got around to perhaps putting his mind to maybe thinking about being almost prepared to consider reconsidering his views on Tess's 'un-intact state', on the grounds that she was, when all was said and done, more fucked against than fucking, and Camilla was as a consequence doubled up and terrifying the gasteropods and lamellibranchiates out of their shells with her howls of pain, I was fairly skipping across the beach, as indeed were my pebbles now fairly skipping across the surf.

When I next looked in Camilla's direction it was to see her back on the beach herself, standing by the water and considering a solitary splash that she'd made, in vain imitation, presumably, of my deft flicks of the wrist.

'You've got to throw low,' I called out.

'I did.'

'You've got to really let it go.'

'I did.'

'You've got to use something very flat and heavyish.'

She was coming towards me and I noticed that she was empty handed.

'I did,' she said.

'What I especially can't stand about the little shit . . .'

'Angel Clare or Hardy?'

Camilla kicked sand at me. 'Don't try that one, Barney. You know they're indistinguishable where it matters.'

There was a time when I would have bridled at this, forcing my features into that expression of concentrated complacency which only clerics or critics can manage, and saying, 'But Angel Clare, however much he resembles his author, could never have written *Tess of the D'Urbervilles*.' But that was an age ago, before life and Camilla had knocked me around. And besides, I wasn't looking for an argument. I was relieved that we were talking again. That Camilla was back by my side, attacking the beach with her strong toes, covering me with sand. 'Go on,' I therefore said, 'tell me what it is that you can't stand about the little shit.'

'The assumption of an advanced moral tone towards female impurity – that's not my word – when it's as clear as daylight that he's simply tossed, like a boat without ballast, between fascination and abhorrence. All that crap about natural Purity! He hasn't got the nerve to admit that Tess is interesting to him *because* of her experience, not *in spite* of it. If he'd been honest he would have given Tess to Alec on every page.'

'Or Alec to Tess,' I chimed in. That shows what an accommodating mood I was in. How pleased I was that Tarquin was forgotten and that we were enjoying ourselves as in the good old days.

But accommodation always gets one into trouble. 'No, not Alec to Tess. You've missed my point. We're not talking about harmonious sexuality here – perish the thought. What the little shit wants, what he really thrills to, is the D'Urberville impress *on* Tess. Rape, but by a better class of person.'

'Like a royal seal?' Boy, was I trying to please!

'Precisely. Have you ever wondered why Hardy is so interested in Tess's genealogy? The answer came to me while I was sitting on the rocks. Her aristocratic background is a metaphor, it's wholly figurative. At the very moment that Angel forgives her and thereby makes her a spiritual virgin again, he has immediately to recall the historical interest of her family, the masterful line of the D'Urbervilles. Because without that, and without Alec's seal upon her, what is she? Nothing. The wickedness that Hardy can't comfortably indulge Tess in the present, he bestows upon her in her past. He ransacks her beginnings, uncovers her original sin – the thing he most wants to dwell upon – and hangs her up by it in the end. It's a compulsive metaphor for intercourse.'

It was a privilege to share a beach with her. I was so proud that I kicked sand myself. And when she tried to

291

escape from me I chased after her and brought her down with what was a pretty professional rugby tackle considering that I'd never played rugby. We rolled over and over, laughing and shouting, so that anyone watching us would have thought we were making a film. But they'd have been wrong. This was the actual thing, real life, true love. Or at least it was for me. I was able finally to pin her shoulders to the wet sand, and then and there, as a token of my appreciation and passion, I whispered an extempore rhyme into her ear.

> In regard to the Impurity of the Pure Woman, Tess,
> Hardy could not admit he wanted more, and not less
> So lacking the courage to bend or up-end her,
> He settled instead for the chance to suspend her;
> And taking the line the pure girl had sprung from,
> He fashioned a loop – and that's what she swung from.

I expected Camilla to be as pleased with my funipendulous poem as I'd been with her umbilical exegesis. That's how these things are supposed to work. Verbal relationships look to democracy even more than do mute ones. So I was surprised to discover that she was struggling violently beneath me and wasn't to be satisfied until she had me flat on my back myself, half in, half out of the water.

'What are you so perky about?' she wanted to know, as she brushed the sand off herself, totally inconsiderate as to where it landed. 'What are you doing composing winning little poems? You're no better than he is. You also want your women stamped with someone else's approval. What do you value in me, except where I've been and what I've done? Or better still, what's been done *to* me. I only excite you when you remember that I've belonged to others. And when that history starts to pall on you, you think you can take matters . . .'

But I didn't hear the rest. A large wave which had

started to gather momentum somewhere not far from the Americas was heading my way. Have I mentioned that I can't swim? I didn't believe that I could count on Camilla's coming to my rescue either – at least not until she'd finished what she had to say, and that could be too late. I was as good as on my own out there. So, although it wouldn't show me in a good light, vis-à-vis Camilla's assault on my manhood, to come struggling out of the waves on my belly, coughing up sea water and with bladder-wrack in my hair, that was what I had to do. By the time I'd recovered breath and some little dignity, Camilla was half-way up the beach on the way back to the car-park, still shouting. She even swung round a couple of times and pointed her finger at me with unmistakable menace. But I didn't catch what she was saying apart from, 'Don't start your fucking Thomas Hardy tricks on me!'

I fixed her though. When Leonard Smith and James Gibson and D.M. Thomas arrived in the village to mark the centenary of Hardy's original journey from Bockhampton to Castle Boterel* – a journey which they had just lovingly re-duplicated themselves – I didn't tell her they were here. I suppose that was a bit tough on them. There can't be any doubt that after two days of seeing only ghosts, meeting Camilla would have been the highlight of their pilgrimage – even if she wasn't on the original Hardy itinerary. But I was damned if I was going to contribute to her having a good time after what she'd just said to me. And besides, in the light of those last remarks of hers, and in the light of how badly my gift of Tarquin had gone down, I couldn't very well show up on Camilla's doorstep with three strange men, each of them imagining he was Thomas Hardy – could I?

* See The Thomas Hardy Yearbook (Toucan Press, 1971).

6

1

Tarquin apart, Camilla had her own reasons for charging me with recidivism. She had first found me interesting – dare I go so far as to say exciting? – when she saw me vilifying Sharon and scaring the living daylights out of Rowland Fitzpiers in scabrous French. Until that moment, in her own words, I had been just another analretentive at a Hardy party. What she didn't say – but what I will now say for her – is that she invited me down to Castle Boterel (or at least didn't actively dissuade me from coming) in the hope that I would scare the living daylights out of her. I'm absolutely certain she didn't know precisely how; she was, in fact, incapable of taking any kind of physical pain – she screamed, for example, whenever she brushed her teeth, she bled easily, the pressure of her earrings tortured her, and no matter how obscene she found the drama of penetration she was very precise (the word might even be narrow) about where she was and was not to be considered penetrable. Just in what manner she was therefore going to accommodate an acolyte of the Marquis de Sade's was a conundrum which I am sure she had not even begun to put her mind to.

It's possible that she wanted nothing other than to hear some French – I've said that she had a gaudy streak, and there's no denying that you can get pretty sick of the Cornish dialect down here. It's also possible that she simply wanted a laugh. A laugh? Yes, well that's what I thought too. But I have to say that *The 120 Days of Sodom* gave Camilla more amusement than any other book I'd seen her read. Don't ask me where she got it; as far as I was aware it was an imprisonable offence just to have heard of such a work. I distinctly remembered Sharon explaining to one of her regular customers that she didn't dare try stocking de Sade, that none of his novels were allowed into England because they gave too accurate a description of the average English civil servant's leisure time activities. Well, Camilla didn't agree with her on availability or subject matter. 'God!' she exclaimed one night, some few weeks after I was almost drowned on Stratleigh beach – it was about three in the morning and I was already wide awake, unable to sleep for her wild laughter – 'You've got to like him. It's so different from English filth. He's so preposterous!'

I rolled over and tried to stuff the pillows into my ears, but I was wasting my time. The bed shook beneath her appreciation, and the ancient timbers of the cottage creaked like a galleon's. Camilla's laughter was an invariably reliable gauge of our relations; the louder it was, the worse they were. Tonight there would have been few people sleeping from Pennycrocker to Penzance.

I took advantage of her having to go to the bathroom and stole a glance at what she'd been reading. She was away longer than I expected, washing her hair. 'Jesus, Camilla,' I said when she got back into bed, a towel around her head like a turban, 'it's all about . . .'

'I know,' she said, beginning to laugh again.

'And when they're not eating that, they're . . .'

'I know,' she said.

'There's a bloke here that fucks the nostrils of a goat.' I don't know why I sounded so outraged; I had no special feeling for farmyard animals.

Camilla clutched her stomach. Her towel had unwound itself and hung over her heaving shoulders. 'You mustn't forget that while that's happening the goat

295

is licking his balls, somebody else is whipping his arse, and a fourth party is . . .'

'So what's so likeable about that?' (I know, I know – I didn't deserve to have a beautiful woman with wet hair in the bed beside me. In retrospect I can only put my humourlessness down to the lateness of the hour. If she were here now, laughing over what someone was doing to the eyelid of a yak, I'd be laughing with her. I would. Believe me.)

She looked at me with utter contempt, as if I were a member of an inferior species, and a poor representative of that, to boot. 'Listen to me,' she said. 'I'll say this just once. And I'll say it without any interruptions from you. The 120 days of Sodom – not to be confused with our 520 days of Boredom – are devoted to the graphic illustration, at the rate of 5 per day, of the 600 extravagancies, contingencies, and ramifications of debauchery, starting with the simple, proceeding through the complex and the criminal, and culminating in the murderous. Don't start twitching – I know perfectly well what you wish to say and I don't wish to hear it. I don't approve of what Hitler did either – at least not in all cases. But if you ask me what I find likeable, then I'm going to tell you. I like the theatricality of it all. I like the treating of sex as a kind of comedy of manners. I prefer publicity to secrecy in sexual matters, as you know. And I like dangerously amusing social occasions. Madame Duclos, who resembles me in having large and perfect breasts, and who is the narrator for the month of November, sits gorgeously rouged and bejewelled on a throne which is mounted on a stage, and delivers her five autobiographical illustrations daily, with great wit and verve and charm, but without – and this should interest you – omitting a single *detail*, no matter how personally revealing or degrading, to an audience which comprises the Duc de Blangis, who is endowed with a monstrous member, the Bishop of X, a faithful sectary of sodomy, President de Curval, who is infrequently erect and Durcet, who is short and squat and somewha effeminate in build and taste, together with one another's wives who are also one another's daughters, a Harem of carefully picked little girls, a Harem of even more carefully picked little boys, Eight Fuckers among whom are to be numbered Hercule, Invictus, Antinous, and Bum-Cleaver, plus all other necessary props and procuresses. These, as you might expect, take a lively interest in Madame Duclos' disclosures, and although a strict timetable has to be respected, are not discouraged from vigorous audience participation. Now all this, Barney – though I can see from the expression on your face that you are not disposed to agree with me – all this seems to me a more amusing theatre for the indulgence of impossible sexual fantasies than the sombre seclusion of a domestic bed. I don't say that one cannot live without an orgy, but if such is one's taste' (I was looked at very punishingly here) 'then it strikes me that it is better gratified with style and wit and varied company, in a setting that doesn't preclude the other social pleasures such as food and drink and conversation, and in an atmosphere at once light and vivifying, that allows one to follow one's *own* predilections and not just those of the person who is whispering pathetically and proprietorially in one's ear. And now can I have my book back please?'

There wasn't any point then, and I don't suppose there's any point now, in my saying that I missed her meaning.

2

In the weeks that followed this candid exchange of views Camilla became increasingly inaccessible to me. She began to devote more of her time to the Alternative Centre than she used to, actually opening the doors when people knocked on them and accompanying her students on their topographico-literary forays. When she got home tired in the evenings she would prepare herself a light snack – I had to fend entirely for myself – and then go straight to her desk where she would whip up a storm of frenzied intellectual activity, typing and swearing and producing pamphlets at a phenomenal rate. Only once did she let me into what she was working on, and that was because we had company and company made her expansive.

Max Loveday, the mentally turbulent proprietor of The Harbour Rock Shop, who hated his shop, the lettered rock and spun filaments of sugar he served from it, and every other detail of his life in Castle Boterel, came to see us once or twice a week. We were the only people in the village he could talk to who had any understanding of how he felt. He could rely on us not to be so naïve as to ask him why, if his life was so awful and he hated selling lettered rock in Castle Boterel, he didn't try to change it and go and sell something he liked more in a place that suited him better. Camilla and I knew all about the fatal allure of misery and discomfort, and why a man might choose to pack himself around with the things he most loathes.

Candy wasn't Max Loveday's only problem either. He had been an academic, teaching French Literature (Robbe-Grillet, Nathalie Sarraute, the text as lexical surface – that sort of thing) to admiring students at one or other of the Scottish Universities, until he had fallen in love with the wife of his professor, or was it until the wife of his professor had fallen in love with him. I'm not entirely certain how it went – Camilla had the details – but it resulted, anyway, in the pair of them making a run for it in a hired furniture van containing, among other things, a grand piano, a hundred tea chests of books, and three of the professor's children. Castle Boterel was the haven their caravan finally came to rest in, and since there was no university specializing in Nathalie Sarraute hereabouts they bought the Rock Shop. By the time Max Loveday discovered that he wasn't all *that* keen on the professor's wife – or it might have been the professor's wife who discovered she was not all that keen on him – it was too late for either of them to do

298

anything about it. They were well and truly at the mercy now of all the paraphernalia, all the actual and emotional clutter that illicit bliss collects once it finds a home.

There's a peculiar bitterness that settles on absconding lovers who are not caught and brought back but are allowed to find their isolated cottage with ivy growing round its windows, a room big enough to accommodate a grand piano, and a little garden running down to the sea. The prompt provision of an earthly paradise seems to intrude into the romantic drama of their lives as cruelly as a *deus ex machina* intrudes into the willing suspense of a theatre audience, leaving them feeling cheated, disgruntled, and dissatisfied.

We get to see a lot of that sort of thing down here. It can have quite a marked mercurial effect upon the property market – and that's only one of the disadvantages of living at the end of other men's rainbows. All right, Camilla – of other women's also.

I'm sure that one of the reasons Max Loveday became our friend was because we didn't mind it when he yelled abuse at us. Naturally private and reserved though his temperament was – he normally spoke with an infuriating softness, for example, forcing anyone who wanted to hear to incline towards him, and he kept his sad eyes always lowered beneath long and even feminine lashes – nevertheless, the moment the first touch of alcohol passed his lips he would begin ranting at us about Barthes or Lacan or the new flavour of rock the wholesalers were pushing on him. He would exhaust the three of us with his tirades, showering Camilla and me with every kind of calumny and malediction, accusing us of all known crimes against the body and the intellect, not the least of which was our disgusting conspiratorial cosy domesticity. Only then, when he had tried our friendship to the limits, did he settle back for ten minutes into his usual demeanour of polite, arch, and difficult-to-hear disputatiousness, prior to kissing Camilla, shaking hands with me, and going off into the night – not happy exactly, but happier in his unhappiness than he'd been when he arrived.

Tonight, sensing that Camilla and I were not so united as usual and therefore not so blatantly susceptible to the charge of gross togetherness, he raged himself out of self-generating rancour early and was therefore reduced to pacing from one room of the cottage to another, scouring Camilla's walls and bookshelves for some pretext to vent spleen. Nothing was spared, from Camilla's old school swimming certificates to dog-eared postcards or paintings pinned to kitchen cupboards. 'Aha! Fans of Vuillard, I see,' we could hear him jeering, rooms away. 'You require a linear narrative drive in pictures too, do you? Well, why not. I'm pleased at least that you're certified to save lives. Who was the last person you saved? Seurat, by the look of it. Pity you bothered.' We let him rant, filling him up with brandy and talking between ourselves, which wasn't easy since we weren't talking. At last – it must have been after midnight – he found something that interested him on Camilla's desk. He fell silent for five minutes, then, through the walls, we heard his guffaws.

'What have you found now?' Camilla called out.

Max came back to where we were sitting, holding out an open book accusingly. It was Florence Hardy's life of her husband. Max raised a quizzical eyebrow at Camilla, as if to say, 'You've a lot of explaining to do now, good woman.'

What he actually did say was, 'From what I can see this Florence Emily Hardy writes much like her husband.' There was a tone of malicious triumph in his voice, as if he'd discovered another cosy domestic conspiracy.

'That,' said Camilla, 'is because she didn't write it. He did.'

'He wrote his own biography?'

'The authorized version, yes. He ghosted it for her, that's to say for himself.'

Beneath his long, soft lashes, Max's eyes glinted malevolently. 'So that's why there's a lie on every page.'

300

But he was wasting his time if he thought to wound Camilla that way. 'By my count there's never less than two,' she answered.

I could see Max calculating that he might have to change sides if he was to get a good argument going, but I could see him calculating also that that wouldn't be easy. 'Why does he claim he cared nothing for social advancement and then list every aristocrat he ever took tea with?' he asked. 'I don't mean why was he dishonest. That's easy to understand. I mean why was he so *transparently* dishonest.'

Camilla shrugged amiably. 'He never needed to be opaque, did he? You know what novelists are like – they spill their guts on every page and claim it's plot. And their readers, who are always sentimental about creativity, believe them. Hardy had got away with it so easily for so long, it was like second nature to him. Look at this,' Camilla seized the book from Max and riffled through it. 'Spitting chips about what the reviewers say about him and boasting Olympian indifference – in the same sentence!'

Max seized the book back from her and flicked himself. They stood for a while shoulder to shoulder, Max reading out extracts, guffawing in unison.

'This is interesting though,' Max said. 'According to Florence – I take your point that nothing is reliably according to Florence – Hardy once saw a dark man he didn't recognize standing by her during one of those miserable teas they gave at Max Gate, but when he asked her later who it was, she assured him that there was no such person present. Years later he claimed that he could still see the man's face vividly. Do you reckon Florence smuggled strangers in? There's a Nabokov story that Barthes . . .'

'Oh no.' Camilla couldn't have been more categoric. 'He would have imagined him all right. He was perfectly capable of that. Notice that it's a dark man. Probably tall too. And didn't you say standing at Florence's shoulder? Well there you are. He even put him in position.'

I thought it was about time that I made some contribution to this conversation. And I was always watchful of the more extreme forms of Camilla's mental daring. 'Are you saying that he actually imagined another person into the room?'

'Another *man*, yes. Why not? A strong imagination can do anything – especially under pressure of nervous possessiveness. Why shouldn't jealousy be able to body forth a rival, finally make it flesh? That's by no means the greatest of its marvels. I love the idea myself – I mean as being something quintessentially Hardyish. He was a ghost-ridden man. He often felt that he couldn't do much more than hover insubstantially himself. I don't doubt for one moment that he projected that dark stranger into the room, fleshed him out and put him next to Florence.'

I wasn't sure what I thought of that. Nor was Max. We both made grunting noises. We were only men, after all. We were only the ones who spirited rivals, that's to say one another, in or out of rooms; we weren't to be trusted with knowing what we were doing when we did it.

Camilla looked irritated with us both for not rising. If she'd had the power I think she would have dematerialized the pair of us.

'He doesn't look to me like someone in possession of strange gifts,' Max said, coming to a photograph of the old forger in old age.

'Who's talking about strange gifts?' Camilla retorted, angrily.

But Max hated to be interrupted. He could drop his voice and mumble for hours if he wasn't allowed his say. 'On the other hand,' he said, 'there is some quality of devilish deception in his face. I'd never noticed it before, but he actually looks quite like Dr Crippen.'

'You're not the first person to have noticed the resemblance,' she told him. Rather archly, I thought. Offering him a fight if he still wanted one. Though of course, like all perversely aggressive men, he no longer did. 'Emma Hardy spotted it before you. At around about the time

302

that Crippen's face was in all the papers, together with the details of how he murdered his wife and eloped with his secretary, Emma noted the resemblance to Florence – Florence, at this stage, being passed off as a sort of friend to Emma-cum-secretary herself. That particular way of smuggling in a mistress, getting her to feign friendship with your wife, fills me with more than usual abhorrence for husbands, by the way. Emma didn't think much of it either. Only let's hope, she said to the wholly humourless Florence, that Tom's resemblance to the little dentist stops at a facial one, and that I don't end up dead in the cellars myself one day. She left the further coincidence of secretaries implicit – naturally. And naturally Florence didn't get the joke. As a rule few people did get Emma's jokes. It was assumed that the wife of an eminent novelist who didn't think highly of her husband could only be funny in the sense of peculiar, not funny in the sense of funny.'

The brandy was beginning to tell on Max. He looked about to see if there were some attack upon him hidden in Camilla's remarks. I confess I did the same. 'We're taking the side of wives tonight, are we?' he finally thought of saying.

Camilla didn't move a muscle. 'I take the side of wives against husbands every night,' she said.

Max's eyes were bloodshot. 'But does that make art?' he challenged her.

I couldn't see to the bottom of that one. But Camilla could. She was ready for bed. 'In this particular case we'll never know,' she said, rising. 'Emma Hardy's "What I think of my Husband" diaries never got to see the light of day. He destroyed them. Burned them. He wouldn't let them be in the world. So we'll never know whether they made art or not. But I'll tell you what, Max, I wouldn't mind making art out of them. I've often thought I'd like to reconstruct them. God knows it wouldn't be difficult, imagining what she thought of him.'

Max fell towards her and poked her in the shoulder. 'Do it then, my girl,' he told her. 'Do it.'

Camilla was miles away, already launched into Emma's thwarted prose. 'That business of installing Florence in the house, getting it to look to Emma as though Florence were *her* friend, is typical of the man,' she said. 'There was a persisting surreptitiousness in him. Or are all men like that? Are all men furtive in their moral lives?'

I looked at Max Loveday. Max Loveday looked at me. We both needed time to think about this.

'Don't bother,' said Camilla, 'I know the answer.'

Max collected his coat, made his usual farewells, once more told Camilla that she should 'Do it', and made off in the direction of his cliff-top cottage where everything he thought he'd ever wanted waited for him. 'But is it art?' I heard him repeating to himself in the pitch black. Only the Trevose lighthouse to the south and the Lundy lighthouse to the north made any impression on the darkness. 'But is it art?' he was still asking, long after he'd vanished from my view.

'Why don't you?' I asked Camilla when we were in bed.

'Why don't I what?'

'Why don't you reconstruct Emma Hardy's diaries?' I sat up and turned to face her, a lesson in loyalty, comradeship, enthusiasm, and support. If there was anywhere in the West Country a man less surreptitious and morally furtive than I was I would have liked to meet him. 'Do it,' I said. 'It sounds a terrific idea.'

'Don't offer me encouragement, Barney. I'll do it if *I* want to do it.'

Bitch. A bit of furtiveness wouldn't have done *her* any harm.

3

Camilla's aggressive absorption in her work however, the renewal of her personal war against Thomas Hardy in which I would gladly have played a part if she had let me, was not the only reason for my unease at around this

304

time. The realization that it was me that Camilla was stamping out on those never silent typewriter keys was hard enough to bear, but how do you think I felt when suddenly, quite out of the blue, scraps of Sadeian miscellanea started to show up around the cottage, not quite on the same scale, but only not *quite*, as that bombardment with Hardiana to which Sharon had subjected me a few years before?

Camilla was, it goes without saying, more subtle than Sharon. She conducted an altogether classier campaign. She never descended to mathematical persuasion, for example, multiplying the 120 days of Sodom by the number of times she had failed to achieve satisfactory orgasm and leaving me in no doubt as to the magnitude therefore of the debt I still owed her. She never made any reference to the coincidence of our birthdays – except once, when she told me that de Sade was very short, shorter even than Hardy, and wondered whether it was my opinion that such was the fate of all people born on June 2, Something-other-and-40. She never organized things so that I would find myself helpless but well-dressed in a room with a regressive hypnotherapist, either, despite Harry Vilbert's presence in our lives. And I'm certain that it never once crossed her mind to sit a photograph of de Sade (Camilla could have found one had she wanted) next to one of mine in a pretty frame on her bedside table. But just like Sharon she took to leaving apposite quotations on scraps of paper in conspicuous places – *L'émotion de la volupté n'est autre sur notre âme qu'une espèce de vibration produite, au moyen des secousses que l'imagination enflammée par le souvenir d'un objet lubrique*, to take one instance, showed up one morning sellotaped to my shaving mirror; *le besoin du mal est le premier mobile de nos caprices* fell out of a packet of breakfast cereal. Sharon-like also, she opened up correspondences with some notable international Sadeians (I put my foot down, by the way, when she proposed that one of us, preferably her, take up an invitation to a

305

weekend conference in a *château* outside Nantes), and left copies of the novels where I would either have to pick them up or break my neck falling over them. *Les Crimes de l'amour* was kept permanently, with its spine facing out, under the bottom left leg of Camilla's bed (the side I entered from), where it served to correct the picturesque slope of the bedroom floor; *Aline et Valcour, ou le Roman Philosophique – Écrit à la Bastille un an avant la Révolution de la France, et orné de seize gravures originaux* doubled as our only coffee table book and indeed our only coffee table when we moved into the Sheep Pen; and I don't know how many *contes et fabliaux*, how many *lettres et cahiers personnels*, ended up open under my nose, having been used as trays to carry coffee and biscuits, or as coasters to stop me putting a dripping wine glass directly on to one of the *seize gravures originaux*. I was particularly shocked one afternoon, when I was helping Camilla to re-hang her bedroom curtains and needed something to stand on, to discover that I'd been handed a limited edition of a German translation of what was still Camilla's favourite – *Die hundertzwanzig Tage von Sodom, oder die Schule der Ausschweifung*. If she's now reading him in German, I thought, then it's serious.

Serious or not, it was impossible for me to avoid the conclusion that Camilla, also just like Sharon, was waiting for some hidden part of me suddenly and marvellously to reveal itself. And was running out of patience.

Yet I was the one who was accused of exerting pressure!

4

The question of the degree of Camilla's seriousness engaged me more than any other now. Was I really being invited to give vent to the terrible side of my nature, supposing I could find it; or was Camilla simply pulling my leg. I recalled her amusement on the first of her 120 days in Sodom, and her exact words, 'You've got to like

306

him. It's so different from English filth. He's so preposterous.' And I took comfort from those, hoping that the
whole thing was just an elaborate tease, a bit of good
unclean fun designed to rouse me from my cowardly
luxorious subjection, to pay me back for my backward
slide into underhanded Hardyishness, a demonstration
in itself of the superiority of the preposterous over the
surreptitious. But I couldn't be sure. I lived in constant
dread that any time – and quite against the grain of
what I thought we'd hammered out together (what she'd
hammered out in me, that is) – I would be called upon to
perpetrate some unspeakable act of vileness upon
Camilla's body – involving the nostrils of a goat for all I
knew – of which I would be wholly and fatuously incapable. The shadow of Melpomene loomed black and
large. Is it any wonder that I quickly resorted to the kind
of cruelty I knew best and dashed downstairs with even
more urgency every morning to collect the mail, and
leapt from my seat like a man with a million guilty
secrets every time the phone or door bell rang – on the
off-chance that that would just about satisfy Camilla as
to pain? I had no other means of keeping myself interesting to her. I was terrified of being rumbled for a
fraud. A shrivelled penis in the presence of Melpomene
was one thing, but what would Camilla have said had
she decided to cower before me and found herself eye to
eye with such a puny threat? 'Ah triple foutredieu,' she
had heard me boast, when the blood flowed freely, 'je
bande!' Well then, lay on and 'Bandes-toi!'

Whatever Camilla's motives, the effect of her campaign was to change things between us. Eventually my
anxiety, making me watchful and tense and guilty,
diminished the pleasure I'd been taking ever since I'd
known Camilla in all the vigorous daily misery she could
cause me. I couldn't flinch in peace. I couldn't tremble
over her body in the mornings with the old disregard to
dignity and pride. I started to feel bad about the whole
way I'd behaved towards her. I realized that all along I'd
been thinking only about my own gratification and had

given – *could* give – precious little in return. I began to feel sorry for her, and once I felt sorry for her I couldn't possibly fear her. For her part, it is my opinion that she was actually grateful for a period of non-belligerence in which she could take a break from the gruelling, punishing business of striking terror into my heart. She seemed to be perfectly content about not spreading herself as a banquet every morning also. By invisible degrees all obscenity slipped clean away from her organs and from mine. It was as though there were some tacit agreement in the air between us that as long as I didn't complain that she was no longer putting the fear of God into me, she wouldn't complain that I was putting nothing into her. To reflect this alteration in our inner lives, our social habits changed also. We began to talk to each other again but we whispered less. We took more walks. We didn't drink so much. We shopped more often than we ever had, looking for unusual cheeses and spiced cooked meats – which wasn't easy – in Plymouth and Exeter and Truro. We found new furniture for Camilla's cottage. We found a new and yet more derelict cottage. Imperceptibly we drifted into that phase known to all lovers who stay together long enough as domestic harmony.

Time passed. We lay side by side in our new bed – the kind that stops either party rolling into the middle – flat on our backs, rigid, staring up at the beams that were even older and prettier and wetter than the last ones, our bodies safely but fondly separated, neither one daring to lay an inflammable finger on the other. A pair of deprived algolagniacs (don't bother to deny it, Camilla), two masochists on a mattress, each having to abjure the thrill that can only come from thrall, the incomparable rapture of rough capture, the unslakable thirst to come off worst. (Don't deny it, Camilla. You sought appropriation to the other sex. The itch for the switch was on you as well.) Until, like so many before us, we decided that since we were already getting nothing of what we really wanted, we might as well get married too.

308

7

'Here's to Barney and Sharon!'

My father's resounding champagne toast, delivered into the very eyes of Camilla and embarrassing, apparently, to everyone but her, remains as the centrepiece of my recollections of our wedding day. Apart from that, everything went just as it might have been expected to go. Cards and telegrams had arrived for us in abundance in the morning – for which the postman never forgave us – amongst them a loving message and a cheque from Camilla's parents (they had given up attending their children's weddings out of a sense of decency), and an envelope from Sharon's solicitors containing a photograph of Asimova in a bridesmaid's outfit. After we had signed the register at Trewoe we were driven by limousine to Trevail from where we made the short journey back into the village in a pony and trap. That was Camilla's concession to rural romance, that and the wild flowers she had braided around the straw hat she wore for all her weddings, for luck. In the afternoon Camilla's favourite fishermen and farm hands turned up in their suits, wrapped themselves around Camilla – where they seemed to feel most safe – and sang until sunset about heartless sailors, pertinacious ploughboys, and saucy fiddlers. Max Loveday and Jeannie, the professor's wife, came round to wish us happiness but couldn't bring themselves to pronounce the word, and the last I saw of them they were having their fortunes told by Harry Vilbert. I can only suppose, since they didn't stay, that Harry had promised them unbroken felicity, that's to say even more of the same. Rabika Flatman, who had accompanied my father since it was definite that my mother wouldn't make the journey, took me aside and complimented my bride and told me that she wished it could have been a double wedding. 'In *all* senses?' I asked, hopefully. But she didn't understand. As I think I've already mentioned, she wasn't Marghanita Laski. In the evening we all laughed and drank and kissed and were at times too familiar with one another – Camilla in particular being too familiar with my father, and Rabika Flatman going (not just out of jealousy, I hoped) just a touch too far with me. But then *we* were friends from way back.

All this was as it always is and as we wanted it to be. It was what took place the following morning that was a trifle odder.

We did not have a honeymoon. 'I don't know about yours,' Camilla had said, 'but all mine have been disasters. Why don't we stay here, refuse to answer the phone, and take a short holiday later?' 'When we know each other better?' I quipped. I didn't demur though. Harmony, as I've explained, was now our principle, mutuality our keynote. Harmoniously we slept after all our guests had left us, and harmoniously we awoke the next morning – our eyes opening at precisely the same moment, for we were synchronized as well as harmonized – to find the light streaming in on our now lawful nakedness. 'How are you?' she asked. 'How are *you*?' I replied. 'Why don't you close the curtains?' she suggested, and that was so unlike her, so contrary to her usual preference as to curtains, that I wondered if there was now to be a merging of all the minor impulses of self in one great symphony of consonance and accord. I slipped out of bed to do as she wanted – or was it to do as she wanted that I wanted? – and when I returned I found her laid out, spread, as she had not been for such a long time now, for me to feast upon. It was like old times, except for this: where her expression had once been quizzical and challenging it was now sweet, and

310

where her limbs had once been splayed wantonly, there was now a subtle hint of modesty in their disposition. She somehow seemed more compact than she used to be also, her breasts less extravagantly full, the swell of her belly less curved, the hairs between her legs less ungovernable. Do not mistake me: she was beautiful still, and voluptuous enough to satisfy the wildest fantasy of every man – but only one at a time. Yes, that's what was different – she was not spread as a banquet this morning, she was spread as a wedding breakfast. She was enough, she was more than enough, she was plenty for me; but she was only for *me*, and there was nothing left over. For the first time since I'd met her at Fitzpiers's party and knew her only as Gertrude Bugler – no, earlier than that, for the first time since I had seen her elusive reflection in every girl I had desired, in every one of those dreams of beauty which she had persistently refused to accept were premonitions only of her – now, this morning, at last, I could feel that she was *mine*. It didn't matter whether or not I was mistaken. It didn't signify what Camilla might have had in *her* mind. The important thing was that this was what I felt, and that no sooner did I feel it than I knew I didn't want it. There and then and once and for all I understood what I never had wanted and never would want – something that was just for me.

Later that same morning I surprised Camilla by going over to the window and opening the curtains. 'What's the matter with you?' she asked. 'You're not usually interested in daylight.'

I wasn't either. I just wanted to check that it was still out there, and to remind myself of it, in the pubs and on the wharves and in the fishing boats and on the tractors – Camilla's murky past and lineage, the madding crowd of her history and future, my Arcadia.

8

1

Light, filtering through the iron bars of one solitary grilled window, loses itself amid the steam that rises from the bathtubs. The shuttered room is hushed except for the violent slaps of the masseurs and the wailing of the lunatics. The latter, male and female alike, wear only a strip of material tied about their loins. They gesticulate extravagantly. On a raised dais the ageing Marquis de Sade, ghastly in red lipstick and powdered whig, bares his back to the whip and retches asthmatically.

'Despite the fact that murder was once the sole proof and reason of my being,' he rasps, 'the very idea of it now revolts and sickens me.'

To illustrate his meaning the lunatics give up their wailing and clutch their stomachs; from every bath and shower cubicle comes the sound of nausea and revulsion. The whip that has so far only twitched teasingly over de Sade's surprisingly youthful back is now withdrawn in earnestness.

'My own prognostications' (Swish – Groan) 'return to mock me. In the streets the women brandish the bloody severed genitals of hated men.' (Swoosh – Moan) 'Month after month the sharpened scaffold blade falls and falls again. My friend, all the spontaneity – aaagh! – has gone out of murder. Revenge – ouch! – has lost its fizz. Brutality has become merely technological.'

The girl who brandishes the whip encourages her breasts to spill out of her frail blouse. The colour of her nipples matches exactly the colour of the blood that runs down de Sade's back. When she raises her arm once more the lunatics fall still and begin to imitate the whistling of the leather thong. They suck in air and rattle their tongues against the insides of their teeth, producing a chorus of sibilant vibration which swells to a crescendo until the moment the lash finally strikes de Sade. Whereupon they exhale their hisses as if to signal the departure from their bodies of spent souls. A moment of frozen silence and then they leap into gibbering exultation, like gibbons wearing diapers.

'They've snitched that from the Aldwych production,' Camilla whispers in my ear. 'only then, Glenda Jackson actually whipped Patrick Magee with her hair. Apparently it was her own idea. She suggested it to Peter Brook.'

I don't question Camilla's authority. These are the sorts of things she somehow just knows, in the same way that Sharon knew who really owned Selfridge's and how Liberty's first started. But I do ask her whether it is Glenda Jackson or Peter Brook we have to thank for the degree of audience involvement to which we've so far – and the play isn't even half over yet – been subjected. We are on the front row (Camilla having been given complimentary tickets) and although I am prepared to forgive, on the grounds of old fashioned authenticity, the soaking I've received from de Sade's post-flagellatory asthmatic spittle, I am less tolerant of the near-naked prancing lunatics who have burst balloons in my ear and blown feathered kazoos in my face, with the intention, I can only suppose, of showing me how like a children's party madness is.

'Do we have to stay?' I ask Camilla in a louder voice than is necessary. 'I thought we had a pact about fringe theatre.'

'We do. But this is different. I've told you – I know the director.'

'Director? You mean someone is in charge of this?' I am not being entirely unreasonable. One of the inmates has just turned his back on me, taken down his diaper, and come within an inch of impaling his buttocks on my rolled-up programme. And another is even now throwing examples of institutional food into the audience. Apparently even the cooking isn't up to much at Charenton.

But Camilla is determined that we remain in our seats. 'Be quiet,' she tells me. 'Look at Charlotte Corday's tits if you can't think of anything else to do. Too late, they're in again. No they're not – here they come. And sit still. I'm trying to get a look at Marat in the bath.'

(Marat, by the way – this being an innovative production – is black. He is also, as they say in theatrical circles, bollock-naked.)

'I am the kind of man who yearns to be defeated,' de Sade declaims, bracing himself for more punishment. And I, settling back in my seat, do the same.

This must have been the longest unbroken stint in one theatre that Camilla and I had put in since we'd known each other. As I think I've said, we were great walkers out of plays. And we didn't go about it in a slap-dash fashion either. Already this season we had succeeded in not sitting through a Christopher Hampton, an Edward Bond, a Howard Brenton, and two David Storeys – all at the Royal Court; a Trevor Griffiths at the National (we knew better than to bother even taking our seats for *Equus*); a Pinter at the Aldwych (directed by Peter Hall – a double reason for not staying); to say nothing of five fringe David Edgars, and of course every Alan Ayckbourn on in town. Peter Brook eluded us in London – he might have been experimenting with silences – but Camilla and I had always found his productions well worth travelling some distance not to sit through, and we finally caught up with one we could walk out on in Paris.

The year – as any ordinarily educated theatre-goer will by now have recognized – was 1973, and since Camilla and I were still married it will be evident that I hadn't acted in haste on the strength of the realization that had dawned on me during my first morning as

314

Camilla's husband. I had neither left her (which would not have been much to the point, anyway) nor encouraged her to leave me. I wasn't, I am pleased to affirm, a totally unfeeling brute. Just because a loving wife could not, by definition, provide me with the form of gratification I most craved – namely, the sensation of being with a wife who wasn't loving – that was no reason to discard all the other pleasures and obligations which marriage exists to confer. I am quite certain that Camilla was making identical accommodations to practicalities in regard to me. If I wasn't an unfeeling brute, neither was I a complete fool. I had never for one moment supposed that she had not found herself, as Mrs Fugleman, in a position every bit as false as mine. Flooding me with wifely irradiance each morning, and making herself look smaller than she was, so as not to frighten me (or herself) with superfluity, was not her idea of a good time either. But like me she made the best of it.

What we did, in fact, to make the best of it together, was go public. We plunged into the life of the village. Camilla became a parish councillor again. I joined the cricket team. Camilla ran raffles and organized sponsored walks to raise money for the local primary school. I learned the words of her favourite pub songs. We became thoroughly conscientious about our responsibilities to the place we lived in, even going so far as to stop smiling at the officers of the National Trust when they waved their sticks at us from across the river. And finally – I can't find any better illustration of our state of mind than this – we traded in Camilla's old MG for a Ford Cortina Estate.

It is always a sad, symbolic gesture in the life of a couple, the transfer from a two to a four or more seat vehicle; it marks the end of bilateral self-sufficiency. I ought, I suppose, to have been pleased. But paradoxically it upset me. I hated seeing the MG go. I had spent the night in it on more than one occasion. And it represented the independent, racy side of Camilla's nature; the thing I'd loved her for.

I didn't like it either – again paradoxically – when

315

Camilla proposed, in our second year of marriage, that we no longer enter the Camelton Carnival in tandem. In the past we had dressed and made each other up meticulously for this event, but this year Camilla accompanied Max Loveday in the Comic Tradesman's category, and came second; whereas I was reduced to joining Harry Vilbert and Lionel Turnbull amongst others in a Walking Historical Tableau for Nine People. We did *And Shall Trelawney Die?* but so did everybody else, and we won nothing.

I mention this only to be scrupulously fair to Camilla. I don't want it to appear that she was hanging on to my arm, waiting for me to determine her fate.

This was a positive time for us materially, though. I plugged the holes in the walls of our cottage and Camilla agreed to think about having a damp-course. We effected major changes to Camilla's school, improving the kitchens and extending its cultural activities to take in guided coach trips (I became the guide) to other literary landmarks near by, such as Westward Ho! and Jamaica Inn, Nether Stowey, Doone Valley, and Lyme Regis, where the Cobb still meant Louisa Musgrove and Jane Austen to me, not Sarah Woodruff and John Fowles. And no matter how much we prospered we were careful not to lose touch with the eager life of the intellect and spirit also, speeding up to London in the Cortina as often as we could, balancing our duties to the Alternative Centre for Thomas Hardy Studies on the one hand, with our obligations to keep up with what was happening in the British theatre on the other.

I cannot deny, however, that strains were beginning to show in our private life, irrespective of our efforts not to have one. If I got too drunk at the pub or at a party I pushed Camilla in the direction of other men. I once deliberately left her alone for two hours with Harry Vilbert; and during an evening we spent with my father and Rabika Flatman at their place in Tooting – we went there after leaving a John Arden early – I actually pushed her in the direction of my father. There was

316

nothing I could do about these impulses, they were released by alcohol or social excitation, and rose like a hot spring from molten rock. Choice scarcely entered into it. My needs were upon me. Men cannot live, you see, by bread alone.

The measure of how seriously Camilla viewed my relapse was our being in this cold and aggressively uncomfortable warehouse in the first place, sitting on old tram seats and watching the Combined London Polytechnics' Theatre of Cruelty Ensemble performing its new adaptation of *The persecution and assassination of Marat as performed by the inmates of the asylum of Charenton under the direction of the Marquis de Sade* – or *Marat/Sade* as it was called by the sorts of people who also referred familiarly, as if they'd had a hand in its writing, to *The Dream*. It didn't matter how well Camilla knew the director, she would never have put us through this unless she had had another motive. I didn't fully understand it at the time, but this was her last attempt to get me to come clean about my uncleanness.

'You just listen to this,' Camilla urged me, prodding me with her elbows whenever she felt that someone was saying something significant. 'And sit up straight.'

2

But I am a long way away, far gone in one of those interminably rambling reveries about childhood – I am actually back at kindergarten, offering my toys to other little boys for them to break – the sort of reverie which in my experience anyway, only the live theatre provides the ideal conditions for. Concerts are excellent for all manner of light musings upon the present, and I find that I can formulate the most vigorous and hopeful schemes for my future in the cinema; but I need the mannered drone of stage voices, I need artifice close and palpable, if I am to set about retracing my steps in earnest to the mud and silt of my origins. Once, half way through a cycle of history plays at Stratford, I actually made it back to the moment of my conception. The sensation was not unlike rising suddenly from a bent position and seeing stars. And on another occasion – I think it was when Camilla and I were in Persepolis for *Orghast* – I retrograded even further. Back, back I went, way beyond that sudden shock of stars. But I have nothing to report of my journey. No smiling face of God, no silver clouds, nothing. Just blackness, chaos, and confusion. Not unlike the second half of the cycle of history plays.

A lively song, performed with gusto by the athletic inmates of Charenton –

> What's in it for the population,
> If there ain't universal copulation? –

interrupts me from my recollections of the day I was presented with my first rattle. Not quite off the stage, and not quite on the stage, but definitely underneath my very nose, lunatics of both sexes are interfering with one another's diapers and suiting their actions to the words of the song. This is known as mime.

Camilla digs me with her elbows. 'They're certainly spirited,' I concede.

De Sade, in the meantime, is peering into Marat's bath. As is Camilla. 'Marat,' he says, 'during my thirteen years rotting in the nick' – have I mentioned that this is an updated version of French history? – 'I came to understand that our greatest imprisonment is a fleshly one, each of us locked in a body that torments and terrifies, each body racked by its own relentless dissidence.'

Beside him, hovering over Marat's now overcrowded ablutions, but lost in a kind of half ecstasy, Charlotte Corday has her breasts out again and is caressing them, allowing the audience to see the knife that nestles between them like a silver serpent.

'For thirteen years, behind thirteen doors,' de Sade continues, 'I put my mind to no other question but the orifices of the body.'

'You listen to this,' Camilla tells me.

'Marat, these pits and dungeons of the self, made

318

crueller by the savage jealousy of imagination, are worse than any incarceration of stone and iron. And for as long as they are bolted your revolution is nothing other than a student demonstration led by some self-satisfied lecturer in sociology!'

Camilla nudges me with her elbow and kicks me with her foot. I don't know what any of this has to do with me. I'm not proposing any revolutions. I can only think that she wants me to understand de Sade's speech as a call to slide back the bolts of self-confinement, to quit the closet of the mind. But she'll get nowhere with me on that one. Especially as she has no alternative to offer me. Why quit the closet of the mind if that's where all the fun is?

  The Revolution's all in vain,
I would have my attendant lunatics intone,
  That lifts the ban on liking pain.
  Reforming zeal can't get much sillier,
I would have them moan,
  Than legalizing scopophilia.
But then I am a merry wag – an incorrigible rogue – am I not?

I didn't realize, as I pulled away from Camilla's kicks and nudges, that this theatrical experience was her ultimatum to me. I was meant to come away from it a different man. Some hope! If she'd mentioned the phrase 'different man' to me I'd have swallowed hard and whispered, 'Go to him.' That's how far I was from understanding that I was in danger.

So we were not destined, Camilla and I, ever to accompany each other to the theatre again. All last occasions for anything are distressing; there isn't one of them – not even the last day at school – that doesn't feel like an intimation of the ultimate in last occasions; but it especially distresses me still, to think that the last play Camilla and I ever went to together – we sat through.

3

When it was all over Camilla took me back stage – or rather, back 'space' – and introduced me to her friend the director. Because this was the final night of the production, a small party was underway. Some of the lunatics were still in their nappies, but Charlotte Corday's breasts were put away inside a check shirt, and de Sade had changed into jeans and a sweater. Camilla's friend, Jonathan, was delighted to see her. 'I'm so pleased you could come,' he told her. 'I only wish you could have been here on Wednesday when we were really good. Everything just came together Wednesday. Tonight was a bit of an anti-climax.'

'I thought it was terrific,' said Camilla. 'We both did.'

'Did you?' He took praise, I noticed, as toast takes butter. He absorbed it, through his skin, as though it were his by custom and by right. I had never seen so much self-content. He actually admired parts of himself – his fingernails, his shirt-cuffs, the knot he'd tied in his shoe-lace – while he talked to us. He was not a close friend of Camilla's, but they'd been students together and kept more or less in touch. Once or twice a year he would send Camilla a postcard from somewhere exotic, always showing a painting rather than a view, and describing in the manner of Keats rather than in the manner of Lawrence what he had perceived about the customs of the natives, the quality of the light, and above all, of course, the state of the indigenous theatre. I formed the impression, even before I met him, that he communicated with his friends only when he was in the very pink of conceit, and that friendship for him was therefore something he chose to sound whenever he wished to congratulate himself on how far he had travelled. In this he was the very opposite to me, who saw old friends as a kind of guarantee of fellowship in disgruntlement. 'How are you?' 'Vile. How are you?' 'The same' – was my idea of camaraderie. But Jonathan didn't know where to begin when Camilla asked him how he was – the subject was so epic.

320

I left them to their congratulations of him and went to talk to some of the actors. Duperret, the Girondist Deputy, turned out to be a second year economics student, and Charlotte Corday, whose nipples I felt I knew better than I knew Camilla's or Rabika Flatman's or come to that my own, was a secretary in humanities. The three of us conversed for a while about the new excitement that could be felt at all levels throughout the British theatre, but I drifted away when they started to tell me how daringly experimental Jonathan was. It was part of that very experimentalism, I discovered as I circulated, that Jonathan should have given parts in his production to foreign students temporarily domiciled in England. Apparently none of the lunatics was a native English speaker and even Marat came from Martinique. Jonathan wanted to suggest that the language of madness is universal, a couple of Dutch boys explained to me.

A half an hour later, after dancing had started and the wine going around in little plastic cups had run out, I came upon Camilla, pinned into a corner and being what I suppose one would have to call nuzzled, by the actor who'd played de Sade. He was younger without his makeup than I had realized, fresher faced, leaner. Fresher mannered too. My presence didn't seem to abash him in the slightest.

'This young man,' said Camilla, laughing and trying to disengage herself from his attentions, 'has been attempting to persuade me to drive him and his friend Pierre – that's Marat, Barney; you know, the one in the bath – to Exeter, where Pierre has got a cousin.'

I didn't want to spoil anyone's fun. Or keep cousins apart. 'Well why not? We can drop them off on our way back tomorrow,' I suggested.

'I've already offered them that. They seem to want to go tonight.'

'Tonight?' I looked at my watch. It was well gone eleven. Then I looked at Camilla who was high coloured, and at de Sade who was still trying to bite her neck, and at Pierre who had just ambled over in a smart blue suit and a stiff white collared shirt. 'I suppose it's not impossible,' I said. 'If we left right away.'

Camilla threw me an icy glance. 'Barney, you know you hate driving on motorways at night.'

I consulted my watch again, as if logistics were all that were on my mind. 'I guess we wouldn't go that way at this time,' I mused aloud. 'We'd have to take the A303 and the A30 down through Andover and Yeovil. It's longer, but we'd see more country.'

'Barney, it's the middle of the night. We wouldn't see anything.'

'J'aime beaucoup la campagne,' said Pierre.

For some reason that settled it for me. 'We'll have to leave right now,' I told them.

The bright and boyish de Sade made one more dive for Camilla's throat and let out a loud halloo of jubilation. Marat/Pierre did a backward flip. Together they were breaking down the artificial barriers of mere language. So was Camilla. She eyed me steadily. There was an interrogation in her look which I had to answer. But since none of us was going in for verbalizing I merely shrugged my shoulders. And I refused to meet her gaze.

'Very well,' she said. 'On your own head be it!'

4

It must have been getting on for two o'clock when Camilla ordered me to stop the car. She had been twisted round in her seat for the whole journey so far, encouraging our multilingual, parti-coloured, but wholly youthful passengers to prattle on about themselves. They were none of them helping me with road signs or looking out for police or paying the slightest attention to the countryside I had kindly offered to drive them through. That is until my headlights picked out that great unsightly tumble of stones, that heap of Druidical litter, which no day or night time traveller on this road can pass by without comment or curiosity.

'What monstrous place – quel endroit affreux – is this?' Pierre asked.

I increased pressure on my accelerator.

'It's Stonehenge,' announced Camilla with authority. 'Slow down, turn left, and stop the car, Barney.'

I did what I was told, these being the first words that Camilla had addressed to me since we'd left the party. As I've demonstrated before, I'll do anything for harmony.

'The heathen temple, you mean?' The young de Sade was beside himself with intellectual ardour. 'This is the place Jonathan has been trying to hire to put on a performance of *Nng* on midsummer's day. He reckons it's pretty ironical that the authorities won't give him permission when all he wants is to restore it to its proper use.'

'It's proper use?' (That was me.)

'Jonathan says it used to be a bronze-age theatre.'

'Was that before or after it was a prehistoric space station?' That was me again. I could be pretty cutting with enthusiastic youngsters. Particularly when I was in an ambiguous relation to their enthusiasm for my wife. 'Actually,' I went on, 'it was used for synchronizing solar and lunar phenomena. It was able to divide the year into precise halves, quarters, or even eighths, by means of highly sophisticated solstitial alignments.'

In fact I didn't believe a word of this and suspected that Jonathan might well have been right – Stonehenge looked to me as though it had been a place for hippie happenings for the last three thousand years. But I wasn't going to admit as much to a couple of kids.

'I favour a more sepulchral/symbolic function myself,' said Camilla.

I didn't like the sound of that. 'Either way it's pretty uninteresting,' I said. 'Shall we get along now?'

'Oh no, oh please let's look around it now we're here,' the two boys pleaded together.

I didn't want to be a killjoy but I had to offer it as my opinion that at two in the morning Stonehenge was unlikely to be open to the public. Camilla though, much as she clung fervently to her right to close her own establishment whenever the fancy took her, was not one to accept the closure at any time of what belonged properly to the nation. On many an occasion she had got me to accompany her over the walls of Dundagel castle in the moonlight, and it was almost impossible for her to pass a property appropriated by the National Trust and not want to make a symbolic trespass on it – to claim it back, as it were, and if only fleetingly, from the new feudal landlords. 'Come on boys,' she said tonight, although it was only the Department of the Environment she was taking on, 'I'll get you in.'

I felt suddenly very sick in the stomach. 'Camilla, there's wire all around it,' I reminded her.

But she was already half out of the car. 'So what? Pierre's an acrobat. You saw him leap out of that bath. He can get us over.'

I shook my head. 'I'm not breaking into Stonehenge,' I insisted.

'I know you're not. You're staying here to mind the luggage. You can keep your headlights on so that we can see what we're doing. Flash them if anybody comes. We won't be too long. Allons, mes enfants.' And she was off, haring towards the wire, with a couple of blooming boys in hot pursuit.

I waited for what seemed to me to be hours – though I'm prepared to concede now that it might have been no more than minutes – and then, locking the car but leaving the engine running and the headlights on, I set off after them. Don't ask me how I got over that wire. I've never been a good climber and I had no French acrobat to help me. Extremity of emotion alone, I suppose, made me careless of my inadequacy and had me air-borne. I was so over-wrought, indeed, that I would have forgotten that I couldn't swim and swum, if a lake had suddenly opened between me and those towering trilithons.

I caught my breath, once I was inside the wire, and rested against the great flaming Sun Stone, itself leaning as if in obeisance towards the vast Sarsen circle and its enfolded mysteries. I peered into the darkness. I could

324

see and hear nothing. I crept stealthily along the ground, the buried secrets of the Romans and the Saxons only inches beneath my feet. I circumnavigated the erroneously named Slaughter Stone (it wasn't erroneously named tonight!) and made for the Sarsen pillars, which, incidentally, are in reality silicified nodules of sandstone, that's to say sand held together by silica cement, and were probably transported from somewhere in the area between Marlborough and Newbury – unlike the Bluestones, which almost certainly came from the Prescelly Hills in Dyfed in Wales. (I include these geological niceties, I ought to say, not to load with verisimilitude this extraordinary turn in my narrative, nor to curry favour with those who like to acquire a little learning when they read, but because I can scarcely bear to recall the terrible events of this night without the support and comfort of the dispassionate labours of harmless scholars. Their love of bloodless stone reminds me that the orifices of the body are not the only study to which the restless imagination of man need sacrifice itself.)

But this was to be a sacrificial, orificial night. I knew as much even as I advanced, an accomplished crepuscular navigator all of the sudden, miraculously aware of prehistoric ditches and jutting flint, my back arching instinctively against the icy pillars of the outer circle, my eyes as untroubled by the darkness as a cat's. I knew it even as I peered around the colossal sandstone doorway into the inner horseshoe (made of spotted dolerite, by the way), and saw giant, even violent shadows, and heard at last a sound that was not the booming tune of the wind upon the edifice, was not a music either which I could say I recognized, although I knew, without a single doubt, from whom it came. To my left the two great trilithons loomed black and indefinite, tremendous and yet oddly inconsequent like all wasted ruins, wanly menacing. A graveyard of smaller rocks stretched out before me, and beyond that the Altar Stone, a massive splinter of micaceous sandstone, measuring 16ft long by 3ft 4ins wide, but trapped like the victim of some blunder on a building site beneath the fallen stone of the central trilithon at one end, and its spilled lintel at the other. And there, splayed out amongst this confusion of masonry, careless of discomfort, druidical decorum, or our marriage vows, my own monumental Camilla heaved and twisted and bellowed, as she'd never heaved and twisted and bellowed on a bed of rock for me, her legs thrown wider apart than I'd ever seen them thrown, in order to accommodate the boy de Sade – the steam from whose nostrils ascended into the night like incense, the glint from whose solitary ear-ring flashed amongst the melancholy bluestone pillars like a falling star; while at her other end, in a squatting position above her uncovered and once more superabundant breasts, the black acrobat and actor Pierre swayed to a monstrous rhythm, his gracefully predacious shadow falling now on this silicified module of sandstone, now on that, according to the extravagance of his movements (or of mine!), his virile member – I didn't have to imagine it, I had already seen it enough times this evening, getting in and out of Marat's bath – his virile member, I say (if I could look, you can), plunged deep into Camilla's throat.

5

It must have been a full hour – I am not exaggerating the time this time – before all activity on or around the Altar Stone ceased completely. At last the sound of breathing, quick and small, was all that issued from the innermost chamber of the ancient temple. Outside, only the distant purr of my boiling engine and the sad, scared scrapings of nocturnal creatures disturbed the silence.

Then Camilla stood up, shook herself, and went forward, neither of the men having moved.

'I am ready,' she said quietly.

9

I

This village is undoubtedly a good place to enjoy jealousy in. I will go further, and venture to affirm that there cannot be many settlements, outside of a fortified Sicilian mountain shtetl or a mixed monastery in the Andes, better situated than Castle Boterel for the cultivation of that most morbid of all manifestations of fidelity. (Fidelity? Why yes. Did I ever love Camilla more single-mindedly than when I wept for her amid the megaliths?) And when I speak of its ideal situation I am not merely referring to its distance from major centres of distraction and refreshment; I am thinking also of its climate, its terrain, the deeply engrained genius of its people for the propagation of hearsay, and the abundant natural provision of vantage points, confluences, o'erhanging crags, freakish acoustical phenomena and the like, all offering unparallelled opportunities for the great devotional vigils of jealousy – for espials, rencounters, speleology, ornithology, and for eavesdropping on an epic scale. Many was the time I lay flat on my belly in the gorse, silent upon a peak, waiting for the wind to carry up a tinkle of laughter or an exhalation of endearment from a thousand feet below me, to hurl it against the opposite cliff face and to bear it thence on a zephyr into the amplifying chamber of my ear. And many a time, too, have I hung like a cormorant from the rocks, careless of the dizzying crash of foam beneath, consumed by the need to know whose tiny fishing boat

Camilla was out in, what he was recommending that she use for bait, and what she was telling him about me.

Yes, Camilla was out fishing again, once more doling out dinner to the gulls like a goddess. She was back drinking too, back singing sentimental songs in The Strangled Stranger and The Broken Vow And Sacrament, roaring in her old piratical manner at jokes and anecdotes she'd heard a thousand times before, to all intents and purposes the Camilla that was, restored to herself as though I'd never been. But older – and therefore sadder. Restorations to an older self always entail bitterness. I could have told her that. It can only mean that the intervening period has been a proof of the impossibility of change or a confirmation that change was never necessary – either way a murderous waste of years. The responsibility for that carnage was settled firmly on my shoulders. Camilla hardly looked at me now, but when she did it was to accuse me wordlessly of the worst of crimes.

This re-emergence of the old Camilla in a new atmosphere of bitter domestic resentfulness was the immediate consequence of our trip to London and Stonehenge. And I do mean immediate. There had been no incubation period, no slow simmer of grievance; there hadn't even been a discussion. The sleeping bag had been tossed down to me the minute we got back – we had driven into the village in one of those ghastly pearl-grey dawns that mock all adventurers of the mind or body – and there I remained for the duration of the summer, sharing the floor with the spiders, whom, in lovelessness, loneliness, and a determination to hang from high places in the hope of catching something, I soon came to resemble.

I cleaned out the school each morning, attending minutely to the written instructions Camilla left me, dogged her footsteps each afternoon and night – literally padding after her, sometimes – and erupted into shameful and largely ignored frustration at the weekends. The only words I could ever get out of her after I'd pleaded, threatened, and on occasions even sobbed, were,

328

'What's the matter with you? I'm giving you what you want.'

'You aren't, you aren't!' I would call after her as she left the cottage, provocatively dressed and luridly made-up to go God-knows where, to meet Christ-knows who, to do the Devil-knew what.

So why, if she wasn't giving me what I wanted – and she wasn't, I swear she wasn't – why did I not simply leave? Why didn't I fold the sleeping bag up neatly one morning, put it back into its bag, pack my three suit-cases, scribble her a note to the effect that I was still her husband in law, could not be expected to suffer such cruel torment any longer, would be in touch with her through my solicitors, and go?

No one who knows the transfixing, utterly mesmeric power of jealousy would ask that question. Nor would anyone who knows Castle Boterel. Go? Go from here? The smallest and least tenuous of those spiders with whom I shared the floor had a better chance of making it up the greased sides of Marat's bath than I had of clam-bering out of this natural wind-blown basin of morbidity. The village lanes ran down, not up. The close enfolding hills enfolded me. The sudden squalls, capable of whip-ping half the slates off a roof, even at the height of sum-mer, identically matched my weekend tantrums – each of us knew how the other felt; there was nothing either of us needed to be taught about unfocussed fury. And when the blow-hole blew its watery raspberries, it blew on my behalf. Does this sound suspiciously like an affec-tion I am describing, a sympathy based on mutual and corresponding interests? Well, why not? Rural life never speaks more poetically than when it addresses an obsessed or broken spirit. Rocked and wrapped around by it in my misery, I actually fell in love with the wretched place!

These penitential morning walks I take began, in fact, at this period, when Camilla was still here. I had less to reprimand myself for then, of course, and they were not the guilt-laden expeditions they are today; but I found a congruence in Nature that surprised me, and I was up early, following the holidaying or honeymooning couples out into the harbour, but not stopping when they did, to grasp each other the moment that they saw the sea, for all the world like the last members of some once vast expeditionary party, struck by the lonely anti-climax of success. I had no success to halt or hinder me. I marched on in the direction pointed out by the bare fingers of slate, past the naked serrations of rock, sliced clean by the wind for a geology lesson, and on to the highest promontory. Here I would pause and sometimes sit, looking back into the village and the rising farms behind it, and down into the harbour from which the waters had receded, leaving the gouged-out sea-bed, the discoloured pools, the tangled mess of vegetation resembling lettuce and cooked spinach, and the boulders tossed in total disregard of form and symmetry – a natural dereliction, just like me.

Then I would rise and start to climb in the direction that Camilla might take, and I would wonder if this was the day I was going to be vouchsafed an aerial view of her, flat on her back on a shingle beach, forehead to forehead with one of her mackerel-smelling friends, the two of them (and me made three) engrossed in the endlessly shocking phenomenon of penetration.

Stonehenge had not cured me of *that*?

How can I explain this? – yes, yes it had; but Stonehenge belonged, as it were, to the old dispensation. It was the last act of a drama that was still somehow for me. It was done to spite me – I knew that, of course – but even that meant that I still had a hand in its production. Whereas the jealousy I was now braving my instinctive vertigo for was the real McCoy. I was out of the reckoning this time. I was the last thing on anybody's mind. I was as good as gone. So if I actually could swing by my heels from these gnawed and crumbling cliffs, ignore the blinding spray and falling rocks, distinguish from the cries of the kittiwakes and the plunge-diving gannets Camilla's gasps of wholly elemental and

330

thoroughly un-connected to Barney Fugleman pleasure, and *still* not plunge puling into the heaving oily sea below, then I would be well on my way to beating this thing, wouldn't I?

Well wouldn't I?

2

The question's academic anyway. I never got to find out what I could beat. Things moved just that bit too fast for me.

On the last night Camilla and I spent under the same roof I dreamed a terrible dream. Generally I slept badly in the sleeping bag. The floor was hard, and Camilla would come and go at all hours, making late snacks and deceptively innocent phone calls. Her only acknowledgement of my presence was to step over me where I lay. She never once kicked me, I'll say that much for her. But I suspect that was only because she didn't want to give me ideas. And she was right to be careful. One inadvertent prod from her foot and I'd have been reduced to a blubbering heap of nostalgia and needs. I would lie for hours, pretending to be asleep, hoping. So you can see why my nights were unsettled. But on this night I had put myself to floor early, after a long fruitless day following Camilla up the coast and finally losing her in a sea mist off Windy Beak. If I hadn't been so tired I'd have stayed awake and read, or watched the spiders. I knew that early nights were not good for me. All my worst nightmares came to me when I retired early, and tonight was no exception.

It was so bad that I actually woke up screaming. I rolled over and unzipped myself and stumbled into the kitchen. I poured myself a glass of water and took it outside to drink. Although it was very late in the summer the weather was still gentle. The night still had some light left in it too. I breathed in the warm air that was blowing off the Atlantic. While I was out there I noticed that Camilla's light was on – the light from the room we used to call ours. She must have come back while I was

dreaming my vile dream and quietly stepped over me. I
didn't stop to think what I was doing. I simply ran back
inside and tore up the stairs and pushed my way into her
room – our room.

She was sitting on the bed looking terribly weary. Her
hair was drawn back austerely and tied at the back, like
a tragic Swede's. That was how she mainly wore it now.
She might have been laughing piratically, like her old
self, in every pub in Castle Boterel, but that didn't mean
she was happy. But I wasn't in any position to pass
comment. She didn't seem particularly surprised to see
me, which was in itself surprising considering that I
hadn't been in the upper half of the cottage for months.
She noticed that I was under strain though.

'What's the matter with you?' she asked. 'You look as
though you've seen a ghost.'

'Worse than that,' I said, 'I've just *been* a ghost.'

I would have liked it if she'd shown a bit of interest. Or
invited me to sit on the bed. Or cradled my troubled head
in her arms. But she did none of these things. All she did
was light herself a cigarette.

'I've been at Max Gate,' I said. 'I've spent the entire
evening standing next to Florence Hardy. It was horrible. Nobody would talk to me or give me any tea. Not
even a cake. *He* seemed to be the only one who knew I
was there. He just kept staring at me. And he seemed to
be able to move me with his eyes. But only in one direction – closer and closer to Florence. It was unimagin-
ably vile. I could smell her clothes and her hair. An
odour of misery and deprivation rose from her. I felt that
if I'd put my arms around her her bones would give – not
crack, just subside. And all the while I was being
impelled closer, closer. Camilla, I want you to tell me –
what am I doing dreaming such shit?'

Camilla puffed at her cigarette and looked up at me. 'I
suppose it's an advance,' she said, 'imagining that
you're someone else's imaginary rival.'

I waited for what else she had to say but there wasn't
anything. 'Is that it?'

332

She shrugged.

'Camilla, I'd like to stay here tonight. In this room.'

She shrugged again. 'Do what you like,' she said. 'I'm going for a swim.'

'A swim? At this time?'

'Why not? The water's still warm.'

She gathered her things together, towels, cosmetics, assorted items of clothing, much more, it seemed to me than she could possibly need – but then I didn't know much about swimming. The goggles and flippers seemed fair enough, but the real question I wanted to ask about those was who'd bought them for her. I threw myself on the bed and watched her. 'Don't go,' I desperately wanted to say. 'Be careful,' I would have liked to warn her. But I was in an enfeebled state. I couldn't trust myself to say anything. So it fell to her to deliver our last words for us. 'See you,' she said, just before she left. And this was such an advance, in tenderness, over any other thing she'd said to me since we'd returned from London and Stonehenge, that I broke up completely.

3

I knew something was wrong the minute I opened my eyes. It was light outside; I was in a bed, not a sleeping bag; and Camilla was not back.

I called out several times on the off-chance that she had decided to sleep downstairs since I was sleeping up, but there was no answer. I looked through the window and saw that the Cortina was not in the path. I threw on my clothes and ran into the street. I thumbed a lift from the milkman. 'True September,' he said. 'Mild and muggy.' My advice to anyone in a hurry is not to accept a lift from a milkman. I arrived at the harbour approaches at last and ran to where the fishermen and a few other privileged souls were allowed to keep their cars. Camilla's car was there. There was no way that I could have known that it stood as she had parked it the night before, prior to diving from the highest rock and striking out for the Mazzard, but I knew it all the same.

The tide was in and most of the fishermen were out. Much as I hated giving them the satisfaction of witnessing my distress, I asked the few who were back whether they'd seen Camilla. They welcomed the opportunity to tell me which boats Camilla was most likely at any time to be found fishing from, but they also told me that she wasn't to be found fishing from any of them this morning. It had been too early a start for her. 'Camilla's not what you'd call an early riser, boy,' one of them dared to inform me. And they were all absolutely certain – since there were no secrets between fishermen, especially where Camilla was concerned – that no boat from Castle Boterel had taken her out this day.

I went in search of Lionel, but I couldn't find him. I scampered to the crown of the highest of the two comatose icthyosauri and looked out over the waters. There was nothing out there apart from a few bobbing buoys marking the whereabouts of lobster pots. Even the gull community was sparse and quiet. Grieving? Grieving for Camilla? I turned and slid down the rocks and headed back towards the harbour where the first walkers of the morning, now breakfasted, were gathering. I stopped everyone I passed, holiday-makers and locals alike, astonishing them with the urgency and I suppose the incoherence of my questions. Had they seen a girl, a lovely girl with fair hair, pulled back, and broad shoulders, wearing goggles, swimming out in that direction? None of them had. As usual, no one had seen anything.

I am not a good person in an emergency. Where others would run for help or start yelling their lungs out, I go self-conscious and fall to fretting over protocol. I knew that I should have alerted the coast guard, but then again, was that really the thing to do, ought I really to trouble them when I wasn't dead certain that I had anything to trouble them about? I was debating this, leaning over the stone arched bridge which joins the northern and the southern banks of the Valency River, when Harry Vilbert found me. He was crossing the bridge on

334

his way to open the Museum. I remember thinking that he was looking greyer and frailer than ever inside his denim suit. And I remember wondering whether I, thirty years his junior, looked any better.

'Camilla's out early today,' he commented.

I started. 'Have you seen her?' The ferocity of my enquiry startled him. I know that I grabbed him by his shoulders because I can remember being startled myself by how difficult they were to find.

'No, I haven't seen her. I just thought that was who you were waiting for. And I noticed her things on the rocks.'

'Her things? Where?'

The Off Wessex Museum of Nugatory Spells and Superstitions, occupying a converted grain store, is the last building on its side of the harbour. Seaward of it, a narrow ramp descends gently into the water. This is used for launching light pleasure boats, rubber dinghies and the like, and swimmers use it also, when the tide is right, to launch themselves. It's convenient for them, too, because the natural ledges of the rocks from which it has been carved are ideal for congregating, for sun-bathing, and for parking their belongings. It was on these rocks that Harry Vilbert, crossing the bridge, thought he'd seen a bundle that he recognized.

He wanted to come with me but he was too old and I couldn't wait for him. I slithered down the ramp and hauled myself up the dripping bank of slate. There was no room for any doubts. That was Camilla's towel. And next to it was a plastic bag containing *her* sun-glasses, *her* hair grips, *her* hand cream, and *her* copy of *The Return of the Native*.

A minute or two later, on Harry's advice, I was hammering at the door of the harbour master's cottage, breathing heavily, making promises I had no earthly chance of keeping, not just to God and to Camilla, but to my mother, to Harry Vilbert, even to Asimova.

I'm sure now that it wasn't entirely his fault, but the harbour master took two lifetimes getting to grips with what I was trying to tell him. First of all he wanted to know how I could be certain that Camilla was in the water; then he failed to understand what reasons I had to be frightened for her if she was a strong swimmer and what was more was wearing flippers; it was only when he realized that Camilla had gone swimming the night *before* that I sensed him catch some of my consternation. But even then he wanted to cross-examine me on why it had taken me so long to report her missing. 'That will take too long to explain,' I explained to him.

He gave me one of those looks that I had all my life been dreading meeting from a doctor or a lawyer or a mechanic – the look that says, for all my professional expertise and wisdom, I don't think there is anything I can do for you now. He shook his head. 'If you're telling me that she's been in the water for upwards of ten hours . . .' He shook his head again.

I had reached that stage of panic where I was not yet wholly convinced that I was marked out to suffer terribly, and yet all the familiar physical details of my life were beginning to take on the slow motion magnification and the high colour of catastrophe. My own voice was strange to me; the harbour master spoke as someone that I'd already met with in a dream. Try as I might, I cannot now re-assemble his arguments for not calling out the lifeboats or sending for the RAF helicopters. I simply know that I found them compelling at the time. I, too, didn't want to trouble anyone. Nor can I remember leaving his cottage with him, clambering into his motor launch, and setting out, just the two of us, in the direction of the louring black rock. But that was what we did. What I do remember is my insistence that that was the only place to look for her. I don't know what I expected to find. Camilla sitting up on its highest peak, combing out her hair? Why not? Nothing else that was happening bore any relation to likelihood or reality. Only my remorse was recognizable to me. That, it seemed, like cockroaches and certain kinds of weed, could survive anything.

Nor was our search fruitless. Floating in the foam that encircled the Mazzard like a frilled collar we found one of a pair of flippers. The harbour master fished it aboard for me to examine. I didn't know one flipper from another – I don't think it had ever even occurred to me that they came in sizes; nonetheless, I knew this flipper to be Camilla's. I held it in both my hands and put it, still running with spumy water, to my chest. I threw my head back. A twitching sparrow-hawk looked me over. A guillemot rode the water like a duck. Two images, two tableaux of the mind, each superimposed upon the other, fought for the attention of my inner eye; one was of me, bent like a hunchback beneath the cruel burden of guilt that was Camilla's legacy, the other was of Camilla, lying on her back on the sea-bed of the harbour, her body stripped by the receding tides, her breasts still full but deadly white, her hair indistinguishable from that mess of vegetation, the shredded lettuce and stewed spinach. Then darkness came into my eyes and I went down, face forward, into the bottom of the boat.

4

I spent the rest of the morning and most of the afternoon in Harry Vilbert's room in the Museum. He had been waiting for me when the motor launch had returned, and with the help of the harbour master had got me out of the boat, up on to the wharf, through the small crowd of tourists who had gathered in the hope of seeing something that would at last make their holiday memorable, and into his office. He then propped me up with cushions in an old armchair, drew the curtains, and closed the Museum. I have no personal recollection of any of this. I am just going on what Harry told me. Apparently he arranged for breakfast to be brought to me, brewed me endless cups of tea, and even sent out for half a bottle of brandy. For all I know he might also have muttered incantations over me, rubbed my limbs with strange unguents, and fed me with an extraction of newts' eyes.

I was in no condition to refuse anything. It's certain that he bound some kind of herbal coronet around my temples, because I found bits of leave and split ends of stalks in my hair later, when I went home and bathed. I realize that I should be grateful to him. He looked after me. He watched over me. For several hours he never left my side. If it had not been for him I might have done something drastic. I owe him, and I should be grateful. But it's not easy.

You see, he was the one that was there when – hard as it is to recover one's senses in a room lined with wall charts illustrating the life cycles of the common, the native, and the exotic wart – I nonetheless *did* recover my senses, sufficiently at least to remember who I was, what had happened, and how many responsibilities now lay before me. He was the one who listened quietly and poured me brandy while I talked about police and coroners and having to break the news to Camilla's parents. And he – Harry – was the one who waited until I declared myself well enough to leave him, until I was out in the harbour even, shading my eyes from the light and feebly shaking his hand in gratitude – Harry let me go *that* far, before fishing inside his denim jacket and handing me a small manilla envelope – a business envelope – which I could see immediately was addressed to me.

I stared at him in stupefaction. 'What's this?' I asked him.

But he didn't want to discuss it. He was half inside the Museum by the time my fingers had closed on what he'd handed me. I had literally to drag him back out.

'Where did you get this?' I demanded. I take it that it is not necessary for me to explain that although my name was the only thing written on the envelope, I recognized who had written it. It had never occurred to me that there would be a note. If there was a note then something more frightful than an accident had occurred. That image of myself with my back bent in an unending pilgrimage of guilt flashed once more before my mind's eye. 'Who gave it to you, Harry?' I repeated. I had taken

338

him by the shoulder again, or whatever that was that felt like a bag of walnuts inside his jacket.

He looked even older and closer to the point of expiry than usual. I believed I actually saw him sway. 'Lionel,' was all he was able to get out.

'Lionel?'

'Lionel Turnbull. He handed it to me this morning . . . while I was helping you out of the boat.' He could barely get his breath. But I understand now that he wasn't at all close to death. It was excitement that he could barely catch his breath for. 'He told me not to give it to you until I had to. Those were Camilla's instructions to him.'

'Hang on, Harry – are you saying that Camilla gave this to Lionel to give to you to give to me, only when you decided that you *had* to? When was that, Harry? When did you decide you *had* to? And when did Lionel see Camilla?'

But I got answers to none of these questions. Harry had broken away from me and was back inside the Museum of Nugatory Spells and Superstitions before I could reach out and haul him back. A minute later I saw him watching me from one of the windows, an ashen face peering out from between the plastic toadstools and the painted phalluses, the whites of his eyes flecked with red spots of exhilaration.

I suddenly had the fancy that the rest of the village was similarly engaged, and that there wasn't a window anywhere that didn't have at least one face in it. But at the same time I felt that it didn't matter. Nothing mattered. I sank into the grassy verge, along which Camilla and I had strolled hand in hand on countless sunny afternoons, and I tore open my envelope, careless of who saw my suffering now, tears rolling freely down my cheeks on to the single sheet of paper containing Camilla's final valediction to earthly joys.

Except that – as any fool but me would by now have realized – earthly joys were the last things Camilla had said goodbye to.

Here's what Camilla wrote to me. I've carried it in my wallet all winter. You'll notice that it doesn't begin with the usual polite form of address – that's the sort of thing that being with an interesting woman means you have to go without.

Barney,
I have asked Lionel Turnbull to see that you don't get this until I am well gone from the village. Don't make trouble for Lionel. A lot of persuasion went in to getting him to take his boat out at night. He is a morning person by nature, as you know. But I pleaded desperation. And he didn't help me to spite you.

Please don't waste your time wondering whether Lionel or anybody else who lent a hand knows things about me or about you or about us that they shouldn't. The best thing is for you to work on the assumption that they do. You'll handle it.

I hope the melodrama of my exit hasn't caused too much trouble for anyone in the village – except you, that is. I wanted you to experience some genuine grief on my behalf, just once. I don't mean that other stuff. But we don't have to go over all that again. The other reasons for my leaving the way I have are between me and Max, and Max and Jeannie, and are nothing to do with you.

Max is with me. We'll be in France for a while and then I don't know what. I don't expect you to bother to follow us. You know your French isn't up to it.

I'll arrange to have my things collected when I know what I want done with them. I won't put you to any trouble. I'll send packers and so on. Stay on at the cottage if you want to. I think you should. I want you to have the School. I think it's yours by right now. You'll do it more justice than I ever could. As Max said, when I told him about your chimerical rival dream, you're a natural. He only wishes that he might emulate you one night and dream himself lost in one of Robbe-Grillet's labyrinths

– a new man in a New Novel. You of course, as you've so often told me, are an old novel man yourself. So run the Hardy centre. You're more suited to it than perhaps you realize.

Please feed the cats and remember to water the plants. Don't punish them for me. Try to remember: I'm giving you the thing you've always wanted.

I have to say that I enjoyed planting my towel on the rocks and taking my last swim in the harbour. I did throw myself into that; I meant it; it was, in its way, a true little death. But it was good to be like that new New John Fowles novel you've ranted so vehemently against, and to give myself an alternative ending.

Camilla.

I'm relieved to be able to transcribe that document and get it out of my system. I never liked it. It gave me quite a lot of pleasure to starve the cats and watch the plants die. And if I do open up Camilla's old establishment I won't be selling Lionel Turnbull alias Lance Tourney's pamphlet in the shop; and I definitely won't be selling any Barthes, Robbe-Grillet, Nathalie Sarraute or John Fowles either. I've squared up to melodrama in my time – I used to give it to the Brontës where it really hurt – I won't lie down to modernism without a fight.

10

Well, I've done it. I've finally made it out of Lyonnesse. I'm writing this on my old desk in Finchley, the very one at which, over twenty years ago, I used to sit and do my homework and hunt for prepositions. Ostensibly, it was a barrage of phone calls from my mother and Menashe, demanding that I come to see them on a matter not only strange but urgent, and a similar battery from Rabika and my father – the first phone call my father has ever made to me, incidentally – that prised me out. But of course I wouldn't have come unless I was ready.

I think it was removing Camilla's letter from my pocket that really did the trick. I felt lighter instantly. And on three consecutive mornings I skipped my penitential expeditions. Lovely mornings they were, too; bright, crisp, purples prinking the main – absolutely perfect for the gratification of guilt. But I'd been having a few thoughts about guilt. I'd always known that it was a dubious emotion – you couldn't read Thomas Hardy and not know that remorse was just a grander name for impotence, a spot of exercise for the slack muscles of passivity – but I'd clung to it because it was an emotion that came easily, suited me, went with the way I looked and dressed, and because I feared that without it I'd lose the conviction that the sky had only fallen in on me because I'd pulled. Lose guilt and you lose the illusion of control. I knew all about it; I'd been walking myself into a delirium of guilty responsibility all winter. Camilla's letter, however, out of its envelope for the first time in months, reminded me that it was pure vanity on my part

342

to suppose that I'd done anything – it had all been done *to* me. Camilla had left on her own account, not because of me. She would have gone at last, whatever I'd done. She could no more bear the tedium of love than I could. It was her mess just as much as it was mine. Hadn't she been at war with someone – with Hardy, with the village, with her brother, with her own height (be still, be still my heart) – long before I'd happened by? So what was I doing, poaching guilt? Let her go walk the cliffs – that's if there were any in whichever structurally symbolic corner of France Max had sequestered her.

I felt bare, finding myself suddenly without remorse – unaccustomed, uncertain, vulnerable even; but I also felt good in a prickly, watchful, spiteful sort of way. So when they wouldn't stop ringing me and asking me to come up, I couldn't see any reason not to comply. That's not meant to sound negative. I was pleased to come, as it happens – but it takes a little time to get used to the idea that you're the fly and not the wanton boy. It's my experience, anyway, that you go a little quiet for a while.

I came up yesterday. I cleaned the cottage, fastened all the windows – unnecessary since it was possible to walk in through the walls – and really raced that Cortina up the hill. I had the radio turned up full blast and I sang along with it, keeping my eyes fixed on the road in front of me, not choosing to look at the sea which was rising like a flood to my left, nor at the picturesque cob dwellings which were receding in my rear view mirror. I didn't get very far though, only half-way round the second hairpin bend, before I saw Harry Vilbert in the road, his right thumb out and a scrap of cardboard saying LONDON hanging round his chest. I had no option. I had to stop. He looked to be at death's door, for one thing. And for another I now saw him as a fellow victim. *He* wasn't troubled by remorse or compunction either. He was another one to whom it had all just happened.

As I've already mentioned, I had only let Harry engage me in conversation once since the day he looked after me in his office at the Museum. And we didn't discuss much then except the superiority of men to women when it came to longevity of devotion. I would have liked to make it a condition of my getting him safely to LONDON that he sit in total silence throughout the journey, but I didn't want to upset him. If he died in my car before we were out of Cornwall then I'd never reach Finchley. So I had to let him ramble on about eggs in baskets, water under bridges, ill winds and manilla envelopes. He clearly felt that he had some apologizing to do, because he talked a lot about manilla envelopes; and it was only when we were just outside Exeter that I realized he really was talking about them in the plural. 'Your memory's going, Harry,' I told him. 'You only gave me one envelope. I remember that clearly. You kept it from me for six hours.'

But there had been another envelope. A bigger one. Harry had no doubt about that. In his excitement at the time he had forgotten to give it to me, and when he went back inside the Museum to fetch it he lacked the courage to come out again, so alternately angry and distressed did I appear. He had brought it up to the cottage later, had not been able to raise me – I was flat out, that's why; flattened, plastered, and prostrate – and not being able to fit the envelope through the letter box either, he had popped it under the doors of the wooden shed that abutted the cottage. He was surprised that I pumped him for so many details. We were going back eight or nine months. 'Do you mean you've not found it yet?' he asked.

I hadn't. I had never been near the wooden shed since Camilla had left. Too many sounds came from it for my liking. I don't mean ghostly sounds – as from the past. I mean too much scuttling of vermin feet; too many hisses of adders fanged. Camilla might have taught me what ragwort looks like, but the country still holds terrors for me. There are doors I still won't open and stones I still won't turn.

'So it's where I left it?' Harry hoped. The idea that there was something, somewhere, that was where he'd left it seemed to fill Harry with a sort of simple pride.

'That's if the rats haven't chewed it.' I sounded

irritated. I wanted to punish him for his stupidity. Pushing it under the doors of the shed indeed. He was the kind of person who slipped telegrams under mats, or dropped urgent pleas for help into rabbit warrens. I knew whose novels he belonged in.

But the significant thing about all this was that I kept on driving in the direction of Finchley. Six months ago – or less – I would have turned around and travelled a thousand miles if need be to lay my hands on something that Camilla had written me. So the signs are all good, as Harry himself might have said.

I'm back.

London didn't work out. The first mistake I made was to try and contact some old friends. Of those that remembered who I was, a good half didn't know I'd been away. Then I went out and got lost on the Tube. Things like that can break the spirit. I decided to cheer myself up by going to the theatre. I found a meaty David Hare to walk out of – *Knuckle* I think it was – but it wasn't the same without Camilla. Walking out is essentially an activity for two. In the foyer, talking of walking, I walked into my cousin Bernice. She had a handsome Israeli on her arm – Yossie she called him – who was even hairier than she was. It left me quite melancholy and bereft, watching them go back into the auditorium hand in hand, knowing that they would be together after the play was over, and perhaps all night, twirling each other's moustaches.

And if that wasn't regrettable coincidence enough, I ran slap into Sharon, Fitzpiers, and Asimova on my first day back, in Harrods food hall. Asimova was screaming and stamping her foot, demanding her own individual hand-raised venison pie as far as I could understand it, and Fitzpiers was searching in his pockets for the money to buy her one. I thought, but only fleetingly, about offering. I had heard that Fitz no longer believed that the future lay in SF and had gone over to the novel of industrial espionage as the genre that spoke most vividly for our times. I didn't know how much truth there was in this but I did notice that Sharon was wearing a rather beautifully tailored seersucker boiler suit tucked into shiny on-site wellingtons, and I let that determine my inference. They didn't recognize me at first. Then when they did they tried hoping that I wouldn't recognize them. It was too late, though; a smile had appeared like a geological fault across the whole width of my face. Fitzpiers was just about able to shake my hand, but Sharon clearly found any form of contact with me impossible unless it was through her solicitor. I was just feeling sorry that that was the case, wishing that we could get on as of old and share a joke about Fitz's predilection for milkshakes, when Asimova started crying again. I think she wanted her own individual smoked salmon this time. 'Daddy!' she screamed. 'Daddy!' That was enough for me; I was off, half-way to the other end of Knightsbridge, before she could scream it a third time.

But it was my parents and the Flatmans who were the real flies in the ointment. The reason they had sent for me – not in concert, you must understand; neither household was in communication with the other except through private detectives and the Jewish secret police – the reason they had separately insisted that I immediately get up to London to see them was that they had finally decided (again not in concert) on marriage. That's to say my father had decided to marry Rabika Flatman and my mother had retaliated by deciding to marry Menashe. I fully realize that it might have been the other way round, that my father might have been the one who was doing the retaliating, but it should be understandable why I am inclined to favour the man in such disputes, just at present. (It's wonderful not feeling answerable to Camilla!) Either way, this flurry of Hymeneal preparation ought not to have posed me any problems: I was absolutely even-handed in my congratulations and good wishes; I wanted them all to be happy in precisely equal measure; and I was as willing to be witness or page-boy or guest-of-honour or whatever else

346

was required of me for the one set as I was for the other. The trouble was that the dates happened upon for my mother to become Mrs Flatman and Mrs Flatman to become Mrs Fugleman coincided. I don't mean that they coincided a bit – that I'd be pushed to get from one lot of nuptials to the other – I mean that they coincided *exactly* – to the hour, to the minute. Two zero five in Finchley; two zero five in Tooting. if I'd owned a helicopter I could not have made it to both; if I'd been Camilla's brother I could not have heard my old mother *and* my new mother promise that they would. As for changing one of the times – that was out of the question. 'Let *them* change *theirs*,' I was told on each side of the river. To a suspicious nature it might well have looked as though the coincidence wasn't a coincidence at all, but a way of getting me to come off the fence, to declare my allegiance once and for all. That was what it came to anyway – whether they'd planned it to or not – a test of my ultimate loyalty. Would I go to theirs or would I go to theirs? Which one of them, or rather which pair of them, did I love the most?

'Actually, that should be "the more",' I explained to my mother. 'If I'm choosing between two pairs only, it's "the more". But if you'd like to throw another couple in . . .'

'When it comes to love, Barney,' Menashe replied for her, 'the *most* is the *least* your mother and I are prepared to settle for.'

'In that case,' I said – and I said it in North London and n South – 'I'll go to neither.'

I have to say that I was disappointed in Rabika's attiude. 'You've been got at,' she accused me. And for the 'irst time since I'd known and revered her I decided that I lidn't like the sag of sun-burnt flesh that swung from ler upper arm after all. But then I was going in for nisogyny, as I've said, as a consequence of having loosened my grip on guilt.

As the days went by the general level of sportsmanship dropped dramatically. Rabika snuggled up to me. She even referred, with wild laughter in her eyes and a bubble of the old mockery on her lips, to the time I'd leaned her over the sink in my parents' bathroom. Was she trying to tell me that if I went to her wedding and not the other person's she would let me lean her some more? Back in Finchley, Menashe dropped dark hints about setting me up in business. He kept leaving his wallet around for me to see also. But it was my mother who introduced the roughest tactics. 'In fact,' she sat me down one afternon and told me, 'your duties and obligations are not equal in the way you think they are. It does you great credit, Barney – and Menashe and I have both commented on it – that you are trying so hard to show scrupulous fairness both to me and to your father, but you ought now to know – I hope you are ready for this, Barney – that your father – here, have some more tea – is not your father.'

Why did every conversation with my mother remind me of some other conversation I'd had with her at some other time and in some other place? 'My father's not my father?' I repeated, and the question sounded so familiar to me that I wasn't in the slightest bit surprised to hear myself repeating it.

She shook her head. I won't go into the details of what she told me. She went into so many herself that I have already forgotten most of them. What she was most concerned to get me to understand was that she had acted as she had, done what she had done, not because she had been bad but because she had been driven. My mother had talked to me of being driven many times in the past; but always by outrage, by a fearless sense of justice, by some moral imperative, or, during the hard years, by simple poverty and want. This was the first time she had ever introduced the idea that she might once have been driven by desire. She didn't use that word of course. She simply said that she'd been driven, flashed her eyes, and left me to put a name to the driver. The one name she did give me, though, was that of her co-passenger. 'Menashe Flatman is your father,' she whispered to me at last.

through the steam that ascended like a mist from the swollen tea strainer.

I did some simple mental arithmetic, the kind that Menashe himself was renowned for. 'Mother, you and Menashe have been, er, driven, for four or five years at a rough count. Now I'm almost thirty-three . . .'

She interrupted me. 'Menashe and I have known each other a long time,' she said. 'Longer in fact than your father has known the other one.'

I couldn't be certain whether this confidence was meant to be a further inducement to me to go to the Finchley wedding and not the Tooting; but it led me to be curious about one thing. 'Does that mean that you drove them . . .?'

She interrupted me again. 'I'm not blaming anybody. You can say that we drove one another. But there are some insults a woman cannot bear. Your father . . .'

This time I interrupted her. 'Which father is this now?'

'Barney, Menashe is your father.'

'Does the father I'm used to calling father know this?'

She pulled a remarkable face. I'd seen some good ones from her over the years but this one was a lulu. It somehow called out from the past a scorn that was older even than I was. A thousand little lines that had been lying in wait for over thirty-three years suddenly leapt into place around her mouth. 'What would *he* care *whose* you are?' I watched her weighing the advisability of her next sentence, but making the mistake of delivering it anyway. '*You're* just the same. You don't care who brings up whose.'

I held up my hand. Asimova conversations were banned in this house. I'd banned them myself since the incident of the wardrobe – my mother's Bay of Pigs. 'What does it mean to say I'm just the same as him,' I asked her, 'if I'm not his?'

'He brought you up, didn't he?'

I suddenly felt very warmly towards my father – that's to say towards the one who had brought me up. I wished he was here, just back from the office, running through the day's freshest examples of parental spite: Gerda Loines and Marie Baddeley and Ilona Gayne. I couldn't summon up any such enthusiasm for Menashe, despite his stupendous memory for my mother's name. I've said that they have sentimental secrets in their lives, these arithmetical city businessmen with their silvered moustaches; but I was damned if Menashe's sentimental secret was going to be me.

I left Finchley almost as speedily as I'd left it on the day I very nearly found Asimova in my old wardrobe. I didn't bother looking in at Tooting. I knew exactly what I'd find there – Rabika Flatman taking unscrupulous advantage of my long-standing passion for her, and my father – utterly confounded by his family's clamour for indivi- duation – distantly amused by something or other, and largely indifferent to Rabika and to me. That, I decided, was the quality I most liked in him. He had never both- ered to get to know me and had never encouraged me to get to know him. He had not been icy, he simply had not been very interested in relationships. How tactful of him, if I wasn't his son, not to have attempted to make me think I was; how civilized of him not to have tried to make me *his*. No wonder I was fond of him.

So it wasn't necessary for me to see him again before I left. I knew what I wanted to know. It was best – just in case I was tempted into some last minute backsliding – to get away quickly. I didn't want to catch myself asking who or whose I was again, just for old times' sake. Not in Finchley or in Tooting anyway. The cliffs were far and away the best places for that sort of thing. There's a democracy of familic confusion out on these Cornish headlands – nobody else knows who he is either.

I am still surprised by how cheerfully I drove back here, the wind before me, the Fuglemans and the Flatmans behind. I was in such prime condition that I ought really to have stopped off at Paddington before I left London and gone looking for Melpomene. But I was eager to be away. I sailed along the motorway, acknowledging the

350

friendly waves of lorry drivers and traffic police alike. For the first time ever I crossed the Tamar without a qualm. I didn't even mind those last, normally spirit-breaking fifteen miles, the ones that tell you you really are leaving the kindly concessions of social man. I whistled down those blind lanes with my windows open, and slowed the car right down to enjoy the spectacle of that ultimate upward sweep of land, its final flourish before dropping sheer into the sea.

I wasn't in a hurry to seek out the manilla envelope that Harry Vilbert had posted into my unused garden shed, but of course I was curious enough about it to have remembered it was there. The rats hadn't got it, but the damp very nearly had. I reckon the odd snake had tossed it around a bit also. The envelope was just about legible. It read, *What I think of my Husband*. And its contents were still legible too. I suppose it was inevitable that they would not contain a single reference to Thomas Hardy. *I* was the husband that Camilla wanted to express her thoughts about.

I don't know what effects this composition would have had upon my peace of mind had I read it when I was intended to – last autumn. I'm sure it would have set my convalescence back by months. But I'm stronger now, as I've proved. I read what Camilla had to say, then I walked down with it through the village, smiling and nodding as I went, out into the harbour, past the Museum and the harbour master's cottage, and up on to the cliffs. Once there I made for one of my most favourite vertiginous ledges, where I sat awhile and peered down into that absurd fuss and ferment below me; then, choosing my current of air as craftily as if I were a kestrel, I up-ended Camilla's envelope and let the pages of what she thought of her husband hang and sway for a moment before floating down with a rocking motion into the opal and the sapphire of that wandering western sea.

THE END